TANGLED LIVES

Hilary Boyd

WINDSOR
PARAGON

First published 2012
by Quercus
This Large Print edition published 2013
by AudioGO Ltd
by arrangement with
Quercus

Hardcover   ISBN: 978 1 4713 3630 0
Softcover   ISBN: 978 1 4713 3631 7

British Library Cataloguing in Publication Data available

Printed and bound in Great Britain by
TJ International Limited

For my mother, Peggy Sandeman-Allen.
I still miss you.

Prologue

Kent, 1967

'It's time.'

Nurse Julie stood beside the bed, but she didn't look up at her. She just continued to stare at the baby, asleep, cuddled in the crook of her arms. He was already washed, and dressed in a brushed cotton nightie, knitted blue matinee jacket, matching booties and hat. The clothes seemed to swamp his tiny form and make him seem heartbreakingly separate from her.

'Do you want any help?'

Annie shook her head and eased herself off the bed, turning to place the baby in the waiting wicker carrycot. He stirred as she laid him on the cool sheet and flung his arms outwards in a small spasm. She gently tucked the soft, white, wool blanket close around him, knowing how he hated being put down. Who would understand him now? Who would give him the minute-by-minute attention that she, despite reminding herself there was no future in it, could not resist providing?

The ten difficult days of new motherhood had gone by agonisingly quickly, as if she were careering towards a cliff edge with her baby son. And as each day had brought her closer to this one, the shadow presence of his father grew ever more insistent. She should have told him; she knew it. But every time she thought about the conversation, she imagined the shock, the distaste, the embarrassment on his face. It would be the

1

same expression her mother's had worn since she'd heard the news. She couldn't bear it. If only he'd been in touch after that night. Why . . . ? Why hadn't he called? But it was too late for all that now. She'd made her decision.

The rest of the morning was a blur. Formalities, kindly smiles, pity; she saw the pity. But it was businesslike and left no room for protest, as if she were no longer important in this drama about her baby son's life, played out in front of her by these competent professionals. Which she wasn't, of course.

And then she was in her mother's car, being driven through the glorious spring day towards London.

'I've had your bedroom painted while you've been away,' her mother told her, in a crisp voice which seemed to Annie like a wall, a barrier that protected her mother from knowing—or wanting to know—what her life had been like over the past four months.

'It's still cream, but it looks terribly smart,' her mother was saying.

'Thank you. I can't wait to see it,' she replied, surprised by her own enthusiasm about the fresh paint on her bedroom walls.

1

Annie Delancey stood in the warm, quiet kitchen and slowly peeled apart the last two pieces of streaky bacon. As she fitted them into the large skillet where the other rashers were already buckling and sizzling on the heat, she felt an overwhelming sense of happiness. It was Saturday. Her family was here for the weekend. She would do pancakes.

She glanced round at the neatly laid table, smiling with pleasure at the vibrant golden daffodils lighting up the centre, competing with the glass jug of freshly squeezed orange juice and the square of yellow butter on its white china dish.

Her son Ed, now twenty-six, worked unholy hours as the manager of a restaurant/bar in Islington, and she hardly saw him, so having him home was a treat for her. But this visit, she knew, was not so much to hang out with his dear old mum as to avoid his freezing Stroud Green flat, where the heating was on the blink. When she'd heard he was bringing his girlfriend, Emma, she'd asked Marsha—her second child and barely a year younger than Ed—to come over for a late breakfast.

She took the maple syrup from the cupboard and set it on the table, then moved to the window and gazed out at the well-kept, mature garden with satisfaction. It was beautiful the way the pale spring sun lit up the frosty landscape. She and

Richard had planted out the garden, mostly from guesswork, when they'd first moved into the house just before Ed was born. And it had worked, despite the inevitable restrictions of a long, narrow London garden. They had tweaked and improved over the years—mostly Richard's doing—adding the inevitable wooden decking a few months ago. This was now bordered with earthenware pots of various sizes, planted up with herbs, ivy, narcissus, and some dark purple and yellow gold-laced primulas—all slow to bloom because of the late frost.

'Mmm, great smell.'

Annie hadn't heard her husband come in. Richard was leaning his tall frame close to the pan, sniffing appreciatively.

'Shouldn't these go over?' he asked a little anxiously, prodding the rashers with the metal tongs.

Indeed, the bacon was already crisp and on the verge of being burnt. Annie grabbed the tongs from her husband and began to salvage the contents of the pan, decanting the rashers onto a plate lined with kitchen towel before putting them in the warm oven.

'Shall I tell them it's nearly ready?' he asked, pointing to the ceiling.

'Leave them,' she said with a smile. 'They'll smell the bacon if they're even halfway conscious.' She looked at her watch. 'Mash should be here in a moment.'

And sure enough, on cue, the front door banged and she heard footsteps on the stairs leading down to the kitchen.

'Hi, darling . . . you look frozen.' Annie put the

oven gloves down and turned to embrace her daughter. Marsha's cheeks were pink from the cold, her blue eyes bright in her oval face, her long pale-blonde hair drawn back into an untidy ponytail. She shivered, slinging the post she'd retrieved from the doormat onto the kitchen table before rubbing her gloved hands together. She eyed the breakfast preparations hungrily.

'Maple syrup . . . I know what that means!' She gave her father a hug and took off her black coat, unwinding her red wool scarf before thinking again and wrapping it back round her neck.

'Shall I wake them now?' Richard asked again. And this time Annie nodded.

*   *   *

Lucy was first down. Annie saw her wince as her bare feet hit the chilly terracotta floor tiles, tugging over her hands the sleeves of a navy jumper that covered her tartan pyjamas. Rounder than her sister, with wavy auburn hair and soft brown eyes, Annie always marvelled that they had produced two such different daughters; different in looks as well as personality.

'It's freezing,' Lucy complained.

Her father smiled. 'My sweater not keeping you warm enough then?'

She glanced down and looked a little sheepish.

'Just borrowing it, Dad. None of mine are big enough.'

'It's only my best cashmere. I don't want syrup down it.'

Annie rubbed buttered paper round a clean pan, and removed the saucer she had put over the jug of pancake batter. She loved the whole process of cooking. The careful preparation, the smells and the warmth and her pleasure in feeding her family. Ladling a small amount of batter out of the jug, she waited till the pan was smoking before pouring the mixture carefully onto the hot surface to form a number of creamy-yellow rounds.

The four of them settled at the large oak table, a steaming pile of pancakes between them. Richard slowly pressed the plunger down on the cafetière. 'We're not waiting for Ed and Emma?'

Marsha shook her head vehemently. 'No way!'

'How was the party?' Annie asked her elder daughter.

Marsha shrugged as she loaded her pancakes with maple syrup.

'OK, the usual media mob. But yeah . . . I met an interesting guy. He had things to say beyond who you know and your latest project. Makes a change—you wouldn't believe the morons out there.'

Annie looked at Richard and raised an eyebrow. This was more information than Marsha usually divulged about her evenings out. A grunt or two, a mind-your-own-business look, a vague 'got smashed', was all they had learnt to expect from the twenty-five-year-old.

'Cute?' Richard ventured, to receive a scornful roll of his daughter's eyes.

'Sorry, who's cute?' Lucy, still half asleep, asked. She had a habit of zoning out of family conversations.

'Nobody,' Marsha muttered, then grinned. 'You should see your faces! Every time I mention a man, you all seem to hold your breath.'

'Tell me about him, Mash, I missed it,' Lucy insisted.

'Nothing to tell. I liked him, but he wasn't my type.'

Lucy groaned. 'Always the case, eh? They're either fascinating but look like a geography teacher, or drop dead gorgeous and brainless pillocks.'

'No way did he look like a geography teacher.'

'So are you going to see him again?'

Marsha shook her head. 'It wasn't like that. We didn't swap numbers or anything, just sat and talked for ages. He's bound to have a girlfriend somewhere.'

Annie noticed a certain wistfulness in her daughter's tone. Marsha hadn't been serious about anyone since Ben, her college boyfriend, who'd gone to Japan to teach English for three months and fallen for a Japanese girl, breaking her daughter's heart.

Richard was checking through the pile of mail. 'All for you.' He pushed it towards his wife. She found a credit card statement, a promotional letter from the gym, next week's copy of *The Economist* in its plastic wrapper. 'You said you'd cancelled this,' she said, waving the magazine at her husband. 'They just pile up and we never read them.'

'I do—occasionally,' he insisted.

The last letter was a brown envelope with a red stamp saying, very indistinctly, Kent Social Services. She turned it over, puzzled. Her name and address were handwritten in blue biro.

'Morning . . . morning, all!' Ed jumped down the last three stairs, coming into the kitchen with a fanfare. Emma trailed sleepily behind him. Despite the chill, he was dressed only in a pair of patterned boxers and an old grey sweatshirt. Emma, luscious and big-breasted with permanently tousled dark hair, huge, soulful brown eyes and a porcelain skin, was almost swamped in the folds of Ed's navy towelling dressing gown.

'Hope you haven't eaten everything.' Ed looked anxiously at the ravaged breakfast table.

'Serve you right if we had,' Marsha retorted.

Annie was surprised at the sharpness in her tone. She had worried from the start about Ed going out with his sister's lifelong best friend and now flatmate. But her worry had been for her son— Emma's reputation as a player when it came to men had been established as far back as her teens. She hadn't thought of the toll the relationship might take on Marsha. Her eldest children had been almost like twins growing up—Lucy a bit of an outsider. Was Marsha feeling left out now that the two people closest to her were so wrapped up in each other?

'How was last night?' Emma was asking Marsha.

'She met a cute guy!' Lucy answered for her.

'Shut up! I didn't. He *was* cute, beautiful in fact, but I told you, he wasn't my type.'

Emma shook her head at her friend. 'Nothing new there then! Can't remember the last time you had the hots for someone . . . well, I can, but . . .'

'Just because you fancy everything that moves,' Marsha interrupted.

Emma laughed. 'Yeah, it's easier that way.'

'Thanks, I'm flattered,' Ed said, frowning.

Emma leant forward and planted a sloppy kiss

on his cheek. 'And so you should be.'

Annie saw her elder daughter turn away, and knew she had been right.

'I'll make some more pancakes in a sec,' she said as she turned the letter over and pulled at the brown flap.

'Oh, Mummeee . . . you spoil us.' Ed bounced round the table and draped his arms round his mother in a tight hug. She returned his embrace, so happy to have him home. But he wasn't looking well, she thought. He'd never had much colour, inheriting her own blonde hair and the same grey-blue eyes, but now he looked almost pallid. No sunlight with all those ridiculous hours he puts in, she thought, noticing the padding that had recently appeared round his waist. He wasn't tall like herself and his father, more stocky, but he was too young to start putting on weight.

She returned her attention to the letter, drawing a single piece of paper from the envelope.

'What've you got there?' Ed peered over her shoulder. But after a cursory glance, she instinctively closed the letter and pushed it under the pile. What she had glimpsed was almost incomprehensible. Like an automaton she got up and went to the frying pan, stirring the batter, reaching for the ladle, heating the butter. Only when Ed and Emma had their own pile of pancakes, and she had retrieved the remaining bacon from the oven, did she find an excuse to leave the room, knowing that if she didn't have a moment alone, she would explode.

'Anyone seen my phone?' she asked, casting a vague glance around the kitchen.

The others all shook their heads.

9

'Probably in the bedroom,' Richard suggested.

'I just need to check the deliveries went out alright. I'll be back in a minute.'

She headed quickly for the stairs, the letter stuffed in the pocket of her grey tracksuit bottoms. Once clear of the basement, she ran up the two storeys to her bedroom and shut the door with exaggerated care. She sat on her bed, her hands cold and shaking as she opened the letter again. This can't be true, she told herself.

She took a few measured breaths and reached for her mobile, which lay on the bedside table.

'Jamie, it's me. Are you around for a coffee? . . . I can't get away right now, everyone's here for brunch, but what about later? . . . Three's fine. The usual? . . . Brilliant . . . No, I'm OK, honestly . . . I'll tell you when I see you. Bye . . . bye.'

Her voice sounded hoarse, but she was surprised any words came out at all.

The phone call seemed to have drained all her strength, and she lay back silently on the bed, clutching the letter in one hand, her mobile in the other. She felt almost ill, her heart clattering dangerously in her chest, but after a few moments she forced herself upright. Checking in the bedroom mirror, she saw that she looked deathly pale. They can't see me like this. She rubbed her cheeks, took a few deep breaths, brushed her fair hair vigorously, then made her way downstairs. Ed and the girls were deep in conversation; only Richard glanced up.

'Everything OK?' She must have looked blank because he added, 'With the deliveries?'

'Oh, Carol wasn't answering. I might drop round later, just to check.'

10

Richard smiled. He had long ago accepted her passion for her work. When Lucy started school, Annie had set up a small business making celebration cakes. It followed on from the job she'd taken, aged nineteen, cooking director's lunches. This was in the days when company directors still had nicely brought-up girls come in to prepare meals for themselves and their clients. It had been her mother's idea, and she did as she was told—at that stage in her life she hadn't felt she had many options. And it was at one such company, an accountancy firm, that she had met Richard Delancey.

Much later, Delancey Bakes had started in the kitchen of their Dartmouth Park house, but moved to small premises in Gospel Oak when orders began to flood in and the hot, sweet smell of baking took over the family home. In those days, she did much of the baking and decorating herself; Richard's accountancy firm in Tottenham Court Road did the books. Latterly she employed four people and a delivery man, but all the cake designs were exclusively hers. Her elegant creations had become famous in London and the South, a Delancey cake a must-have for any credible wedding, party, christening or anniversary. But even now, she kept a keen eye on every detail of the business, and prompt, efficient deliveries were crucial.

She went to fill the kettle. 'Who wants more coffee?' She needed to keep herself busy and calm the panic bursting inside her head.

2

The cafe was full of weekend families, the atmosphere steamy, and thick with the noise from the large coffee machine and crying children. The walk had done her no good. Normally, exercise was Annie's panacea; she believed almost every ill could be cured by a brisk walk over the heath, fifty lengths of the gym pool, a vigorous game of tennis with Richard. But today she could hardly contain herself for the ten minutes it took to reach the cafe. The east wind made the air bitter, but she didn't care as she ran along the slippery streets, the letter burning a hole in her pocket.

Her friend—dark, neat, handsome, and tanned from a hiking holiday in Crete—was already there, guarding a cramped corner table by the window, texting furiously on his mobile. She had known Jamie since she was a child. He had lived in the same London square as she, and they had played together in the communal gardens, although her mother had never approved. 'That Walsh boy' was how she referred to Jamie, as if he were some tubercular street urchin, when in fact his parents were mild-mannered professionals (his father a respected osteopath) who just happened to fall outside her mother's snobbish and exacting social boundaries.

She edged her way past a toddler spitting croissant onto the flap of his high chair, peeled off her hat and coat and crammed them by the window.

'Whoa . . .' Jamie searched her face. 'You look

manic. What's up?' He rose to embrace her across the table.

She returned his kiss, then dithered for a minute, trying to find the words but failing. So she just unfolded the crumpled letter from Kent Social Services and smoothed it out on the cafe table in front of him.

'Wow! That's wonderful!' he said when he'd read it. He glanced up at her, and she saw his smile become uncertain. 'Isn't it?'

Annie found she was cold, even in the over-heated cafe. 'I never thought . . .'

'What is it? Thirty years? No, more. Thirty-five.'

She nodded. 'I'd given up thinking I'd ever see him . . . I just never imagined . . . after all this time . . .'

'Nor me. The children must be a tad surprised.'

She winced at his understatement.

'They don't know. Nor does Richard. It just came this morning when we were all having breakfast. I was so shocked I didn't know what to say, so I said nothing. It was hell, pretending everything was normal.'

Jamie raised his eyebrows. 'I must admit I never thought he'd pitch up. But you'll see him at last. That's brilliant, darling.' Despite Jamie's words, his eyes were bright with concern.

She dropped her face into her hands, the background noise fading as she tried to make sense of her emotions. A pulse thudded in her head.

'I want to see what he's like, of course, but . . .'

Jamie looked puzzled. 'But what? Isn't this exactly what you've wanted all these years? To meet Tom again, to know what happened to him?'

13

He glanced down at the letter again. 'Well, Daniel now.'

'Daniel ... Daniel Gray,' Annie whispered, turning the name over on her tongue. Strange to think he'll never have known the name I gave him. It had been Tom from the moment he was born. She had dreaded the birth, longed for it at the same time. She'd just wanted it over, to forget the whole thing had ever happened and get back to her life. But by the time they came to take him away, she knew every inch of him by heart. She counted his breaths, marvelled at the perfection of his newborn skin, the velvety cap of strawberry-blonde hair, gazed into his dark eyes, felt the squeeze of his starfish fingers, pressed her nose to his body to inhale the warm, milky scent. Never, not for a moment, did she imagine that her nineteen-year-old self would fall in love with that tiny, scrumpled form. She could still feel the softness of his skin beneath her fingers as she sat in the crowded cafe today.

'How on earth did they trace you?'

Annie shrugged. 'No idea.' She paused. 'Mother? But she's moved since then.'

'Anyway, she wouldn't do that without telling you, would she? Pass on your details like that.'

Such faith! Jamie's forgotten what she's like, she thought, even though he's borne the brunt of her spitefulness for years. He had, in the end, won her mother's grudging respect with his charm and good manners, despite the fact that he'd declared himself gay at the age of twenty-one and gone on to train as a nurse—a series of events that had made her mother's eyes widen in horror. 'I did warn you,' Eleanor had declared self-righteously,

14

'there was always something not quite right about that boy.' Jamie, however, despite Eleanor Westbury's caveat, had been very successful. He was currently in charge of the ICU at a busy north-London hospital.

Jamie tried to get the attention of the frenetic waitress.

'What can I get you?' the Russian girl snapped, daring them to hesitate for even a second before making their choice.

'Cappuccino, extra hot, double strength, no chocolate, please.' She spoke fast, eager to get back to the subject of Tom. Jamie asked for English breakfast tea.

'You want milk with that?'

'Please.'

'You don't sound very keen to see him,' Jamie commented after the waitress had gone.

'No, I am. Of course I am.'

'So what is it? What's bothering you? I mean I know this is a big moment, but . . .'

'I suppose it's telling the children,' she interrupted. 'Richard knows, of course. But having to admit to the others that I haven't been exactly truthful all their lives.'

Jamie raised his eyebrows. 'Why would they care? They'll probably be gripped to meet their brother.'

'You think so?'

'Well, it's intriguing, isn't it? Meeting a rel you didn't know you had? I'd be excited.'

She smiled at her friend's enthusiasm. Was it that simple? Wouldn't they be upset she hadn't told them? It was such a huge secret. And what about Ed? Maybe the girls wouldn't mind having a

15

brother, but how would he react to not being her only son?

'Anyway, darling, you can't *not* see him, you'd go mental knowing he was out there. You know you would.'

This was true. She had wanted this, as Jamie said, since the day they took Tom away. But it was the baby Tom she yearned for. This Daniel person, although just as much her son, obviously, was now a thirty-five-year-old man. All previous imaginings would be meaningless.

She took a deep breath. 'Won't he hate me for what I did to him?'

Jamie didn't reply for a moment. 'Depends what happened to him, but he can't be wanting to see you just to say how much he hates you. That'd be perverse. Unless he's . . . well, I'm sure he's not.'

'Not what?'

'I was going to say unless he's a nutter.' Jamie shot her an apologetic grin, but she wasn't really paying attention.

'They'll think it was a terrible thing I did . . . giving my baby away.'

'No, they won't. You can explain why. It's not as if you were the first teenager ever to have an illegitimate child in the sixties. I'm sure I'd have had one myself if it was possible.'

When Annie didn't respond, he went on, 'Come on, Annie, buck up. It's a bit of a shock, I'll grant you, but it's basically good news. Your long-lost son is back!'

She suddenly realised what he was saying. 'No, you're totally right,' she said slowly. 'I'm being pathetic. Of course I'll meet him . . . and finally see how he turned out.'

16

Jamie patted her hand approvingly. 'Atta girl! Feel the fear. Live the dream!'

She laughed. 'Shut up, will you? You're making me sound like some half-witted reality-TV contestant.'

'Hmmm . . . now there's an idea. Has it been done?' He paused, head on one side, then spread his palms in the air, gazing, dewy-eyed, into the middle-distance. 'I can see it now: mothers reunited with their long-lost children, lots of sobbing and regret, bit of stagey rage, but mainly LURV. We could call it *Mum Swap*, or *Family Makeover* . . . what about *This Is Your Mum?*'

'Giving your baby up for adoption isn't funny, Jamie.'

Jamie looked contrite. 'No. No, sorry, of course it's not. But I genuinely think it'd be marvellous to be reunited with a child you gave up. This has been hanging over you for thirty-odd years, Annie, even though you never, ever mention it. Well, now you can finally lay your past to rest and be, well, free.'

I'll only be free, she thought, if Tom forgives me. As Jamie said, she didn't talk about it, but that didn't mean she hadn't felt guilt, a lasting regret, since that day. Her life had been good, she had three other beautiful children, but that didn't negate her feelings about her firstborn.

As they left the restaurant and walked arm in arm along the icy pavement, Jamie stopped and dragged Annie round to face him.

'I've had a thought. Suppose he wants to meet his father too?'

Her eyes widened.

'I mean, if he's after his gene pool, you won't be the whole story, will you?'

17

'What are you saying?'

'Well, you'll have to tell *him* too.'

'So?' She pretended nonchalance. Tell Charles Carnegie that he has a son? The thought of it made her feel slightly sick. Jamie and Marjory were the only people in the world who knew Tom's father's identity, and that included the man himself. Even Richard hadn't wanted to know who he was.

'Let's cross that bridge when we come to it,' she replied. 'You know, I get the feeling you're enjoying this, Mr Walsh,' she added, digging her friend hard in the ribs as they began to walk again.

*   *   *

Annie found her husband in his office. Unlike the rest of the house, she hadn't been allowed a hand in decorating Richard's room, and the result was a calm, uncluttered, functional space: a manly mahogany bookshelf neatly filled with accountancy manuals and historical tomes, a black leather desk chair, burgundy curtains, and a large Scottish landscape on the wall opposite the window giving a splash of, albeit muted, colour. Richard was poring over the usual spreadsheets on his screen.

'Where are the children?'

He looked up, surprised at her tone. 'Umm . . . Lucy's gone out to meet Rosie, I think. The others are slumped in front of the TV downstairs. Why?'

She sat down on the black padded leather chair beside Richard's desk as her husband's eyes slid back to his screen. 'Richard, something's happened.'

Richard, clearly engrossed in a riveting

18

spreadsheet, reluctantly dragged his eyes away from it and waited for her to speak.

'Tom . . . the baby. He's contacted me.'

'The baby? What baby? Sorry, not sure what you're talking about.' He was still miles away.

She took a deep breath. 'Please, this is important, Richard. My baby, the one I gave away.'

His eyebrows shot up. 'Oh . . . Oh, God.' He looked almost panicked. 'He's been in touch? When?'

'This morning. I got a letter from Social Services saying he wants to meet me.'

Richard stared at her in silence for a moment.

'OK . . . and will you?'

'Well, yes, I'd like to. But it means telling the children, of course.'

He frowned. 'Do you have to tell them at this stage? Couldn't you just meet him first and see how it goes?'

'I could, but why shouldn't I tell them now?'

'Oh, I don't know . . . just seems a big thing if it's going nowhere.'

'What do you mean, "going nowhere"?'

'I've heard of this before, Annie, and often it doesn't work out. You know, no connection beyond the DNA.'

He made it sound so heartless.

'This is my son, Richard. And the children's half-brother.'

Richard laid his hand gently on hers. 'Of course. Sorry. Not sure how to react, that's all. If you want to tell them now, then you should. Up to you.'

But do I? she wondered. Do I really want to open this box?

'Maybe I'll write back and see when he wants to

meet,' she said.

Richard nodded approvingly. 'Seems best for now.'

She felt shaky and weak as she made her way slowly upstairs to the bedroom. Jamie and Richard can't possibly understand the real significance of that letter. I'm not sure I do either. Except I'm seeing my son, my very own firstborn, for the first time in thirty-five years.

3

It was Monday night, and Ed was on his way home to his flat—now heated, thank goodness. As he walked from the Tube station he rang Emma for the third time to see if she wanted to meet up.

He was sure she said she'd be at home tonight, but her phone went straight to answer. Where *was* she? When he got in he grabbed a beer from the fridge. His flatmate, Mike, was in his room on his computer. Mike was an addictive gamer, often playing war games late into the night, and they rarely saw each other except to squabble over who finished the milk. He checked the phone again. Nothing. The familiar twisting in his stomach started up again. No matter how much Emma said she loved him—and she'd said it a lot since they began dating three months ago—he found it hard to believe her. Ed knew her reputation, of course. Like the rest of the family, he'd listened endlessly to Marsha's lurid stories of Emma's love life as a teenager, but he understood. She'd had a rubbish upbringing—which was why she'd practically lived at their house—a mother who mostly left her with a string of au pairs, but when she was home flew into unpredictable rages and criticised her endlessly. And a father who lived in New Zealand with his new family and saw her once a year if she was lucky.

He'd got together with Emma when she was on the rebound from that psychopath Lewis, who by all accounts had been hideously jealous when he was with Emms. It got to the stage where he didn't even trust her to go out without him, and began stalking the TV production company in Soho where she worked as a researcher. Emma had been terrified. But now he was going out with her, Ed could almost see Lewis's point of view. There was something so mercurial about Emms. You thought you were holding onto her, but she was never quite there, even when she was actually in your arms. And then your mind began to play tricks.

He took a deep breath and called his sister.

'Ed . . . how's it going?'

'Hi, sis . . . is Emms there?'

There was a pause on the other end of the phone.

'Mash?'

'Sorry, I'm here. Just painting my toenails and it's got a bit crucial. You can't stop mid-nail or it goes lumpy, so I was wedging my phone on my shoulder. Go on . . .'

'I was supposed to be working tonight, but I swapped tomorrow's shift with Andy—he has to go to some family thing. So I thought I'd see Emms and she isn't answering her phone.'

'Sorry, she's not here. I haven't spoken to her

since this morning.'

'No probs, I'll keep trying. If you see her, let her know I called.'

'Sure . . . see ya.'

He hung up, embarrassed at his neediness, but he still couldn't believe a girl as beautiful as Emma would give him a second glance. She was surrounded by those cool, Oxbridge media types at work, all of whom must be hitting on her twenty-four seven. Shut up! He needed distraction, and sat himself down in front of some ludicrous television show with another beer.

The next thing he knew he was stretched out on the sofa, his phone, which he'd left on the cushion beside him, buzzing in his ear.

'Eddie?'

'Hi, babe.' He sat up, glancing at his watch. It was midnight.

'Sorry I didn't get back to you. God, I am so bloody knackered,' he heard her say.

'Working late?' he asked.

'I had to stay to make a couple of calls to the West Coast. They couldn't talk to me till their afternoon and of course they're eight hours behind. Anyway, one of them didn't even answer and the other was fucking useless.'

'Is this for the prison doc?'

Emma yawned. 'Yeah . . . and then Bryan insisted we go for a drink, and one drink led to another, you know how it is.'

'Nightmare,' he said, making every effort to trust what she was saying. Bryan was Emma's boss. He'd met him. He was paunchy and old and only talked about himself. No problem there.

'Listen, got to go to bed. Talk tomorrow. 'Night

. . . love you,' Emma was saying.

'Love you too.' And he did love her. He'd loved her—worshipped her—since he was about sixteen. But it had almost been easier before, loving her from afar, certain she'd never look at him in that way. Now he seemed to live in a perpetual state of fear that he would lose her.

*   *   *

'Mother, it's me,' Annie shouted into the intercom, and, after a certain amount of predictable fumbling Eleanor let her in to her elegant first-floor flat in Cadogan Gardens, two minutes' walk from Sloane Square.

'Darling, how lovely.' The brittle, almost stagey delivery of her mother's greeting always made it sound false to Annie, even when perhaps it wasn't.

'Mother.' She air-kissed the ageing, powdery cheeks, inhaling the timeless scent of Joy.

They went through to the large, high-ceilinged drawing room, where Eleanor sat down heavily in her armchair, adjusting the navy padded hairband that held her grey bob back from her face. Her mother had been considered a beauty in her youth—or so she had always told Annie—and even now she had the air of believing that still to be true in the way she held herself erect and proud.

The middle-aged Spanish housekeeper was dusting the rosewood table by the window, crammed with a variety of glass paperweights and silver-framed photographs.

'Morning, Mercedes.' Annie was very fond of the long-suffering woman. She was patient and kind with her tiresome mother, and she knew she would

23

do anything, literally anything, to make sure Mercedes never left. She gave Annie a smile and discreetly disappeared, duster and spray-polish in hand.

Annie watched as Eleanor swept the room with an imperious glance, checking, Annie knew, for any faults in the housework. Finding none, she turned her attention to her daughter.

'How are you?' Annie asked, sitting opposite on the brown velvet sofa. The room was freezing, but her eighty-two-year-old mother seemed not to notice.

'No complaints, darling. I could do without the wind, but otherwise I'm as busy as ever.'

Did she mean the April wind, or some internal complaint? Annie wondered. She'd never tell me if it was the latter, she decided, unless the situation was a dire medical emergency.

'Yes, it's been bitter for April.'

'Caro and I went to a superb lecture at the V&A yesterday. It was that marvellous man you see on that antiques programme. Can't remember his name . . . Morley something. Then we had a jolly lunch in the cafeteria.'

'Sounds fun. How is Caro?'

Eleanor pulled a face. 'Oh, you know. So-so. That woman always has something to moan about. If it's not her knees it's her wayward son or the price of lunch—which I thought very reasonable, if a trifle slapdash. All those tiresome help-yourself places are. But dear Caro never lets up.'

Annie could picture the two old ladies in the V&A cafeteria, politely sniping at each other but enjoying every minute. The smile she couldn't control received a reproving look from her mother.

'Moaning is unattractive and, what's more, it's very bad manners. Always think of others before oneself. That was my mother's motto and it's been mine. Follow that rule and one can't go wrong in life.'

True in essence, Annie thought, but perhaps her mother wasn't the best advertisement for this oft-repeated mantra, since she seemed to have gone through life never considering *anybody* but herself, except in her strict adherence to the finer points of etiquette.

For a while they chatted about the usual inconsequential things that Eleanor always saved for her. It mostly involved society tittle-tattle about people mercifully far removed from Annie's life now. Get on with it, Annie admonished herself, and took a deep breath.

'Mother . . . I've got something I want to tell you.' She heard her own voice sounding alarmingly portentous.

Eleanor, stopped in her tracks, raised her eyebrows and waited, fingering the string of pearls around her neck.

'Sounds ominous,' she said.

'It is. Well, "ominous" isn't the right word. It's more . . . well . . . I wasn't going to tell you, but . . .'

'Stop mumbling, darling. I can't understand a word you're saying.'

Annie drew herself up, leaning forward on the sofa, steeling herself for her mother's reaction. Does it really matter what she thinks, she asked herself.

'I've heard from Kent Social Services. My son wants to meet me.'

'Your son?' Eleanor looked as puzzled as Richard had, then horrified. 'You mean the adopted one?'

'Well, I'm not talking about Ed, Mother.'

'That's outrageous! What does he want? It must be money. He's heard you're successful with those cakes of yours and he wants a handout.'

'Mother!'

'Well, darling, really. Think about it. He must be what, thirty-something by now? Why has he suddenly come out of the woodwork? I hope you're not going to indulge him.'

'What sort of a woman wouldn't want to meet the baby they gave away?'

'A very sensible one, in my opinion. You're soft, Annie, you always have been, just like your father. That's how you got yourself into this mess in the first place. Take it from me, no man of that age needs a mother. He'll just use you.'

'Thanks.' She got up; she'd had enough. 'Anyway, I thought I should let you know.'

Eleanor tutted. 'No need to take umbrage, darling. I'm just warning you. I'm sure dear Richard has said the same thing.'

Here we go, she thought crossly, the Dear Richard moment. He didn't remotely fit the bill for Eleanor's Ideal Husband. He wasn't aristocratic, didn't have inherited wealth, land or a title, hadn't gone to Eton or Oxford, didn't buy his clothes in Jermyn Street or have his hair cut at Trumpers. Yet to Eleanor he could do no wrong. Richard played up to her mother, tongue in cheek, but in fact the two got on surprisingly well.

'He hasn't, actually.' Annie reached down to give her a chilly peck on the cheek.

26

'Well, he should have. This chap . . . you know nothing about him. Just because he's your son, you think he's bona fide, but he could, for instance, be violent. You have no idea who adopted him. They weren't necessarily nice people you know, darling. Not like us. They could have been drinkers, or criminals. Feckless, at any rate. One can't rely on his having our values.'

Our values! she spluttered silently. Our values? Would they be the ones that ran her daughter out of town, a teenager and pregnant? He'll be lucky if he doesn't have our values, she thought.

'We don't even know the exact provenance of his genes,' Eleanor added, her look sly.

'I'd better get back to work,' Annie said, ignoring the pointed remark.

'Be angry with me if you like. But promise me, if you do see the boy, make sure Richard is there too. Please, darling. I'm serious.' The old lady looked anxiously at her.

'Yes, Mother,' she replied, her heart softening at her mother's obvious, though surely misplaced, concern.

Even the raw wind was a relief to Annie as she made her way across Sloane Square to the Tube. It was Richard who had insisted she tell her mother before she told the children—Daniel was, after all, her grandson. She was glad it was over; the conversation with her mother reminded Annie of so much she'd tried hard to forget.

*   *   *

Lucy was sitting at the kitchen table cradling a mug of tea when Annie got home.

'Not at work?'

Lucy shook her head. 'I took the morning off. It's the interview on Friday and I need to practise.'

'Interview?' Annie frowned.

'You know, the volunteer NGO job? I told you.' Lucy looked a bit put out that her mother hadn't remembered. 'Which is great, but I'm hopeless at interviews. I get so nervous my voice shakes. Will you go through the sort of things they might ask? You know, coach me?'

Annie's heart sank. She knew her youngest was hell bent on saving every child in Africa. It had started in her teens when she watched a documentary about AIDS orphans. She and Richard had been sure it was just a phase, but Lucy had gone on to choose a degree in Social Anthropology at SOAS, and was now utterly committed to working in an African orphanage.

'Of course.' She paused. 'But you don't think Dad would be better qualified to help? I've never been for a proper interview in my life. Mother secured all my jobs.'

'I suppose that was one of the advantages of your posh upbringing.'

'Hmmm. Well, without sounding like a brat, it certainly didn't seem like an advantage at the time because it was always the job that Mother thought would be suitable. I didn't have any say.'

'Couldn't you tell her you didn't want to do it?'

'I suppose the problem was that at that stage I didn't know what I wanted to do. If I had, I'm sure I'd have stood up to her.' She didn't add that, at the time, she had lost all confidence in herself, that she hadn't cared much *what* she did, as long as it was something that stopped her having too much

28

time to think about the baby.

Lucy was silent for a minute, then said, 'You know I really appreciate you and Dad not trying to stop me going to Africa, Mum?'

Annie smiled. 'You shouldn't thank us. We would if we could.' In fact Richard had broken out in a sweat when he thought of his precious daughter in such a potentially dangerous environment. 'She'll be all on her own. She's sure to be kidnapped, or killed . . . I can't bear to think what else.' But Annie, no more sanguine than her husband about the danger, but considerably more realistic when it came to Lucy's determination, convinced him there was nothing either of them could do to stop her.

'Yeah, I know,' Lucy said. 'And that's why I love it that you're supporting me.' She paused. 'God, I can't imagine you telling me what work I should do.'

'No, well, different times.'

'So will you help me? You've interviewed loads of people for the bakery—you must know what makes you take one person over another. And Dad'll just get hysterical and say dumb things about how there are lots of children in this country who need saving.'

'He's probably right.'

'Don't start!' Lucy began gathering up the stack of papers on the table. 'I'd better get going, I'm going to be late. Can we do it tonight? Just grill me a bit so I get my courage up?'

Annie nodded.

'This is the only thing I've ever wanted to do, Mum. It might be hard, but I have to go. It means everything to me.'

Her earnest face, with the brown eyes full of compassion and missionary zeal, tore at her mother's heart.

'No, I know, darling. But we're your parents. We worry.'

Lucy shook her head in amused despair, and waved goodbye to her mother.

4

Dear Tom,

I know you are called Daniel now, and I shall call you that from now on, but Tom was the name I gave you when you were born. I am writing to say that I would be very happy to meet you. If you are still keen, I suggest we do so at the house of Marjory Best, the lady who took me in when I was pregnant with you and who's happy to host our meeting. She lives in Kent, about eight miles from Canterbury, and her nearest station is Faversham. I don't know where you live, but I hope this isn't too inconvenient for you. I thought it would be better to meet there than in a noisy public place.

I have suggested two o'clock on Saturday April 27th to Marjory. I hope these arrangements suit you, Daniel, but if not, please don't hesitate to suggest an alternative.

With best wishes,
Annie Delancey

She had written and re-written the letter until her head spun, then left it burning a hole on her laptop, unable to do any more about it.

'Should I be more loving?' Annie asked Richard now, reading the letter out to him one final time before sending it off. 'It sounds so formal.' She clutched the print out in her hand, hovering over her husband as he sat on the sofa in the sitting room, trying to read the paper before supper.

'At this stage, "loving" would be a little weird,' he muttered, not taking his eyes from the page.

'Well, do you think it's too personal then? The bit about naming him Tom? Perhaps I should leave that out?'

Richard lowered the paper, smiling up at his wife. 'No, I like that. It's good to have something about your connection with each other in there.'

'So is it bossy to be the one to suggest the time and place? Maybe he should be the one to take the lead on this. I mean, he's a thirty-five-year-old man. He can presumably make his own decisions.'

'Up to you, Annie. But I don't see there's anything wrong with making your own suggestion. If he has another idea, I'm sure he'll say so.'

'Yes, but I don't want to put him off before he's even seen me.'

'Annie! You've written a brilliant letter. Just send it, for God's sake.'

But she wasn't to be mollified. This was too important.

'He's probably got a car. I think I'll leave out the bit about the train. He can Google it anyway, if he needs to get one. I don't want him to think I'm being patronising.'

Richard just shook his head, picking up his paper again.

'OK, OK,' she walked over to her desk in the

corner. After adding Marjory's address and a covering letter to Kent Social Services, she pressed 'print', collected the letters from the tray, signed them, read them through just one more time, and folded them into an envelope before she had time to change her mind.

*   *   *

Annie arrived at the bakery with some relief. She had spent the last two days, since sending the letter off, obsessively thinking about Daniel, imagining what they would talk about, how he would look: Will he resemble me? My side of the family? Or will the Carnegie clan be dominant? She tried to recall exactly what Charles looked like, but the image had become blurred by time. He was handsome—she remembered that much— tall and blond, his hair wavy and a little long—it was the sixties—and cringed as she remembered her eighteen-year-old self thinking him almost godlike. Perhaps his eyes were blue? She couldn't be sure. And the set of his features wouldn't materialise at all. She hoped Daniel didn't favour his father too much; it would be hard to take.

She hurried down the steps of her floury, sweet-smelling kingdom. Here she was in control and knew exactly what she was doing. She loved it. And the beautiful thing about a cake was its mechanical simplicity. People panicked about cakes but the truth was that, if you followed certain steps, you got certain results. Nothing in her life had ever been as uncomplicated as her cakes.

The room was large and light. Although it was a semi-basement beneath a two-storey sixties block

32

of offices behind Gospel Oak station, the high windows, which faced onto a small car park at the rear of the building, ran the length of the bakery and took up almost a third of the back wall. So although the strip-lights were on except when there was very bright sunlight, the room never suffered from the claustrophobia of a basement.

Four long, laminated work surfaces stretched across the space, a bank of ovens sat against the north wall, an industrial-sized fridge on the opposite side. Metal shelving ran above the work surfaces and against the walls, stacked high with baking tins, cake-stands, boards, cutters, tins of icing, flour, sugar-craft, ribbon, dowels to hold the tiers in place—everything needed to make a celebration cake.

Each of her four employees momentarily stopped work to greet Annie. Jodie, her manager, a tough, lively woman in her thirties, was in the corner office responding to orders on the computer.

'Morning, Annie.' She rolled her shoulders and pushed the desk chair away from the computer. 'Masses of orders, all weddings so far today—and mostly for September.' She smiled at her boss as she reached back to re-knot her dark ponytail.

'Great. The autumn surge never lets us down.' Annie sat down at her own desk, which was pushed tight against her manager's in the small space.

Jodie nodded agreement. 'How's things?'

'Good, yes.' The fact that her long-lost son was trying to contact her seemed somehow unreal in this mundane work environment. She'd hidden it away in a secret compartment of her brain.

'Coffee?'

Annie nodded enthusiastically. 'Please, that would be wonderful.'

She looked through the glass of the office wall, and saw the other three employees hard at work. Carol, a plump, middle-aged baking genius, was levelling cake mixture in four deep tins. Kadir, a young Turkish boy who spoke little English, was painting edible silver colouring onto icing scrolls on the top layer of a wedding cake. Annie hadn't known how he would fit in when she had taken him on a year ago, but she soon found he had artistic flair and one of the steadiest hands in the business for decorating the cakes. Lisa, the last of the crew, was the general factotum. In her twenties and from the estate opposite, she cheerfully cleaned, cleared, mixed ingredients, listed supplies, set ovens. Without her, Annie knew, the more delicate egos of Carol and Kadir wouldn't be able to function.

Jodie placed a mug of coffee on the desk beside her.

'Kadir's come up with some ideas for the Chandos wedding.' Jodie pushed across a sheaf of sketches. 'I think the first one's great.'

Annie looked at the drawings, happy that Kadir was beginning to take over some of her design work. She pointed. 'This one?'

Jodie checked and nodded.

Annie considered it for a moment. 'Yes, very good. Complicated and time-consuming, but he and Carol are more than capable.' The sketch in front of her was for a lavish concoction consisting of flowers in pink and white—roses, apple blossom, honeysuckle, lilies, dog roses—spilling elegantly from a wooden gardening trug, the handle tied with a huge bow. 'That should satisfy Madam.'

Stick-thin Serena Chandos, who looked as if she would faint with fear at even the smell of cake, had nonetheless insisted on coming to the bakery, though she was hardly able to negotiate the steep concrete steps in her designer stiletto boots. She wafted a sharp perfume, at odds with the sugary ambience of the room, and produced from her Burberry bag a raft of hideous designs that no self-respecting cake would be seen dead in. She had wanted something that reflected her husband-to-be's market-gardening business, which he ran from his vast Yorkshire estate. Annie had needed to be very diplomatic.

Jodie laughed. 'It'll cost her, but she went on and on about how money's no object. She seemed to think it impressed us.'

'You mean she thought we loved her because she was rich, whereas in fact it's only the money we love!'

'Yeah, 'fraid so. Although I reckon women like that don't actually give a toss about what people like us think.'

Carol, her round face framed by a white-cotton peaked cap encompassing her greying hair, stuck her head round the door.

'Sorry, ladies, but I need some input.' Annie beckoned her inside. 'You know the Carnegie cake ... the chocolate one with a yacht on top?' Both women nodded. It was for a diamond wedding. The couple lived on Hayling Island and had been obsessive sailors. 'Just checking. The spec. says "alcohol"? Not sure what that means.' She waved the plastic pocket with the specifications at Annie.

Annie took it absentmindedly. The name: Carnegie. She had heard it last week, and months ago when the order was made. It wasn't the first cake they'd made for the family, but although the name always resonated uncomfortably with her and prompted mild conjecture, it hadn't held the significance it did today.

'Annie?' Carol said, when she didn't reply.

'I'll look,' Jodie volunteered, giving Annie a puzzled glance while she brought the order up on the screen. 'Carnegie ... yeah, I remember. He drinks, she doesn't. The daughter says she thinks it would be OK to put booze in if it's not too strong. She was leaving it to us.'

'It tastes nicer with a wee tot,' Carol suggested.

Annie handed the spec. back to Carol, but couldn't focus, her gaze still far away. Could this be Charles's family? His parents, maybe, or an uncle and aunt? Would Charles himself be at the anniversary party?

'Use your judgment,' Jodie was saying. 'If it were me, I'd put some in. Once it's baked it doesn't taste of alcohol anyway, it just tastes better.'

'As long as she's not allergic or anything.'

Jodie shook her head. 'The daughter would've said, surely. Anyway, they've been married sixty years. If she croaks after a bite of anniversary cake, at least they'll have had a good run for their marital money.'

Carol chuckled. 'Mightn't be too hot for business if the clients start keeling over.'

'True, but he must be almost dead himself if he's been married that long.'

'Mind boggles. I've done twenty-eight and that's nearly killed me!'

'Not quite what I meant,' Jodie grinned.

Annie heard their banter, but couldn't respond. She shook herself. 'Sorry, missed that.' She looked apologetically at Carol.

'We were just speculating about Mrs Carnegie's demise, Snow White-style, from a bite of Carol's booze-infused sponge,' said Jodie, trying to control her laughter, but Carol obviously noticed Annie's blank face and gave her a questioning look.

'I'd better get on,' Carol muttered, before making a quick exit.

'Are you OK?' Jodie asked.

'Fine. I'm fine,' Annie assured her manager. 'Can I just take a look at the Carnegie order?'

Jodie frowned. 'I don't think there's a problem. The daughter definitely left it up to us to decide on the alcohol content. We were only joking about Mrs Carnegie.'

'No, I know that. I just wanted to check something.'

Jodie moved over. Annie took her seat, and examined the detail of the order. It was from a Mrs Laura Mackenzie. Charles's sister, she remembered, had been called Venetia. She let her breath out slowly. There must be hundreds of Carnegies, but she remembered her mother saying Charles's parents had a boat. Had he another sister? Daniel would surely want to meet his father, however disastrous it might prove. Her mother could track him down, no doubt. Eleanor kept up with many of her previous pupils from the days when she ran the smart finishing school for 'young ladies' in Knightsbridge that she'd named the Westbury Academy. But the thought of finally telling her mother the name of Daniel's father filled her with dismay. She could already hear the recriminations.

'OK,' she said to Jodie, closing the document and repressing a sudden desire to confess everything to her. Her mobile bleeped. A text:

> *Thanks for getting back to me. Yes, I can make 27th. Look forward to meeting you then. Regards, Daniel Gray.*

*　　　*　　　*

Annie's mobile rang as she was preparing supper that evening. She grabbed the phone eagerly.

'Annie?' Marjory's husky voice sounded expectant.

'Marjory, hi. Thanks for calling back. I just wanted to say that we're on. He's coming . . . yes, yes, very exciting . . . see you then.'

'Who's coming, and why is it so exciting?'

Annie jumped and spun round. She hadn't heard Lucy come in.

'Umm . . . oh, just . . .' she could feel the colour rising to her cheeks and turned quickly back to the stove, bending to open the oven door. 'I'm taking Jamie to see Marjory next weekend. They haven't seen each other for years.' It wasn't a lie exactly, just not the whole truth, but it grated on Annie's conscience.

'That'll be fun,' Lucy said.

When the flush had finally subsided and Annie looked at her daughter again, she could see Lucy was regarding her carefully, a small frown on her face.

'Work OK?' Annie asked.

38

'Mmm, yeah. Nothing special.'

Lucy wandered over to the stove.

'This looks like a bit of a feast, Mum. What's the occasion?' The 'feast' included rolls of smoked salmon sprinkled with lemon and pepper, each roll pierced with a cocktail stick and arranged on a round wooden platter; a large roasted sea bass nestling in foil with thin slices of fennel, spring onion and lemon caramelising on the top; rosemary potatoes; pak choi with ginger and soy sauce, and a chilled bottle of Sauvignon Blanc.

'Oh, nothing. Just felt like cooking. You know me.'

'You're being unusually, well, sort of kind at the moment.' Annie caught her daughter's questioning gaze again, but continued scraping the small, crisping chunks of potato from the roasting tin and spooning them into a warmed white china serving dish.

'Aren't I always the kindest and most considerate mother on the planet?' She raised an amused eyebrow at Lucy.

'Uh, well, reasonably so, I suppose,' conceded Lucy with a grin. 'But this last week you've been particularly, well, sort of extra kind.'

'Have I?'

'For instance, you offered to pay for my Africa trip if I get the job, even though you think it's stupid and dangerous. You didn't go off on one when Mash said she was getting a tattoo on her ankle—which, by the way, she totally won't. You agreed with Dad about the new car, even though you hate those Honda hybrid things. And you didn't even nag him when he put the plates in the dishwasher without rinsing them. That's a first!'

Annie laughed. 'I hadn't noticed. Right: can you give Dad a shout? Supper's ready.'

But Lucy wasn't to be put off.

'Dad,' she said, as soon as her father appeared, 'have you noticed Mum being a bit sort of *different* recently?'

Richard kept an admirably straight face.

'Different in what way?'

Lucy frowned again, her gaze darting between her parents.

'I don't know . . . something . . .'

Richard put his arm round her, gave her a squeeze. 'Can't say I have,' he lied.

Annie shot him a grateful look. It amazed her that Lucy hadn't clocked something was up before this. She knew she'd been distracted, almost euphoric at times, since the letter had arrived. And her daughter had always been overly sensitive to atmosphere.

Lucy shrugged, shook her head. 'OK, don't tell me then. As long as it's not cancer or one of you having an affair.'

There was silence for a moment, then Annie and Richard both let out an awkward laugh.

'You've got too much imagination,' Annie told her.

'Drink?' Richard pressed a glass of chilled white into his daughter's hand.

*   *   *

'So . . . have you arranged the meeting yet? With the boy?' Richard asked, his voice lowered, even though Lucy had gone upstairs to bed a while ago.

Annie nodded. 'Saturday week at Marjory's.'

'Great. I'll drive you down.'

She didn't reply for a moment.

'Thanks, darling, but I've asked Jamie to come. I thought . . . well, he was there at the time, and he knows Marjory . . .'

She winced as she saw the hurt flash across his face. 'I know Marjory too,' he said.

'Richard, I'm so sorry. I didn't think you'd want to be involved at this stage . . . it being my past, before we met.'

'It may be your past, but I'm totally involved in everything in your life now, aren't I?'

He still looked upset, which she couldn't bear. They'd never talked about her baby, and she'd always thought it was because he didn't want to imagine her with another man. Most people of her generation had some sexual history, but often it was hidden or merely hearsay. She still found she was embarrassed by this living, breathing evidence of a life before she'd met Richard.

'Come with us then. Please, Richard. It would be great to have you there.'

He shook his head. 'You're probably right . . . and we don't want to frighten him off with great crowds of us.'

'It wouldn't be crowds.'

'No, but perhaps it's better, this first time, that you keep it simple.'

She reached for his hand. 'I'm sorry. I should have discussed it with you.'

'Doesn't matter. No harm done.'

5

Annie's bed looked as if she were clearing out her cupboards for a jumble sale. Discarded clothes lay in untidy heaps as she tried on one thing after another. She paused to look in the long mirror at the latest—navy trousers and a blue pastel cashmere V-neck—then ripped them off again. Nothing looks right, she wailed silently. It feels exactly like when I was young and dressing to meet a new date.

She was passionate about clothes, her style classic yet individual. When she had the time, she would spend hours in the local north-London charity shops where, to the irritation of her relatively impoverished daughters, she would ferret out designer gems for less than five pounds. But what on earth do you wear to meet a long-lost son?

Richard poked his head round the door. 'Jamie's here.'

She turned from the mirror in a panic.

'Already? What's the time?'

'Nearly ten,' Richard's expression was solemn. She wasn't sure he had quite forgiven her for the arbitrary way she had organised the meeting without him.

'But I'm not ready!'

'You look great.'

She pulled a face, turning back to the long mirror. By now she had on black jeans, a white tee shirt and a dusky-pink fitted Chanel wool jacket with bold pink and gold buttons she had picked up in one of her charity-shop forays many years ago.

'I love the jacket,' Richard added, 'but isn't it a bit smart for Marjory's kitchen?'

She sighed impatiently and ripped it off. 'I know, but I feel good in it. Well, what should I wear then? Some hideous old cardie?'

'As if.'

She picked up a charcoal wool tunic. 'This'll have to do. What do I care if he thinks I'm a frump?' She pulled it quickly over her head and began to fiddle with her hair, which she'd had cut just above her shoulders the day before and which was, in her opinion, much too short. While wondering what Daniel would look like, she wondered as well what he would make of her. She knew she favoured her late father more than her mother. She had strong cheekbones, her father's elegant, aquiline nose and wide-set grey-blue eyes. She knew she wasn't beautiful, but hoped she passed for good-looking. People said she looked much younger than she was—not too much sagging and bagging yet, thank goodness—but would her son approve?

'OK . . . that's it. I can't do any more.' She cast an agonised look at Richard. 'I'm scared.'

Her husband smiled sympathetically. 'Of course you are.'

'You could still come with us?' She reached to kiss him on the cheek.

'Thanks, but no. I've got work to catch up on,' he replied. 'You'd better get going.'

*   *   *

Annie drove. She had long since refused to go in Jamie's car. He not only drove like a boy racer, but

43

kept the interior so immaculate that if she so much as breathed he would tut and whip out a wet-wipe.

'How do you want to play it? Do you want me to stay in the room while you meet him?' Jamie asked, as they sat in the Saturday-morning traffic clogging up Lewisham High Street. 'Or hover? What?'

She shook her head. 'I just can't imagine it. I mean, what will we do? Hug? Shake hands?' She drove in silence for a while. 'And what will we talk about?' She glanced over at her friend. 'Can you stay at first? Make it a bit more normal, so it's not just him and me.'

'Well, if you think I'm normal, or Aunt Best for that matter! Let's hope he hasn't led a sheltered life.'

She laughed nervously. It had been Jamie's suggestion she meet Daniel at Marjory Best's house in Kent. Annie had first met Aunt Best—as she was known to the girls—one freezing day in December 1966. Six months pregnant and terrified by the unexpected turn her life had taken, she had arrived at the comfortably chaotic vicarage, dropped off by her mother as if Eleanor was unburdening herself of an awkward pet. At that time there was one other girl staying in Marjory's sanctuary for unmarried mothers—a shy, annoying seventeen-year-old who spent all day crying. Annie, who'd been brought up never to cry unless seriously injured, and then as little as possible, looked upon Clemency with a disdain worthy of her mother. But Marjory had taught her compassion, shown them both respect. And, indeed, love.

'Marjory's not legging it, is she?' Jamie was

asking.

'No, so you can talk about the weather or her beloved magnolias while Daniel and I get used to each other.'

'Yeah, see how it goes. If you want us to leave, just cough loudly, or scratch you nose—whatever—and we'll make ourselves scarce.'

'I'm terrified, Jamie. I keep getting goosebumps when I think of seeing him.'

He didn't respond for a moment, then said, 'He's going to want to know what happened, isn't he.'

'You mean why I gave him away?' She sighed. 'It's haunted me since the day they took him.'

'What will you say?'

'What can I say? I wasn't some poor girl from a starving family with eighteen to a bed and coal in the bath. I was rich by most people's standards. At least Mother was rich. We had a house large enough for five Toms ... Daniels.' She looked across at her friend. 'Not much leeway there.'

'Just tell it how it was, darling. If he doesn't understand, there's not much you can do about it now.'

They pulled off the motorway, following signs for Faversham. It had begun to spit slightly and the windscreen wipers dragged noisily across the car window. This was a familiar route for her. She had spent much of the year after Tom's adoption driving down from London to be with Marjory—like a murderer revisiting the scene of her crime. But it was comforting to have a friend who was prepared to talk about what had happened and listen to how she was feeling. Her mother certainly wasn't.

The Georgian vicarage looked just the same,

elegantly decaying in its mature garden, neglected now that Marjory couldn't physically indulge her passion. Annie hadn't been down for over a year, but she met Marjory in London every few months, collecting her off the train at Charing Cross and walking slowly with her to the National Gallery. Marjory had always chosen which work she wanted to view that day; it could be anything, modern or ancient, sculpture, watercolour, oil painting or a drawing. Her friend was eclectic in her taste. She would settle down in front of the piece, silently absorbing the whole at first, then talking in detail to Annie about how it was created, its provenance, the artist, the period, why she liked it. It was a treat for Annie, who had been introduced to art by her Uncle Terence but had had no formal education in the subject. Then, when the old lady had decided the painting had been given due respect, they would wander down to the gallery cafe and have lunch.

*   *   *

As the car drew up on the weed-ridden gravel drive, Marjory appeared in the doorway, propped on a thick, ebony cane. She looked every inch the artist she was, her tall, lean figure, silver-haired and elegant even in baggy corduroys, a black polo-neck sweater and a red knitted scarf slung casually round her neck, gave the appearance of being younger and more robust than Annie knew her to be.

'God, she hasn't changed a bit!' Jamie exclaimed as he got out of the car and went to greet the old lady.

'Jamie, dear, this is such a pleasure for me!' Marjory embraced him, then moved to kiss Annie. For a moment Annie clung to her, wallowing in Aunt Best's reassuring love.

'Sorry, guys, need a pee.' Jamie carefully sashayed past Marjory into the hall.

'End on the left,' Marjory called, looking after Jamie. 'He hasn't changed at all. He still looks so young.'

'That's exactly what he said about you.'

'Would that it were true.' Marjory shook her head, a wry smile lighting her washed-out blue eyes. 'I'd make a pact with the devil to be mobile again, but the bastard hasn't made me an offer yet.'

They went through to the kitchen, where Marjory had set out lunch on the oak table. Unlike the rest of the large house, the room was warm. What will Daniel make of this place, Annie wondered, glancing around with a new eye now that she had her son in mind. It had not been redecorated in at least two decades and was gloriously untidy, filled with piles of books, newspapers, sketches on torn-off scraps of paper, paintbrushes soaking in jam jars full of murky water. She knew Marjory still had her 'morning woman', as she called Mrs Blundell, but Joan was almost as ancient as Marjory. Annie revelled in the familiar chaos. She sank gratefully into the worn armchair by the Raeburn, almost hoping that her son wouldn't come, as she listened to Marjory and Jamie catching up on the decades since they had last met.

'Sit, sit,' Marjory urged her guests, pouring a glass of red wine for each of them. They ate the

47

smoked mackerel, potato salad, sliced beetroot and brown bread in silence for a while, perhaps nobody wanting to be the first person to mention the reason why they were there.

Marjory eventually took courage. 'He's coming at two?'

'He said so, yes.'

'He knows how to get here, I assume.'

'I only gave him the address. Do you think I should have sent him detailed directions? It's not that easy to find.' Annie began to panic.

Jamie laughed. 'He'll ring if he's lost, darling. We live in the twenty-first century now. He's not a child.'

Annie was upset by her friend's remark. For a moment Daniel's missing childhood hovered between them. She looked yet again at the large station clock ticking loudly on the wall beside the wooden dresser. It said one thirty-five, three minutes later than when she'd last checked. Her heart was fluttering and her mouth dry. She wished she hadn't had the glass of wine. Would he smell it on her breath?

'Shall we sit in here when he comes?' Marjory asked. 'I've done a fire in the sitting room, but it's still not very warm in there.'

Annie glanced at her two friends, waiting for guidance.

'Let's stay in here. It's properly cosy . . . love it.' Jamie declared, throwing his arms wide to embrace the mess as if it were an artwork. 'OK if I just go for a wander in the garden before he gets here?' he asked, getting up from the table.

Marjory nodded to him.

'I don't really know what to expect,' Annie said,

when they were alone.

'Expect nothing if you can, dear.' Marjorie reached across to pat Annie's hand. 'Because there might be disappointment. You might not relate to him, or you might not even like him. He might be angry, or needy . . . just plain dull.'

Annie said nothing, not believing a word of what Aunt Best was telling her. Of course I'll like my own son, she said to herself.

'I'm not saying it *will* be like this, of course. It's just he's spent a lifetime out of sight, and genes don't guarantee love. You know as well as anybody, parenting is about familiarity, Annie. You see your child every minute of every day, for decades. You build on your primary instinct to love. But with Tom, you only have the fact that you're related, and the memory that you loved him once. It might be enough to begin a relationship, but then again it might not.'

'It's hard to think like that.'

'I'm not trying to put a dampener on things.' Marjory eased herself out of the chair and stood still for a moment to steady herself with her stick before moving slowly across to the sink. 'I just think it's important not to have too many expectations.'

Annie felt a surge of anxiety at Marjory's words and realised she couldn't think beyond this first meeting. I don't have any expectations, she thought, beyond actually setting eyes on my firstborn child again.

'We'd better clear up a bit.' Marjory bent stiffly to open the dishwasher, and Annie began collecting the glasses.

'I asked Mrs B. for one of her Victoria sponges.

Men always like cake.'

The thought of the sponge cake brought sudden tears to Annie's eyes. Every day when she was pregnant, gathered round this same table, Aunt Best would insist on the ritual of tea. Whoever was in the house, and anyone else sensible enough to drop by at three thirty, was encouraged to join in. It was a time for conversation, for catching up with the day, for laughter, for sharing worries.

Back then Marjory baked too: flapjacks, banana bread, lemon cupcakes—nothing fancy. Her baking was enthusiastic rather than consistent, and there was much merriment at the failures. But Mrs Blundell had the magic touch. Her cakes were creamy, light and melting, always utterly delicious. It was memories of Joan Blundell's Victoria sponge that had set Annie on the path, many years later, to Delancey Bakes.

She went up behind Marjory and put her arms round her thin shoulders.

'That was the dearest thing to do,' she said. Nothing bad can happen to me, she thought, under the auspices of Aunt Best, and Joan Blundell's Victoria sponge.

There was a sudden clatter of feet on the flagstones in the hall, and Jamie burst into the kitchen.

'He's here! Quick, he's just getting out of the car. And tell you what, he's absolutely GORgeous!'

Annie closed her eyes for a moment and took a steadying breath.

'Let's do it!' Marjory's authoritative voice urged Annie forward, through the kitchen, into the hall, towards the open front door and her reunion with her son, Daniel Gray.

Jamie's right, he *is* beautiful, was her first thought. Really stunning. And the spitting image of Uncle Terence.

'How do you do. I'm Marjory Best.' Marjory was shaking the man firmly by the hand. 'Please, do come in.' The afternoon was still overcast and drizzling; a typical April day.

'Hi, I'm Daniel.' He introduced himself, his voice surprisingly strong and confident. He glanced quickly between Jamie and Annie, his gaze settling on Annie. She tried to speak, but no words came out, so she just held out her hand to him. The glaring genetic connection was so startling that it was almost like a physical blow.

Daniel was tall with broad shoulders, his thick wavy hair a dark auburn and falling just below his ears. He had her own grey-blue eyes, strong, sculpted features—more beautiful than handsome —dominated by her father's nose, but otherwise Terence Sinclair seemed incarnate in front of her. Her flesh and blood, no question. And not a trace of Charles Carnegie, she thought with a twinge of childish satisfaction.

'Annie Delancey,' she said eventually.

For a moment they clasped hands in silence. The others were moving off towards the kitchen, but she and Daniel continued to stare at each other. Just as she had when he was a baby, she wanted to gaze at him forever.

'Come through,' she heard Marjory call.

Daniel waited, gesturing politely to her to go first.

Marjory filled the kettle and put it on the Raeburn. Jamie took down the cake tin from the dresser and carefully lifted the sponge onto a white

51

plate with a blue rim. It looked perfect, cream and jam poking temptingly from between the golden sponge layers, icing sugar dusting the top like a light fall of snow. Annie hovered, hardly daring to look at the man.

'Do take your coat off,' Marjory urged him. 'There are hooks just outside the door to the right.'

Daniel obediently removed his battered black leather jacket and disappeared to hang it up.

'OK?' Jamie mouthed at Annie, smiling encouragingly.

The ritual of tea and cake took up the next half-hour. Conversation was light and mostly conducted by Marjory and Jamie, who adopted a breezy normality that wasn't matched by the other two. It was Jamie who asked the questions: Had he found the house all right? Did he know the area? Where had he come from? What shocking spring weather they were having. Yes, Marjory was an artist. No, Annie didn't live round here, but in north London.

Annie listened and watched. This was basic information, but it was daunting, reminding her how much she didn't yet know about her own son. Apparently he lived in north London too. In a rented flat in Finsbury Park—no distance from her at all. I could have bumped into him anytime on the street, in the supermarket, and never known, she thought.

He'd been brought up in Brighton, had only passed through Kent on his way to the ferry at Folkestone, so no, he didn't know the area. He wrote plays. So far he'd had short ones put on in pub theatres and the like. He'd been to

Cambridge, started as a copywriter in advertising, then made the leap to theatre—his one true love. He seemed shining and confident to Annie, articulate as he took the grilling with good grace. How can he not be nervous? she asked herself, in awe.

When Jamie got up to fill the teapot, Marjory turned to Annie.

'Why don't you two go through to the sitting room? It'll have warmed up by now, and it's more private.'

Annie felt suddenly panicky at being alone with him.

'Daniel?'

He nodded, but she could see in his uncertain smile the first sign that this meeting was hard for him too.

The sitting room was warm and quiet, the furniture soft and yielding with age. They sat opposite each other in worn chintz armchairs, the fire between them making the air sharp with wood smoke. The gold carriage clock ticked like a sentinel on the mantelpiece. Neither of them knew where to look. Where there had been too little intimacy in the kitchen, now there was almost too much.

'This is so strange.' Daniel was the first to speak.

She nodded. 'I've imagined it a million times since ...' She couldn't say it. But her heart suddenly soared with happiness. This is Tom. This is him. This is my son.

'Am I as you imagined?' he asked quietly.

'I only knew you for a few days,' she paused, 'I can only remember you as you were then. A baby.'

'So not quite as you thought then,' he joked, his

confidence returning.

'You're the spit of my uncle—your great-uncle—Terence.'

She saw him waiting expectantly.

'My father died when I was young, and Uncle Terence sort of took over. He was a gorgeous, flamboyant character, a life-enhancer in every way. I loved him very much. He was my mother's brother.' How much could she fairly say about Mother, the pivotal figure in both their histories . . . ? 'I don't know . . . for some reason I never expected such a strong family resemblance. I suppose I hadn't dared think about it . . . about you . . . as part of my family.' She knew she was babbling, but she couldn't seem to stop herself.

'It's odd,' he replied, 'because you know every bit of my genetic history, and I know absolutely none. Was my father . . . was he important in your life?'

She gave a small sigh. 'Your father was . . . not really important, no.' She wouldn't utter the words 'one-night stand'.

Daniel looked at her, waiting for her to continue, but she didn't know what to say.

'So you weren't in a relationship with him when I was born?'

'No. No, I wasn't,' she said quickly. He mustn't think there was a perfectly good couple who'd chosen to give him away. She looked her son straight in the eye. 'We were never in a relationship. It was one night. He wasn't interested after that.'

Daniel glanced away. 'But you . . . liked him? At the time?'

'At the time, yes, I suppose I did.' She didn't want to say that she had quickly made up her mind

54

that Charles was an arrogant prat—good-looking and rich, the perfect profile of the man her mother had brought her up to desire. She had been naïve and inexperienced; he had taken advantage. That's what she had told herself. But she had to admit that it hadn't been entirely one-sided.

'Are you in touch now?'

She shook her head. 'We never spoke again.' How bleak to have this as the beginning of your life. No love, no friendship, no connection at all. Just a hasty, fumbled lust.

'So he really didn't want anything to do with me?'

'No, it wasn't like that. I never told him. He doesn't know about you to this day. Almost no one does.'

Daniel turned away from her, but not before Annie had caught the surprise on his face.

'Wow! *That* bad. So he might not even be alive.'

She kicked herself for her insensitivity. Did he really have to know that his very existence was like a dirty secret? He must now be wondering if things would have been different if she'd chosen to tell his father—a question she'd asked herself endlessly.

'I think my mother would have heard via the grapevine if something had happened to him,' she told him. 'His family knew my mother quite well, not friends exactly . . .' She paused. 'My mother ran a finishing school for girls in Knightsbridge: the Westbury Academy. His sister was one of her pupils. He came with her to the end-of-year dance and that's where I met him.' For a moment she had a flash of what had been, for her, a magical night. But her past seemed so shallow and redundant in the telling. A finishing school? Knightsbridge? Hardly the profile of a disadvantaged single mother driven by economic circumstances to give her baby away.

'What was his name?' Even Daniel spoke about him in the past, as if he no longer existed.

The name stuck in her throat. 'Charles Carnegie.'

There was a knock at the door and Marjory peered in.

'All OK in here?'

Annie turned. Her face felt flushed by the heat of the fire. 'Yes . . . yes, fine, thank you. We won't be long.'

Marjory waved her hands expansively. 'Take as long as you like.' She eyed the fire, then Daniel. 'Put another log on, would you, dear? I don't want it going out now it's lit.'

Daniel jumped up immediately and took a couple of logs from the wicker basket by the fire, riddling the glowing ashes with the poker before efficiently tenting the two pieces of wood for maximum draw.

'I was thinking a glass of wine might be appropriate?' Marjory suggested, nodding her approval at Daniel's work.

Annie longed for one, but Daniel hesitated. 'I've got to drive, but perhaps a small one.' He grinned at Marjory.

'Right, well, I'll leave you to it. Come through when you're ready.' The door closed quietly behind her.

Annie wanted to say something personal, acknowledge him somehow as her son, but she didn't know how.

'Why did you choose to find me now?' she asked instead.

Daniel shifted awkwardly in his chair at the question. 'My mother died, a couple of years ago.'

His mother. Annie felt her heart contract. 'I'm sorry,' she said.

'It was sudden, a stroke. She lived for twenty-four hours, then . . . I wouldn't have looked for you while Mum was alive. It might have upset her.'

'She was a good mother, then?' Her emotions as she spoke were too complicated for her to analyse. How conflicted would I be if he said, No, she was a terrible mother, I had a hellish childhood?

Daniel nodded. 'Wonderful.'

'And your father?'

'Dad? He's a . . . how would I describe him?' He gave a short, almost cynical laugh. ' "Complex" sort of covers it.'

'But you see him? You're still in touch?'

'Hardly. We haven't been close since Mum died. He was a teacher at Brighton College, physics and chemistry. Now retired. He—well, from what Mum said, Dad didn't particularly want me. It was Mum who pushed for the adoption, apparently. Dad's just not a child person, not at all, even though he taught children.' He shrugged. 'And I was rubbish at science.'

He joked, but Annie could hear the hurt. Was he looking for a replacement father in Charles, she wondered. Because unless some Damascene conversion had taken place in Carnegie's life—which was highly unlikely, because he'd have been too stupid to recognise it—the man would make a dismal excuse for a father. She wished she could protect Daniel from finding this out.

57

'Me too! I was rubbish at most things at school.' She paused, fiddling with a rough bit of skin on her thumb as she mustered her courage.

'Daniel . . . it means so much to me . . . you finding me. All these years, I never stopped thinking of you. You were always there, in the back of my mind. I was desperate to know what your adoptive parents were like, whether they were looking after you properly, loving you . . . as much as I would have done.' She paused, making a huge effort to stem the incipient tears. The relief that the wondering was over for her was tempered by re-newed shame that she had given him away in the first place, making her suddenly hot and uncomfortable. 'It was so hard, thinking you were out there somewhere, and that I had given up the right to know you. Every birthday I thought of what I might have bought you, I calculated how you might have grown, wondered what you were good at, at school. I'm so sorry.' Her vision blurred with tears.

Daniel cleared his throat. 'Please . . . it's just great that we've met at last.'

She let out a long, slow breath. 'I was young. I didn't realise the implications at the time . . . how much I would regret what I did. But at the time I felt I had no choice. My mother was horrified, she refused to support me . . . And I was so unworldly.'

Daniel didn't reply at first. His head was turned towards the fire and she had no idea what he was thinking. Should she tell him the details of his adoption now, or wait until he asked? she wondered.

'I can't imagine what it was like for you,' he said, finally looking across at her.

There was an awkward silence.

'There's so much I want to tell you, if we can keep in touch?' Her question was tentative. She heard Richard's words ringing in her ears: no connection beyond their DNA.

'I'd like that, if you're up for it.'

'I could bring the albums next time. You must want to put faces to some of your ancestors.'

'That'd be great.'

As they got up to leave the room, Daniel stopped her, laying his hand lightly on her arm.

'One thing I haven't asked—' he frowned slightly '—along with a thousand other things of course.'

She waited.

'I wondered . . . do you have a family?'

She tried to look him in the eye, but failed. In that moment, her lovely life with her husband and three other children seemed the ultimate betrayal.

'Yes . . . yes, I have a husband, Richard, and three children. A son and two daughters.'

Daniel nodded slowly.

'Do they know about me?'

'Richard knows. But there never seemed a good time to tell the others. I should have. And of course I will now. I hope you'll meet them.'

'Big secret. But then I guess everything's easy with hindsight,' Daniel replied, his voice hardly more than a whisper.

*   *   *

It was getting dark by the time Annie and Jamie began the journey home. They waved a final time to Marjory's upright figure standing in the doorway, backlit by the light from the small chandelier in the hall.

'I hate leaving her alone in that huge house,' Annie said, as the car crunched over the gravel.

'She wouldn't be happy anywhere else.'

'I know, but what if she has a fall or something?'

'Marjory would shoot herself if she had to hang out with some dodgy carer referring to her as 'we' all the time . . . *Do we need a little nap now?* You know the sort of thing.'

She nodded, but her thoughts were elsewhere as she negotiated the lanes to the main road and she didn't answer.

'Well, he's definitely the most beautiful thing I've seen in decades,' she heard Jamie say. 'Fancy waiting thirty-five years and then finding a son so handsome and clever. I mean he could have been a dog.'

'You're so shallow! Although he was beautiful, wasn't he?'

'Gorgeous!' Jamie repeated, and she realised he was probably a little drunk. 'So, come on. What did it feel like?'

'It was . . .' She stopped, unable to find the words to describe what had happened.

'Did he seem like your son? I mean, did you sense a link to the baby? Or was it like being with some random stranger?'

'He looked so like Uncle Terence that I couldn't help feeling the family connection. But it was hard to believe after all this time that he was really Tom.'

She drove in silence for a while, the headlights of the oncoming cars almost hypnotic in the gathering dusk.

'Did he ask the dreaded question?'

'Why I'd given him away?'

Jamie nodded.

'No, but I half told him anyway. Not the details—he didn't ask. He wanted to know if I had other children. And he asked a lot about his father, which of course I couldn't tell him. I suppose I can tell him next time.'

'Maybe he didn't want to face the rejection thing,' Jamie suggested.

'Maybe. But it wasn't personal.'

Jamie snorted. 'I'd say it was highly personal!'

'No, you've missed my point. It wasn't personal enough. At the time, although I couldn't help loving him, I don't think I allowed myself to think of him as a real person, as my son. I only thought about him as something getting in the way of the life that had been prescribed for me. Seeing him today, so obviously my flesh and blood, brought it home to me that we've been separate his whole life because I refused to properly acknowledge him. I could only see him as Mother did: a problem that needed sweeping under the carpet.' She paused. 'Of course it hit me later, but by then it was way too late.'

'I know what you're saying, but we can't second-guess how he feels about it.'

'I'd be angry, if it was me.'

'Please . . . I think we've done the blame thing, darling.'

'OK, OK, easy for you to say.' She glanced across at her friend. 'Well, next step, telling the others.'

But oddly, now she'd met him, she knew this would be easier. She would be telling them about a living, breathing presence called Daniel Gray, not the shifting memory of a tiny baby.

'Where have you been, Mum?' Lucy jumped up as her mother came down the stairs to the kitchen. 'It's after nine. I called your mobile hours ago, and Dad's. Neither of you were answering. I thought something had happened.'

Annie gave her a brief hug before sitting down at the table. 'Sorry, sweetheart, it must have been off. I was with Jamie, we went to visit Marjory Best and you know how it is when Marjory and I get together. I did tell you.'

'Oh, yes. You did. I forgot. Did you have a good time?' She looked relieved, but Annie felt Daniel's presence hovering between them. She hated lying to Lucy, and her guilt drove her to a sudden urge to reveal all then and there, not waiting for the others. But she held herself together and fought down the instinct.

'Isn't Dad home?'

'I haven't seen him all day. Are you OK, Mum? You look really pale.'

'Do I? It's a long old drive back from that bit of Kent.' She paused. 'I'll give your dad a try.' It was something to do. Her head was still bursting with Daniel; she could think of nothing else. She dug her mobile out of her bag and a piece of paper fell to the tiled floor. It was Daniel's contact details, scribbled on the torn-off corner of an old envelope—one of many such pieces of scrap paper lying about Marjory's chaotic kitchen. She grabbed it quickly and stuffed it back in her bag, but Lucy was putting the kettle on and didn't notice.

'It's me,' she said, unnecessarily, in response to Richard's greeting. 'Where are you? . . . oh, of course . . . no . . . yes, it was good . . . no . . . alright.

See you later.'

Lucy looked questioningly at her as she ended the call.

'I'd forgotten he had to speak at this conference thing. He says it went well but he'll be late. Why don't I do us an omelette? Or some scrambled eggs?'

'It's OK, Mum, I've eaten,' Lucy answered. She gathered her stuff from the table. 'I think I'll go up now. Do some emails.' She gave her mother a quick kiss. ' 'Night.'

'Good night, darling. Sleep well.'

Annie was relieved to be alone and have a chance to run over the day's events in peace. She replayed everything Daniel had said, wondering most about his adoptive mother. She couldn't help feeling a twinge of envy for this unknown woman who had chosen to nurture her son. She had loved him. Nothing else matters, she told herself, ashamed of her envious thoughts.

There was some white wine in the fridge from the previous night. She poured herself a glass, reached for her phone and scrolled through to Daniel's number.

Loved meeting you. Hope we can again
soon. Regards, Annie. X

She read it over and deleted the kiss. Then, for the next hour, she checked every few minutes to see if he had responded. But there was nothing. It reminded her yet again of being young and waiting for a boyfriend to call. She went to bed but couldn't sleep, gradually convincing herself that she had not measured up to Daniel's high standards of what a mother should be. She was relieved to hear her husband making his way upstairs.

'How can we get them all together without telling them why?'

Richard, still half dressed in his shirt and boxers, frowned at her. 'Ed can never do Saturdays, and you know what it's like getting him to change those nightmare shifts. We'll have to make it Sunday.'

'Can't we just say we want a family get-together? That we haven't had one for a long time. Something like that?'

'But we have. We had one only a couple of weeks ago. To be honest I think Lucy'll be relieved to know what the atmosphere's been about.'

'Maybe. She keeps giving me those intense looks of hers. You know the ones.'

Richard nodded and smiled as he put on his blue cotton pyjamas and climbed into bed. They lay side by side in the wide bed, not moving, saying nothing, like two stone effigies.

'I'll be glad to get it over with,' Richard muttered.

'Me too.' She glanced at her husband. 'Will they mind?' Her stomach fluttered when she envisioned the three faces staring at her as she exposed her past.

'Mind? I doubt it. It was before they were born. They'll be surprised, but once they've got over the shock . . .'

Annie heard Richard's reassuring words, but the young girl who had been berated by her mother for being a 'slut', for bringing shame on the family honour, for betraying her beloved father's memory, came back to haunt her. It was the girl she was then, the girl who had given her baby away, not the mother they were so familiar with,

64

who she'd be presenting to her children for the very first time. She hoped they'd understand.

What will it feel like, letting the secret go? she wondered. She had learnt repression at her mother's knee. So well, that by the time she was grown up she was perfectly trained to withstand her own emotions. Not speaking about Tom to the children had been second nature to her: a closed compartment in her mind. It was hard to imagine that compartment would soon no longer exist.

6

Ed watched as Marsha vigorously beat butter into the potatoes with a wooden spoon. He had a handful of knives and forks in one hand, but he made no move to put them on the table. Marsha glanced up at him.

'What? You look miles away.'

Ed shook himself. 'Oh, nothing. Just thinking.'

'Always a mistake.'

Emma appeared in the doorway. 'What is?'

'Thinking,' Marsha replied, indicating her brother with a nod of her head.

Emma went over to him and laid her cheek against his for a moment. 'Love you,' she muttered in his ear. Which was what he'd been thinking about: love. He would like to talk to Marsha about this love thing when they got the chance. It confused him and made him feel uneasy, in some ways dishonest. Because it felt too easy, Emma loving him like this. Suddenly. Not that it wasn't what he wanted. And the sex was mind-blowing—

he couldn't get enough of her. But he just wasn't sure if she really meant it, or whether it was just something she said sort of automatically when she was in a relationship.

The flat doorbell rang. 'That'll be Lucy. Get it, will you?' Marsha said.

'So, Sunday it is.' Lucy helped herself to a couple of sausages. 'The mystery will finally be revealed!'

They all looked at her.

'Mystery?' Marsha asked.

'Yeah, about Mum. I told you the other day. I knew you weren't listening.'

Marsha laughed. 'OK, so tell us again.'

Lucy sighed. 'She's been weird for two weeks now. Sort of preoccupied, but then really generous, and cooking all these huge meals. Can't explain really . . . it's as if she's hiding something.'

'And you think she's going to tell all on Sunday?' Ed asked.

'Well, don't you think it's odd she is so insistent that we're all there?'

Ed shrugged. 'Mum's always insistent we're there. It's her thing, all that nurturing stuff.'

'You didn't tell me about Sunday, babe,' Emma chimed in.

'No, well, she said just us three . . .' He saw Emma's eyes flash and knew he was in trouble.

'Did you ask if I could come?'

Ed nodded. 'Of course I did, but she said just family.'

'And I'm not family?'

'Emms, this isn't about you, OK?' Marsha spoke sharply. 'Go on, Luce. You really think there's something up?'

Ed could hear the worry in her voice.

66

Lucy nodded. 'Yeah. I can't think what, but something. I don't think I'm imagining it.'

Emma got up and stamped off to the bathroom. Marsha rolled her eyes at her brother.

'And did you ask her why she was being weird?' Ed asked Lucy.

'I did, but she and Dad fobbed me off. Sort of pretended I was deluded. But I saw the look between them.'

'So Dad's in on it too?'

For a moment there was silence. Emma came back to the table and plonked herself down, her face set in a sulky pout.

'What are the options?' Ed asked them, pouring out more wine.

'Maybe they're splitting up,' Emma volunteered, her interest sparked.

'Very helpful, Emms.'

'Just saying . . .'

'I don't think it's anything bad. She seems distracted rather than miserable,' Lucy said.

'Maybe Mum's just about to sell her cake business for millions, and they're going to up sticks and move to the south of France.'

'Not!' Ed laughed at Marsha's suggestions. He envied his parents' focused lives. They seemed always to have known the direction they wanted to take, then taken it.

'Can we change the subject, please, guys? They'd have told you if it was anything serious.' Emma sounded bored, but Ed knew she was just pissed off. She wouldn't let it drop that she hadn't been included in the brunch.

'Well, come Sunday, we'll know.'

67

Annie took the blueberry muffins out of the oven and laid the baking sheet carefully on the top of the stove. The muffins sat plump and golden in their waxed cases, the tops dotted with crystals of coarse baking sugar.

'Smells good.' Richard cast an amused glance at the table, laden with fresh croissants, pains au chocolat, dishes of apricot and blackcurrant jam, hard-boiled eggs in their shells, fresh orange juice in a glass jug, thick slices of ham beside a wedge of Manchego cheese on a white china platter. 'Are we feeding five or five hundred?' he teased, but Annie was used to it. After all, she had first met him in the tiny galley kitchen his company used for hospitality, and even on first acquaintance he had been in awe of her culinary zeal.

'Normally we just get cold ham and salad,' he'd told her back then, looking longingly at the crusty chicken pie just out of the oven and the buttery new potatoes. 'You don't have to go to so much trouble, you know.' Annie had sent him a scathing look and said, 'But I *like* cooking. Where's the fun in ham and salad?'

Now she said, 'You know it calms me down.' She spoke lightly, as she lifted the warm muffins into a basket. 'Will you do the coffee, please?'

'Sure.' But before he did so, he came up and put his arms around her. 'I know you're nervous, but there's no need to be. They love you.'

Annie sank back against his chest for a moment. She was hot from the cooking, but she felt a sudden shiver, as if her nerves were short-circuiting.

'I hope you're right, but thank you . . . thanks for the support.' She took a deep breath and returned to the soothing task of arranging the muffins in a loose pyramid.

'Morning.' Lucy came into the kitchen.

'Hi, sweetheart,' Richard responded.

'The others not here yet?'

Annie glanced at the clock. It read just before eleven. 'I'm sure they're on their way,' she said.

Lucy helped herself to a sliver of ham and for a moment there was silence in the kitchen.

Ed and Marsha arrived together. Annie thought they seemed a little subdued. She wondered what Lucy had said to them.

'Coffee?' Richard was bright and businesslike as he handed out cups of coffee. 'Sit . . . sit,' he encouraged.

Annie felt her stomach churn. She glanced over at her husband, his eyebrows raised as he urged her on.

'Muffin? They're blueberry.' She indicated the basket.

'Mum!' Lucy's voice sounded like a pistol shot. She didn't need to say more. Annie took a deep breath and stood up. It felt better to be free of the table. She leant her back against the cold porcelain of the butler's sink. The expectation in the room was suddenly palpable, everyone avoiding everyone else's eye.

'I have something to tell you,' she began. 'Something that I should have told you years ago, but I didn't know how. It never seemed the right time.'

She paused, mesmerised by her children's expectant faces, frozen in the moment. Richard

69

pointedly cleared his throat.

'I have a son.' She forced the words out. She'd rehearsed all sorts of versions, but in the end she forgot everything and just told the bald truth. But hearing what she'd just said, she quickly corrected herself. 'Another son. I gave him away for adoption when I was nineteen.'

She waited. Ed and the girls were just staring at her in stunned silence, their faces no longer expectant but bewildered.

'I told your father when we first met . . . at least, when I knew we were serious about each other. But at the time I thought I would never see Tom— I called him Tom but he's called Daniel Gray now—I never expected to see him again. I looked after him in the hospital until he was adopted . . . in Kent.' The hot flow, once started, of hitherto secret history felt like a sort of balm. She wanted to go on talking about him forever now. Her children, however, were still gaping in astonishment, as if they didn't understand a word she was saying.

'Adopted children didn't have the right to find their birth parents in 1967, nor the other way round. Then the law changed.'

'And he's found you?' Lucy asked.

'Yes. That's where I was the other night. I met him at Marjory's last Saturday.'

Ed was silent, his head dropped.

'Why did you give him away?' Marsha's expression seemed puzzled rather than disapproving.

Annie was aware of a strange lightness in her body, as if the secret, now expelled, had had a material weight. It made her feel almost dizzy.

Here was the question at last.

'I ... well, I ... it was too late to have an abortion. I didn't realise I was pregnant till I was four months gone.' Lucy looked surprised, Ed still said nothing. 'And anyway, it wasn't so easy to get an abortion in those days.'

'Who was the father?' Marsha asked.

'Just a boy I met. He ... wasn't important. A mistake really.'

'And he didn't want anything to do with the baby?' Lucy queried.

'I didn't tell him.' Annie heard the questions as if they were familiar stations on an Underground map. She had repeated them to herself so often, over so many years, and they were all interconnected, all leading one to another to another, but she had never arrived at a final destination, a reply that would end all questions.

'It was such a different time,' Richard said. 'Your mother had no economic independence. She felt she didn't have a choice.'

She knew she should have been grateful to her husband for his support. But in fact she felt a surge of annoyance.

'Don't, Richard ... please. I *did* have a choice. I knew of other girls who kept their children. But my mother was so horrified at how it would look to the parents if I was suddenly toting an illegitimate baby around her precious academy that I gave in. I was weak. And I'd led such a sheltered life.' She paused again. 'Mother sent me off to Marjory Best. That was how I met her and became friends. She took in pregnant girls like me, who had nowhere to go.'

'What's he like?' Ed finally spoke. The face she

71

knew so well was suddenly inscrutable.

She took a long breath. 'Well, he's . . . he's great. He's thirty-five, he used to be in advertising, but now he writes plays, he read English at Cambridge. He's really beautiful, he looks incredibly like Great-Uncle Terence. I thought he was charming, easy to talk to. I really liked him.'

'So this is why you've been so weird!' Lucy said.

'Yeah,' Marsha added. 'We've been trying to work out why for days. You'd have laughed at some of our suggestions.'

'You worried us,' Ed stated, his tone faintly hostile.

'So,' she said, unsure what to say next. 'You're not shocked and horrified?'

There was a small silence, then Marsha said, 'Well, Mum, I'm surprised, sure. Shocked even, I suppose. But why would we be horrified?'

'I think it's exciting, having a new relly,' Lucy declared.

Annie turned to her son.

'I don't understand why you didn't tell us before.' He wouldn't look her in the eye.

'I've always felt so ashamed of what I did. I thought you'd think I was a terrible person for giving my baby away.'

There was another short silence.

'And it was hard, when you were children, to find the right moment,' Richard added.

'I can't imagine having my baby adopted.' Lucy said quietly. She reached across the table and took her mother's hand in hers. Annie held it tight.

'But *why* couldn't you keep him?' Marsha persisted, ever the truth-seeker. 'Grandma had enough money. She could have paid for you to get a flat on the other side of London so those stupid parents wouldn't be offended.'

Annie felt a pricking in the back of her throat and swallowed hard.

'You're right, of course. But at the time . . .'

'I'm sure you'd have kept him if you could've, wouldn't you?' Lucy said.

Would I? She thought. Would I have kept him if my mother had supported me? I suppose so, but not happily. The truth is, I was young and thoughtless, I wanted my freedom.

'Mum . . . he really *is* your son, is he? I mean, how do you know?' Ed's voice was full of suspicion.

Annie was surprised.

'Well, of course . . . I suppose I don't know for certain, but he got in touch through Social Services. And, like I said, there's a strong family resemblance.' Not for a moment had she thought that Daniel was not who he said he was.

'It's just you hear of people conning families by pretending to be a long-lost heir and copping all their money.'

'Ed!' Marsha glared at her brother.

'Look, I'm only *saying*. For Mum's sake as much as anyone's. She should make sure.'

'I think we can be sure, Ed,' Richard intervened.

'Have you met him, Dad?'

'No, but —'

'He's not after my money,' Annie interrupted. 'He just wants to know who his parents are, which seems fair enough. His adoptive mother is dead.' She hated the thought that Ed was essentially taking her mother's position.

'So did you *never* tell the father about him? Even

later on, I mean,' Marsha asked.

'I haven't been in touch with him since that night.'

'But you know him . . . you know his name?'

'Of course I know his name.' She didn't say any more.

'What is it then?' Ed asked, his voice still carrying an edge of hostility.

She hesitated before naming Charles, unwilling in the last resort to bring him into the family consciousness.

'You won't know him,' she stalled, then caught the look on her husband's face. It was tense, waiting.

'OK . . . his name's Charles Carnegie.'

She saw Richard relax; obviously the name meant nothing to him. None of the children said a word.

'Daniel wants to meet him too,' she added.

'Wow!' Lucy leant back, tipping her chair precariously on two legs. 'Must be too weird, not knowing your real parents till you're thirty-five.'

'I think he sees his adoptive parents as his real parents,' Annie corrected her.

'Yeah, but you'd still feel the genes, or lack of them, I reckon.'

Richard laughed. 'Good way of putting it, Luce.'

'It's not going to be fun, having to tell this Charles person that you forgot to mention the baby.' Marsha's look was full of sympathy, 'Don't envy you that, Mum.'

Annie nodded in agreement, not wanting to think about Charles right now. She felt suddenly tired. What a strain it had been, holding her children at arms' length since the letter had

74

arrived.

'I think it's great, Mum,' Lucy said. 'It must be amazing for you, finding him again after so long.'

'What did it feel like, seeing him as an adult?' Marsha asked.

But before Annie could answer, Ed pushed his chair back loudly, the wooden legs screeching on the tiles, and, without a word, stomped off up the stairs.

The others looked at each other, each face registering surprise and bewilderment.

'He was bound to take it badly,' Richard said.

'Was he? Why?' Lucy asked.

'Mum's only son . . . then not her only son,' he explained.

'Don't understand why it's different for him.'

Marsha was looking after her brother with concern. 'I'll go and talk to him,' she said, also getting up.

'Perhaps I should go,' Annie suggested.

'No, Mum. Let me. He's probably just a bit shocked.'

They watched Marsha leave in silence.

'I still don't see why he should be more upset than us,' Lucy went on stubbornly. 'You hardly know Daniel . . . he can't be jealous of someone you've just met, can he?'

Annie shrugged. 'I suppose it is different. You're my daughter, and you've always shared me with Marsha in that respect. Whereas Eddie, he's been my one and only.'

Marsha, breathless, came back into the room. 'He's gone. I went out, but he was already driving away.'

'Leave him,' Richard counselled. 'He's being a

75

brat.'

'Dad! He's upset. It's not an easy thing to find out.'

'You and Lucy aren't upset . . . are you?'

'No,' Lucy said quickly.

'Nooo . . .' Marsha's response was more equivocal. 'But it is a bit of a shock, finding out you've got a half-brother out there you've never met. Perhaps if we'd known earlier . . .'

'That was a mistake . . . not telling you all. I'm sorry about that, but, as Dad said, there never seemed a good time while you were growing up.'

'It doesn't matter now, Mum. Although it might have been a problem if me or Luce had met him and fallen in love with our own brother!'

'The chances of that happening are about as likely as winning the lottery,' Richard said.

'Yeah, and someone does that practically every week,' Marsha countered. 'What shall we do about Eddie?'

'I'll ring him later, maybe meet up if he wants to,' Annie replied, wondering how she could have handled it better. She didn't want to show the girls that, although she and Richard had predicted Ed might be the one most affected, she was taken aback by her son's response—it had seemed almost mean-minded. He's never been as demonstrative as the girls, she thought, but surely he must know how much I truly love him.

*   *   *

Emma came round as soon as she got Ed's call. He took two beers from the fridge, and they settled on the sofa. Mike was at a video-games convention at

Earl's Court so they had the place to themselves.

'Mum was cool as a cucumber . . . oh, by the way, I've got another son who's totally *gorgeous* . . . and he went to *Cambridge*. Oooh, well, how clever is that?'

'Eddie . . . stop it. She was probably freaked out having to tell you. It's a fuck of a long time to keep that sort of massive secret.'

He looked at her in exasperation. 'This isn't just about Mum though, is it? Everyone's feeling sympathy for my mother, but what about me?' He knew he sounded peevish, but he didn't care, he was furious.

Emma put her arm round his shoulder. 'Come on, it's not the end of the world. What exactly is it that's upsetting you? Having a new half-brother? Or the fact that he went to Cambridge?!'

He didn't know. All he knew was that he felt hideously jealous, like a stabbing, painful feeling, which was too ridiculous to say out loud. Sad to say, but Emms might be right, he thought. It was Daniel's degree that got up his nose as much as his relationship to his mother—university, especially bloody Oxbridge, rang a very sour note for him.

He thought back to the terrible day he'd got his A-level results. He'd suspected all along that he wouldn't do brilliantly. Not that he'd slacked on the revision, he just found it hard, but he hadn't been prepared for the disaster of two Cs—and an F in economics. Economics: his father's favourite subject! His mother had been a bit too effusively kind and 'it doesn't matter' supportive. But his father . . . he still winced when he remembered the anger and disappointment on his face. They'd wanted him to do retakes—his father had argued with him for weeks about it—but he'd stubbornly refused. Do the year again and probably still fail? That was so not going to happen, even though it meant giving up any chance of uni—where all his friends were headed.

And then he'd had to watch his sisters shine. Both of them getting As and Bs, Marsha with a couple of A-stars. He didn't begrudge them, of course, but the comparison with his dismal results was painful, even today. Added to which, he hated his poxy job at the bar.

'Being able to earn enough money is what's important in life.' His father's tone had finally been stalwart, making the best of a bad job. And what he said was partially true. But you had to enjoy *how* you earned it, didn't you? The trouble was that he didn't know exactly what he did want to do, even at the ripe old age of twenty-six.

'It was the way she spoke about him, as if he was this god. So good-looking and clever and charming and just like Great-Uncle Terence ...' He mimicked his mother's voice. 'Almost as if she was in love with him.'

'Don't be dumb, Eddie. Of course she's not. You're jealous!'

'I know I am ... and I know it's pathetic,' Ed mumbled.

Emma kissed him firmly on the lips. 'I'm sure he's totally grisly. Probably up himself and fake sucky to your poor mum. I loathe him already!'

Ed laughed. 'Yeah, me too.'

'Will you have to meet him?'

'I walked out before we reached that point. But I'm sure Mum will do one of her lunches and we'll all have to gather and play nice. You can bloody well come too.'

'Oooh, I wouldn't miss it for the world. I shall hiss at him from the sidelines.'

Ed's mobile rang. He checked the display. 'Mum. That's the third time. I don't want to speak to her.'

'Oh, go on, answer it . . . don't be mean.'

When Ed made no move to do so, Emma grabbed the phone from his hand.

'Annie . . . hi. Yes, sure, he's right here.' She mouthed, 'Be kind,' as she handed him his phone. Ed made a face but took the call nonetheless.

*   *   *

'Ed seems to have calmed down a bit, thank goodness.' Annie closed her phone. But she had heard the tension in her son's voice and it cut directly into her heart.

'What did he say?'

'He said it had been a shock. He said . . . well, not much really. He didn't sound particularly happy—or sorry, for that matter—but at least we spoke.'

Richard took her in a firm embrace which put a stop to her slightly manic clearing of the table. 'You must be pleased it's all over, that you've finally told them.'

'I am, very . . . except for Ed. He's never done that in his life before. I can't remember even having a row with him, except about tidying his room.'

'There was bound to be some fallout, Annie. And we did predict it would be Ed. Leave that, I'll make some tea.'

She sat down reluctantly and watched him fill the

kettle and pick two matching mugs from the mug rack, take the lid off the Chinese-pattern tin caddy, rinse out the teapot with warm water, open the fridge for the milk and the drawer for the spoon. The familiar ritual itself was as comforting as any tea would be.

'It'll be better when they've met. I'm sure they'll get on. It'll be good for Ed to have a brother . . . and for Daniel too.'

Richard turned from his task. 'Whoa, don't get too carried away here. They might get on, of course, but you can't manufacture family.'

'You sound like Marjory . . . manage your expectations blah, blah.' Why did everyone have to be so cautious, so negative? Daniel was charming. She couldn't imagine anyone not liking him.

'Marjory's a wise old bird. You should listen to her.'

'I do! But I just want everyone to like Daniel, to welcome him into the family. That's not so much to ask, is it?'

Richard didn't reply and went back to measuring out the spoonfuls of tea.

They carried their mugs up to the ground-floor sitting room. This was Annie's favourite room. She had painted it in very pale cornflower blue, more a wash than a colour, the sofa and deep armchairs were rich cream, the stripped pine floor covered partly by a Turkish rug in a darker blue and rust. It was always peaceful, and was now flooded with afternoon light as they settled in their chairs.

'So this Carnegie guy,' Richard began, not looking at Annie. 'Will you get in touch with him?'

'If Daniel asks me to.' Daniel had replied to her text. They were meeting the following Saturday.

She watched her husband's face go still. 'You don't mind, do you?'

Richard raised his eyebrows, gave a quick shrug. 'No . . . no, of course not. Why would I?'

'Obviously I hate the idea of seeing him, but it'll just be once, to fill him in. Then it's up to Daniel.'

He nodded slowly. 'What was he like? Charles? You never said.'

'I thought you didn't want to know. I'd have told you if you'd asked.'

Richard was silent.

'Richard?'

'Were you . . . were you in love with him?'

She stared at his bent head, felt the tension behind his question. Please, she thought, don't make this more difficult than it already is.

'I was eighteen. I thought I was. As you do at that age.'

'But you don't regret your decision not to tell him about the baby?'

She still, after all these years, found it hard to answer that.

'Charles is the long-dead past, Richard. I'm married to you and we have three beautiful children. How could I regret something that might have prevented that?'

He nodded, but still there lingered a measure of tension in his face.

'I wouldn't see him if I didn't have to,' she assured him, her voice quiet but firm in her attempt to assuage his fears. 'But you can't tell a man over the phone that he has a grown-up son he's never met.'

Richard gave a rueful grin. 'I suppose not.'

7

Annie saw her mother through the window from Jermyn Street, sitting at her usual table in Fortnum & Mason's Fountain Restaurant. She loved this place. She could remember when it had been styled as a soda fountain, with dark red plush decor and a bar with high stools, from the times when she'd been brought here as a child, a special treat before returning to boarding school. She would have a Dusty Road sundae, with vanilla and coffee ice cream, macaroons, whipped cream and delicious butterscotch sauce. They still had it on the menu, but the taste had changed. Or maybe she had, and she never ordered it now.

'Darling, how lovely.' Eleanor Westbury smiled briefly as Annie bent to kiss her mother's cheek.

'This place,' Eleanor made a dismissive gesture with her right hand, eyeing the most recent refurbishment with rank disapproval. 'I simply don't understand it. They spend all this money, and it's still beige.'

'It's not quite . . . more greeny . . .' Annie looked around. 'No, you're right, it's definitely beige. They probably did a psychological survey and discovered beige was the most sympathetic colour for digestion.'

Eleanor snorted. 'It's not sympathetic, it's enervating.' She wagged her finger at her daughter. 'And it's everywhere. Maybe there's a glut, like fish in the days before those dreadful foreigners stole all our stocks.'

Annie laughed. Her mother was awful, but in this

instance she was also right. The colour, or lack of it, was a bit depressing.

'You should write and complain.'

'And have the place close again for months while they find another shade? Where am I supposed to have lunch?' Eleanor sighed. 'No, one must put a brave face on it. Just accept this is the way things are nowadays.'

'Beige?' Annie teased, to receive a sharp look from her mother.

The waiter, a plump, older Italian in a dark suit, who had been corralled by her mother to do her every bidding on her weekly visits, came to the table and bowed obsequiously to Annie. 'Madam, it's good to see you again.'

'Hello, Giorgio. Good to see you too.'

'Are you ready to order, or shall I give you a minute?' Giorgio asked with a broad wink—their private joke. Annie and her mother always had the same thing: Eleanor, a single Welsh rarebit with a tomato, mayonnaise on the side; Annie a double with bacon. They would share a green salad, and Eleanor would finish with a black filter coffee, Annie a strong cappuccino.

'I'll shock you one day and order a ham sandwich.' Annie smiled at Giorgio as he removed the wine glasses from the table.

'Now,' said Eleanor, settling comfortably in her beige chair, 'to what do I owe this honour?'

'Does a daughter need a reason for having lunch with her mother?'

'She doesn't need to, but she usually does.' Eleanor's smile was benign.

Annie couldn't help laughing. 'OK, you win.'

Her mother's blue eyes, faded now by age but

just as beady, watched her daughter expectantly. Eleanor, for all her protestations to the contrary, loved gossip.

'Well, I saw him. My . . . my other son.'

Eleanor raised her eyebrows.

Annie waited while Giorgio poured tap water into the two tumblers. 'He's the spit of Uncle Terence.'

For a moment her mother's expression clouded. Eleanor had been very close to her brother. Closer, Annie had often thought, than she was to Ralph, her husband. Annie knew Eleanor still badly missed Terence, ten years after his death. Eleanor's brother was all that she complained her husband was not: a man of distinction and probity.

Annie remembered her father as charismatic, certainly: handsome, tall, blond, a chain-smoker, always laughing, and twanging his scarlet braces to amuse her. But probity, it turned out, was not one of his virtues. He hadn't been home much, but when he was, he brought energy and a semblance of happiness to the stifled atmosphere of the house. Annie couldn't say she had known him properly—not like her own children knew Richard—but then neither parent had been particularly involved in her early upbringing. That had been left to a succession of nannies, none of whom lasted long under Eleanor's iron hand.

At six o'clock, after she'd had her tea of bread and butter, cake and warm milk, the current nanny would take her down to see her father, on the rare days he came home in time. Just in from work as a headhunter in the City, he would already have a whisky in his hand, the ice cubes clinking merrily in the cut-glass tumbler, the high-ceilinged drawing room pungent with smoke. For a while he would be all hers, balancing her on his pinstriped knee, teasing and tickling her, and playing Strauss waltzes very loud on the gramophone as he danced the length of the parquet floor in his silk socks, Annie high in his arms. Her mother would sit and watch from her armchair, but make no move to join in. Then, when she'd been there barely half an hour, the drawing-room door would open slowly.

'Time for bed,' the nanny would say. And her father would wrap her in a tight, smothering hug, whisper on his smoky, whisky'd breath, 'I love you, Annie-bee,' then hand her over. She never wanted to leave him, but knew better than to cause a fuss.

But to Eleanor, as Annie later discovered, Ralph was a useless drunk, a waster who'd been over-indulged by family money, who spent most nights boozing and losing his fortune at illegal gambling parties which one of his aristocratic friends set up. And her mother had a point. Her father died leaving his family nothing but massive debts.

Giorgio arrived with the Welsh rarebits, setting them down on the white tablecloth with a Mediterranean flourish. 'Salad and mayonnaise on its way,' he said, before Eleanor had a chance to remind him.

'So what does he do? Your son,' Eleanor asked. Her mother always wanted to know what someone 'did'. That and where they went to school.

'He went to Cambridge, then into advertising. Then gave it all up to write plays.'

'Not a very sensible choice for a bright man. Unless he's successful, of course.' Eleanor's look was sceptical.

Annie shook her head. 'I don't think so. Not yet.'

Her mother harrumphed. 'No wonder he's so keen to hunt you down.'

Annie didn't react. 'He's wonderful, Mother. But it was strange, knowing he was my son, seeing Uncle Terence in him . . . yet not knowing him at all.'

Eleanor was silent, her head bent as she sliced small pieces of rarebit and carefully added a smear of mayonnaise with her knife.

'Do you regret it?' her mother asked.

'Seeing him again? No, of course not. Although I never thought I'd get the chance.'

'I meant giving him away,' Eleanor corrected, not meeting her eye.

Never, in the thirty-five years since the baby's birth, had Eleanor asked her this question. There had always been the assumption that the adoption was the right thing and brooked not even a discussion, let alone regret. Now she posed the question reluctantly, as if she were getting something over with but didn't really want to hear the answer. And although Annie had the opportunity to say how she felt at last, she hesitated. For years she had blamed Eleanor, as she blamed Charles Carnegie. Easy to do. But in that moment she couldn't help remembering how relieved she herself had felt in the weeks after the adoption. Relieved in an ashamed way. The regret came soon after, a gradual thing which crept up on her and refused to go away.

'I regret it, yes,' she replied, slowly. 'He was my baby. I believe it's a terrible thing to do to a child, unless your circumstances are dire.' Her mother's gaze remained fixed. 'But it was my choice. I could have kept him, and I didn't.'

Eleanor raised an eyebrow, her expression full of disdain, no doubt for what she saw as Annie's misplaced sentimentality.

'Damn good thing too. It would have ruined your life.'

'Why?'

'I hardly need to explain, Annie.' Her mother looked around for Giorgio.

Conversation over. But Annie remembered her real purpose, and held her temper.

'You know the Carnegies? From the school?' Annie spoke lightly, with a lack of emotion that did her mother credit. 'We had an order at the bakery for an anniversary cake. A diamond wedding. The name was Carnegie, and I wondered if it might be them?' She paused. 'Of course, there must be millions of Carnegies.'

'Not millions. It's certainly not a common name,' her mother said.

Annie persevered. 'The order was placed by their daughter, but her name was Laura Mackenzie. I remember Venetia, but was there another sister?'

Eleanor's attention sparked up. Annie knew she couldn't resist reminiscing about anything to do with her beloved Westbury Academy.

'No, there was only the one girl. Venetia, as you say. And an older brother ... Charles, I think. Such a charming family. Angela and I kept in touch for years. Henry Carnegie was at Brooks's with Terence, of course. And I seem to remember the boy was something in wine. He was involved with one of those warehouse places that sell in bulk, made a vast fortune, Angela said.' Her mother sighed nostalgically. 'But after Henry died, we rather lost touch. Caro seems to think Angela's no longer with us either, but as one gets on it's impossible to keep up with everybody. A Christmas card is all I can manage now. If I don't send them out, everybody thinks I'm dead.' Eleanor chuckled merrily, as if her demise were high comedy.

Brooks's, thought Annie. If Charles's father had been a member of the gentlemen's club in St James's, then Charles would quite possibly be one too—people like him lived for tradition. She could try leaving a letter for him there. I'm amazed he's made a success of his life, she thought; he'd seemed so indolent and spoilt back then.

'You're very far from dead, Mother,' she assured her, as they waited for their coffee.

'As we speak, darling.' Eleanor nodded. 'But the reality is, I could keel over at any second.' She attempted a look of pathos, but it was ruined by her clear enjoyment of the self-centred melodrama.

'Well, so could I, for that matter.'

'One day you'll be sorry you didn't take me more seriously,' Eleanor complained good-naturedly.

'I do take you seriously, Mother. How else could I take you?'

Her mother gave her a shrewd smile. 'You make it sound a bit of an effort, darling.'

As she left the restaurant and waited on Jermyn Street for a taxi for her mother, Annie thought about Daniel. She was seeing him on Saturday and her heart filled with delight at the prospect.

*   *   *

Marsha, Emma and Ed sat in the corner of a wine

88

bar in Wardour Street. Ed glanced impatiently at the clock on the wall above the bar. 'Where's Lucy? Not like her to do overtime in that crap job.' This was the first time they'd got together since his tantrum at his parents' house, and he hoped he wouldn't get a hard time from any of them.

'She's getting her visa for Tanzania. You know, that hideous volunteering job she went for?' Marsha replied.

'I didn't realise she'd actually got it.'

Emma groaned. 'Hardly surprising. Can't think who else'd want to do it.'

'No, well . . . we've got more pressing things on the agenda today.' Marsha paused. 'Sorry, can't wait for Luce, I need a debrief. Now!' She widened her eyes at the other two. 'I don't know about you guys, but I can't get my head around what Mum told us. It's been driving me nuts.' She glared at her brother. 'And you weren't much help, running off like a greyhound out of a fucking trap.'

'Sorry, I don't know why I did that. She was so . . .' He tailed off when he got a warning look from Emma.

'What?' he mouthed. But Emma just shrugged.

'I know it was childish, but I got pissed off because Mum seemed so gushing about the man. As if she'd fallen in love with him.' He was ashamed of his words and waited for his sister to object.

'No, I get what you mean,' Marsha said. 'It was weird.'

'The whole thing's weird,' Ed commented. 'Not just the fact of him, but Mum hiding it.'

'It just makes me look at her differently,' Marsha went on. 'I mean, can you imagine giving your baby up and not mentioning it to *anyone*, including the father, for thirty-five years? Bizarre.'

'Why would you do that?' Ed asked, as much to himself as to the others. He wasn't one for secrets, everyone always knew what he thought—perhaps to his detriment. As a child he'd had such a reputation for blurting things out that no one would tell him what they'd got the others for Christmas. 'Not being able to cope with a teenage pregnancy in the sixties is totally understandable. But it seems perverse to hold on to such a huge secret even with your children.'

'I don't think it's that strange,' Emma commented as she drew a doodle in some spilt beer on the wooden table. 'I can imagine with something like that you don't say anything at first, then gradually the secret gets trapped and massive, and then there's no easy way to bring it up.'

The others gazed at her in silence, considering what she'd said.

'But hey, it's not my mum,' she added.

'Do you think she was in love with this Carnegie guy?' Ed asked, the thought an odd one. He was still having trouble marrying the two images of his mother the announcement had evoked. The one, a starry-eyed adolescent caught out by a night of passion. The other, his present-day mother, all conservative, nurturing efficiency.

'She didn't have much time to be in love, if it was only one night. Perhaps it was just a sixties party thing? Booze, dope, back of a car . . .' Marsha suggested, pulling a face.

This was a step too far for Ed. 'Eugh! Mum plus drugs plus sex? Stop it.'

'If she'd been in love with him, surely she'd have

90

told him about the baby?' Emma said.

'You'd have thought so.' Marsha shrugged. 'I don't know . . . maybe Mum having a wild moment is cool. Ruins the honest, straightforward, sort of conventional image I've always had of her, but is that a bad thing?'

'Here's Lucy.' Emma looked towards the door.

'Hi, sorry I'm late.' She brought a stool from the next-door table and sat down heavily. 'What have I missed?'

'Everything,' Ed said with a grin. 'Drink?' He got up.

'Thanks. Glass of white, please, Eddie.'

'So how's things back at the ranch? Any repercussions from Sunday?' Marsha asked.

Lucy shrugged. 'Not sure . . . Dad's definitely been a bit quiet.'

'What do you mean?'

'Don't know. Sort of careful around Mum, a bit brooding. Not his usual self.'

Ed felt a small twinge of satisfaction. So this love-fest for Daniel wasn't shared by everyone then.

'Maybe he's jealous.' Emma looked pointedly at him, but he ignored her.

'Of Daniel, or the father?' Marsha asked.

Ed gave a short laugh. 'Both, probably.'

'Well, it could be hard for him too,' Emma put in. 'Even though he's known about it all along.'

'Mum does talk about Daniel rather a lot. Can't wait to meet him, see what all the fuss is about.' Lucy's face was alight with anticipation.

'Me too,' Marsha agreed.

'He'll be a twat.'

Lucy sighed. 'Here we go . . . It's you that looks

like the twat, Ed, having a mood every time his name's mentioned. Especially as you haven't even met him.'

'Yeah . . . don't do this, Eddie. You'll just upset Mum, and even if Daniel's grim—which I accept he may well be, of course—Mum doesn't deserve you being antsy about him. Especially if Dad's a bit wound up by it all. It isn't her fault this guy's popped up out of nowhere.'

Emma nodded in vigorous agreement with her friend's words.

'OK, I get it.' He stared back at the three stern faces and frowned. 'I'll try and behave, but that doesn't mean I have to like him.'

Ed just didn't understand why they were so eager to welcome a complete stranger into the family. He remembered the Prodigal Son story from RS at school. He'd always thought it grossly unfair, even as a child: one son at home slogging his guts out for little thanks, then the other one rocks up, a full-on no-good waster, and the father brings out the fatted calf. He couldn't remember the details—or even the point of the story now—but it rang bells with this Daniel fellow.

'You never know, you might surprise yourself,' Marsha was telling him.

*   *   *

As Annie took the short walk to Hampstead Heath that Saturday, she rejoiced in the warm sunshine, the light breeze, the scent of pollen: new life slowly blossoming around her. She was always anxious about getting cold—she blamed her low blood pressure—and today, despite the temperate

92

weather, she wore a fitted tan suede jacket over her white shirt and jeans.

She saw Daniel before he saw her. He was sitting on a bench at the Parliament Hill entrance, where they had arranged to meet. He sat very still, his hands clasped in front of him. She hung back for a minute, and watched him. How beautiful he is! His thick, auburn hair glinted in the spring sunshine, his intelligent eyes and strong family nose conferred a quiet nobility on his face. She realised she was very nervous. This time they would be alone; there would be no buffer state in the shape of Marjory or Jamie. She hoisted the large picnic bag she carried onto the other shoulder and went to greet her son.

They walked past the ponds and north towards Kenwood, then veered west, neither concentrating on where they were going, making small talk about the Heath, the weather, the dogs, until Annie spotted a bench away from the Saturday crowds and they sat down.

'You shouldn't have gone to so much trouble.' Daniel looked on in awe as she decanted the contents of the cool-bag onto the bench between them. She had made plump brown-bread egg and cress sandwiches; small, crisp chocolate-chip cookies; lemon cupcakes with soft, creamy citrus icing. She'd fried up some chipolata sausages, still warm and nestled in tin foil. There were cherry tomatoes, organic crisps and homemade lemonade. And a thermos of tea. This is like a children's tea party, she thought with horror, as she laid everything out on the bright blue cotton tablecloth. She realised she was blushing.

'Trying to recreate your childhood,' she said,

with an embarrassed laugh.

'It looks wonderful,' Daniel declared, not meeting Annie's eye.

'I hope you didn't have lunch,' she went on as she poured the tea. 'I'm afraid this is what I do. I bake.'

Daniel grinned and shook his head. 'I'm starving.'

She handed him a paper plate and waited while he helped himself. She had no appetite, but she took a sandwich anyway for the sake of politeness.

'Did you tell the family?' he asked. 'About me.'

'Yes. Last weekend.' She hesitated, immediately thinking of Ed, who was still being distant with her. She'd rung him a few times during the week, but he'd only taken one of her calls, and then been carefully polite and too busy to talk. And Richard. Since their conversation about Charles, he'd seemed pensive, not really responding when she'd wanted to talk about Daniel. But Daniel didn't need to know all this.

'Were they surprised?'

She nodded. 'Very. They asked a lot of questions.' She gave Daniel a brief smile. 'It's a relief to get it out in the open at last.'

'They weren't upset?'

'They . . . I think they were intrigued more than anything. You know, Mother's secret past . . .' She knew her responses sounded stilted, almost cagey. But there was so much she had to edit out of the scene in the kitchen last Sunday. 'They're looking forward to meeting you,' she said.

Daniel's face broke into a shy grin. 'Great! I'd love to meet them too.'

'I thought we might aim for the weekend after

next, if that suits you? I'll check with the others . . .
Ed works shifts, but he can usually change one if
he has enough notice.' She refused to think about
what her son's reaction would be when she asked
him to do just that.

Daniel nodded. 'That's good for me.'

The sudden silence between them was filled by
Annie offering him another sandwich, pressing on
him the foil wrap of sausages, 'before they get too
cold'.

'Tell me about them. Your family.'

Almost reluctantly, as though her family was
something to be apologised for, Annie began to
talk about her children, her husband, her work.
And as she talked, she realised she was editing out
the happiness. Stupid, but it didn't feel right to
dwell on the fact that she'd had a good life, a
successful life without him.

'And you?' she asked, when she thought she'd
said enough.

'Oh, you know . . . normal, I suppose. Mum
didn't work, outside the home, I mean,' he added,
smiling. 'She was a brilliant woman. She made
things—clothes, jewellery, painted a bit, was mad
for redecorating the house—much to my father's
dismay. Always had a project.' He paused, his
expression distant, obviously remembering. 'And
she read a great deal: novels, poetry. I suppose she
was a bit of a hippie, and huge fun to be with.
People loved her . . . I loved her. I owe her
everything.'

'You must miss her a lot.' Annie stifled an
unjustified spike of resentment at the word
'everything'.

'Every day of my life.' His eyes lit up with tears,

95

but he wiped them quickly away and reached for another sandwich. 'Sorry.'

'Don't be.'

Neither spoke for a moment.

'Did you know you were adopted from the beginning?'

'Oh, yes.' Daniel nodded. 'I can't remember not knowing. Mum used to go on about how she fell in love with me at first sight and knew we'd been destined to be together because my eyes were as blue as hers . . . which can't have been true at a couple of weeks old!' He paused. 'But Dad . . . he's never really mentioned it.'

'I'm glad you were loved . . . happy,' she said.

Daniel looked off into the distance. 'Happy? I suppose we were.'

She wondered what he meant.

'I think you're incredibly brave to have found me.'

'I've been thinking about it for a long time.' He paused. 'Not that I'm trying to replace Mum with you—please don't think that.'

'No, of course not,' Annie answered hastily, relieved in a way. She was so familiar with mothering her other children, but she felt at a loss with her elder son. She refilled his cup with tea, handing him the plate of cupcakes.

'I hope . . . I hope you won't just disappear, now you've met me.'

A large brown Standard Poodle suddenly leapt up to the bench and began sniffing at the picnic. Annie stroked it and pushed it away from the food. Its owner shouted from the distance and the dog bounced elegantly away. The other people wandering the paths of the Heath seemed very far off, in another world.

'Beautiful dog,' she commented.

'I . . . I would like to get to know you and your family,' Daniel said, looking after the leaping dog, 'if that's OK.' He turned his gaze to her. 'But everyone's told me not to expect too much.'

She smiled in agreement. 'They've said the same to me. Relentlessly.'

'I was told it was quite likely you wouldn't want to see me . . . It often happens, apparently.'

She couldn't answer for a moment, remembering her instinctive response to the letter.

'Are you an only child?' he asked.

'Yes.' She found it odd that he didn't know even this about her. 'And you too?'

Daniel nodded. 'Dad probably thought Mum wouldn't cope with two. She was . . . quite a nervous person.' He looked uneasy as he spoke, as if he felt disloyal telling her this.

'I wish I'd had siblings. It would make dealing with my mother so much easier.'

'Is she that bad?'

'Oh, worse! Much, much worse. But I shouldn't be mean. She went through a lot when my father died. Anyway, you'll meet her one day and you can make up your own mind.'

'Do I want to?' he asked, laughing.

'In for a penny . . .'

He nodded. 'I suppose.'

The atmosphere between them relaxed over the afternoon. She found him easier to talk to as they began to unravel their separate histories. As the day wore on, the warmth of the sun disappeared and she was glad of her jacket. Daniel had only a T-shirt on.

97

'Aren't you cold?

He shook his head. 'But perhaps we ought to get going.'

'Yes. Oh, I forgot. Before you go . . .' Annie pulled the photograph album she had selected out of her bag. It was her own childhood album her father had compiled from holiday snaps, but it also included a few photos of her mother and her father when they themselves were young. The record came to an abrupt end when her father died; Annie had never seen Eleanor with a camera. She had considered bringing along more recent albums, to show Daniel her other three children and Richard, but that seemed too much like rubbing salt in a wound.

'Mother . . . my father.' Annie pointed to a photo of Eleanor and Ralph, arms linked and looking uncharacteristically happy, on a terrace in the south of France—so the caption, in her father's flamboyantly cursive script, stated. 'Them as children . . . this one's me . . .' She turned the page. 'That's Daddy's mother, Grandmother Westbury . . . Uncle Terence and his friend Paul—they lived together for nearly thirty-five years, and Mother always referred to Paul as her brother's "lodger"! But look, can you see?' She pointed to Terence's face. 'Can you see the resemblance to you?'

Daniel peered more closely and nodded uncertainly. 'I suppose. But it's always hard to know what you look like to someone else.'

She continued to leaf through the album, stiff and creaky with age, the faces staring out from the black cardboard pages, similar in kind to millions across the globe, yet also entirely specific to herself, and now to her son.

Daniel scrutinised each face with great care, going back and forth through the pages as she talked, asking questions about each one. This was his first proper glimpse, she realised, of his ancestors. There was silence as she closed the book.

'So do we pass muster?'

Daniel laughed. 'Definitely. I think I do look a bit like your ... well *my* great-uncle.' He seemed pleased by this connection. 'But the others ... I have to keep telling myself that these people are my bloodline.'

'Yours and mine,' she said with a smile.

'May I borrow it for a while?' he asked.

They began to gather up the remains of the food and pack it away in the cool-bag. There was a lot left; she had eaten virtually nothing. As they walked back the way they had come, this time in a companionable silence, Annie enjoyed the evening light, the golden radiance beautiful across the spring landscape of the Heath.

'I asked my mother, not telling her why I was asking, about your father ... your biological father.'

'Oh?' Daniel looked at her eagerly.

'She said *his* father used to be a member of Brooks's club. Like Uncle Terence. And if Carnegie Senior was a member, then Charles'll quite probably be one too—it's the old male bonding ritual, helped along by too much brandy, butlers and mulligatawny soup.'

Daniel chuckled. 'You're just bitter because they won't allow you to join in.'

'God forbid! Mulligatawny is filthy.'

'I don't even know what it is.'

99

As they joined the main path which led to the park's exit they were slowed down by the steady procession of people strolling home. Families mostly, trailing small children on scooters, dogs, buggies, all displaying that weary contentment brought by a day out in the fresh air and sunshine. She had a sudden urge to take Daniel's arm, to stroll with him as she might have done with Ed. But she didn't have the confidence.

'So I could write to him at the club,' she went on, 'and see if it throws up anything.'

'That would be great . . . but are you OK with it? Seeing as he doesn't know about me.'

He's so polite, she thought. I wish he'd say what he really thinks. Just tell me that I let him down, that he's angry. He must be a bit angry, surely.

'Of course I'll do it . . . for you.'

'It might be a can of worms.'

'That's no way to talk about your father!' she retorted, and they both started to laugh. As she watched him laugh, she tried again to remember clearly what Carnegie had looked like.

'But, Daniel, I have literally no idea what he's like. As I told you, I never knew him really, and I haven't seen him in over thirty-five years. He might be horrible and refuse to see you. Or he might simply be horrible. Or you might loathe him and regret ever meeting him. Are you sure you're up for it?' She found herself repeating a version of Marjory's caveat.

'I've risked it once,' he grinned at her. 'And that's worked out better than I hoped.'

She blushed. 'I'm so glad you did.' But she wasn't looking forward to confronting Charles Carnegie.

8

Annie stretched her thin rubber swimming cap over her head and began the usual struggle to contain her thick hair within it. It was seven in the morning. She had posted the letter to Daniel's father that morning—care of the ridiculous gentlemen's club—on the way to the gym. But part of her hoped, cravenly, that he might be dead.

She stood at the edge of the pool, looking at the fast swimmers' lanes, bodies pounding up and down in each other's wake. They were all men with strong, clean, rhythmical strokes, but she could sense their frustration at being penned up like this. Normally she came later, when these young bloods had taken the Northern line to the office and the pool had a more relaxed clientele. She glanced at the slow lane, where two middle-aged women were climbing out of the water, then dropped into the shallow end, fastened her goggles and set off at high speed in the empty lane. As soon as she got into her rhythm, she began to review the picnic, and what Daniel had told her. They had talked about his work.

'How do you finance yourself?' she'd asked.

Daniel had shrugged. 'Not easily, if I'm honest. Apart from the plays, which are hardly a source of income, I do articles, reviews for papers and mags, any writing work I can get. But it's freelance of course—which means you die of starvation before anyone pays you.'

She had been asking because she was interested in how an artist survived, but Daniel had looked at her cautiously.

'I don't want your money, you know.'

'Mother thinks you do, but that's Mother for you. I didn't mean to seem nosey. I was just curious.'

'Look, I could have stayed in my mind-numbing but lucrative copywriter's job at JGW. But no, I chose to suffer for my art. The play I've just written is being put on with two others at the Edinburgh Fringe by this small theatre company.' He'd pulled a face. 'I'm terrified. It's such a chance if the critics like it. But they might not even see it, let alone review it . . .'

'I wouldn't have the faintest clue about how you go about putting on a play.'

Daniel had shaken his head. 'Yeah . . . and I wouldn't have a clue about making a celebration cake.'

'Thanks . . . but that's a very polite comparison. Anyone can make a cake. I could teach you in a second. You'd never be able to teach me how to write a play!'

She swam on. Twenty lengths, thirty. Charles was young back then, we both were. I didn't give him a chance. And even if he's rubbish, Daniel has a perfectly good father. Although perhaps not so good. She sensed Daniel was keeping something back about the science teacher. It was clear he adored his mother, but he seemed to clam up whenever she asked about his dad.

As Annie got out of the pool, slightly breathless, her heart beating pleasantly fast from the exercise, she vowed not to be childish about meeting Carnegie. Daniel deserved to know what everyone else knew. She didn't remember ever being specifically aware that those two people she called her parents represented what Daniel had termed her 'bloodline', yet the sense of family had been part of a natural cohesion, a grounding, that she had taken completely for granted. The photograph she had shown Daniel, of her parents leaning against each other on the balcony in the south of France—something Daniel would never have of his own mother and father—*that* was her origin. For better or for worse, Annie knew where she came from.

*   *   *

'Daniel's working so hard on this play he's writing. Every time I call him he says he's polishing it, or seeing designers or actors, talking to the director. It's bloody impressive. I'm lucky he's taking time off to meet up tomorrow.'

'You're seeing him *again*?' Richard asked, from the bathroom. 'That's about five times in two weeks. You're always on the phone to him. *And* he's coming to lunch next weekend.'

Annie exhaled slowly as she stood in front of the mirror, rubbing night cream into her face. 'Don't exaggerate. This'll only be the third time. Surely you don't mind?'

There was a tiny pause from the bathroom.

'No . . . I just thought we might go and see a film, or do an exhibition, play some tennis. We haven't had a game all year.'

She refused to feel guilty. 'We could do that on Sunday.'

'You've forgotten.' The reply, almost accusatory, echoed to the sounds of splashing water. 'It's the

Andersons' silver-wedding lunch.'

'You won't mention Daniel to them, will you?'

'They'll have to find out sooner or later,' she heard him say, his tone still sounding sulky.

Was he really jealous of Daniel? She hoped not, because she wasn't prepared to pass up time with her son; she had a lifetime to catch up on. She went through to the warm, steamy bathroom. Richard lay with his eyes shut, his arms crossed peacefully over his chest, like a corpse. He'd taken his rimless glasses off and hooked them over the edge of the bath. Her husband had a good face. Nothing remarkable, but his regular, open features spoke of honesty and quiet humour. His short hair, brown mixed with grey now, and slightly receding at the front, was damp from the bath, his cheeks pink. She'd taken a long time to fall in love with Richard. She had seen him every lunchtime as she chopped and stirred and baked for him and his colleagues, but there had been no spark at first, just a friendly banter between them. She'd known he liked her, of course; he made that very clear, even with his shy, diffident manner. But she was wary, well defended against attacks on her heart. Richard had persevered, however, and gradually, without her being aware, she realised she had begun to look forward to seeing him each day. The love, when it came, had been a quiet, grounded love. Not the trembling, churning obsession that Charles had represented.

'Richard?' He opened his eyes. 'I know I'm focusing a lot on Daniel at the moment. But it's important to me. You understand, don't you?'

Her husband pulled a face and reached for his glasses. 'I do, but I think you've got to get a balance, Annie.'

His self-righteous tone made her bristle.

'I mean, all you ever talk about is Daniel these days. Daniel said this, Daniel said that, Daniel did the other . . . you're obsessed with him.' He paused to rub the steam off his glasses. You've still got three other children, you know. And a husband.'

She couldn't believe what she was hearing.

'Richard—'

'Of course it's important that you get to know him. I'm not stupid, I understand that,' Richard interrupted, drawing himself up, sending water sloshing over the back onto the black and white tiles, not looking at his wife. 'But everyone's sick to death of the subject. You're not doing the man any favours by turning us all against him.'

Annie's eyes widened. ' "Everyone"? What are you talking about? OK, Ed's still not happy with it, but the girls . . .' She wondered if what he was saying was true. But they hadn't seemed annoyed when she talked about their half-brother. 'I'm so, so sorry. I didn't realise I was being such an obsessive pain in the neck.'

'No need to be nasty,' Richard retorted, heaving himself out of the bath and reaching for the large white towel.

'I'm not the one being nasty.' She stalked out of the bathroom and plumped down hard on the bed. A moment later, Richard sat down beside her.

'I'm sorry, Annie. Maybe I was being harsh. If I'm honest, I suppose I feel a bit left out. Childish, I know. But it's like you've suddenly fallen in love with another man.'

His arm went round her. For a moment she resisted, then she leant into his embrace.

105

'I suppose, in a way, I have,' she whispered. 'But not in the way you mean.'

Maybe when they meet him, she thought, he and Ed will both relax. Daniel will stop being this bogeyman. They'll see there's nothing to be jealous of.

*   *   *

It was a warm, breezy late-spring day, perfect for lunch outside. Annie hadn't slept well the night before, and got up early to begin preparations for the family event. She'd checked the weather forecast online at least twice, not believing the weather would hold for a barbecue. But by eleven o'clock it seemed set fair.

She began by marinading the spare ribs, then moved on to the pastry for the *tarte tatin*, setting it to rest in a plastic bag in the fridge while she scrubbed the new potatoes for the salad and put them on to boil. Lucy had said she would be down to help her mother, but there was no sign of her yet.

Please, she sent thoughts upwards into the blue sky as she wiped down the wooden table on the deck and scrubbed off a large patch of dried-on pigeon mess. Please let them all get on.

'Hi, Mum.' Lucy looked washed and smart in a flowered skirt and white cotton T-shirt. 'How's it going?' She looked round at the already advanced preparations. 'Looks like you've done it all already.'

She gave her daughter a brief hug. 'If you could lay the table . . .'

For a while they worked companionably

together, both singing along together when the radio played Dolly Parton's 'I Will Always Love You'. Annie's mobile, which was in her apron pocket, buzzed loudly. It was Daniel. Don't let him be ringing to cancel, she begged silently.

'Just checking the address,' she heard him say.

She told him, not mentioning that she'd already sent it in an email. He must be nervous too.

'See you at one thirty,' she rang off.

Lucy looked questioningly at her.

'Daniel . . . lost the address.'

'Don't worry, Mum. It'll all go brilliantly.'

Annie pulled a face. 'Thanks, darling. I'm worried about Ed more than anyone. Have you spoken to him? He never talks to me, just texts. He's not going to throw another wobbly, is he?'

Lucy shook her head. 'He'll be fine.' But her daughter's tone was tinged with doubt.

'I just want Daniel to have a good time, to feel . . . well, to feel welcomed.'

'Ed'd never be rude, Mum, not in front of a stranger.'

'No . . . no, of course he wouldn't.' She didn't like Daniel being called a 'stranger', but she didn't challenge Lucy. To them he was. She set Lucy to chopping the cucumber for the salad and went to change into her dress, trying to stop working herself up about her younger son.

The front door banged twenty minutes later and Ed, Marsha and Emma clattered down the stairs. Annie, her face flushed from the oven, greeted them with relief. She hugged Ed tightly, but he clearly hadn't forgiven her; there was little returned warmth in his embrace.

'What are we having, Mum?' Marsha looked

107

around at the preparations.

'Barbecue. Now you're here, will you light it for me, please, Ed? I don't know where your dad is, but he always leaves it till the last minute, then sprays lighter fuel over everything.'

The kitchen was suddenly alive with activity.

Annie saw Lucy pulled Marsha aside and slide her eyes meaningfully in her brother's direction. It wasn't encouraging.

By the time the doorbell rang, just after one thirty, everything was ready—Annie's organising almost military in its precision. So they all stood about making desultory conversation round the smoking barbecue, waiting for the honoured guest.

She watched with pride as Daniel, escorted by Richard, made his entrance into the kitchen. He looked so handsome, so smart in his pale blue shirt, jeans and dark jacket. His auburn hair was shiny and smelt of shampoo when she hugged him, but she noticed the expression in his grey-blue eyes was hesitant, much more so than when she'd first set eyes on him at Marjory's. She began the introductions, but was interrupted by Marsha, whose eyes were wide in disbelief.

'You!'

She saw a blush creep up her daughter's cheek as an answering one appeared on Daniel's.

'The party ... Jason's flat ...' Daniel looked away in confusion.

Annie, bewildered, glanced quickly from him to her daughter.

'You've met?' And suddenly she remembered the moment—the day of the fateful letter—that Marsha had mentioned meeting a man at a party who wasn't a media moron. Please, dear God, don't let them ... She searched her memory for what her daughter had told them about the evening. No, she'd definitely said he wasn't her type—they'd all laughed at Lucy's remark about geography teachers—although she also remembered a certain wistfulness in Marsha's tone. She felt a small shudder pass through her body, but she didn't have time to consider the implications now.

Richard was oblivious to the drama. 'Drink, anyone? There's cold beer in the tub in the garden, or white wine. Daniel?'

'Umm ... thanks, a beer would be great.' Daniel seemed to make a big effort to pull himself together.

'Why don't you all go outside while I finish off the lunch,' she said, shooing them towards the deck. Although apart from turning out the tart, which couldn't be done till the last minute, there was precious little left to do. She watched the group from inside. Ed was largely silent, nursing a bottle of beer and staring out across the gardens while Emma and Lucy were both looking up at Daniel and laughing at something he was telling them ... She caught the name of a famous actor. Marsha was ignoring them and helping her father turn the spare ribs and sausages over on the grill. Annie felt cold suddenly. I should have told my children about Daniel, I should have warned them. But what were the chances of them meeting like that? She was sure, from what Marsha had said at the time, that nothing had happened between them. But it could have, it could have ...

'Annie tells me you run a bar in Islington. Which one is it? I'm often around that neck of the woods.'

Daniel addressed his half-brother.

They were seated round the table at last. The sun had come out and, to the untutored eye, it looked like a normal family enjoying a normal Sunday lunch in the warmth of an early-summer afternoon.

'Red Desert, it's newish. On Upper Street, just before the Almeida on the left.'

Nothing about Ed's demeanour reassured his mother about his state of mind. He looked tired and dull, slumped over his food, which he just pushed round his plate. By comparison, Daniel seemed in his element, seated between Emma—who had purposefully manoeuvred herself into the chair next to him—and herself, but entertaining the entire table with stories from his life in advertising. Her heart went out to her younger son.

'The owner an Antonioni fan, then?' Daniel was asking.

Ed looked blank.

'You know, Eddie, the guy who did *The Passenger* with Jack Nicholson?' Emma glanced at Daniel knowingly. '*Red Desert* is one of his.'

'The owner's Moroccan. They have red sand in Morocco, I'm told.' Ed made no effort to hide his satisfaction in snubbing Daniel.

'You like it there, don't you?' Annie tried to encourage her younger son to open up. But she heard herself sounding like the mother of a ten-year-old asking about school.

Ed raised his eyebrows. 'No, Mum, I hate it. It's slave labour and boring as hell. But—' he shrugged at Daniel '—a man's got to earn a crust.'

Daniel seemed not to notice Ed's sullen tone and

grinned sympathetically. 'Yeah, unfortunately you do. God, the jobs I've done to keep body and soul together. I sometimes wonder if this writing malarkey is worth it.'

'At least you're doing something you care about, along with the shitty jobs,' Ed replied.

'I suppose so. What would you care about if you had the chance?'

Annie held her breath. They were really talking at last!

'I've always wanted to work with wood ... you know, carpentry, joinery ... design and make my own furniture,' Ed said quietly.

Emma looked puzzled and Lucy burst out laughing. Marsha was sitting in silence down the end of the table and hardly seemed to be listening to the conversation.

'Make furniture?' Lucy exclaimed. 'Since when? You've never mentioned that before.'

Richard harrumphed, but didn't comment.

Ed's face flushed angrily. 'Since forever, actually. I'm not just some loser in a bar,' he added, glaring at his father for a split second.

'Come on, Luce, he's done lots. That table in our flat, Mum's bread bin.' Marsha came to life in her brother's defence, and Annie noticed Ed shoot her a grateful glance. 'They're good,' her daughter added.

'I'd love to work with my hands,' Daniel responded. 'It must be the most satisfying thing in the world.'

Annie saw Ed eye him suspiciously, as if to check if he was making fun of him. But, to her at least, Daniel's comment seemed entirely sincere.

She went inside to get the pudding, beckoning

111

Marsha to help collect the plates. Her daughter did as she was bidden and followed her into the kitchen.

'Listen, I owe you a big apology,' Annie told her in a whisper, her voice breathless with anxiety. 'I made a terrible mistake not telling you all about Daniel. I was being selfish, I realise that now. Only seeing it from my point of view. I never thought . . . That night, at the party . . . I mean, obviously it's a one in a trillion chance, but it happened. You should have been warned.'

Marsha didn't meet her eye. 'Yeah . . . well, not much we can do about it now, eh?'

'Are you angry with me?'

'Mum, I'm not *angry*, but—' her eyes filled with tears '—just really, really shocked. Suppose we *had* done something? Had sex, for instance?'

Annie recoiled. 'You didn't, did you? You said . . .'

Marsha shook her head. 'No, we didn't. I told you at the time, he's not my type. But we might have.' She paused. 'Can you imagine if I'd let my own brother make love to me? How horrible would that have been?'

Annie was shaken.

'What's up, guys?' Lucy came inside, balancing a stack of empty bowls in both hands.

Marsha pulled away from Annie's embrace and wiped away the tears.

'Nothing, it's fine,' she mumbled, and hurried to the small loo in the corridor.

'Mum?'

'Marsha's upset because of meeting Daniel at that party.'

Lucy looked baffled. Then it dawned on her.

112

'Oh, you mean . . . She didn't . . .' her eyes widened in shock. 'They didn't . . . ?'

Annie quickly shook her head. 'She says not.'

'God!' Lucy shot a glance out towards Daniel on the terrace.

'Don't say anything to the others, will you.'

'Of course not.'

Annie handed Lucy the pudding plates and a small porcelain jug of double cream in silence. She heard laughter and saw her elder son grinning as he finished another anecdote. Emma's beautiful face was alive with pleasure. She couldn't see Ed's, his back was to her, but he seemed to be laughing too.

She brushed away the dark thoughts about Daniel and Marsha and hurried outside, laying her *tarte tatin* in the centre of the wooden table. The chunks of apple nestled plump and buttery, a deep golden brown, in rough circles on top of the crisp pastry, the caramel juice leaking temptingly around the edges; the vanilla ice cream, homemade of course and delicately flecked with dark pinpoints of vanilla seeds, scooped smooth and rich from the container; the gold-rimmed floral-patterned Ironstone plates set off the pudding to perfection, but her pleasure was overshadowed by what Marsha had said.

It was only when the pudding had been carefully divided and served, the ice cream handed round, the cream poured, that Richard raised his glass.

'I'd like to propose a toast. To meeting Daniel!' Everyone round the table echoed his words, 'Daniel . . . Daniel.'

Annie glanced round at all four of her children—together for the first time—and saw only the

113

smiles she had longed for. Her eldest had won them over with his charm and humour as she'd known he would. Marsha was putting on a good show; even Ed looked almost mellow.

'So, what's the verdict?' Marsha asked, directing her attention to Daniel as she poured the coffee and passed the small demi-tasses round the table. 'On your long-lost gene pool?' She grinned cheekily at him.

Daniel didn't flinch. 'It's been wonderful today,' he smiled at the faces round the table. 'I really appreciate being here.'

'Our pleasure,' Richard said.

'What's it like? Meeting us?' Lucy voiced what each of them had been thinking.

Annie had gone over versions of this conversation in her mind so many times before today, and she found she was almost holding her breath.

'Odd, I suppose. And for you too ... not knowing I even existed till recently,' Daniel replied.

There was an awkward silence.

'Yeah ...' Marsha began, then stopped.

'We were ... surprised,' Lucy added. It sounded to Annie as if this wasn't quite what her daughter had been about to say.

'I can imagine.' Daniel shifted his gaze to the horizon, fiddling with the edge of his napkin.

Annie was just wracking her brains to find something to say, when Emma spoke up.

'I've got some cousins I've never met.' She didn't sound as if she'd even noticed the awkward lacuna in the conversation. 'On my father's side. My dad's eldest brother ... they fell out about twenty years

114

ago over some stupid money thing. I've sometimes thought of looking them up.'

'Often happens in families.' Richard nodded. 'So where did you say you were living, Daniel?'

Annie smiled at her husband's deft change of subject.

'Umm, Islington at the moment.'

'Do you share?'

Daniel shook his head. 'I'm on my own. But not for much longer. The landlord is selling up and I have to move out in two weeks. There's some subsidence problem he can't be bothered to deal with, so he's offloading it cheap.'

'Is this sudden?' Annie asked, wondering why he hadn't mentioned it to her. 'Where will you go?'

'Friend's sofa in Stoke Newington, then I'm up in Edinburgh, rehearsing. I haven't got time to look for another place before that—there's still so much to do on the play.' Daniel was beginning to look uncomfortable under this scrutiny, but Annie persevered.

'But that's weeks away. Won't it be a nightmare, not having a proper place? Especially when you're working.'

'I'll be fine, honestly. I've done it before.'

'You could stay here,' Lucy interrupted, to receive shocked looks from the rest of the family.

'No . . . no, please. That's very kind, but no way . . . I couldn't possibly do that.' He held his hands up in protest. 'I didn't tell you so you could ask me to stay.'

'Why can't you, though?' Lucy persisted, looking between her parents. 'We have the room. Marsha and Ed don't live here any more.' Her mother noticed her twiddling a length of her auburn curls—a gesture she'd developed as a child when she was nervous.

Annie wasn't sure how she felt. She had wanted Daniel to be part of the family, but her daughter's suggestion seemed too sudden, too soon. She glanced at the others, but they looked back at her with a neutral gaze, perhaps waiting for her reaction.

'It does make sense,' Annie said slowly, against her better judgment but not wanting Daniel to think she wasn't keen. 'It's only for a few weeks . . . and at least you'd have a proper room of your own.'

Daniel shook his head, smiling at them as if they were daft children. 'I've only just met you all! I can't just suddenly move in.'

'It's just a room. We're out during the day,' Lucy went on, clearly warming to her theme. 'You'd have the place to yourself. We'd hardly notice you were there . . . would we, Mum? Dad?'

'Will you at least consider it?' Annie asked, raising her eyebrows at her husband, who still said nothing.

But Daniel shook his head firmly. 'I can't.'

'Tell you what . . .' This from Marsha. 'Why don't you give it a go, and if it doesn't work, you can move out again and kip on your friend's sofa.'

Lucy nodded. 'What's to lose?'

'Richard?' Annie waited.

Her husband nodded slowly. 'It's up to you,' he said, not looking at her.

'Well . . .' Daniel still hesitated. 'It seems such an imposition, considering you hardly know me. But obviously it would be a great solution from my point of view.'

'Brilliant!' Lucy said. 'It's a deal. You can go in Eddie's room.' Annie saw her glance at her brother, who gave an imperceptible shake of his head. 'You don't mind, do you?' Lucy went on. 'You hardly ever come home.'

'It's fine,' Ed mumbled.

Annie searched Daniel's face. Was he comfortable with this? Wasn't Lucy railroading him a bit?

'Please . . . if anyone has any objection to my coming here, you'd say, wouldn't you?' Daniel begged.

Marsha smiled. 'Hmm, not necessarily, Daniel. Us Delanceys aren't exactly renowned for telling it how it is. We can be polite to the point of ridiculousness. Like Mum not mentioning you for thirty-five years.'

Daniel looked awkward, clearly not knowing what to say.

'That wasn't to do with politeness, Marsha. And it's not very polite of you to suggest we might be lying about wanting Daniel here,' Annie pointed out, giving her daughter a questioning stare.

'I didn't mean that, Mum,' Marsha said quickly. 'I'm sure you're very welcome here, Daniel. But generally . . . I just thought I'd mention it, if you're about to spend time with the family.'

Daniel seemed to have recovered his composure. 'My own family's never been that hot about airing stuff either. And whatever the intention, it doesn't make things easy.'

'Probably a generation thing,' Ed put in. 'The parents come from the stiff-upper-lip school of emotions: never tell anyone anything even remotely personal if you can get away with it.

117

Whereas us lot spill every bit of dirty linen we can dig up, preferably on TV, preferably in front of millions.'

While they all laughed, Richard could be heard to mutter: 'Nothing so great about that, is there? All that eternal sobbing. Haven't you noticed? Every film you see today, the slightest thing sets 'em off. Can't even say hi without the entire cast— including grown men—tearing up.'

'Men should be able to cry,' Marsha retorted.

'Cry for a good reason, of course,' Richard agreed. 'But crying because they think that's acting? Doesn't do it for me.'

'Ah, Dad,' Lucy leaned over and put her arm affectionately round her father's shoulders. 'It's stiff upper lip for you then. Don't let the bastards see the whites of your eyes.'

*   *   *

As Daniel was leaving, Annie drew him aside. She wanted a private moment with him, out of the glare of the rest of the family.

'Don't feel pushed into anything,' she said. 'I'd love you to come, but if you're not comfortable with it . . .'

Daniel shrugged. 'Are you absolutely sure about this? Shouldn't you think it over? I mean, I love it that you and I have had the chance to bond a bit, but your family don't know me from Adam. Perhaps Lucy's being too kind.'

She smiled. 'She is kind, but we do want you to come. Please . . .'

He hesitated, perhaps making some calculations in his head.

'Well . . . if you're sure. Please feel free to change your mind at any time though, Annie.' He seemed relieved, but there was also a note of uncertainty in his voice.

'Thank you, but I'm sure we won't.'

'And thanks for an amazing lunch. I think your family is wonderful.'

She looked up at him. 'Your family too, now.'

*　　*　　*

When they'd all gone, Annie went outside and sat for a moment on the deck, enjoying a heavenly sense of relief. It was only now, when the shadow of her long-held secret had begun to fade in Daniel's presence, that she felt she could properly let go. No longer, when she thought of her baby, would she have to imagine him adrift out there in the world, not knowing how he was growing up, or with whom. It felt good.

'You must be pleased.' Richard interrupted her reverie.

She stretched luxuriously, looking up at him with a smile. 'Wasn't it brilliant! Daniel fitted in so well, as if he really belonged. Maybe blood is thicker than water after all.'

Richard, now in his corduroy slippers, slopped across the deck and began pulling at a stray tendril of potato jasmine on the far wall.

She waited for him to comment on Daniel, but he said nothing. 'You liked him, didn't you?'

Her husband turned to face her, a handful of slim branches in his hand. 'I thought he was very charming,' he replied.

She waited. She knew him so well. Never a

gusher, Richard had his own quiet way of expressing enthusiasm, and he wasn't doing that now.

'It's just . . . well, I think you made a big mistake in allowing our kind-hearted daughter's offer to go so far.' He turned away, dumping the plant clippings on the ground.

'You think it's too soon?'

Richard gave a sigh and turned back to face her. 'Annie, we hardly know the man! It's like going to Kentish Town and stopping the first person you see and inviting him home to stay for six weeks.'

Annie felt her pleasure at the lunch melt away. She had the same fears as her husband, but she wasn't sure why.

'You could have said at the time that you thought it wasn't such a great idea—before the decision was made.'

He stared at her, his eyebrows raised. 'Could I?'

'Of course you could. Anyway, what have you got against him coming? I understand it's sudden, I felt that myself. But I *do* know him, Richard. I've met up with him—as you'd be the first to complain about—quite a lot recently, and I hardly need references. He's my son.'

'It would still have been better if you'd asked for time to think about it.'

'Maybe, but I didn't. And nor did you.'

He wasn't listening. 'I don't blame Lucy. She's bent on saving the world. And we've said it before, her bleeding heart will always get her into trouble. But you shouldn't have gone along with it so easily.'

Pompous idiot, she thought. 'You make her sound like Care in the Community.'

120

'It's just . . . well, once he's here, supposing he gets settled and wants to stay?'

Annie knew this was just Richard inventing excuses for the position he was taking. The truth is, she thought sadly, he doesn't really want anything to do with Daniel.

'He's got a play on in Edinburgh, remember? It's hardly likely he'd forgo that rare privilege just to hang out with us.'

After a solid silence, broken only by the click of the kettle reaching the boil back in the kitchen, she added, 'We have everything in life, Richard. We have a huge, half-empty house, we have money, we have a close family. Can't we be generous for once, and ask someone in need to share all that?'

Richard harrumphed. 'Now you're making *him* sound like Care in the Community.'

Annie couldn't help smiling at that, and Richard finally saw the funny side and smiled too.

'I just think you're taking things a bit too fast, that's all.'

'I agree.'

'OK. Well, let's try and make the best of it then, shall we?'

'I hope having Daniel here is better than just making the best of it.' She firmly resisted his doom scenario.

'Well, I hope so too.'

9

Ed was wandering round the supermarket the following morning. He liked shopping, found the mundane predictability soothing. Emma had said she'd meet him there—she'd had to drop in on her mum for an hour—but he started pottering along the aisles without her, picking up stuff she'd probably put back when she turned up. She favoured loads of vegetables—mostly green—fruit, and nasty things like wholewheat spaghetti and muesli bars. Whereas he, despite his mother's similar fixation on healthy food while he was growing up, went for stuff like a good honest pie— steak and kidney, mince, or even fish, he wasn't fussy—tinned beans, cereals with heaps of sugar. It was a running gag between him and Emms, but they usually came to some reasonable compromise.

As he pushed the trolley, his mind went back, not for the first time, to yesterday's lunch with Daniel. He'd surprised himself with his outburst about making furniture. True, he'd often fantasised about a quiet life in the country, doing practical work such as making tables and cabinets outside a picturesque cottage with a river and a dog, but he'd only said it to say *something*. Daniel would keep on about his writing, and he didn't want to appear like some deadbeat. But saying it out loud had sparked an old thought. He decided he'd investigate carpentry lessons, despite the dismissive response he'd got from his father when he'd mentioned it in the past. He didn't need his approval now—he could afford to pay for the lessons himself.

He caught sight of his girlfriend walking past the end of the aisle and called out to her. 'How did it go?' He kissed her lingeringly on the lips in greeting, aware that most of the other guys in the supermarket would be dying of jealousy.

Emma shook her head. 'Oh, you know . . . the usual bollocks. I'm not sure she's taking her meds.'

Ed laughed. Emma's mother was not on medication as far as either of them knew, but Emma always joked she should be.

'That bad?'

'Not really, I suppose. I'm just always waiting for her to kick off. It's not very restful.'

'Mothers seem to make it their business not to be restful these days,' Ed muttered.

She linked arms with him as he pushed the trolley. 'Come on, babe. Annie's a walk in the park compared to mine. You're not still sore about the lunch, are you?'

'It's OK for you to be so laid back about Daniel. It's not *your* saintly half-brother risen from the dead to take up residence in your old bedroom.'

'But he was great. You can't honestly say you didn't like him? I saw you laughing at some of his stories, and he was nothing but charming to you, despite your snippiness. Imagine what he *could* have been like.'

Ed paused before answering. 'It's not to do with liking him or not liking him. Sure, he was charming, in a smug sort of way. And don't think I didn't see the way you were hanging on his every word. Flirting with him . . .'

Emma pulled her arm away from his. 'For

123

heaven's sake, Eddie, what's your problem? It's fucking boring, this. You getting off on how much you hate him all the time. I'm not going to apologise for being nice to him.'

'Emms ...' He reached out to her, but she moved away.

'No. I don't want to hear another word on the subject. Daniel's no threat to you, and the sooner you realise it the better. You should count yourself lucky you've got such an amazing family.' She stalked off down the aisle, flashing a flirtatious smile at a guy getting a tub of ice cream out of the freezer cabinet. She just can't help herself, he thought.

'Emma, where are you going?' he called after her, clocking the smug grin from the man at the freezer.

'To get salad,' she shouted over her shoulder.

He followed her sheepishly with the trolley. He knew he was being a pain in the bum, but he couldn't seem to help himself. Emma didn't get it. She didn't know what it was like to feel you'd let your parents down, then be faced with the replacement perfect son. OK, her family was a train wreck, but her parents weren't to be respected, they didn't set standards to live up to. His did.

*   *   *

'You did book, didn't you?' Annie cast a nervous glance at her husband as he manoeuvred the car into a tight space—the only one they could find on a Sunday—at the opposite end of Cadogan Place from the restaurant.

124

'Bit late if I haven't,' Richard teased her. 'But do I look like a man brave enough to tell Eleanor Westbury her favourite restaurant's full?'

'Nobody would be that brave. But then she thinks you're so bloody marvellous you could probably stab her and still be awarded the Dear Richard medal.'

Her husband put on a theatrical smirk as he turned the engine off.

'So what's Eleanor's position on Daniel?' Richard asked, as they walked along beside the fenced gardens.

'How do you mean?'

'Well, is he a contentious issue? Can we talk about him?' He glanced at her. 'Only asking. You know how tricky she can be.'

Annie felt a frisson of anxiety. 'I don't know. I don't see why we shouldn't be able to talk about him, but as you say . . .' She could imagine the tight expression of disapproval on her mother's face. Lunch would be a nightmare if her mother chose to start on about Daniel being 'feckless', or after Annie's money. Especially as Ed was coming.

'Best to leave it this time, perhaps?' Richard suggested. 'Until she's met him and things have . . . settled?'

Did she sense Richard was relieved? Or was she being oversensitive? They had barely talked about Daniel's impending arrival since the decision was made the week before. Richard had made her so conscious of bringing him up in conversation all the time, that now she hardly dared mention his name.

'I suppose. I still haven't told her that Charles is Daniel's father.'

The Rib Room at the Carlton Tower was comfortingly familiar to Annie. Like Fortnum's, her mother had been bringing her here since she was young. It had first opened in the early sixties, and the unchanging decor—luxurious but understated—the low lighting, the warmth, the thick white tablecloths and immaculate tableware, the all-encompassing fragrance of roast meat, gave her a curious sense of safety. Even her mother seemed to annoy her less at the Rib Room.

Ed, Marsha and Lucy were already seated. Her mother was precisely fifteen minutes late. This was part of the carefully choreographed birthday drama—Eleanor was only ever selectively late. Annie hoped she could make the day perfect for her exacting parent.

'Isn't this splendid!' Eleanor entered the room with her usual flourish, guided to the table on the arm of a charmingly attentive maître d'.

Ed and the girls all jumped up and greeted their grandmother, wishing her happy birthday. Richard took over from the maître d' and settled his mother-in-law carefully on the squashy banquette. The birthday present and card had already been placed on the table, and Eleanor clapped her hands at the sight of them.

'How kind you all are!' She made no move to open the slim parcel, which contained a very expensive cashmere print scarf from Liberty, just looked around at her family with what seemed to Annie—so used to her caustic humours—like real pleasure.

'So, children. Tell me what you've all been up to.' Her glance roamed the three, then settled questioningly on Lucy.

'I've been accepted to do this volunteering in an orphanage in Tanzania in September, Grandma. Did Mum tell you?' Lucy's excitement shone from her face.

Eleanor raised her eyebrows disapprovingly. 'Heavens! Is that wise? Your mother mentioned the possibility, but I hoped you'd grow out of the idea.'

Lucy laughed. 'I'm twenty-two, Grandma. I think I'm a bit past growing out of things.'

'Well, if you're that old, you shouldn't be gallivanting about in foreign parts. You should be marrying some nice chap and settling down on his country estate to breed.' Eleanor cocked her head as they all laughed at her joke. 'I'm perfectly serious,' she added, but there was a mischievous gleam in her eye.

'Well done, Eleanor! I keep telling her exactly the same thing, but she pays absolutely no attention to me,' Richard agreed, to receive an approving pat on his hand.

'Of course you do,' Eleanor went on. 'I can always rely on you, dear Richard, to be the one with common sense in this family.'

'Toady,' Annie mouthed, looking pointedly at her husband as her mother turned away. So far, so good, she thought. She had tried to sit next to Ed, hoping she could break the ongoing silence between them, but he had carefully sandwiched himself between the two girls and was saying very little.

'Come on, Grandma, open your present,' Marsha urged, laughing. She and her grandmother had always had a close bond. Marsha loved the old lady's sharp wit. 'I chose it myself.'

'Well, now. Let's see . . .' Eleanor reached for the package and began slowly to untie the pink velvet ribbon and pull open the thick, floral paper. She'll love it because Marsha's chosen it, Annie thought. If I'd picked it out it would be the wrong colour, or the wrong pattern, or she already has one just like it. Eleanor would be polite and overtly grateful, but she would know she had failed.

'It's perfect!' Eleanor quickly draped the soft blue wool over the shoulders of her immaculate navy Chanel suit and Annie breathed a sigh of relief.

They ordered, the chilled Puligny-Montrachet was poured, the conversation flowed. Annie began to relax.

'It's a shame Emma couldn't be here.' She leaned across the table to address her son.

'Yeah. She had to see her father. He's making one of his royal visits from New Zealand.'

'Poor Emms,' Annie commented, knowing how stressful the girl found time with her father. But Ed just nodded and turned to say something to Marsha.

The chef arrived with his silver-domed trolley containing a huge side of roast beef. Eleanor and Richard requested theirs rare, the others wanted medium, and the chef, in his high white toque, set to work carving thick, mouth-watering slices of brown-pink meat and laying them reverently onto the heated white plates stacked beside the joint.

Annie was passing a plate down the table to Ed, loaded with meat and puffy golden Yorkshire puddings, when her mobile rang. Nooo, she thought, glancing quickly over at her mother for a

128

predictably disapproving reaction. But Eleanor was laughing at something Richard had said and hadn't noticed. The display said private number, but it might be the oven man. She *had* to answer it. The thermostat on the huge industrial oven at the bakery was malfunctioning, burning everything Carol put near it. It had to be fixed today or they would be in danger of defaulting on orders, something Delancey Bakes had never, *ever* done— a celebration cake was completely pointless if it was late.

She mouthed an apology to the table and got up, quickly leaving the dining room as she answered the call.

'Hello?'

'Er, hello. Am I speaking to Annie Delancey?' The voice had a plummy drawl, not in the least like the service engineer's northern brogue.

'Yes . . . who is this?'

'Well, it's Charles Carnegie, actually. You wrote. You have something of considerable importance to tell me?' The man sounded amused, almost playful. Her heart seemed to somersault in her chest.

'Charles? Charles Carnegie?' She hardly managed the words. His voice sounded older, of course, but it was recognisably the same voice that had set her alight, a lifetime ago now.

' 'Tis I.'

'Oh . . . thanks for getting back to me.' She fell back on politeness while she got her breath. 'Yes, yes, I do—have something of importance, I mean.'

There was silence for a moment.

'God, it must be thirty years since we . . . er . . .' the voice paused. 'So, are you going to tell me

129

then?'

'Not on the phone, no. I can't tell you on the phone, it's too . . . I'd just rather see you face to face. Somewhere private.'

There was a short laugh. 'Oh, I say, this is beginning to make me nervous. I hope it won't be disagreeable.' The playfulness had gone and been replaced by mild suspicion.

'No, it's not in the least bit disagreeable,' Annie retorted, amazed that he seemed to have no inkling about what she wanted to tell him.

'That's a relief. Well, I'm off to Paris on Friday week, but normally I'm up in town Tuesdays and Wednesdays. This Tuesday any good?'

Annie thought quickly, glad that he was suggesting an early date. She could get it over with before Daniel arrived. 'Yes . . . Tuesday's fine.'

'Do you want to come to the flat? I'm in Onslow Gardens. Shall we say six-ish? I'll text you the address.'

They said goodbye and she hung up. She realised she was shaking. She knew she needed to go back into the dining room before the family came to find her, but she was incapable of facing them just yet. She hurried down the corridor to the Ladies'. He sounded exactly as she'd imagined he would, she thought: smug, facetious, arrogant. There was no way the man on the other end of the phone would be interested in being a father to Daniel, and this knowledge came as some relief to her. She didn't want him in her own life, not even peripherally.

'Who was that, Mum? You've been ages.' Ed looked at her suspiciously when she returned, and she knew he thought it had been Daniel on the

130

phone. 'We got them to take your food away to keep warm.'

'Thanks ... Sorry, everyone.' She glanced at Richard, knowing she looked pale, begging him silently not to draw attention to it. 'It was the oven man. He says it's the thermostat, which we all knew already, but he says it's not going to be easy to fix because the oven's so old.' She lied fluently, waiting for some sharp comment from her mother.

But Eleanor shook her head sympathetically. 'The usual story. They can't mend anything these days. Built-in obsolescence, they call it. I call it rank incompetence.' She wagged a finger at her. 'Be careful, darling. Don't let him bully you into buying a new one you don't need.'

She smiled gratefully at her mother. There's an upside to having a selfish mother, she thought. Like I never really know what's going on inside *her* head, she doesn't know what's going on inside mine either.

'You're right, Mother, he mentioned that. But, give him his due, he's still trying to fix it.' Annie felt suddenly anxious about the oven, and realised she was beginning to believe her own lie. But even so, she reached into her pocket to turn her mobile off. She certainly didn't want the real oven man ringing right now.

'Who's having pudding?' Richard spoke into the silence.

*   *   *

Annie's head was spinning with the implications of the Tuesday meeting. Blast the man for existing, she thought crossly, as the car pulled out into

131

Sloane Street after lunch.

'I really enjoyed that,' said Marsha from the back seat. 'Grandma's so witty.'

'Yeah, she really makes me laugh. She loves pretending to be spiteful, but she doesn't mean it,' Lucy replied.

Annie and Richard exchanged a knowing glance.

'I wish I'd seen her when she was running her finishing school,' Lucy added. 'She must have been awesome.'

'Monstrous, more like. They were a spoilt bunch, but Grandma showed no mercy.'

'Training a girl to get a husband . . . sounds so weird now,' Marsha commented.

'Oh, I don't know,' Richard said. 'A little French, tennis here, art galleries and theatre there, how to dress properly . . .' he glanced at Annie. 'Even how to get into a car without exposing too much leg, you said. Sounds too good to be true. Nothing wrong with training a woman to be the perfect wife!'

The general hilarity that greeted his words was drowned out by the blaring siren from two speeding police cars careering round Hyde Park Corner.

'Seriously though,' Richard added, 'Eleanor did an amazing job setting up that school, however ridiculous it seems now. It can't have been easy— she'd never worked a day in her life. I know she can be difficult, but I take my hat off to her for that.'

Annie nodded. 'I know. I sometimes forget how hard it must have been.' She so often found herself firefighting with her mother, keeping just ahead of the niggling and the jibes, that she lost sight of the fact that Eleanor, left with overwhelming debts—mostly from gambling—racked up by her husband, had pulled them back from the brink of destitution. And had even made a tidy profit from the ridiculous fees she got away with charging the twenty-five pupils she took on every year. That, and the sale of the huge house in Ovington Square, had provided her mother with a very comfortable old age.

'Can you drop me at Green Park, Dad? I'll take the Victoria line.' Ed interrupted her thoughts.

'Wouldn't it be quicker to go from Camden?' Richard asked.

'The Victoria line's off every weekend till the autumn,' Marsha put in.

Ed groaned. 'Bugger, I forgot. Are you sure it's *every* weekend?'

'Don't you believe me?' Marsha asked.

'Yeah, sure I believe you. OK, I suppose it'll have to be Camden.'

He's in such a hurry to be shot of us, Annie thought sadly.

'If you're meeting Emms,' she heard Marsha say, 'she probably won't be back till later, but you could come home with me and hang out, if you like.'

'Can't. I've got things to sort out at home.'

She heard the cagey tone in her son's voice. Ed's not just avoiding me, he's avoiding his sister as well.

'I wonder how Grandma will react to Daniel. Will she like him, do you think?' she asked, directing her question to the back of the car. There was silence for a moment. Annie turned to look at her children.

'He's charming and clever. Grandma likes

clever.' Lucy smiled at her.

Annie waited for Ed or Marsha to volunteer something.

'Mum . . .' Marsha began. 'What happens now? With Daniel?'

'How do you mean?'

'Well, he's coming to stay till he goes to Edinburgh, but will he come back afterwards? I mean permanently?'

'Of course not,' Richard snapped.

Annie frowned at her husband. 'No, he won't be coming back, Mash.'

'He might if he hasn't got anywhere else to live, mightn't he?' Lucy asked.

She saw Richard's what-did-I-tell-you look and wanted to smack him.

'He's just staying for a few weeks. He has no intention of living with us. Why would he want to?' Annie tried to control her irritation.

More silence greeted her question.

'Don't get me wrong, I don't mind one way or another,' said Marsha lightly. 'I was just asking.'

Asking on her brother's behalf, Annie thought.

'He counts as family now, I suppose,' said Lucy.

Ed finally spoke, his tone suddenly vehement. 'He's *not* family. Not in the way we all are. I mean, was that the last time we'll have a Daniel-free family get-together, Mum? Is he always going to be around from now on?'

Annie didn't reply for a second. Don't antagonise him.

'I don't know what's going to happen, Ed, if you want the truth. I've never been in this situation before, obviously. I'm just feeling my way . . . like the rest of you.'

She turned again and saw the concerned faces looking back at her. It reminded her of when they were young, lined up on the back seat on the way to school, to and fro to parties, swimming, the supermarket, on holiday in Scotland or Normandy.

'Can we just let things take their course? I'm not going to foist someone on the family that nobody wants around.'

'You're not upset, are you, Mum?' Lucy asked after a moment.

Annie said no, but she had to turn away, not wanting her children to see her incipient tears. They were tears as much of frustration as anything else.

'I really don't want this thing with Daniel to come between us,' she said, swallowing hard. 'I couldn't bear that.'

'Nor me.' Lucy's tone was stalwart. 'Can I come to yours for a bit?' Annie heard her ask her sister in a low voice.

'So what was going on at lunch?' Richard asked, as soon as they'd dropped the others off.

'Charles Carnegie called. We're meeting on Tuesday.'

'That explains it. You looked positively ill.'

'I didn't want to mention his name in front of Mother.' She sighed. 'I'll be glad to tell him though . . . get it over with finally.'

'Where are you meeting?'

'Where?' She was puzzled by the question. 'He suggested I come to his flat.'

Richard's head shot round. 'His *flat*? Why can't you meet in a pub or a bar?'

'What does it matter where we meet?'

He didn't reply.

135

'Richard?' She could hardly bear another round of bickering.

'Just seems a trifle odd, meeting in his flat when he hardly knows you.'

'I don't see what's odd about it.' She tried to keep the irritation out of her voice as she added, 'Anyway, we've made the plan now.'

'Should be very cosy,' Richard muttered.

She didn't bother to answer.

*   *   *

The two sisters sat at the kitchen table in Marsha and Emma's flat in Canonbury—a third-floor corner flat with two bedrooms and a view across to the overground station. Both cradled a mug of tea.

'Are you as sick of all this as I am?' Marsha asked her sister.

Lucy nodded. 'Sure am. Being with the Delanceys these days is like hanging out with the Addams Family—no one's entirely normal.' She paused. 'It's the tension that drives me nuts.'

'Will things get better, I wonder . . . when the unwitting cause of it takes up residence? Or will that make it worse?'

'I don't know . . . better, I think. It's not as if Daniel's a pain. Won't Dad see that and relax?'

'And Eddie?'

Lucy shook her head. 'It goes deeper with him.'

'Yeah . . . typical that Mum's long-lost son pitches up with the face of an angel and a sodding Cambridge degree.'

'I'm worried about Ed and Mum, Mash. He's being such a dick at the moment, and Mum doesn't help by being so focused on Daniel all the time. I mean, I totally understand why she is, but still . . .'

'It's a mess.' Marsha gave her sister a rueful smile. 'But it seems like we're stuck with it.'

They sat for a while, sipping their tea, neither speaking.

'When you met him—Daniel—at that party, I know you said he wasn't your type, but . . .'

Marsha didn't answer immediately. 'Can't go there, Luce.'

Her sister's eyes widened.

'No, I don't mean that. We talked. I promise you, we only talked.'

She brushed off Lucy's question, but she was still in shock and angry with her mother. Maybe the connection she'd felt for Daniel the night they'd met had been just a strange blood-tie thing, which she'd confused with sexual attraction on her part. But seeing him again, this time as her brother, had totally freaked her out. It wasn't Daniel's fault, obviously, but she was with Eddie on this one. She wished he would just go away.

10

'I'm not sure why you need to make such an effort.' Richard was standing in the hall, eyeing her from top to toe as she walked down the stairs. His tone was deceptively light.

'I haven't made "such an effort",' she insisted. 'I've had a shower and washed my hair, which I always do before I go anywhere.' But, in fact, she had been in a state about how she would seem to

Carnegie, ever since his phone call. I shouldn't give a toss, she told herself, because he probably hardly remembers our evening together. But a girl has her pride.

Richard was staring at her unhappily. 'Is there any reason why I can't come with you to meet Chelsea boy?'

Annie went up to him, touching her hands to his shoulders and looking him straight in the eye.

'None at all. I told you, you can come if you want to. I just think this is something I'd rather do on my own. It'll be awkward for both of us. I think he'd find it worse with an audience.'

'I hate the thought of you seeing him at all . . . prick.'

'*You* hate it!' She smiled brightly and gave him a tender kiss on the cheek. 'I'm doing this for Daniel,' she said with deliberate resolution, as much to give herself courage as to remind her husband that she would never willingly have put herself in the same room as Charles Carnegie again. At least by the time Daniel moved in she would have some idea about whether his real father would play ball or not.

It was at moments like this, when her normally grounded, dependable husband seemed about to pick yet another fight about Daniel, that she lost heart. She and Richard had always been on the same page, united in their endeavours. It hadn't necessarily been easy. When she'd been starting up her cake business, working all hours, Richard expanding his accountancy firm, and the children still small, there had been real tensions. But they'd both had a common purpose: the family.

Finding Daniel was of no obvious benefit to any

of them, she realised sadly, as she gathered her jacket from the peg. And Richard hasn't a clue how much I've wanted to see him again, because of my own daft notions of secrecy. Serves me right, I suppose, if he doesn't understand what's happening to me. Before he'd had calm, organised Annie and now he's got obsessive, emotional Annie. Who wouldn't be put out?

'I won't be late.'

He nodded resignedly. 'Good luck then.'

* * *

The red-carpeted stairs up to Charles's pied-à-terre seemed endless. The house was an end of terrace, with a grand white-pillared porch supporting a wrought iron balcony on the first floor, overlooking the communal gardens. As she climbed, the ceilings got lower, the staircases shorter, the carpet more worn, until she arrived on the top landing: the one-time servants' quarters.

Charles opened the door of his flat before she had time to catch her breath.

'Well, hello there.' He grinned and gestured her inside. She had to squeeze past him as he stood on yet another narrow flight of stairs, which led up to the landing of his apartment. He smelled very clean, fragrant with ginger and citrus.

She remembered him at once. He seemed not to have changed much. He was tall and slim; his thick, wavy hair, still wet from the shower, brushed back and just lying on his collar, was now grey-blonde. He wore a fresh blue cotton shirt, open-necked, with his monogram, CC, stitched to the pocket, navy cords, and old tan loafers, no socks.

'Please, come in.'

'Thanks.'

Both hovered awkwardly in the small sitting room, Annie checking out the view across London over the top of the attic balustrade, Charles standing in the doorway looking at her curiously. He rubbed his hands together, grinned uncertainly, then said, 'Drink? I've got a lovely little Chablis waiting in the fridge.'

'Thank you, sounds great.' She remembered her mother telling her he was 'something in wine'.

He came back in with the bottle and two glasses, which he set down on the coffee table. The room was elegant and immaculate, as if no one lived there, the colours bland taupes, creams and browns, the furniture French Country style, the pictures nondescript line drawings of famous gardens. He must have seen her eyeing the decor.

'I know, frightful, isn't it? My wife had one of those interior-decorator chaps in, and now it looks like an expensive hotel room.'

Annie hesitated. 'Not really.' She was being polite and they both knew it. 'Where do you live when you're not here?'

'Hambledon Valley . . . Henley way.'

She looked puzzled. 'Isn't that only about forty-five minutes from London?'

'Correct. But I was done for being over the limit,' he grinned ruefully, '*Way* over the limit, a while ago, and I'm in wine . . . I drink. Louisa, my wife, insisted we get this place, and she was right, I really can't afford to lose my licence again. They'd throw away the key.'

He took his glass by the stem, holding it delicately as if it were a rare object, and swirled it

140

twice, plunging his nose into the top of it and inhaling deeply. 'Mmm. Heaven. Smell that.' He looked over at her as he took a sip. She also put her nose to the glass and sniffed. 'I love this wine,' he went on. 'It's so fresh and citrusy, not too sweet . . . and with those wonderful flinty undertones.'

She smiled at his enthusiasm; he sounded like a wine review. She tried hers. It was indeed delicious. He nodded his approval.

'So . . . you're here on a mission. Shall we get it over with?'

She saw his boyish good looks suddenly cloud over. He must have worked it out, surely, she thought, her heart beating slightly faster as she put her wine down on the coffee table.

'Alright. Well, I'm not quite sure how to put this.' She took a slow breath. 'Not sure what you remember about that night . . . with me . . . all those years ago . . .'

Charles looked away, clearly embarrassed. For a moment, Annie allowed herself to go back. It was summer, 1966. She had met Charles properly for the first time at the Westbury Academy's graduation ball—Eleanor insisted on the grand name, although it was really an end-of-year dance for the girls and usually comprised around a hundred and twenty people—'graduates' and their guests—at the Rembrandt Hotel in Knightsbridge. Annie had tried to get out of it; she loathed the sight of the snobby girls and their parents—they seemed to epitomise all that she hated about her mother's aspirations—although she accepted she was probably classed as one of them back then. She had seen Charles around before that, picking up his sister, Venetia. He seemed like a god to

Annie, with his blond good looks and devil-may-care posing against the iron railings of the building—part of which was her home, the other part her mother's finishing school.

She'd just left school, feeling heady and thrilled by the prospect of being loose in London, free from formal education and the constraints of her Sussex boarding school. Her mother had told her she had a year, during which she would be expected to learn shorthand and typing, cooking, and how to drive. After that, she'd have to work, as a secretary, perhaps, with one of Eleanor's chums in the City. Annie was happy with this; at that moment she had no ambition but to enjoy herself.

Her partner for the dance was one red-haired Torquil McVitie, a friend from childhood, but never a boyfriend. They'd gone to ballroom dance classes together at Miss Vacani's in Knightsbridge, although she'd always known that Torquil's genius lay in his wit, not his feet. Charles was at the same table, and had flirted outrageously with her all night. He had danced with her too, swirling her round the room with great panache. 'Everyone's watching,' he'd whispered in her ear. Three agonising days later, he'd called. She remembered the weather being unbearably hot and humid that week.

'Come round to my house,' he'd said. 'We can sit in the garden. My parents have gone to France for the summer and I've got the place to myself.'

She hadn't told her mother she was seeing him. Eleanor would have panicked, Charles Carnegie being viewed as a 'catch'. She would have begun nagging her daughter as to what to wear, how to stand, how to eat, which topics of conversation

142

might amuse him—as if these things hadn't already been instilled into her daily, for what seemed like her entire lifetime. She lied, said she was going to a nurses' party with Jamie.

They had sat on two padded loungers in the garden of the Carnegie house, off High Street Kensington, drinking cold champagne filched from his parents' cellar, and eating from a cereal bowl full of crisps. She hadn't eaten all day, from nerves, and became very drunk very quickly. But Charles was easy to talk to, a beguiling companion. As the light faded, he brought a silver candelabra into the garden with three tall cream candles and put Otis Redding on the gramophone, opening the doors wide to the relaxed soul rhythm. They'd sucked orange ice lollies from the freezer and then lain on the cool grass and kissed, their lips and tongues still frozen. She remembered the clean, masculine heat of his body, the delicious softness of his mouth. Later, he had taken her hands and pulled her to her feet, guiding her, wobbly from desire and too much champagne, upstairs to his room.

The sex was surprising, a bit painful, and not that great for her. But she didn't care. It was only part of the whole. She was lying naked with a man, and not just any man—Charles Carnegie. She was drunk, alive, free at last to be a woman.

She'd never heard from him again.

Charles was silent, maybe lost in the past as she had been.

'You do remember, don't you?' She was both amused and shocked that he might not. The seminal moment of her life, upon which so much had hinged, and this man maybe didn't even recall it?

Charles laughed. 'I *do* remember. Of course I do. Not senile yet. It was hot, we were in the garden . . .' He paused, his face taking on a look of doom. 'Do I see where this is going?'

She nodded. 'I thought you'd have twigged before now.' She looked him directly in the eye. 'We have a son together: Daniel.'

There was a moment of stunned silence. Charles looked blank, as if his brain was refusing to take in what she'd just said.

'You mean . . . you mean you've brought up my child all these years—what is it? Thirty? More?—You've brought him up and never told me?' He stared at her in disbelief.

She held her hands up to stop his injured tirade. 'No. No, I didn't bring him up. I . . . I gave him up for adoption when he was a baby.'

Charles took a huge breath, getting to his feet to pace the small room. He turned, his hands on his hips, and looked at her in shock and bewilderment.

'Wait! Let me understand this. You got pregnant that night, didn't tell me, gave him away—again without telling me—and now . . . why are you telling me *now*?'

'He got in touch. I've met him.'

He shook his head. 'Christ . . .' He slumped back in his chair, his head in his hands.

'Do you have children?' she asked.

He looked up, nodding distractedly. 'A daughter. Amelia. She's nearly twenty-five.'

'Look, Charles, I'm really sorry. I know this must be a terrible shock for you. I should have told you at the time.'

'Well, yes, you certainly should have.' He threw his arms in the air. 'I can't believe it.' He paused,

144

thinking for a minute. 'Why didn't you have an abortion? Are you Catholic or something?' His voice was accusatory.

'I didn't realise I was pregnant till it was too late,' she said softly. 'I was still having my periods . . . it happens sometimes.'

Charles shook his head again, reaching for his wine glass.

'What was I supposed to do? You never called me,' she said, suddenly defensive. 'After that night I never heard from you again. Why would I have thought you'd be interested in being a father . . . ? Would you have been?'

'Don't make this my fault.' His tone was curt. He was looking at her with suspicion now. 'Are you sure it's . . . he's mine? I mean, we were all sleeping with anything that moved back then. How do you know for certain?'

She'd been expecting this. 'I have no concrete proof, if that's what you're asking. You know I'd never had sex before that night, but you only have my word for that.' She shrugged. 'Without DNA I can't prove a thing.'

He seemed to accept that she was telling the truth, because he nodded.

'Would you have been interested in being a father, at twenty-one, or whatever you were then?' she asked again.

Charles pulled a face, shook his head in bewilderment. 'That's an impossible question. I don't know. How can I know what I'd have felt this long after the event?' He paused and there was a heavy silence in the small room. 'No, probably not, if I'm honest. But these things aren't that straightforward, are they? I certainly had a right to

145

know, to make the decision for myself. This is my son you're talking about, Annie, not just yours.'

She had known he would be angry.

'I know, and I've said I'm sorry. I was in the wrong, obviously, but hindsight, etc. Think of it from my point of view. It was months after we'd had that night in the garden and I hadn't seen hide nor hair of you since. I was only eighteen, in shock, my life ruined. Mother was kicking off about the shame, the shame, and hustling me away to the country.' She glared at him. 'Frankly, Charles, you were the last thing on my mind.'

This wasn't true, of course. She'd thought about him endlessly, both during her pregnancy and after Tom was born. But a stubborn streak, the same one that refused to acknowledge what was really happening to her, had prevented her from calling him. Charles was silent for what seemed a long while.

'No . . . no, I take your point,' he said eventually. 'Must have been hell for you. Especially back then when our parents still clung so rigidly to the no-sex-before-marriage drama.'

She was touched by his words.

'It *was* hell. The worst was giving him away. My mother refused to support me if I kept him. In fact, she never even countenanced the possibility that I'd keep him. And at the time, I suppose I couldn't really face taking on motherhood alone. I ran away.'

'It's understandable. Different times.' He proffered the bottle and topped up her glass.

'He wants to meet you.'

'I was afraid you were going to say that.' There was silence for a moment. 'What's he like?'

146

'He's . . . great.' She couldn't help smiling as she told him a bit about Daniel, unable to keep the pride from her voice.

'You say he looks like your uncle—doesn't he look at all like me?' Charles laughed at himself. 'Vain bastard that I am.'

'He's really handsome, beautiful really. I thought he looked like my side of the family until I saw you tonight. But in fact he does look like you too . . . around the eyes, the shape of him.'

'You're just saying that.'

'Well, see for yourself.'

Charles shook his head, but didn't immediately reply.

She watched him and waited nervously. She realised now that she didn't want him to refuse.

'I'm not sure. I mean, what does he want from us?' Charles was saying. 'Not money, I hope, although God knows I have enough of that to support twenty sons.' He didn't seem to be boasting, merely stating a fact.

'I suppose he just wants to understand where he comes from. It's a fair enough request. We both know exactly what our heritage is, for better and worse. It's important, don't you think? To know?'

'Yup . . . yup, it is. Very.' He sighed. 'Bit of a shock though, all this. Not sure I could bond . . .'

'I suppose it's different for me. I carried him, gave birth, looked after him.'

'Sad, really,' Charles commented. 'I hope he was happy with his other parents.'

'Reasonably so, I think.' Although the more Annie talked to her son, the more she realised his childhood hadn't been that easy. It seemed his mother, although the life and soul of the party, was

147

also an intensely neurotic woman who had leaned heavily on Daniel. The father seemed to be a distant, rather cold man who scared them both. Daniel hadn't complained, exactly, but she thought she had read accurately between the lines.

Charles stretched his arms into the air. 'I'm exhausted by all the drama! Are you hungry? I could make you a fried-egg sandwich. I'm afraid that's the extent of my repertoire. That and cheese on toast, but the egg one is generally more successful.'

She smiled and shook her head, glancing at her watch. 'God, how did it get to be after ten? I'd better go.'

'You're married then,' Charles said, clocking her flustered look as she gathered her bag and her jacket from a nearby chair.

'Yes. And he's not too keen on your profile.'

'Seems a bit unfair,' Charles protested mildly. 'I didn't do anything . . . except lose touch, perhaps. I agree that wasn't very gentlemanly.'

She got up. 'Why *didn't* you ever phone me, by the way? Was I such a disaster?'

Charles thought about this for a moment. 'We had fun, and I definitely liked you. I suppose I just took off to France for the summer and got distracted by too much booze and French totty. Can't really remember.'

'How flattering!'

He chuckled as he escorted her to the stairs. 'I didn't mean it quite like that. But you know what boys are like at that age . . .' He stopped, embarrassed.

'So what do I tell Daniel? About you. He's staying with us for a few weeks—between flats—

148

and I'd like to be able to let him know the plan.'

For a second they both stared at each other. Annie was suddenly overwhelmed. This is Charles Carnegie, she thought. She had never thought to see him again, any more than she had thought she'd see her son. And she had demonised him for more than three decades.

'He knows you're here presumably?'

She shook her head. 'I thought I'd wait till I was sure you really existed. I don't want to disappoint him, but I can't lie about you.'

'No . . . no, I wouldn't expect you to. Can you give me a bit more time to think about it? I don't want to promise anything and then renege. But it's a big thing for a man, a son.'

She smiled. 'A very big thing.'

*   *   *

Richard was lounging on the sofa in the sitting room, nursing a half-empty glass of red wine in his lap, when she got home. He looks a bit drunk, she thought, surprised he was still up. Normally, by this time of night he would be tucked up in bed with one of his history books. He sprang up when he heard her come in, his eyes bleary.

'Well? How did it go? What's he like?'

She flopped down opposite him, suddenly tired. 'He was . . . OK.'

'OK?' He gave a short laugh. 'What does "OK" mean, exactly?'

She ignored his needling tone. 'It means he was a lot, well, *nicer*, than I thought he'd be.'

Richard slumped back onto the sofa, draining what was left in his glass.

149

'A bit pissed off not to have been told about the boy, surely?'

'Yes. But more shocked than angry, I think. He was surprisingly sympathetic about me not telling him. But he's not sure he wants to see him . . . at least, he said he wanted more time to decide.'

Richard raised an eyebrow. 'Could he really refuse?'

'Well, he could, I suppose. Of course he could. People do all the time. But I don't think he will. He's curious, I could tell. And he has a daughter, but no son. Men are keen on sons, aren't they?'

Richard nodded perfunctorily, but didn't answer, and Annie suddenly felt upset for Ed. Richard had never said in so many words that his son was a disappointment to him—beyond being frustrated about his academic failure—but the two had never really had much in common. Since Ed moved out, Richard, despite Annie's urgings, seldom phoned his son, or made any effort to see him separately from the others. He would call Marsha for a chat, but hardly ever Ed.

'I suppose Charles will get in touch when he's decided.'

She saw her husband roll his eyes.

'So what'll you tell Daniel?'

'Nothing. Not yet.'

'Christ . . .' Richard muttered, heaving himself off the sofa. 'Well, at least now you've told him, you'll never have to see the man again.'

'I suppose not,' she said, slowly to receive a suspicious look from her husband.

'Do you *want* to see him again?'

She shook her head, more at her husband's tone of voice than in response to his question.

150

He set his glass down on the table with the careful gesture of a man who knows he's had too much to drink.

'I'm going up. Coming?'

'In a minute.'

She sat for a while in the cool silence of the sitting room. The meeting with Charles had disturbed her on levels that she couldn't quite understand. We're linked so closely, our genes both joined in Daniel, yet I hardly know the man. I liked him. He was generous about my situation back then, and . . . good company. I didn't expect that. I know Richard is disappointed. He wanted me to come back and rant about what an arrogant prat Carnegie is. But he's not.

11

Annie got up at six the day before Daniel arrived, keen to get Ed's room ready. Excited and nervous in equal measure at the prospect of having him living with her for the first time, she had lain awake many nights that week in anticipation, praying he wouldn't change his mind, praying he would. But she couldn't help imagining the times she might have with him, hanging out at the kitchen table, or in the garden, going for walks or to the cinema, meeting for coffee. Like normal mothers and sons did.

Ed's room was tidy and blank, smelling airless in the way of an unused spare room. She sat on his bed in her turquoise satin dressing gown for a moment, her bare feet cold on the wooden floor.

151

She looked around at the touching remains of her son's youth: a lurid poster of the band Metallica, one of Sinead O'Connor looking like an elfin child; Ed in the cricket team when he was about ten; cycling magazines—a phase he had passed through quickly in his late teens, until he discovered the less challenging pleasures of a car—and piles of videotapes: films like *Mad Max*, *Terminator II*, *Goodfellas*.

He'd been an easy child, quiet, not given to tantrums or boyish violence. But if she were honest, although she loved him deeply, she'd always felt he held back from her. She wondered if this was her fault, if she'd been looking too hard for a replacement for Tom, which no future son could have possibly provided. She remembered the first time she'd held Ed in her arms. There had been joy, of course, and love. But also a terrible sadness for the one she had lost, and overwhelming guilt that she didn't deserve this second chance. Perhaps Ed had unconsciously sensed her equivocation.

Richard stopped on his way downstairs and stood in the doorway watching her scraping the dried-out Blu-Tak from the edge of the Metallica poster as she prepared to take it down.

'Have a heart, Annie,' he said. 'That's Ed's poster. Don't take it down, he'll be gutted.'

She looked at him in surprise. 'But it's so old and tatty.'

'Old and tatty and Ed's.'

She shrugged and pressed the corner back on the wall, but it wouldn't stick and the paper flopped forward.

'He doesn't live here any more,' she complained,

trying again with the poster, annoyed that her husband was probably right.

'Nor does Daniel.' His voice was curt. 'There's more Blu-Tak in the kitchen drawer.' He disappeared downstairs, and by the time Annie got to the kitchen, he was draining his cup of coffee and gathering his briefcase, ready to go to work.

'Richard . . . please,' Annie began. 'I know you're not happy having Daniel here. But we said we'd try to make a go of it. It's not for long.'

Richard looked innocently at her. 'Have I said I won't?'

She shook her head. 'No, but I know you well. You were irritated just now, about the poster.'

He sighed, glancing at his watch. 'Stop looking for the insult, Annie. Listen, I'd better get going.'

He dropped a perfunctory kiss on her temple and was gone.

*   *   *

That night she lay in bed waiting for Richard to come home. Where was he? He was almost never late, and always said if he would be. She'd rung his mobile three times during the evening, but it had relentlessly gone to voicemail. Was this some sort of payback for Daniel? she asked herself.

In the end she'd fallen into an exhausted sleep, only waking to the morning light. The other side of the bed was empty, untouched. Shocked and worried, she got up quickly and padded downstairs. The house was silent. Her mobile was on the kitchen table, and she called Richard's number immediately. The ring-tone came from both her receiver and from somewhere in the

153

house.

Following the noise upstairs, she realised it was coming from Ed's room. She opened the door. There was Richard, sprawled across the bed, half-covered with the clean duvet she'd put on for Daniel, still dressed in his shirt, pants and socks, his jacket, trousers and shoes in a heap by the bed. The room had the sharp, chemical reek of stale alcohol.

'Richard?'

He didn't stir. She went over and prodded him roughly. 'Richard! Get up.'

He started awake, sat bolt upright, his eyes bloodshot, his face shaded with stubble. 'Annie? What . . .' he looked around, then covered his face with his hands. 'Oh, God . . . sorry . . .'

'What the hell are you doing?' She stood over him. 'Where were you? Why did you sleep in here?'

Richard swung his bare legs off the bed and groaned.

'Sorry . . . I didn't want to wake you, it was so late.'

'Where were you?' she repeated.

'Just some work thing. It got a bit out of hand. God, I feel rough.' He stood up, wobbled and sat down again hard. 'It was that last brandy that did it.'

'I made this bed up clean for Daniel. He'll be here in a couple of hours.' She turned on her heel.

'You've never done that before,' she said to Richard when he had showered and changed and come down to the kitchen looking sorry for himself.

'Annie, I've said I'm sorry. It was just a boozy

night. We were entertaining some clients, and it went on a bit, that's all.'

'I understand that, but you've never, ever stayed out that late without even so much as a phone call, and you've never not come to bed.'

'It's not such a big deal, is it?' His voice was plaintive. 'It was just one late night.'

Am I missing something? she wondered as she watched him make a strong cup of instant coffee. He seems to think his behaviour is quite normal. And for lots of men I'm sure it is. But it isn't for Richard.

*   *   *

'Here are the keys to Fort Knox,' Annie joked nervously, when Daniel arrived at the house soon after Richard had left for work. She handed him the spare set after she showed him Ed's room— Metallica still in situ, duvet fresh, windows open to get rid of the smell of stale alcohol. Daniel clutched the keys.

'No one ever realises how hard it is for someone else to use their keys. If you hear stones at your window, you'll know I've failed.'

'You'll have to be a good shot. We're in the attic. But I take your point, and this one *can* be tricky. You have to jerk the front door outwards to undo the mortise lock. Come outside and give it a try.'

She saw him hesitate, his beautiful blue-grey eyes almost bewildered.

'Annie . . . I want you to know how much I appreciate being allowed to stay here. It's saved my life. My friend with the sofa also has a French girlfriend who parties all night and snorts God

155

knows what up her nose. It would have been hell, staying there for any length of time.'

For a moment she couldn't reply, her throat tightening with emotion.

'You're very welcome,' she said brightly, when all she really wanted to do was hug him to her, to tell him that he could stay forever in her home if he wanted to.

*   *   *

Daniel had been with them for five days now, but things were still tense at home. Annie couldn't wait to talk to Marjory, whom she was meeting off the twelve o'clock train.

The painting her friend had chosen today was small, entitled *Portrait of a Lady* by a sixteenth-century Flemish artist, Catharina van Hemessen. The lady sitter, still unnamed, was dressed in a black gown with soft, raspberry velvet sleeves, a lace cap framing her face. The background was dark. There was an intimacy about the painting, a moment caught, as if the artist had known the subject well. The only bit Annie didn't like was the ratty little dog the lady had tucked under her right arm.

'She has a beautiful face.'

'Sympathetic rather than classically beautiful, I'd say,' Marjory replied.

'You'd want to have known her, though, wouldn't you?'

Her friend agreed. 'It would have been hard for van Hemessen to be a painter. She would probably have been taught by her father, the painter Jan van Hemessen. But she obviously has a talent. Most of

156

her work is of this ilk: portraits, women, small canvasses. There's a lovely self-portrait in Basel. Maria of Austria, also known as Maria of Hungary, became her patron, and she spent some time with her in Spain.' Marjory paused. 'Look at her hair. There's not much of it, but it's almost photographic in its realism. And those delicate strings at her neck, the detail on her organza chemise—is it organza? Or perhaps lawn ... chiffon? I'm never quite sure what lawn looks like.'

For a while they talked about the painting in front of them. Marjory expanded on Catharina and her father, on other Flemish renaissance painters. The National Gallery was quiet on a Tuesday afternoon and Annie was absorbed in the lecture, happy to be distracted from her worries.

'Shall we go outside for tea?' Marjory asked, as they began walking through the galleries to the lift, her ebony cane gently tapping on the parquet floor. 'It's too beautiful for the cafe.'

Annie left her friend sitting on the edge of one of the fountains in Trafalgar Square, and went to buy some sandwiches and tea from Prêt a Manger, then they walked slowly across the Mall to St James's Park and sat on the grass. It was a glorious June day, and Annie felt her spirits lightening as she breathed in the warm, scented air.

'Of course, I'll never get up again,' Marjory joked, as she lowered herself gingerly to the dry grass with Annie's help. Annie had favoured a bench, but the old lady had insisted. It's not a picnic if you sit on a bench, she'd declared.

'Hmm, so Richard's playing up,' Marjory commented, when she'd listened to Annie's account of the previous evening.

She'd told Richard she and Lucy were planning a supper with Daniel. Richard had said he'd be there. But, like the week before, he hadn't come home, hadn't called—rolled in at two in the morning.

'Annie? Annie, are you awake?'

Annie had heard his whisper. But although rigid with irritation and thoroughly awake, she hadn't responded.

'I'm not drunk, if that's what you think.' He'd flopped into bed and attempted to snuggle up to her, laying a heavy arm across her body, the smell of alcohol rank on his breath. She'd pushed him off.

'Why didn't you ring me?' she hissed at him in the darkness. 'You said you'd be home and we waited for you. It was embarrassing in front of Daniel.'

'I did ring . . .'

'You didn't.'

'I'm sure I did,' he'd protested.

'I don't know who you think you called, but it certainly wasn't me.'

'Whatever.' He'd sounded almost surly; there was no hint of contrition in his voice. 'I was just working.'

'And you couldn't tell me that?'

'I'm sure Daniel didn't mind.'

'That's hardly the point!' The anger she'd felt had made her heart race uncomfortably. She'd tried to calm herself with a few deep breaths.

Richard had rolled over, turned his back on her. After a moment, his breathing slowed. Then she'd heard him mutter, 'You wanted Daniel here so you could get to know him. Well, I'm not stopping you.'

She'd lain there, listening to his snoring, for what seemed like hours.

'He's never done this before—stayed out late, not phoned me, and so obviously been drinking,' she told Marjory, plucking dispiritedly at the daisies. 'Well, maybe about fifteen years ago, after a friend's stag night. And now twice in as many weeks? It can't be a coincidence.'

'Maybe he really is just wanting to leave you and Daniel to get to know each other?'

'I wish I thought that. And although the girls have been great, really supportive, Ed's hardly spoken a civil word to me since I told him. He avoids most of my calls.'

Marjory cradled her takeaway carton of tea in her lap and was silent for a moment. Then she turned to Annie. 'You really can't blame them, dear. A few weeks ago it was all normal and cosy at home. Things were going well for you all. Then up springs a cuckoo and it all begins to fall apart.'

'Daniel's not a cuckoo!'

'He is to Ed. And to a certain extent to Richard, too.'

'You think I shouldn't have let him stay?'

The old lady shrugged. 'Hard to say . . . perhaps it was a bit soon.'

'But Ed doesn't live at home, and Richard never sees him! Daniel isn't up when Richard leaves for work, and when he comes home, Daniel's often out. And then the one time I ask him to be there . . .'

'No, it's not good.'

'And it's not *like* him, Marjory. He's always been so solid, so there for me. Why is he behaving like this?'

'You know why. He's jealous.'

'But I'm not having an affair with Daniel. He's my son!' She was exasperated. 'He's a grown man. Can't he see how important this is for me?'

'I'm sure he can. Things will be fine, I'm sure, once Daniel goes off to Edinburgh and Richard has time to reflect.'

There was a sudden squawking and two swans on the lake across the path rose from the water, their wings beating the air, their beaks snapping angrily at each other. Both women watched in silence for a moment, until the birds settled again as if nothing had happened.

Annie sighed. 'He's not much of a one for reflection, Richard. He's an accountant.'

Marjory gave a laugh. 'I'd never heard accountants were immune to self-awareness.'

'No, well, it's all about logic and sums with Richard. Daniel staying obviously doesn't compute rationally and it upsets him.'

She began to gather the remnants of their sandwich packets together, angrily scrunching the paper cups into tight balls. Marjory watched her.

'You and Richard have had such a good marriage, Annie. You've been happy—you fit together much better than most. He's a good man. Don't let this ruin things.'

'*I'm* not ruining things. It's Richard who refuses to consider Daniel part of the family.'

'Listen . . .' the old lady paused for a minute, obviously choosing her words carefully. 'It's quite possible that Richard—or the others for that matter—will *never* consider Daniel family. They might like him, they might be pleased to see him occasionally, but I told you, they haven't the

160

familiarity that makes family, and it's too late for that now.'

'I don't believe that.'

Marjory shrugged. 'I know, and I understand why. But if you don't accept that this is at least a possibility—I'm not saying an inevitability—then there's a danger you'll fall out with Richard and Ed over Daniel. Can you afford to do that?'

Annie fought back the tears. She hated being distanced from either of them; she loved them both so much.

'Do I have to give in to their small-mindedness then? When Lucy and Marsha have been so generous to Daniel?'

Marjory reached over and patted her hand. 'It's hard, dear, I realise that. I'm just saying find a way to connect with them again, if you can. This is your family.'

'Alright . . . I'll try, I suppose, but I gave in to other people's demands before over Daniel, and I won't do it again.'

'You obviously feel very strongly about it, and you must do what you think is right. Just don't expect too much from everyone else.' Marjory gathered her bag and stretched out her hand. 'Come on, hoick me up, my bones are beginning to crumble.'

*   *   *

'Anyone home?' Annie called up the stairs when she got back from the picnic with Marjory. Daniel's head appeared round the banister.

'Hi. Good day?'

She nodded up at him. 'It's lovely out there. Do

you fancy tea on the terrace?'

'Sounds extremely civilised. I'll be right down.'

They settled in the wooden deckchairs outside with their tea, surveying the summer garden.

'It's so peaceful here,' Daniel said, turning a grateful smile on his mother.

For a while they talked, discussing his plans for the play, his move, where he might live when he got back in September. There's so much I want to say to him, she thought. So much that I want to hear. The days since his arrival had sped past, with precious few of the opportunities to talk with her son that she had envisaged.

'I keep meaning to ask you. My—um—other father. I suppose that's what you'd call him . . .' Daniel spoke into a silence. 'Did he ever get back to you?'

'I had a drink with him on Tuesday.' Annie looked cautiously at him. 'He asked me not to say anything yet, he wants to think it out . . . about seeing you. It was a bit of a shock.'

'I can imagine that.' Daniel gave a short laugh.

She ignored what sounded like a pejorative tone. 'I'm sure he *will* see you. He didn't seem against it as such, but he didn't want to let you down.'

'What's he like?' Daniel glanced across at her.

'Not quite how I remembered him, actually . . . sort of nicer. I liked him. He's tall like you. Good-looking, charming.'

Daniel gave an embarrassed grin. 'I'm glad it wasn't as bad as you thought. I imagined from your write-up he'd be a bit of a posh arse.'

'Posh, but certainly not an arse.'

'Would it have made any difference, do you think,' Daniel went on, 'if he'd known about me

162

right from the start?'

'I have no idea. I imagine a shot-gun marriage would have been arranged by my mother.' She gave a bleak smile. 'I honestly don't know.'

'It must have been really hard, not telling him. Weren't you tempted, when the adoption was being set up?' He must have seen her expression, because he added quickly, 'I'm not blaming you, Annie. I'd just like to know what happened.'

Maybe it would have been better for him if I had married Charles, even if it hadn't worked out, she thought. At least then he'd have known both his real parents.

'I thought I might hear from him. Hoped like hell in fact. And if he'd called and wanted to see me, I would have told him, obviously. But I hated the thought of us being press-ganged into marriage when he clearly didn't want to be with me.'

Now, telling the only person who really mattered about why she had done what she'd done, the excuses seemed so selfish, so empty of meaning. She swallowed hard, not trusting her voice.

'The truth is, I didn't want a baby then.' The words fell cold and heavy into the summer air.

'Me, you mean.'

She forced herself to meet her son's eye. 'Yes. I know what you're saying, and I agree. It wasn't just a baby, it was *you* I abandoned.'

She saw a frown flit across his face.

'I'm so sorry, Daniel.' She stopped. 'Sorry is such an inadequate word to tell you how badly I feel, how ashamed I am. I could have kept you, I *could* have done it.'

'You were young,' he said, without much conviction, then threw his hands up in the air. 'It's

163

stupid. Mum was wonderful . . . the most loving mother anyone could wish for. She was everything to me. I don't know why this all matters so much to me.'

He got up and began to walk down the garden, his hands stuffed in his jeans pockets. She got up too and followed him.

'Of course it matters.'

The afternoon was so perfect: the air still, warm, fragrant with the scent of flowers and mown grass, only the sounds of small children splashing and shouting in a blow-up pool two gardens away. Daniel stopped near the shed at the bottom of the garden and turned to Annie.

'I can't possibly know what you went through. It's easy to say now that you could have kept me, or that you should have told my father, and your children. You didn't, and I have to accept that . . . have to respect your reasons.' Daniel's speech was resolute, as if he were determined to do the decent thing by his birth mother.

She stooped to pick up a large twig from the grass.

'What does it feel like? Being adopted?' She couldn't help asking him something that had long tormented her.

He looked as if he were about to tell her, then thought better of it.

'Look, I've been lucky, Annie. I was loved. And if Mum hadn't told me I was adopted, would I have felt anything but completely normal? In a way it would have been easier if she hadn't told me.'

They stood there on the lawn, not looking at each other. She reached over to a stem of yellow

164

roses just off the path, picking at a browning petal on one of the blooms. The sun felt very hot suddenly.

'You ask what adoption feels like,' he went on, 'but it's almost impossible to define. And I'm sure it's different for everyone.' He seemed to be analysing his position rather than engaging his feelings. She waited for him to go on, pressing the silky petal between her thumb and forefinger.

'I suppose it's as if I don't have a solid anchor,' Daniel said eventually. 'Like I'm blowing in the wind. I'm sure other people feel like that too, for different reasons, but I've always thought it was part of being adopted.' He paused. 'It's a sort of loneliness, I think. Maybe loneliness is too strong a word, but a confusion about who you are . . . a gap, a void. You don't truly belong to anyone. And you can't help wondering how it might have been.' He looked at her, his eyes suddenly full of concern. 'Please . . . don't look at me like you pity me. I don't want you to feel sorry for me. You asked how it feels, and I'm trying to tell you. But not so you can beat yourself up about what you did.' He shrugged. 'I mean, would I have been happier if you'd kept me? I'll never know, and it's dumb to look at happiness in such a relative way.' He looked hard at her. 'I am not unhappy. I *wasn't* unhappy. Really I wasn't. Please believe me.'

She wasn't sure she did. There was a sadness behind his words she didn't understand.

'And finding us? Does that change anything?'

'It makes me nervous.'

'Nervous?'

'Yeah. Suppose I'm not good enough . . . suppose I'm a disappointment to you or I don't fit in with the family, suppose you reject me for some reason.' He shook his head. 'You can't help thinking like that. It's why so many people never do it, I reckon.'

'I felt the same before I met you. I wanted you to approve of me so badly,' she said. 'But it's been worth all the agony to finally know you. At least, for me it has.'

'And for me too,' Daniel said. She noticed the slight flush to his cheeks and looked away to save him further embarrassment.

Her phone rang. 'Hi, Richard . . . oh . . . OK . . . why? . . . No, I see. OK . . . yes, see you later.'

Daniel looked questioningly at her.

'Richard says not to wait, he won't be home until ten-ish.'

'I get the feeling he's not too keen on me being here.' His voice was hesitant.

'Oh, no. He's fine with it. Just got a lot on at work.' She wasn't going to drag Daniel into a discussion about her husband's behaviour, but the now familiar anxiety about the distance opening up between them cast a shadow over the afternoon. 'But Marsha's coming over. She and Lucy are meeting for a drink in town after work and she thought she'd come and say hi.'

* * *

Supper that night was a low-key middle of the week meal, with chicken salad, cheese and fruit; it was warm enough to eat on the terrace, the candles she'd insisted on lighting still pale in the falling light. The conversation was easy-going, desultory; they were all tired from a long day and

166

no one seemed inclined to make a special effort. She liked that. It was how normal families were.

She was in the kitchen, unwrapping the Brie and the goat's cheese and putting them on the board, when she heard Marsha ask Daniel: 'So . . . do you have a girlfriend? Or boyfriend maybe?'

She winced at Marsha's cheek, but waited eagerly for her son's response. This had been the one burning question she hadn't managed to ask, and Daniel had so far volunteered no information whatsoever on the subject.

She heard his laugh, then a short silence. 'There is someone, but it's early days.'

'Lucky you,' Marsha replied. 'Well, me, I'm fed up with the whole male species. They're either wimps or predators.'

'I get the predators, but how do you class a wimp?' Daniel asked.

'Oh, you know, media types who think they're God's gift because they write for a broadsheet, but couldn't even change a light bulb or wash a sock.'

Annie heard the laughter.

'So you're after a Real Man? Capital R, capital M.' The amusement in her son's voice made her smile too.

'Yeah . . . someone who has muscles that weren't bought in a gym. Someone who could build a house, mend a burst pipe, ride a horse—or a motorbike . . . sail a boat across the Atlantic single-handed. That sort of thing.'

She'd never heard Marsha talk about the sort of man she wanted.

'But is clever and could read a book as well?' Daniel asked wryly.

'Do I detect a certain contempt—jealousy

maybe—for Real Man?' Marsha countered. 'News flash, Daniel Gray! Being practical and strong doesn't rule out being literate.'

'Well, the poor guy won't have much time between building houses and riding about mending pipes to read anything significant!'

'Sneer as much as you like,' Marsha declared. 'I know what I want.' There was silence outside for a moment.

'I agree with Mash,' Lucy joined in. 'I'm in love with Real Man already.'

'Well, you stand more of a chance of meeting him than I do, Luce. You'll come across loads of those earnest, shorts-wearing Médecins sans Frontières types in Africa. They have to fix dodgy generators and beat off snakes and bandits all the time. But I work in a PR company in Soho.'

'Aren't there more snakes and bandits in Soho than in the whole of the African continent?' The question was Daniel's.

'Too bloody right!'

Marsha persisted. 'So what's *your* type?'

'As a self-confessed wimp I'd definitely go for someone who could put up shelves and unblock the sink . . . when I get one, of course.'

Marsha's mobile rang at that moment. Annie took the pears and cheese outside to find they were talking about a politician in the news that day.

12

Annie had neglected her mother of late, but it was still with a good deal of reluctance that she walked up the marble steps of the Cadogan Gardens flat. She knew she had to tell Eleanor about Daniel's paternity herself, before the news filtered back to her via the gossip grapevine. She would never be forgiven if that happened.

It was a good half an hour into her visit, however, and she still hadn't plucked up courage to reveal her long-held secret.

'Charles Carnegie?' her mother almost shrieked when she finally told her. 'Angela Carnegie's boy? *He's* Daniel's father?'

Annie nodded, almost enjoying the shock on her mother's face.

Her mother was speechless for once. They were in her drawing room, just about to walk down Sloane Street to Harvey Nichols; Eleanor wanted some face cream.

'Wouldn't P.J.'s be closer?' Annie had asked, but Eleanor was scathing in her reply.

'Peter Jones is a very sensible shop, darling, and it certainly has its uses. But it has none of the *flair* of Harvey Nicks. I want to browse,' she had told her, with a childish gleam in her eye.

'But . . . but,' spluttered Eleanor now, 'why didn't you tell me it was him at the time? I thought it was some lout you picked up at one of those parties that Walsh boy was always dragging you to. I assumed you didn't even know the man's name.'

'Thanks, Mother,' she replied through clenched

teeth.

'Well, darling, you can forgive me for being a little suspicious, seeing as you waited thirty years to tell me who he is.'

'What's that got to do with it?'

'Don't be rude, Annie.' Her mother went quiet for a moment, and Annie wondered what she was thinking.

'You're a very stupid girl not to have told me. Carnegie would have married you.'

'I doubt it. And if he had, it would have been against his will. Not a very promising start to a life together.'

'But his family is *ancient*,' Eleanor objected, a faraway look in her eye. 'It could have been marvellous.'

'So if I'd have told you the baby would be part of the "ancient" Carnegie dynasty, would you still have insisted I give him up for adoption?'

'Well, no, of course not.' Eleanor looked outraged at the suggestion. 'We would have come to some arrangement with Angela and Henry, I'm sure.'

Arrangement? She was beyond speech herself. God! It was as if they spoke a different language sometimes.

Her mother's beady eyes suddenly narrowed. 'You never told me you were going out with the Carnegie boy. Why didn't you tell me? How long were you seeing him before . . . ?'

Eleanor paused and Annie didn't answer. I could lie, say that it had been going on for weeks and weeks. She'd slip into a coma if she knew I'd had sex on a first date. But she held back, said nothing, and Eleanor didn't press her.

'So when can I meet Daniel?' Her mother looked excited by the prospect.

'Oh, are you sure you want to, Mother? Won't you be worried he'll be violent, or feckless? Not share our values?'

'I don't like your tone of voice, Annie. Of course I want to meet Charles Carnegie's son. He's my grandson, don't forget.' For the first time, and for all the wrong reasons, her mother had finally owned her own flesh and blood. But it brought Annie no joy.

She sighed. 'Come on, Mother, let's go to Harvey Nicks.' What else had she expected? 'I have to get back to the bakery soon.'

'Go, if you have to. I don't want to delay you,' Eleanor said airily, making no attempt to stand up. 'I'm not sure I want to go out at the moment, anyway.'

'Don't be like that.' Now she's taken umbrage, she thought. 'I've plenty of time to walk down with you.'

Eleanor said nothing, just stared at Annie as if she wasn't seeing her. She looked at her mother more carefully. 'Are you alright?'

The old lady sank back in her chair. 'I'm perfectly fine. I've remembered I've got a few things to do, that's all. I expect I'll pop out later in the day.'

She went closer. 'Are you sure you're alright, Mother? You look tired.'

'I said, I'm fine. Stop fussing, will you?' Eleanor seemed to have revived, and was impatiently brushing Annie away. 'Hadn't you better be off?'

'OK . . . well, I suppose I should get going.' She kissed her goodbye, more tenderly than usual.

'Talk tomorrow,' she said. Her mother raised her hand without a word.

Annie heard Mercedes in the kitchen, and crept through to talk to the housekeeper.

'Everything OK?' she asked.

Mercedes looked at her questioningly.

'I just thought Mother looked a bit tired,' Annie went on.

Mercedes threw her arms up in the air. 'She do too much, your mother. She up early, she no sleep much. I hear the radio in the night *mucho*, *mucho*. She always go out, see too many of those people.'

Annie nodded, smiled.

'She old lady now, your mother. But she no think so,' Mercedes added with a shrug.

'No, well, that's not going to change,' Annie agreed.

'I say nothing.' Mercedes' voice dropped to a whisper. 'She get very angry if I say she do too much. She say it not my business, I just work for her.'

'That's not very nice.'

Mercedes laughed. 'Your mother is sometimes not nice. But I used to that.'

'You're a saint.'

'Your mother is not bad person. She not know what she says.'

I'm not so sure about that, Annie thought, but it was neither the time nor place to debate her mother's bad manners.

At that point, Eleanor came round the door of the kitchen. 'I thought you were in a rush,' she said pointedly.

Annie saw Mercedes look immediately nervous.

'I was just having a chat with Mercedes.'

172

'How nice.' Eleanor smiled icily, and Annie took her leave, hoping there would be no unpleasant repercussions for the Spanish housekeeper.

* * *

Later that day, when she was at the bakery, her mobile rang.

'Annie . . . ? Charles Carnegie.' His tone was businesslike.

'Hello,' she replied. She was annoyed with him. It was ten days since they'd met and this was the first communication he'd made.

'Er . . . how are you?'

'I'm fine.'

'You don't sound it.' She heard a low chuckle and his voice dropped to a whisper. 'Listen, I thought I'd have a moment to talk, but I've just seen my three o'clock on the horizon, so can I call later? Better still, meet up?'

Jodie sat opposite her, busy tapping away on the computer, but Annie could tell she was listening.

'What for?' What did they have to say to each other that they hadn't said already?

'Well, there's been a bit of fallout from our discussion the other day. That's why I've taken so long to get back to you.' He paused, and she heard him greeting someone called Mark, telling him he wouldn't be a sec. Then the sound of his shoes echoing across a hard surface. 'I can't talk now, but I'd really appreciate a chat about . . . Daniel, if you have the time.' He spoke his son's name hesitantly, as if he wasn't sure it was the correct one.

What did he mean by 'fallout'? 'OK . . . if you like.'

'I'm around this evening,' she heard him say. 'I'll come up your way if it suits, or we could meet halfway. What about the Ritz?'

She laughed.

'What's so funny about the Ritz?'

'Nothing, I suppose. I was imagining more a quiet corner in a north-London pub.'

'Eurgh! Hideous thought. Can't be doing with pubs. And there's no such thing as a quiet corner of one. No, let's do the Ritz. Great cocktails, and the bar's reopened after the refurb. Looks like an ageing Lothario's gin palace. Love it. You must have been there.'

'Of course I've been to the Ritz.' Cheeky sod! 'But not for about thirty years.'

'I didn't take you there, did I?' There was another chuckle. 'Just joking . . . but so much of my youth is lost in a haze of, well, cocktails, I suppose. Got to go.'

She didn't respond to his comment. 'I'll be there at six,' she said, and ended the call.

'Hot date?' Jodie teased, perhaps assuming she was talking to Richard. Then looked taken aback as Annie, to her horror, found herself blushing. There was an awkward silence while Annie concentrated hard on her mobile, checking non-existent texts. She hadn't told the people at work about Daniel yet. It's not really their business, she'd told herself. But the truth was she was worried they would be shocked by what she'd done and see her in an unsympathetic light.

'How's the Pilkington cake coming along?' she asked Jodie, quickly forcing her feelings under control.

'Finished,' Jodie replied, stretching and yawning.

174

'Go and take a look. Carol and Kadir have done a fantastic job.'

Annie got up from her office chair and went through to the bakery. Radio 2 was playing Glen Campbell's 'By the Time I Get to Phoenix' at full volume. The music took her back, and for a moment she was lost in her youth. Carol was clearly enjoying it too, swaying to the beat as she poured sugar in a thick stream into the industrial mixer. When she saw Annie she waved her over excitedly.

'Have you seen it?' Carol walked over to the work surface and drew the lid off a large white cardboard box set beside the fridge in the area where the finished cakes were boxed up, waiting for Wes, the always-grinning dreadlocked delivery man, to collect.

Annie peered into the box. The cake was a masterpiece: a glittering castle in silver and white, with turrets, mullioned windows, a drawbridge and fluttering white ribbon pennants. The bride and groom, resplendent in golden medieval robes, stood high on the ramparts, overseeing their fairy-tale kingdom.

'Wow! It's really wonderful. Thanks so much, all of you. They wanted kitsch, they got it! Tragic, as always, that it has to be eaten.' In awe, Annie carefully checked out the extraordinary detail around the cake. She patted Carol on the back, waved at Kadir. 'Genius!'

Carol nodded, her red face beneath the white baker's cap lighting up with pleasure.

'Don't forget to take a photograph for the website,' Annie reminded Lisa.

As Annie walked back to the office, her thoughts

returned to Charles. And Richard. What would he think of her swanning off to the Ritz with Carnegie? He'd been so emphatic about her not seeing Charles again after that first meeting. And what did Charles want to talk to her about anyway? This man, who seemed to take everything with a large pinch of salt, had sounded serious for once.

She realised suddenly that Charles reminded her of her father. He showed the same mischievous humour and intemperance that, in Ralph Westbury, had driven her mother mad. She wondered, not for the first time, if her father's death had been, in the marital sense, a relief to her mother.

That dreary November Sunday had been, she knew, the defining moment of her own life. Aged nine, she was awake early and reading J.M. Barrie's *Peter Pan* by the light of her torch. She heard some noise from her parents' bedroom across the landing, but thought nothing of it; her mother was an early riser. Then the telephone rang—in those days a rare event, especially at that time. But her book was absorbing and she read on.

It was just getting light when the bedroom door opened, the dull, grey dawn rendering her mother's dressing-gowned figure almost ghostly. Eleanor sat down on her bed.

'Your father's dead,' she had announced dully. 'He was ill . . . he died this morning.'

Annie had looked at her blankly. She had no idea what her mother was talking about. She had waited for some sort of explanation, some clarification. But Eleanor had merely laid a hand on her pyjama'd shoulder for a second, then got up

176

and left the room.

Her next memory was of sitting at the kitchen table. Maria, the middle-aged Irish nanny who'd been with them for over two years—longer than any of the others to date—was red-eyed and silent. She plopped a boiled egg into the egg-cup in front of Annie and tapped the top of the shell with the wet spoon. Maria was normally never seen on a Sunday, and Annie had been curious to see her dressed in her best, obviously on her way to church. For a moment Maria had hovered uncertainly beside her. Then she had bent and put her arms tight around her.

'You poor, poor child, losing your father so young. And such a lovely man he was. Such a gentleman. It's a tragedy, it surely is.'

She remembered freezing in the woman's embrace. She was not used to being hugged, especially not by Maria, who was normally quite brusque with her. But then something had snapped, perhaps it was the sound of Maria's crying, and she had turned, her own tears hot on her cheeks, and buried her head in the nanny's bosom, sobbing her heart out as she began to have an inkling of what had really happened that morning.

They had been interrupted by her mother, standing silent and disapproving at the door to the basement kitchen.

'Maria . . .' She didn't need to say more. Maria loosened her grip on Annie immediately and turned back towards the Aga and the boiling kettle.

'Annie, finish your breakfast quickly and come and say hello to your grandmother.' She stood for a moment, regarding her daughter's tear-stained face, and added, not unkindly, 'Wash your face before you come up, please.'

Annie had complied, of course. Today, as she thought back, she marvelled at the combined strength of will, the sheer, almost bloody-minded repression in the house that day. Her mother and grandmother (this was her father's mother, all other of her grandparents were dead), were in the drawing room, both seated in front of the empty grate, both dressed and powdered as usual. Except for the silence, there was no evidence that anything had happened. Mrs Westbury senior was normally loquacious; a busy, bossy, high-coloured woman whose raison d'être was society gossip: who she knew and which title they held or were related to; their often disastrous liaisons with chancers and gold-digging arrivistes; to whom they left their money; how dismally their offspring had turned out.

'Hello, Grandma.' Annie had kissed the proffered cheek reluctantly that morning. She hated the sickly smell of her grandmother's perfume—Elizabeth Arden's Blue Grass, although she hadn't known the name of it back then.

'Uncle Terence will be here in a minute. He's going to take you for a walk. He'll bring you back for lunch.'

At school the following day, she hadn't known how to tell her friends; the teachers didn't mention it. So, when asked, she'd recited, dry-eyed, the poem she'd learnt on Sunday afternoon after a silent lunch with the grown-ups, and had the strange realisation that she was now forever changed, different entirely from all the girls sitting

178

staring expectantly up at her.

She pulled herself back to the present and rang Richard. 'I'm meeting Charles this evening,' she told him. 'He has a problem he wants to discuss about seeing Daniel.'

'What sort of problem?'

'He didn't want to say over the phone.'

She heard Richard's wry laugh. 'Can't be said over the phone? Ooh, must be serious then.'

'Don't be like that. Anyway, I won't be late.'

'Doesn't matter, I'll be late myself. More work.' His voice sounded almost smug. 'Where are you meeting him?'

'In town somewhere . . . he's texting me later.' It was the first time in the whole of their long marriage that she'd ever deliberately deceived Richard. She'd done it quite spontaneously and she wasn't even sure why, except that where she met Charles had seemed such an issue for him last time. He might prefer Charles's flat to the Ritz, she thought, almost amused. The Ritz smacked of hedonism—and privilege. Richard wouldn't like that.

13

Ed and Marsha both grinned as Lucy dumped her jacket on the chair and took a bottle of wine out of the orange supermarket bag.

'Great. We got a couple too.'

Ed examined Lucy's contribution. 'Screw-top,' he said, nodding approvingly, then disappeared into the kitchen to get glasses. He emptied a whole tube of Pringles into an earthenware dish and put it on the ancient, stained coffee table he'd made himself when he was in sixth form. He was touched Marsha still kept it. 'Emms is on her way,' he said.

The sash windows of Marsha's flat were wide and high, letting a lot of light into the L-shaped sitting room/kitchen. Marsha had pushed them right up to get as much breeze as possible on this warm summer night.

'OK, Lucy,' Ed said, pouring them each a glass of wine. 'You're the resident spy in Maison Delancey. Is it going any better with the new inmate?'

Lucy groaned. 'Not really.'

'Let me guess. Daniel's annoying everyone with his endless stories—'

'It's not Daniel,' Lucy interrupted. 'He's fine, I hardly see him.' She drew her legs up onto the sofa and clutched them to her, her chin balanced on her knees. 'It's Dad.'

They waited for her to go on. 'He's started doing this thing of not coming home till late. Sometimes really late.'

Marsha sat up. 'What, every night?'

'No, not every night, but quite often. He says he's got some big drama on at work ... some merger thing. I haven't asked for details, but he's stayed out twice already this week, and it's only Thursday.'

'How late's late?' Ed asked.

'Oh, after two the other night. I heard him stumbling around on the stairs. He woke me up.'

'God. What does Mum say?'

'Mum is obviously annoyed with him—they niggle at each other all the time—but Dad doesn't help. He's all nonchalant, as if he hasn't done

180

anything wrong.' Lucy shrugged. 'I asked her if things were OK between her and Dad and I just got one of Mum's looks—and she said "absolutely fine". End of.'

'I'm sure he's just avoiding Daniel,' Ed said. 'You can't blame him. He didn't want him there in the first place.' He had to admit that he'd hoped things wouldn't go so well with his half-brother's visit, but he'd never thought his parents' enviable closeness might be affected by Daniel's presence in the house.

'Maybe, but you don't think it's serious, do you? You don't think they'll split up?' Lucy asked, her face a mask of anxiety.

'No, Ed's right. Dad's just taking it out on Mum. Daniel's going soon.' Marsha sounded reassuring.

'Mum and Dad are solid, Luce. You know that,' Ed added.

'Yeah ... maybe. But why is he drinking such a lot, then? I heard them arguing about it again this morning in the kitchen. Mum was saying she was fed up with him coming home "stinking of booze". I mean, Dad's not even a big drinker normally.'

Ed didn't know what to say, and Marsha didn't respond either.

'And he does things like not phoning to say he's working late. You know Mum never kicks off if he's got work to do, but not to phone and tell her ... ? It's just not like Dad.'

'He's probably just skulking in a pub somewhere,' Ed suggested.

'At two in the morning? And Dad hates pubs.'

'God, Luce. Poor you.' Ed stroked his sister's knee. 'Must be grim being stuck in the middle.' He suddenly felt a pang of guilt about his mother. He

181

knew how upset she would be by his father's behaviour, but he couldn't bring himself to get involved with it all while Daniel was still there.

'It is. They're so nasty to each other. They don't shout—it might be better if they did—it's just sort of quiet and mean.' She looked pleadingly at her sister. 'Will you say something to Dad, Mash? Please . . . he'd listen to you.'

'I could . . .' Marsha thought for a minute. 'But what'll I say? It's kind of awkward accusing your dad of being a dirty stop-out. And he'll just blame Daniel.'

'Mum left a message saying they were off to Cornwall for a couple of days, for Cousin Enid's ninetieth. Maybe with Daniel out of the way they'll bond again,' Ed suggested.

'Let's hope,' said Lucy. 'I just want Mum and Dad back as they were before all this happened. Nothing's been right since she got that bloody letter.'

'I wish he'd never existed,' Ed muttered. 'Everything was fine before he pitched up. Now he's going to be hanging about forever being handsome and clever and annoying . . . not to mention ruining our parents' marriage.'

Even Marsha nodded wearily. 'You're exaggerating as usual, Eddie. It's not his fault. But yeah, it might have been easier if he hadn't got around to finding us.'

Ed suddenly cocked his head. 'Hmm . . . I've got an idea! If they're going away, why don't we have a party at the house? It'd be fun . . . get rid of all this bloody tension, have a bit of a laugh. Mum never minds so long as we clear up. And Emms's birthday isn't far off.'

182

'Daniel will still be there,' Lucy warned her brother.

'Oh, pish! We can deal with him,' Ed replied. 'He can go out if he doesn't like it.'

'Where is Emma anyway?' Lucy asked. 'I thought you said she was on her way.'

Ed sighed. 'She said she was.'

Things hadn't been so good with Emma recently. It was his fault, he knew that. She was tired of his moods and his constant grouching about Daniel. Even the sex, usually so incredible, hadn't been so hot with him in this distracted state. He told himself he had to get a grip. He didn't want Daniel wrecking his relationship too.

'Everything alright between you and Emms?' Marsha, as always, picked up on his mood. Or had Emma said something to her?

'Yeah . . . great.'

'Guys . . .' Lucy wasn't listening. 'You don't think . . .' she began again, her anxious brown eyes darting between her two siblings. 'You don't think they've decided to split but—'

'NO!' Ed and Marsha shouted in unison, each picking up a cushion and bashing Lucy over the head in an attempt to drown out her fears—and their own—once and for all.

*   *   *

Annie was early for the drink with Carnegie. She wandered up to Boots on the other side of Piccadilly and paced the aisles, testing creams and lip-gloss to pass the time. It was raining and she hadn't brought an umbrella, but refused to buy another, remembering the piles in the hall basket

183

at home. She felt a wreck, exhausted and grubby from work, shamed by her deception, her hair beginning to frizz in the moisture. What was she doing, seeing him again? Why couldn't he just get on with it and meet Daniel without involving her in his problems? When she finally crossed the road to find Charles cosily ensconced in a leopard-skin chair in the centre of the glitzy bar, she greeted him with a certain froideur.

He rose as she approached and reached to kiss her cheek in welcome, but Annie held him off with her handshake. He pulled a face.

'Bad day at the office?'

'I'm not in the mood.' She plonked herself down on her own leopard-print armchair, feeling totally out of place in the extravagant, glamorous surroundings—although the clientele at this time of night looked to be mostly businessmen or ageing American tourists.

'That bad . . . time to get the drinks in.' He motioned to a waiter. 'What'll it be? Manhattan? Mojito? Bullshot? Maybe a glass of fizz? Name your poison.'

She hesitated. 'What's a bullshot again?'

'Vodka, consommé, lime, tabasco,' Charles intoned before the waiter had a chance to reply.

'I'll have a glass of champagne, please.' She threw a charming smile at the waiter.

'Good plan. We'll have a bottle of the—' he thumbed the wine list he'd been perusing when she arrived '—make it the Cristal.'

She refused to let Charles see she was impressed as the waiter nodded politely and disappeared.

It was tempting to down the first glass of champagne in one, just to lift her mood. But it was too delicious for that, and for a moment they both sat savouring the eye-wateringly expensive wine in silence. It seemed to her that Charles was reluctant to say what he had come to say.

'So?' she enquired, her tone now kinder as the champagne began to work its magic. 'What was it you had to see me about in person?'

Charles sighed. 'Not easy, this,' he began. 'I'm not sure what it's all about ...' He looked her straight in the eye. 'But Louisa really isn't keen for me to meet Daniel.'

She was puzzled. 'Why not?'

He shrugged. 'I know, don't tell me she hasn't the right. I realise that. But there are issues . . .' He tailed off, seeming reluctant to explain.

Annie waited. A woman in a sleek black dress, heels staggeringly high, tottered past, trailing clouds of a heavy, musky scent which caught in her throat.

'She's . . . well, how do I put this? She's a bit unstable. There have been various times over the years when she's been really upset about something and . . . and once she tried to kill herself.' Charles looked embarrassed.

Was he serious? 'You're worried she'll kill herself if you see Daniel? Why would she? You probably didn't even know her back then.'

'Nope . . . all true. I don't know much about these things, Annie. She's been to all sorts of doctors and therapists, and it gets better for a while. But she's fundamentally paranoid about me . . . who I see, who I talk to. She suspects me.'

'Of having affairs?'

'That, yes . . . I can't even glance at another woman.'

185

'But what's that got to do with Daniel?'

'I wish I knew.'

'I hope she's not jealous of me. That would be ridiculous!'

Charles pulled a tragic face. 'You mean you don't fancy me any more? I'm gutted.' She ignored his remark. 'She's fiercely protective—too protective in my opinion—of our daughter, Amelia. Maybe she feels threatened.'

'But have you had affairs?'

He looked uncomfortable, didn't answer.

'A yes, then.'

For a second his face fell, all trace of roguishness gone; he looked exhausted. 'It's not been easy, Annie,' he said quietly, then, almost immediately pulled himself together, straightening his back, brushing his grey-blond hair off his forehead and swallowing a large swig of champagne. 'But hey, no point in moaning. That never changed anything.'

'So are you saying you're going along with your wife? That you won't see Daniel because if you do she might attempt suicide?' She stared at him. 'I find that really hard to believe. This isn't some phony excuse, is it?'

He held up his hand. 'Wait a minute, that's not fair. I *want* to see him. I decided that the day you told me about him. I'm curious, of course I am, but I need time. I can't risk . . .' he paused, took a deep breath. 'God, I'm sure I'm overreacting. It's ludicrous, as you say, to think she might do something stupid, but I have to find a way to see Daniel that doesn't upset her.'

'And how will you do that? I mean, if Louisa holds this terrible threat over you, what will change?'

186

'No idea, I'm afraid. She's convinced it'll be disruptive, that our family's fine as it is. She seems worried this might damage it in some way,' he muttered, almost to himself. He looked up at her. 'I'm sure none of that's even remotely true . . . is it?'

'There have been, um, a few problems,' she spoke cautiously, not wanting to spell it out.

'Your other children cut up rough, did they?'

She nodded. 'My daughters have been brilliant about it. But Ed, my other son . . . he's not found it easy adjusting to Daniel. Not really his fault, he's not the most confident of people. To be honest, I don't know what to do about him.' She wasn't going to mention Richard's behaviour, it seemed so petty.

Charles was looking at her with concern, and she felt the tears after he must have seen them. She loved Ed so much.

'I don't really want to talk about it,' she said, quickly delving in her bag for a tissue and blowing her nose.

'So perhaps Louisa isn't so stupid after all,' Charles suggested gently.

She shook her head. 'Not stupid, but wrong. Wrong to forbid you to do anything. Wrong to manipulate you with such a terrible threat.'

'She didn't "forbid" exactly. She's ill, Annie.'

'Alright, but still.'

'There's another issue,' Charles went on. 'She always wanted more children . . . a boy, and it . . . well, it never happened.'

Neither of them spoke for a moment. The room was noisier now as the bar filled up and people began to relax. It seemed as if the two of them were marooned on a separate island. Charles reached over and took her hand.

'I've been thinking about it, and I can't imagine how hard it must have been to give the baby away.'

She blinked back the tears and for a second clung to his hand.

'Giving him away *and* getting him back,' she muttered. 'If only everyone would just let me get on with it. I'm not doing anything hurtful, am I?'

Charles sighed and let go of her hand. 'Of course you aren't. But you're not giving me much incentive to get involved!'

'No, I suppose not. But all the same, you will meet him won't you, Charles? Just once. We owe him that.'

'I'll try to work something out. I honestly will try.'

She could hear that he meant it. But she also realised that where his wife was concerned he was weak. As I would be, she thought, married to someone that volatile.

'Don't do anything you're not sure about,' she warned. I don't want the death of Charles Carnegie's wife on my conscience.

Charles shot her a rueful smile. 'Oh, Annie. One night of pleasure and we ... or mostly you and Daniel, of course ... are still paying for it decades later. Doesn't seem quite fair, does it?' He shrugged. 'Come on, drink up. I'll take you to dinner.'

*   *   *

Richard wasn't there when she got home. Which was just as well because it was her turn to be

188

drunk. For once she didn't much care where the hell he was, just wanted to get into bed and sleep, pillow spin notwithstanding. First she tottered down to the kitchen and drank two large glasses of water. *Thank God he's not home.* Then she went upstairs, stumbling round the bedroom, throwing her clothes about and barking her shin on the sharp wooden corner of the bed, drawing blood. *I haven't done anything wrong, but he won't understand about Charles. She didn't understand about Charles . . . or that manipulative wife of his.*

Dinner had been fun. He'd taken her to an old-style Italian in Jermyn Street. She felt strangely at ease with him, considering she hardly knew him. But they'd shared a similar childhood in fifties Kensington; they'd both been packed off to boarding school and hung out in the same social group in London; they were joined by the common bond of their son.

She hid her debilitating hangover from Richard the following morning, and also what Charles had told her. In the cold light of day it seemed spineless not to be able to stand up to your own wife over such an important issue.

'How's the work going?' she asked through her pounding headache. She had no memory of Richard coming in, so it must have been late, but she could hardly take him to task this time.

He looked up briefly from spreading Marmite on his toast. 'Very labour-intensive. But we're getting there. It'll be a few weeks yet.'

'But it's going well?' She tried, unsuccessfully, to focus on the sell-by date on the milk carton. She sniffed the contents. It was definitely on the turn and she nearly threw up.

'Yes, yes, I think so.' His expression seemed unnaturally wide-eyed and vacant to her, but perhaps she was imagining it. 'How was your evening?'

'Fine,' she replied, but she could tell he was just going through the motions, not actually engaging in the exchange.

'Good.' Richard went back to his toast.

So he didn't want to know about Charles. She'd expected the third degree, so his sudden lack of interest was like a slap in the face, almost worse than his previous jealousy. But she felt too fragile to tackle him then and there and they didn't speak again. Richard got up to go, gave her a cursory peck on the cheek, and left the house. She retired back to bed.

*   *   *

'I've got a meeting with Gary this afternoon,' she reminded Jodie when she got into the office later that morning, feeling a little better physically, but still smarting from Richard's indifference. Jodie pulled a face.

'Good luck! Temperature's going to be over twenty-three, the forecast said.'

The web designer, who was doing a much-needed update of the Delancey Bakes site, was an IT genius, but he also had a serious hygiene problem.

'Has to be done.'

She parked in the Chinese car park in Newport Place just before three o'clock and sat in her car for a moment to call Richard. She'd decided they had to talk, and not at home with Daniel and Lucy

190

around.

His mobile went straight to answer, so she left a message: 'It's me. I'm in town seeing Gary the website man. Can we meet for a drink later? Give me a call.'

The afternoon with Gary was arduous. His Soho office was cramped and boiling, the tea mugs layered with stains and no doubt bacteria, and she had to hold her breath every time the big man moved. Added to which she hated everything technical, and Gary would insist on peppering his conversation with a baffling array of initials—CSS, SEO, RSS, HTTP, URL. 'What part of "I don't have a clue what you're talking about" don't you understand, Gary?' she finally asked, with more asperity than she intended. But Gary was so disconnected from the world and from people who weren't rooted in nerd-speak, that his small brown eyes just looked nonplussed by her question.

When it was over, she stood on the pavement outside, breathing deeply and checking to see if Richard had called. There was no message. He'll be stuck in a meeting, she told herself, wandering off down Old Compton Street in the general direction of the car park. She looked at her watch: five past six. Suddenly she made a decision and began to stride purposefully up towards Tottenham Court Road. It was still unpleasantly humid and hot, the streets filthy from days without rain and packed with tourist crowds meandering in gangs across the pavements, making it hard for Annie to weave through.

Richard's office was on the first floor above an electronics store. The faded brown door buzzed without her saying who she was.

'Annie! How are you? Long time no see.' Trish greeted her warmly, getting up from her desk to give her a kiss on the cheek. Nearly twenty years as Richard's office manager had forged a mutual liking and respect between the two women, although most of their relationship was conducted on the phone.

'Roasting, isn't it?' Trish was fanning herself with a handful of computer printouts.

'Nightmare.'

'Is he expecting you?' she asked. 'He's still in with Kate.'

'Who's Kate?' Annie asked in a low voice.

Trish looked surprised. 'Kate Martin? Haven't you met her? Small, dark. She's been with us at least three years now. I'm sure she was at the office party, but you probably didn't notice her. Anyway, she and Richard are working together on the Vanquist deal.'

Annie wracked her memory. 'No, I do remember,' she said, although the image was vague. 'Can I interrupt for a minute?'

'Of course, you know where it is.'

She knocked on her husband's door.

'Come in.'

He was sitting in front of his computer in his shirtsleeves, a small fan gently whirring on the edge of the desk. A pretty girl in a cool mint-green shift dress which showed off her tanned arms sat on the other side of the desk in front of a pile of spreadsheets, a yellow highlighter clamped between her teeth.

Seeing Annie, Richard jumped up, looking pink and flustered.

'Annie . . . what are you doing here?' He waved

192

her in, introduced her to the girl. 'You remember Kate, don't you?' Kate gave her a wide smile and made an excuse to leave the room.

'Didn't you get my message? I've just been with Gary Toomey. I thought we could go for a drink.'

Richard hesitated, picked up his phone from under a pile of paper and gave it a distracted glance, then put it in his trouser pocket. 'Sorry, it's been so busy. Umm . . . do you mind if we just go straight home. I'm absolutely knackered.' As if to add verisimilitude to his words, he yawned, stretching his arms above his head.

'No . . . no, that's fine.' She was tired too.

The Northern line was full and they were crammed by the doors, hanging on reluctantly to the sweaty overhead bar.

'You look exhausted,' she commented.

'I told you. There just isn't enough time in the day.'

'I wasn't accusing you, Richard. But all these late nights must be wearing you out.'

'What do you mean, "all these late nights"? It hasn't been that often.'

'You know it has.'

Richard turned away.

She sighed. 'I know why you're doing it.'

'What do you mean? I said . . . I've been working.' He stared intently at her.

They must have been raising their voices, because she was suddenly aware of an uptake in interest from the people around them. Oh, good, a lively domestic to pass the time till High Barnet, she imagined them thinking. Richard must have sensed it too, because his next remark was almost a whisper.

193

'Will Daniel be there tonight?'

'I've no idea. We didn't plan anything.'

Richard was silent as the train drew into Camden Town and disgorged a number of passengers, then sat with the doors open. Annie gulped in the cooler station air gratefully. After a while a chirpy disembodied voice came over the loudspeaker: 'Sorry for the delay, folks. We're being held at a red signal, but should be on our way shortly.'

Richard rolled his eyes impatiently.

'It's just it'd be nice to have the place to ourselves for once.'

She moved to make room for a Camden Goth, smelling strongly of incense and resplendent in black fishnets, leather choker and purple dreads. 'He hasn't been in for most of this week, but you wouldn't know that since you've been out too.'

'I haven't been "out", I've been working.'

'Same thing,' she muttered and turned her back on him, taking her free evening paper out and pretending to read.

In the end neither Daniel nor Lucy was home. But she was too tired to have it out with Richard and, anyway, what was the point? She knew why he was behaving in this way. And she knew he would go on denying it. So they sat through a drearily silent meal of fishcakes and salad, each being carefully polite, if they talked at all, sticking to neutral subjects that were least likely to spark a row. Richard went to his study immediately after supper, and she sat in front of a tiresome, overheated television drama about a child murderer. She hoped that Daniel might come home early—she had hardly seen him all week.

When he wasn't back by eleven and she was falling asleep on the sofa, she gave up and went to bed.

*   *   *

But she couldn't sleep. Richard was snoring peacefully, but she was wide awake. She crept out of bed and made her way downstairs in her bare feet. She got a glass of water, and on her way out of the kitchen she noticed the light was shining under the television-room door. She walked towards it and heard low voices: Lucy and Daniel. She was just about to open the door, but for a moment she hesitated.

'I went for a drink with this guy from work, and I thought we'd eat,' she heard Lucy say. 'But the tight-wad only bought me one solitary packet of cheese and onion crisps.'

'Couldn't you have bought some more yourself?' She heard the amusement in her son's voice.

'Not the point. He earns way more than me. And it's not like he's the most thrilling company in the world.'

'So you only love him for his cheese and onions?'

'Something like that.'

Annie heard Lucy giggle. Was she a bit tipsy?

There was silence for a moment, and Annie was just about to move away when she heard her daughter's voice again.

'Seen the parents tonight?'

'No, they must have gone to bed early.'

'Probably to cut the arguing time.'

'They do seem to bicker a lot.'

'Yeah, you got that right.'

'I'm sure you hate it, but it's better than my

195

parents. Mum used to do her damnedest to pick a fight with Dad over something trivial, but he just refused to react. He'd give her the superior, silent treatment, as if she was an annoying child, then walk out of the room . . . then she'd cry for hours.'

Annie felt suddenly guilty, eavesdropping on this personal stuff that Daniel obviously hadn't wanted to share with her. She began to tiptoe away when she heard Lucy go on.

'I think both are just as horrible. Mum and Dad didn't used to fight at all, ever.'

'I hope it's not my fault.'

Annie heard the edge of worry in his voice.

'It's never anyone else's fault. People argue about stupid things—like your parents did—because they can't talk about what's really winding them up.'

There was another silence on the other side of the door.

'Mum loves you being here. Finding you has been one of the best things that ever happened to her, Daniel.'

'And your father?'

Annie waited for her daughter to reply, silently thanking her for telling Daniel how much he meant to her.

'Dad's never been one for the unexpected.'

'Mine's the same. A real dyed in the wool . . . traditionalist.'

He makes the word "traditionalist" sound like a dirty word, Annie thought.

'Families, eh? They're all the same,' Lucy said. 'Can't live with 'em, can't live without 'em.'

There was the sound of movement. Annie hurried away up the stairs. The last thing she heard, as the door opened and light flooded the corridor, was Lucy saying, 'I'm off to bed. Sleep well.' And Daniel replying, ' 'Night, Lucy. And you.'

14

'Yes?'

'You always sound so cross when you answer your phone,' Charles said.

'Only to you.' He was the last person Annie wanted to hear from. She reluctantly tore herself away from the screen in front of her, where she was doing a lengthy invoice. Jodie was out getting a coffee.

'That's a bit brutal.' Charles put on a wounded voice.

'Sorry, but I'm really busy, and not in the mood for another will-I-won't-I-see-my-son discussion right now.'

'Whoa . . . you certainly got out of bed on the wrong side.'

'Charles,' she ignored his comment, 'I'm really getting to know Daniel, now he's staying with us. And I'm loving it. But it's made me realise how insulting your position is. He's your son. So see him or don't, I really don't care any more what your problems are on that score. But make your bloody mind up about it once and for all so he knows where he is.'

'Blimey . . .' Charles was laughing now. 'That's telling me. Well, you can stop berating me, Annie, because that's why I phoned. I'd like to arrange a

197

meeting.'

The wind was taken out of her sails. 'Oh, good. What changed your mind? Or your wife's?'

There was a short hesitation. 'I haven't actually told Louisa.'

'For God's sake, Charles!'

'I know, I know. But she's away for a few weeks in the French house, and I thought . . . if I saw him . . . I could say it happened by accident or something. And when the deed is done, she'll probably be fine about it. She's better with reality.'

'Sounds like quite the reverse to me, but you should know,' she said. 'Anyway, it's not my business—as long as Daniel doesn't get hurt. He's been abandoned once, Charles, and we can't know how that's really affected him. You must be very clear about what you're prepared to do. Don't make him any promises you can't keep.'

'You're making him sound like a neurotic five-year-old. Can I still change my mind?' She didn't respond. 'OK . . . joking.'

'Right . . .' She heard Jodie coming back with the coffee. 'Let's do it then. What about this Thursday?'

There was silence at the other end of the phone. Then, 'Thursday it is.'

'OK, I'll check with Daniel and get back to you. You choose the venue.' She wanted to get him off the phone before he changed his mind.

'Fine by me. Talk later,' Charles agreed.

*   *   *

Annie and Jamie sat in the upstairs bar in the Curzon Soho, waiting for the start of the sci-fi film

Jamie had booked tickets for. Jamie was obsessed with science fiction, about which she knew nothing.

'Not sure why I let you persuade me into this,' she muttered, sucking her organic apple juice through a straw.

'Come on, you'll love it! Sci-fi's still drama, just in a different milieu. Once you've accepted that, it carries you along like any narrative, but it has this other, magical dimension. That's what makes it so compelling.'

'But all the sci-fi I've seen just seems so stupid and unbelievable.'

Jamie's eyes widened at her sacrilege. 'You've never seen the good stuff though, have you? It *is* fantasy, but that doesn't make it unbelievable. There is a distinction.' His tone was indignant.

'OK, OK . . . I'm here, aren't I?'

'So catch me up on the goss.' His eyes twinkled expectantly until she said nothing, when he looked at her face more closely.

'Annie?'

She pulled a face, irritation boiling up inside her. 'Shall I tell you what's up? Men, is what's up. I'm like a wagon being circled by the Sioux and it's bloody stressful.'

'O-ka-ay . . . you say "men" in the plural.'

'Oh, yes. There's more than one.' She held up her hand to Jamie, her index finger pointing upwards. 'One: that silly sod Carnegie has only just agreed—after weeks of prevaricating because of his demented wife—that he'll see his son.' Her middle finger joined the first one. 'Two: my up-till-recently totally virtuous and supportive spouse is drinking like a fish, staying out late and may even be getting his leg over Kate-with-the-unreasonably-tanned-arms in the stationery cupboard.' The third finger leapt up. 'Three: my dear son Edward is treating me like I'm Judas Iscariot making off with the silver.' Her indignation ran out, but she slowly brought her fourth finger alongside the rest. 'Four: and this isn't Daniel's fault . . . but having him in the house is stressful, viz. points two and three already stated.' And with that she burst into stifled tears.

Jamie rested his hand gently on her shoulder. When she finally focused on his face, he looked torn between laughter and concern.

'Things do sound a little fraught.'

'You always were master of the understatement.'

'Hmm . . . maybe we should focus on number three.'

Annie sighed. 'Three? Must we?'

'Seriously, darling. Who is this tanned Kate person? Surely Richard isn't playing away? I find it hard to believe.'

'Well, so do I. But she's pretty and young and, well, *there* . . . working with him day in, day out—maybe night in, night out.'

'But has he mentioned her . . . significantly?'

She shook her head, reaching into her bag for a tissue. 'He hasn't mentioned her at all.'

'And you've asked him.'

She sighed. 'Of course not. Richard would never cheat on me, we both know that. Stop looking at me like that, will you.'

'Like what?'

'Like I've just told you I've got an inoperable brain tumour.'

'Sorry, but I can't work out how serious you are

about Richard and this girl.' He paused. 'You know there's no such thing as a man who would *never* cheat, Annie? Only some who probably wouldn't.'

Annie stared at him. 'You're such a cynic, Jamie.' It had been a throwaway line, the remark she'd made about Richard and his young colleague. But now she saw Jamie's expression, she felt a stab of concern. Was that what was going on? Was Richard getting revenge by having an affair?

'I'm bloody angry with him, Jamie. He's not playing fair, even if he's not cheating. We can't seem to have a conversation these days without fighting.' She remembered Lucy's conversation with Daniel a couple of nights back; she wasn't exaggerating.

'Be patient. It'll come right in the end.' Jamie patted her hand.

'You're sure about that, are you?' She blew her nose again. 'Because my family is the most important thing in my life. Cakes you can do without. Family you can't.'

Jamie looked at his watch. 'We should go down, it starts in about five. If you're still up for it, that is. I'm easy. But it might take your mind off the Sioux.'

She grinned feebly. 'Bring it on.'

They wandered down the stairs to the basement level and took their places amongst the sci-fi 'anoraks' in the crowded theatre.

'So when's Daniel meeting his father?' Jamie asked when they were seated.

'Tomorrow,' she said. 'And then me and Richard have to go to bloody Cornwall on Friday.'

She hadn't meant to whinge to Jamie, but there

was a baffling emptiness at her core. She'd dreamed so often of meeting Daniel again. She'd known it would be complicated—Marjory certainly warned her. But she was facing problems she'd never envisaged, problems she didn't know how to address.

*   *   *

That Friday, Lucy sat on her mother's bed, watching her pack.

Annie stopped folding her sweater and looked over at her. 'You'll be OK while we're away?' she asked, but her mind was elsewhere, on the meeting the previous evening between Daniel and Charles.

Lucy laughed. 'Yeah, Mum. I'll be just fine, seeing as I'm a fully functioning, competent, even reasonably sane twenty-two-year-old. And you'll only be away for three nights.'

'Just checking. Daniel . . .'

'And Daniel—for similar reasons—will be absolutely fine too.'

'So I can relax?'

Lucy shook her head. 'Well, I doubt you'll do that, Mum. But put it this way: don't fret on our account.'

'Try not to,' Annie said with a laugh.

'I'm envious. St Mawes is awesome. Remember that holiday we had when I was about nine? We swam every day in that bay, out to the blue raft.'

'It was freezing in fact, but you didn't seem to notice.' Annie paused. 'I wish we didn't have to go. It's not that I don't want to be there for Enid, but there's just so much going on. Still, nothing I can do about it. Only typhoid or a tsunami could save

202

me now.'

'Bags not get the typhoid,' Lucy replied, which made Annie smile.

*　　　*　　　*

Two days of back-to-back socialising with people Annie hardly knew had taken its toll. Even between being present at the scheduled events for Cousin Enid—such as the Friday drinks party, the big birthday lunch on the Saturday or the final supper for the stragglers on Sunday night—they were ambushed by one or other of her enthusiastic entourage (who peppered the Cornish seaside town from end to end) and required to explain Richard's family tree and his relationship to his cousin yet one more time. Enid herself was tireless. She still swam in the sea every day from May till October, her energy and drive the stuff of local legend, and hardly stopped talking, thrilled to see her guests gathered around her, perhaps for the last time in such numbers.

But the real the strain for Annie was the tacit truce she and Richard had called on all things relating to Daniel. It's what we needed, she told herself, as she smiled and smiled and smiled. Just to reconnect with normal things. But the tension sat like an unexploded bomb between them.

'I'm going to get some air,' she whispered to Richard as supper finished on their last evening.

'Wait, I'm coming too.' He looked panic-stricken that she would think of abandoning him. They scuttled out of the restaurant and walked to the end of the promenade, turning off the road onto the concrete slope leading down to the beach.

Benches sat at intervals on the incline, looking out to sea; at this time of night they were all empty.

It's like something out of a fairy tale, she thought, as they settled on the middle bench in silence. So romantic, I wish I could enjoy it more. A full moon, its nimbus glowing like a huge halo, washed the bay in silvery light. The sea swelled softly, hardly a breeze disturbing the black water, the foam of the breaking surf picked out brightly in the moon's rays. On the cliffs to the left you could just see the beam from St Anthony's lighthouse, and across the bay Falmouth beckoned with rows of twinkling lights. She heard Richard sigh. It was a slow, sad sound.

She wasn't sure she wanted to ask him what was wrong.

'Annie . . .' He turned to her, and his expression looked suddenly desperate.

'What is it?'

'Yoo-hoo, guys! I knew I'd find you lovebirds along here somewhere.' Canadian Morag's round, eager face appeared over the sea wall above them. 'Don't move, I'm coming down.'

Richard covered his face with his hands. 'I can't do this.' He got up and hurried up the slope, pushing rudely past Morag on her way down. 'Sorry, Morag, off to bed . . . 'night.'

'Whoa, he seems in a helluva rush. Everything OK here?' She sat down close to Annie, huffing and puffing from her walk. Morag, some distant cousin of both Richard and Enid and the good-natured scourge of everyone's weekend, pulled down the zip of her purple anorak to retrieve her camera from an inside pocket.

'Isn't this awesome . . .' Her voice had dropped

from its customary yell. 'D'you think it's too dark for a shot?' She aimed her camera at the sea. 'Rhona and the kids just won't believe all the rellies I've met this week. I wish they could've been here, but, you know, we went online back in November last year ...' She was off. No conversation with Morag was complete without the tiniest details of all her online bargains—from plane tickets to kitchen whisks to four-wheel drives.

Annie just let it wash over her, wondering what her husband had been about to say.

'I'd better go and check if Richard's OK ... he wasn't feeling too good.'

'Lordy, I hope it wasn't something he ate.' Morag clutched her chest. 'Did he have the chicken? I thought it had a weird—'

'No, he had the pasta.' She cut Morag short and produced a final smile. 'It's been so nice meeting you ... safe trip home.'

The Canadian looked disappointed. 'I hope he's not sick. You know where I am if you need anything. I've a whole trunk full of medication ... can't be too careful.'

'You certainly can't.'

The hotel room was in darkness when she got back, and there was no sign of Richard. She went down to check the bar, but it was closed. Getting back to the room, she called his mobile, but the responding buzz came from the bedside table. What was he about to say? The question kept repeating itself over and over in her mind. But although her heart fluttered with anxiety, her brain refused to acknowledge the possibilities.

She sat on the bed, channel-hopping on the flat

wall-mounted TV. There was nothing she could do but wait. At some point she must have fallen asleep, because the red digital display said 2:07 the next time she looked, the television still burbling quietly on. He'll have gone for a drive, a walk . . . be sitting somewhere by the sea. He'll be back in a minute. What was he about to say? The room was hot and she got up and opened the window wider. The soft sea breeze cooled her cheeks as she stood listening to the rhythmic beat of the waves. She took long slow breaths. A man of almost rigid probity—essential for someone in charge of other people's money—Richard had rarely showed signs of temperament in the past. Yet Daniel's arrival seemed to have changed him, almost overnight.

'Annie?'

She jumped out of her skin. Richard was standing within inches of her, his face haggard with tiredness, bluish from the chilly night air.

'Where have you been?' Her voice sounded hoarse.

'Sorry . . .' He stood there, arms hanging by his sides, and just looked at her. The expression in his eyes frightened her.

She pushed him gently backwards until he flopped down on the bed. 'Please . . . what is it? Tell me.'

He gazed at her for a moment, as if he were almost puzzled by her presence in front of him. 'Oh, Annie. I hate what's happening to us. We used to be so happy . . . before all this.'

'I know things haven't been easy. But we're getting through it, aren't we?'

Richard's expression was sceptical. 'Are we? I don't see it. I feel I'm married to a woman I don't even know.'

'I know I've been distracted, but is it really that bad?'

'Distracted? Is that what you call it? You're tense all the time, always complaining that I'm late, or I don't call enough, or I drink too much. We never talk any more, not least because you're so wrapped up in Daniel—or his father.' He gave a deep sigh. 'For instance, when was the last time we made love? The last time I touched you, you jumped away from me as if I'd scalded you.'

'That was the night you came home late and hadn't called me. I was angry. Angry that you hadn't called and angry because I thought you were avoiding Daniel.'

He shrugged. 'I'm under enormous pressure, you know. This merger is a massive amount of work . . .'

'I know, I appreciate that. But it's not fair to put all the blame on me. You *have* been late and drinking more than usual . . . and you *have* been avoiding Daniel.'

Richard raised his hand in objection, but Annie cut him off. 'Please . . . don't deny it.'

A dull silence filled the room. She moved away from the bed and sat in one of the faun and brown-striped armchairs in the window bay. She felt too tired to keep up this circular argument.

'Look, I'm sorry,' she finally muttered.

He stared at her for a moment as she waited for another onslaught. But suddenly his gaze softened. 'What are we to do? I hate fighting with you.'

She nodded agreement. 'Can't we just do what we've always done? Pull together?'

Her husband shrugged. 'If only Daniel hadn't

207

moved in . . .'

'Christ, Richard! He'll be gone in ten days. Will you be happy then?' Her words flew across the space between them.

'You'll still be obsessed.'

She was heartily sick of his repeated use of that word.

'That's unfair and you know it.'

He slumped forward, covering his face with his hands. When he raised his face she was shocked to see the beginnings of tears. Richard never cried. He lifted his glasses, sweeping them away quickly with his fingers. 'I love you, you know I do.'

She came to his side, leaned against him as they sat on the bed. His arm went round her, clutching her fiercely to him. She felt a surge of relief.

'And I love you too.' She sighed. 'I've been so paranoid. I'd convinced myself that you were just about to leave me . . . or were having some stupid affair with someone.

'Don't be daft, Annie.' His voice was even. 'We'd better get some sleep, don't you think? Long drive tomorrow.'

15

'Where shall we put the ice bucket?' Emma was standing next to the lurid yellow-rubber container, looking helpless.

'On the deck?' Marsha suggested. 'We don't want it in here because of all the water.'

'When's Ed coming with the ice?' Lucy looked up from her task of removing garlic bread from plastic wrappers and placing them on a baking tray. 'It's five already. The beer won't be cold if he doesn't hurry up.'

Emma looked at her watch too. 'I'll call him.' She wandered out into the garden.

'Lucky it's not up to her to get things organised.' Marsha shook her head indulgently at her friend's retreating figure. She looked at the baking tray. 'God, Mum would have a fit if she saw that.'

Lucy laughed. 'Yeah ... and the ready-made pizza and plastic coleslaw and Iceland cheesecakes. We'd better destroy the evidence.'

'Hope they're having a good time in Cornwall.'

'Ed's on his way to pick up the ice, but he says he's not feeling that great.' Emma was back, looking worried and waving her phone in the air. 'He says he's got a stinking headache and feels, like, shivery and sick.'

'No! Tell him to get something to take ... Lemsip, Neurofen ... anything.'

Emma put the phone to her ear again. 'Hear that? Just get over here, then you can lie down and we'll minister to you.'

'What's with the "we"?' Lucy snorted.

Ed stumbled in half an hour later, looking like death, lugging a huge plastic bag of ice.

'Go and lie down.'

'Can't. Bloody Daniel's in my room.'

'Well, go up to the parents' room then,' Marsha urged. 'Have you dosed yourself up?'

'Yeah. I took some of Emms's hayfever pills. I found them in the glove compartment in the car.'

Marsha groaned.

'I'll go and get him something stronger.' Emma looked around for her bag. 'You've got to be fit enough for tonight, Eddie.'

'Should we light the candles?' Lucy asked later, when all the preparations were finished and they were sitting round the table in the garden with a cup of tea, all dressed up, a buzz of contained excitement between them. Just a small breeze stirred the warm evening air, mixing the scent of lavender with the girls' perfume.

'Too early . . . it won't be properly dark till nine-ish.'

'Thank God it didn't rain.'

'Hi . . .' Daniel put his head round the French doors. He held up two blue carrier bags. 'I brought some wine, and crisps and stuff.'

Emma jumped up, smiling at Daniel. 'Great.' She took one of the bags and peered inside. 'Yum. Love Doritos. Well done, you.'

'Anyone ready for a proper drink?' Daniel asked. 'The white's cold.'

The three girls nodded enthusiastically and he disappeared into the kitchen, to arrive back a couple of minutes later with a tray containing four paper cups, a bowl of Doritos and an opened bottle of cheap Chilean white.

'You all look very gorgeous,' he commented with a smile, glancing round at them as he poured the wine. Marsha had on a short red dress with spaghetti straps, her blonde hair loose around her shoulders. Lucy was in a knee-length white lacy dress, more demure and bohemian. Emma looked like the poster girl for Agent Provocateur in a black, tight-laced bustier dress, her ivory-cream breasts barely contained, her lips a startling red. Marsha saw Daniel's eye linger on her friend and wished her brother was here.

'Where's Ed?'

'He's upstairs sick . . . flu or something.'

'He isn't coming to the party?'

'He'll be down later, he's had a ton of medicine,' Emma assured them blithely, lighting a cigarette and turning her beautiful head to blow the smoke away from the group.

'Not sure about that. He looked pretty rough to me when I went up,' Marsha commented.

'Oh, Eddie's tough. This was his idea. He won't want to miss anything.'

*   *   *

Much later, Marsha stood with Daniel just inside the kitchen, a cup of red wine in one hand, a chunk of cold garlic bread in the other. It was after midnight and she was pleasantly drunk. The music had been turned down half an hour ago, as a nod to the tolerant neighbours, but the slow, heavy beat of the bass lent an erotic note to the warm summer night.

'Good party,' Daniel said.

'Yeah, it's gone OK. Shame Eddie didn't make it down.'

'See anyone you like?' he asked, sweeping his hand towards the crowd in the garden.

She shook her head. 'Na. I know them all. You?'

'I'm not looking at the moment.'

She giggled. 'Aren't we always looking . . . whatever we pretend?'

Daniel didn't reply and she looked up at his handsome face. 'No?' She still couldn't get her head round the fact that they were related. And the brother thing wasn't happening for her. Never would, she was sure about that.

He hesitated, as if he was considering whether to tell her something, then obviously decided against it and shrugged, giving her a half-smile. 'Maybe you're right.' They were silent for a moment, watching the action on the terrace. 'Emma's not overdoing it, is she?'

'Never does anything else!'

She watched her friend dancing in a circle of men, her body gyrating slowly to the music, alabaster skin almost iridescent in the candlelight, her features softened, louche with too much alcohol. Emma must have seen them watching and waved, blowing a pouting kiss to Daniel and holding his gaze, in Marsha's opinion, for just too long.

'She's a very beautiful girl,' Daniel mused.

Marsha felt a frisson of jealousy. Why didn't I pick a dog for a best friend? She laughed silently at herself because, despite any frustrations, she adored Emma, had done since they were eight and both pigtailed new girls in Lower Fourth.

*   *   *

'Mash . . . Mash, wake up.' She felt a hand tugging at her arm, then the same, urgent voice: 'Marsha, wake up, please. *Please* wake up.' She forced herself upwards through layers of sleep, finally opening her eyes. In the beginnings of the dawn light she could just make out Emma's face, tear-stained and puffy, hovering within inches of her own.

She shot up. 'Emms? What is it? What's the matter?'

212

Emma collapsed on the bed beside her. 'Mash . . . something terrible's happened. I can't bear it.' She began to cry, sobs that shook her body but were almost silent, a stained tea-towel clutched to her face.

Marsha tried to focus, pulled herself up against the headboard. She reached over to her friend and held her bare arm, which was cold to the touch. Emma was still dressed in her party clothes, her feet bare, the blue checked rug from the TV room slung half around her shoulders.

'What is it? Tell me, Emms, come on,' she urged, yanking the tea towel free of her friend's face so that she could see her properly. 'Why are you still up? It must be nearly morning.' Marsha herself had gone to bed around two, leaving the remaining stragglers with Daniel, who'd promised to lock up. Her friend took a few shaky breaths, trying to control herself, then fixed her huge dark eyes, bright with tears, on Marsha's face. 'Daniel . . . he . . . Oh, God, I don't know how to tell you . . .'

Daniel? What was she talking about?

'Just say it, will you?'

'He . . . he came on to me. He forced me to kiss him, then he . . .'

'*What?*'

'He was really strong, and he . . . you know . . . he grabbed my breast. I was so frightened.' She dropped her head in her hands. 'I tried to tell him no, to fight him off, but he wouldn't listen to me. It was disgusting . . . and with Eddie asleep upstairs.'

'He didn't . . . ?'

Emma looked up again. 'No, he didn't actually rape me, but he would've if I hadn't threatened to scream. Look.' She held her arms out, where there

213

were large red marks on the pale skin above both elbows.

Marsha stared. 'Where were you when this happened?'

'In the TV room. I was on the sofa. Everyone had gone, and I suppose I must have dropped off because the next thing I know, he's leaning over me, his hands everywhere. Oh, Mash . . . I can't believe he'd do this, he's always seemed so polite, so . . . decent.'

Would Daniel do that? Had she got him so wrong? Marsha wondered.

'Have you told Ed?'

Emma shook her head. 'I can't tell him. He must never know, he'd go absolutely mental.'

'You can't just ignore what's happened, Emms. Where's Daniel now?'

'No idea. I've been sitting downstairs for ages, not daring to wake you.'

Marsha got out of bed. 'I need to speak to him.'

'No . . . no, don't do that. Nobody can find out, specially not Ed. Please, Mash . . . don't.' She clutched onto Marsha's T-shirt.

'I mean Daniel, not Ed. I need to hear what Daniel has to say for himself.'

Marsha gently prised her friend's fingers from the cloth, grabbed her cotton dressing gown from the chair and crossed the corridor to knock on her half-brother's bedroom door. There was no response, so she knocked again, louder this time. She heard a muffled groan and pushed open the door.

Daniel's head rose a small way from his pillow. 'Marsha?'

She went into the room and closed the door

214

behind her, standing at a distance from the bed. 'Daniel . . . we need to talk.'

He blinked sleepily, but sat up at once, pushing his auburn hair back from his face. 'What's happened?'

'Don't you know?'

He shook his head. 'Know what?'

'Emma? Ring any bells?'

'Sorry . . . ?'

'Daniel, Emma's in my room right now, almost hysterical, saying you came on to her and would have raped her if she hadn't threatened to scream and wake the whole house.'

He gaped, hauling himself out of bed until he was sitting on the edge in his T-shirt and shorts. He didn't speak for a moment, then held his hands up.

'Listen, I'd never have told anyone this, it wouldn't be fair . . . she was so drunk. But it was Emma who came on to me, not the other way round. I had to push her off. She was really out of it, Marsha. I didn't take it seriously.'

'So you didn't force her to kiss you, touch her breasts?'

Daniel looked horrified. 'Christ! Of course not. Is that what she's saying?' His expression was beseeching. 'I'd never do a thing like that—come on to Ed's girlfriend when he's upstairs sick—or at any other time for that matter. Marsha, you know I wouldn't. It'd be crazy in my situation . . .'

Those were Marsha's own thoughts exactly. Why would he jeopardise his relationship with all of us like that? Her head spun. Who could she believe? she wondered.

'Does Ed know?' Daniel asked quietly.

She shook her head. 'Not yet. But she can't not

215

tell him.'

Daniel threw his hands up in frustration. 'But it's not true! I didn't touch her.'

'There are the beginnings of bruises on both her arms.'

'Yeah ... well, that might have been me, I suppose. I was trying to hold her off.'

'But why would she lie?'

He shook his head. 'I have no idea.'

'She's in a terrible state, Daniel. She was pretty bloody convincing.'

'Marsha, I DIDN'T DO IT. You have to believe me.' He stared at her desperately. And, looking into his eyes, she could see no trace of guilt.

*   *   *

Marsha sat with Lucy, both cross-legged on the grass in the garden.

'Thank God you're here,' Lucy said. 'They'll be home in a minute.'

'Yeah, well, they weren't too happy about it at work, but I couldn't let you do this on your own.'

It was Marsha who heard the front door. 'Here we go!'

'You tell them,' Lucy whispered, then leant back on her elbows as if she was trying to seem relaxed.

'Hi, darlings!' Her mother came out onto the terrace. 'I didn't expect to find either of you here. What a nice surprise.'

They both jumped to their feet.

'Mum ... hi.' Marsha could see at once that her mother had clocked something in her expression—she was looking at her so intently.

Lucy gave her mother a hug.

216

'Sorry. Did I startle you?' Annie asked.

Marsha shook her head and put on a bright smile. 'Uh, yeah, I was miles away. How was Cousin Enid?' She kissed her father.

'Her usual amazing self,' he replied.

'Is Daniel in?' her mother asked, as her dad moved off to put the kettle on.

'Marsha?'

Marsha took a long breath. Sunday morning had been a nightmare. It'd all blown up as soon as Emma told Ed what had happened. Marsha had been getting dressed when she heard the rumpus outside her door. She'd found them all in the corridor.

'You fucking bastard!' Ed was shouting. 'Who the fuck do you think you are? You barge into our lives and think you're fucking God. How dare you? I should fucking kill you.'

'Eddie, stop it, Ed . . .' Emma was screaming hysterically. Marsha watched in horror as her brother suddenly pushed Daniel violently in the chest. He held a handful of Daniel's shirt in his right hand, his closed fist up under Daniel's chin, his other hand pinning his half-brother's shoulder to the corridor wall. She saw the watercolour of Leeds Castle clunk sideways in the fracas.

Lucy emerged from her room on the other side of the corridor. She was still in her pyjamas. 'Guys! What the hell's going on?'

Marsha stepped forward and grabbed her brother by the arm.

'For Christ's sake, Ed. Get off him.'

Ed spun round. 'Oh, take his side, why don't you? He's only fucking nearly raped my girlfriend, and you're standing up for him.'

217

Daniel, looking pale and shocked, shook himself and stepped back, his arms held up defensively. 'Look . . . I promise I didn't touch her,' he said, his voice flat.

'Yeah . . . well, you would say that, wouldn't you?' Ed sneered.

Emma was crying again. Marsha saw her try to take her boyfriend's hand, but he brushed her off angrily. Marsha thought how absurd she looked, done up like that in broad daylight. But she also looked a proper mess. She could see why Ed was upset—something must have happened.

'Ed, please, let's go upstairs. I need to change . . . please, come with me,' Emma begged through her tears.

Ed was still glowering at Daniel, but Emma managed to pull him away and upstairs to the parents' room. Marsha went down to the kitchen with Lucy and Daniel. The place was a mess, and Marsha, still in her pink dressing gown, began silently emptying the scattered paper cups of any wine dregs and throwing them into a black plastic bin bag.

Daniel just stood outside on the deck, his arms folded tight across his chest, staring out across the garden.

'Mash,' Lucy whispered, 'what happened? What did Daniel do to Emms?'

She gave her a tired, clipped account.

'Wow! Do you think he did it?' Lucy cast a glance at the tall, still figure of her half-brother.

Marsha shrugged. 'Who fucking knows?'

'If he didn't, then why would she make something like that up?' Lucy asked.

Daniel turned and came back into the kitchen,

his feet bare on the tiles. He glanced between her and Lucy. 'I swear on my dead mother's life that I never touched Emma last night, except to push her off. She was very drunk and she came on to me. There was nothing I could've done to stop her.'

'Well, Ed believes her.' Marsha shook her head, bewildered. One of them was lying.

Daniel looked oddly hopeful. 'But you don't?'

She hesitated. Emma was her best friend. Could she take his side over Emma's? Did she want to?

'I don't know what to think,' Marsha muttered finally, turning away to look for more debris.

'I think I'd better leave.'

'Leave?' Lucy asked, surprised.

'It's best if I do. I don't want to cause any more trouble. If I'm not here, maybe things'll calm down.'

Marsha immediately thought of her mother. 'Please don't go, Daniel. Not without seeing Mum. She'll freak if you're not here.'

'She'll freak anyway,' he replied, his expression darkening at the thought.

Lucy looked at her sister. 'Mash?'

'I don't know ...' Marsha stared blankly at Daniel. 'I don't have a clue what's best.'

She remembered Ed and Emma upstairs.

'Maybe it'd be better if you weren't here when they come down,' she told him. 'I don't want Ed attacking you again.'

Daniel nodded. 'I'll go.' But he looked bewildered and she felt sorry for him.

'I'm sure we can work this out,' she said, without much conviction. And he shrugged an acknowledgement.

'Thanks.'

'Where will you go?' Marsha asked.

'Oh . . . a friend, I suppose.'

*   *   *

'Umm . . . Daniel's not here,' Marsha answered her mother now. 'I'll do the tea, Dad, you sit down. You must be knackered after that drive.' She hurried over to the sink. 'Go and sit in the sunshine, I'll bring it out.'

She looked out to see her mother sink gratefully onto the padded lounger and heard her say, 'Great to be home!'

'She's not going to think it's so great when we tell her the good news,' Marsha muttered to Lucy as they got the tea ready.

'You tell them . . . you're better at it than me,' Lucy begged.

'Better at what? I've never done anything like this before in my fucking life. And never want to do it again, for that matter.'

Lucy took the tea and cups out on a tray. Marsha followed with a plate of chocolate digestive biscuits. Her father grinned up at her from his lounger.

'You don't appear to have wrecked the place. Can't have been a very good party!'

She and Lucy sat patiently while their mother and father regaled them with stories about the weekend. They laughed in all the right places, but Marsha wasn't really listening. Her brain toiled round and round the night of the party, but could find no satisfactory resolution.

Ed and Emma hadn't stayed on Sunday, just taken off without a word—they must have thought

Daniel was still downstairs. So she hadn't seen them to talk. She'd tried her brother's number, but he'd been almost curt with her. 'She's surviving. She wants to stay with me tonight,' he'd told her, clearly wanting to get off the phone.

'Go on,' Lucy mouthed, catching her eye and smiling sweetly.

Her mother had clocked the look between them and raised her eyebrows at Marsha. 'Darling? Is something the matter?'

Marsha knew it was down to her, and took a moment to decide what to say.

'Uh ... OK. This is a bit tricky ...' She paused. Her parents looked at her expectantly, but she could see her mother was already frowning. She ploughed on. 'There was a bit of a set-to after the party on Saturday night. Emma accused Daniel of coming on to her. Well, more than coming on to her, really sexually harassing her and —'

'No!' Her mother interrupted her. 'No. I don't believe it.'

'Let her finish,' Richard said quietly.

'There isn't much more. Daniel denied it, of course. Ed—who'd been sick and hadn't come to the party—tried to hit him when he heard. Ed and Emma won't talk to us and stayed at Ed's last night. And, well, Daniel thought it best that he leave.' She took a deep breath as the dismal litany ended.

Annie gasped. 'This is complete rubbish! Daniel would never do a thing like that. What are you saying? Has he really left?'

'Mum, for one thing, we didn't want Ed going for him again,' Lucy chipped in. 'He's gone to stay with a friend. Until things calm down.'

221

'Christ.' This from her dad.

'You don't believe him, do you?' Her mother was staring at her and Lucy. She was really pale suddenly.

Marsha sighed. 'I don't know what to think. I find it hard to believe Daniel capable of doing it, and, bottom line, it would be daft for him to behave like that under our roof, surely. But Emms was in a bad way, Mum. You should have seen her, she was terribly upset. And none of us can work out why she would make up something so horrible.'

'It's obvious, isn't it?' Her mother looked furious. 'She's protecting Ed. She knows he's had his nose put out of joint over Daniel, so she's made up this ridiculous story so that Daniel will be disgraced and chucked out of the family and Ed won't have to put up with him any more.'

'Mum! Are you saying Emms actually *planned* this? That she's deliberately smeared Daniel's name? She'd never, *ever* do something so vicious.'

'She wouldn't, Mum,' Lucy added, her voice indignant. 'I know she can be a pain, and a flirt. But no way is she that wicked.'

Her mother seemed to accept this. 'No, well, maybe not planned it. But how do you explain her behaviour then? Because Daniel did not come on to that girl. To Ed's girlfriend? You can't believe that.'

Marsha felt her hackles rise. She's taking his side without even finding out the facts. Not that there were any to find out, only versions, but still, she might be a bit less obviously on Daniel's side.

'You weren't there, Mum. You have no idea what happened. None of us have. You can't know for

222

sure that Daniel isn't somehow to blame.'

'No, you can't.' She was glad her dad agreed.

'Sorry, but I can. I don't care what any of you tell me, Daniel . . . did . . . not . . . attack Emma.'

Marsha glanced at Lucy.

'Lucy?' Her mother was pinning her sister with a ferocious stare and Marsha could see Lucy wavering.

'I'm with Mash, Mum. I think it's really super-unlikely that Daniel would do something like that. But it doesn't make sense. Maybe he did a bit . . . maybe they were both drunk . . . and then Emms got freaked and, like, exaggerated? I don't know . . .'

But her mother wasn't having it. 'She's lying. Look at her track record, girls. She's regularly stolen other people's boyfriends. Had an affair— aged fifteen—with her maths teacher. Run two men at once, basically acted any way she felt like at the time, with no thought for anyone else's feelings? Why would you trust her?'

'Annie,' Richard said, 'you've known Emma since she was a child, and Daniel for about ten minutes. OK, her reputation's not great, we all know that. But can you be certain that she's the one in the wrong here? What you're accusing her of is very serious.'

'Yes, and it's precisely *because* I've known Emma for so long that I can see what she's doing. You know quite well—you've said it yourself often enough in the past, Richard—that girl is capable of anything when it comes to men.'

'I know she isn't altogether to be trusted with guys, Mum,' Marsha said. 'Even though she's my best friend—in fact Emma herself would agree

223

with you. But this is a step too far, don't you think? I just can't believe she would make us think that about Daniel if there isn't at least *some* truth in it.' She couldn't forget the admiring glance he'd cast at her friend at the party.

Her mother got up. 'I'm going to call Daniel. God, poor bugger. He innocently moves in with us—against his better judgment, I might add—and then finds himself in a proper nest of vipers.' Marsha saw her mum shoot an angry glance at her dad.

'Shouldn't you call Ed too?' her father called after her mother, but she didn't answer.

Annie waited until she was in the safety of her bedroom, out of earshot of the others, before making the call to her elder son. Of course she would ring Ed, but he wasn't the injured party here.

Daniel answered his phone on the second ring.

'Welcome back,' he said wryly.

'Where are you?' Annie asked.

'Uh . . . I'm on the Heath.'

'Can we meet up? Not here.'

'Yup, OK.' He sounded resigned rather than angry.

'Usual place? By the Parliament Hill Fields entrance?'

She throbbed with indignation as she made the short walk to the Heath. She knew she'd been curt with her daughters and Richard, and that what they said was perfectly reasonable, but she just couldn't cope with the feeling that somehow Daniel had been set up.

He was sitting on the wall near the entrance, waiting for her. He looked very young suddenly and, unsurprisingly, pale and tired. He got up slowly when he saw her, and offered himself to be embraced. She hugged him fiercely against her, meeting little resistance.

'Let's walk,' she said, and they set off.

'I didn't do it,' was the first thing Daniel said, striding along, his hands buried in his jeans pockets.

'I know you didn't.'

Daniel glanced sideways at her. 'Why are you so sure?'

'I just am.' She threw herself down on a patch of grass up the hill from the main path and looked steadily at her son.

'So tell me. What happened?'

Daniel looked utterly bewildered, pushing his hair off his face in a gesture that had become very familiar to her. 'It had been a fun party, nobody caused trouble ... they were a good bunch. Marsha was tired, but there were a few stragglers—including Emma—out on the deck, so I said I'd stay and make sure everything was shut up after they left. Emma disappeared and I assumed she'd gone up to bed, but after I'd locked the doors to the garden I went to turn the lights off in the TV room, and she was on the sofa. She told Marsha she'd been asleep, but I don't think she was.' He paused, tearing small clumps of dried-out grass from the dusty ground in silence. 'When she saw me, she beckoned me over. I could see she was drunk, and I went to help her up. But she clung to me, and began stroking my face ...' he shot an embarrassed look at her, 'then she kissed me, pressing herself against me ... Annie, she was really trying it on. I don't want to spell it out, but

225

you can guess.'

'And you weren't tempted? Even a little bit?'

Daniel made a short, angry sound. 'So you don't *entirely* believe me.'

'I have to ask,' she said. She knew all too well the lethal level of attraction Emma inspired in the majority of red-blooded males. They would happily risk their marriages, their careers, their dignity to bask in a momentary glance from those dark eyes. Why should Daniel be any different?

'I tried to pull away, but she clung to me, and in the end I had to hold her off—I probably was responsible for the bruises on her arms—and push her back onto the sofa. She was furious.'

'Not used to rejection.'

'Whatever . . . but she called me a bastard, said I was "up myself" and that Ed thought I was a jerk.'

He appeared defeated as he sat there cross-legged on the grass. How upsetting, she thought, to know that people dislike you merely for your existence.

'He doesn't think you're a jerk.'

Daniel raised his eyebrows.

'I'm not denying he's jealous of you.' Her heart went out to her second son. What hell he must be going through, thinking Daniel had tried to make a move on his girlfriend. He's insecure about Emma on a good day. And none of this is his fault.

'It doesn't really matter what Ed thought of me before though, does it? He sure as hell hates me now.'

Annie nodded reluctantly. 'Right at this moment, that's probably true. But I'm sure Emma will tell the truth in the end.'

He shook his head doubtfully.

'I can see why she did what she did now. I suppose she thought you'd tell someone—Lucy, Marsha—and she wanted to get in first and blame you. It makes sense.'

'I thought of that, but it's not really much consolation.'

'I suppose not.'

'I mean, it's hardly in her best interests to tell the truth at this stage, is it? It'd be the end of her relationship with Ed, and probably the rest of the family.'

'But at least I can tell the others what happened . . .'

'My version . . . they know that already, Annie.'

'And I think Marsha and Lucy trust you—they just thought perhaps there might be blame on both sides.'

Daniel sighed. 'Well, fair enough. Even you had your doubts.'

She wasn't going to deny it. She had. But her silence was obviously a beat too long for her son. He gave her a disappointed look.

'Look, there's something I haven't told you. I didn't want to tell you like this. But if it's the only way you'll believe me . . .'

Annie's phone rang. She looked at the screen.

'Sorry, I have to take this . . . Ed?'

'Mum, where are you?' His voice sounded dull and heavy with stress.

'I'm on the Heath.' She dreaded him asking if she were alone, but Daniel was getting to his feet. She gestured urgently for to him to wait, but he just shrugged and turned away. She watched helplessly as he gathered pace, almost running towards the path and the exit to the main road,

227

then turned her attention to her other son.

'Did you hear what he did?' Ed demanded.

'Marsha told me.'

'What are you going to do, Mum?'

She sighed. 'I don't know what I can do, darling.'

'But the bastard assaulted my girlfriend!' Ed's voice was full of rage. 'You're going to throw him out, aren't you? You can't have him in the house after what he's done.'

'He's gone already. He went yesterday.'

There was silence on the other end of the phone.

'Emms is in a terrible state, Mum. I don't know what to do about her. She keeps crying and crying. I want to kill him for what he's done to her. Bloody, bloody bastard.'

It was horrible hearing the anguish in his voice and not knowing what to say, how to help him. Not knowing, either, if Emma's tears were tears brought about by guilt, or by trauma. Nor if Ed himself really believed her.

'Just give her time, darling. She's bound to be upset.'

'Have you talked to . . . *him*?' He asked, spitting out the last word as if it were poisoning him.

'Yes . . .'

'And? Told you he had bugger all to do with it, no doubt.'

Annie was lost for words. One son pitted against the other.

'He said he didn't do it, Ed.'

There was an explosion of anger at the other end of the phone.

'Well, he would, wouldn't he?' She heard a brief silence. 'But you didn't believe him, did you, Mum?'

'I don't know what to believe, darling. The whole thing's a nightmare.'

'Right, well . . . let me know when you've made up your mind.' Ed's voice was suddenly dangerously quiet, then the phone went dead.

*   *   *

For a long time after Ed had hung up, she just sat there on the grass. This is my fault, she thought. I was the one who went along with Daniel moving in. I should have listened to Richard—and to my own instincts. Ed wouldn't have resented him nearly so much if he hadn't been living in his bedroom. I wanted him near me, to get to know him better. But I've handled this all wrong with my stupid naiveté. And now I may have lost them both.

It was only on her slow walk back to the house that she began to mull over what Daniel had said, just before Ed called. Something he had to tell her. Something that would make her believe his innocence. What did he mean? She tried his mobile, but it went straight to answer. 'Please, ring me.' She left the message on his voicemail with little hope that he would.

*   *   *

'Did you talk to them?' Richard asked, finding Annie sitting alone in the kitchen later, nursing a glass of white wine.

She nodded.

'And?'

Annie shrugged. 'Daniel told me what he told

229

the girls.'

'And Ed? What did he say?'

'He's angry with me.' She shook her head. 'It was really upsetting listening to him, Richard. He was in such a state.'

'Poor Ed . . .'

Richard picked an opened bottle of red wine off the shelf by the sink and sniffed the contents. 'Smells alright. Do you think it's safe to drink?'

'I wouldn't risk it if I were you.'

He sat down opposite her, still cradling the wine bottle. 'What are we to do now, Annie?'

'I was being ridiculous earlier, saying Emma had plotted Daniel's downfall. It just seemed so wrong. I'm sorry, I lost it.'

Richard's look was almost sympathetic.

'And Daniel?'

'Oh, he's gone. So . . .' she glared at him, 'a result.'

But Richard held his hand up in protest. 'I didn't say a thing.'

'You didn't have to. Please, don't pretend you aren't delighted he's gone.'

'That's not fair.'

She shrugged. 'Maybe not. But what happened on Saturday night was just a symptom,' she told him. 'We . . . *I* . . . brought him into the family too soon. This, or something like this, was bound to happen.'

She felt utterly miserable as her thoughts swung between her two compromised sons. I'm prepared to take most of the responsibility, she thought. But what's Emma's part in all this? For a mad moment she wanted to take that silly, spoilt girl by the neck and strangle her.

230

16

Annie retreated to the bakery, where she threw herself into her work: making new designs for cakes, chatting up clients, chasing advertising, telling the others the highlights of her Cornish weekend. She forced herself to put the previous days behind her, and the warmth and sweetness of her floury empire welcomed her like a womb. Here they didn't even know that Daniel existed.

Jodie came back into the office with a fresh cup of coffee for her. 'Good weekend?'

'Yes, lovely. Cornwall is stunning. We had a fantastic time.' She could hear her leaden tone of voice belied her words, but Jodie didn't seem to notice.

'Never been, myself. Not sure what the point of the seaside is . . . all that sand.' She grinned.

'No, well . . .'

She had phoned Daniel several times in the three days since he'd left, but he hadn't answered and hadn't returned her calls. She had spoken to Ed, but the call was just a miserable repeat of the previous one. She'd wanted to cry, hearing the antagonism in her son's voice.

'Can I do the Huntingdon-Wheatley cake?' Annie asked her office manager.

Jodie looked puzzled. 'Do it? You okayed the design last week. Do you want to change it?'

'No, I mean make the cake itself . . . actually physically make it. I used to do all of them.'

Her manager raised her eyebrows. 'Of course you can.' Annie saw her glance out through the glass to where Carol was lining up the ingredients. 'She looks as if she's just about to get going on it.'

Jodie thinks I've lost my mind, and perhaps I have, she thought. But she had an overpowering need to indulge in the physical act of measuring, mixing, smoothing, baking. It was why she had started Delancey Bakes, and right now it was the only thing that made sense to her.

Carol moved aside with a cheerful smile. 'Think you can still work the magic?'

Annie laughed. 'Bloody nerve. 'Course I can.'

She fetched a white coat from the cupboard, pushed her hair into the cotton peaked hygiene hat and gave her hands a good scrub. She felt better already.

For the next half an hour Annie was absorbed in creating the birthday cake. Carol had pushed the order, in its see-through plastic folder, along the counter to her boss. Specification: rich chocolate cake, chocolate buttercream filling, chocolate fondant icing, three layers, eight-inch, square.

She diced the soft, slippery butter into the metal mixing bowl, poured on the caster sugar, lowered the beaters onto the ingredients and stared as the mixture became pale yellow and fluffy. In went small quantities of beaten egg as she watched like a hawk for signs of separation. Then the chocolate pieces, melted in a glass bowl over steam. Then the soft light puffs of flour carefully folded in. She smoothed the chocolate cream into the waiting greased and lined tins and took them on a tray to the oven. She looked across the room and saw Carol sipping tea, covertly watching her preparations.

'Not so bad,' Carol called out, grinning.

'We'll see.'

Annie had been in the zone during the making of the cake. But now it was in the oven, she felt as if she were coming down off a high. She set the timer and went back to the office. Jodie looked at her questioningly.

'It's good to stay in touch,' Annie said quietly.

Jodie nodded. 'Funny, I've worked here for nearly six years now, and I've never made a cake in my life.'

'You should try it some time. It's very therapeutic.'

Jodie laughed. 'You in need of a bit of therapy today, then?'

It wasn't a serious remark, but it hit a chord. Suddenly, to her horror and to her office manager's clear embarrassment, Annie burst into tears.

The whole story came out. Jodie, who usually kept a professional distance between herself and her boss, was obviously unnerved, but listened sympathetically to Annie's tale. At one point Kadir came to the office door, but the manager shooed him away.

'I've made such a mess of it.'

'Don't beat yourself up. It's families. They're all like that. I'm not being funny, but you may have got off lightly so far. Believe me, my lot are constantly at each other's throats. That's why I never see them unless I have to.'

'But I don't want it to be like that,' she said.

Jodie shrugged. 'Nobody does. And I'm sure you can paper over the cracks if you really want to.' She laughed. 'I just don't want to. I'm not sure I even like my family much. They might be blood, but they're a pretty sad bunch ... except for my mum.'

Annie stared at Jodie, wondering how she could be so sanguine. 'I thought I did like mine,' she said. 'But I've seen sides to them over the Daniel thing ...'

'Most men don't know how to behave on a good day,' Jodie replied cheerfully. 'You can't really blame them.'

Annie smiled. 'Do you think I'm being unfair to them?'

Jodie considered Annie's question. 'Not for me to say, but I'd sort it out if you can. It's so much bloody trouble having everyone at each other's throats.'

'Supposing I can't sort it out?'

Jodie pulled a face. 'Well, I guess that's life.'

The timer went off and Annie went through to get her cake, baked to perfection, out of the oven.

*   *   *

She didn't want to go home. After the bakery had closed up for the night she began the walk home, but stopped for a moment in a bus stop, sitting alone on the red plastic bench. She thought over what Jodie had said about family and felt tears pricking in her eyes. She loved Richard, she loved all her children. But she and Richard had had another fight that morning. It was one of those quiet, cruel rows, as repetitive as a stuck record, where everything has been said before, but is no less painful because of it.

'It might be a good idea if you actually tried to *see* Ed and talk it out with him properly,' Richard had said, his tone mildly lecturing, as he pulled the end of his navy tie through the knot.

'I *have* tried to see him. But when we spoke, all he wanted me to say was that I was on Emma's side, not Daniel's. And I couldn't do that. I offered to do anything he asked—'

'Can't blame him,' Richard had interrupted curtly, and the fight had begun.

Her mobile rang, interrupting her recollection. She dragged her phone out and saw Charles's name. She took a deep breath. 'Hi.'

'You sound gloomy. How's it going?'

'On a scale of one to ten, ten being the gloomiest, about five hundred.'

'That bad,' Charles chuckled. 'Well, I'm about, if you fancy *un petit coup* and a chat. We haven't caught up properly about the other night ... meeting Daniel.'

She only hesitated for a second. 'Nothing I'd like more,' she said, her heart lifting. 'But I look a wreck, so it'd better be at yours. I can't be seen out.'

'I'll try to cope,' came back the amused reply. 'Champers on ice as we speak.'

'About forty-five minutes then.'

Annie felt a pleasant frisson of wickedness as she set off to hail a taxi. She texted her husband: 'Meeting Charles for a drink tonight. He wants to talk about Daniel.' This was spiteful and she knew it, but she told herself she didn't care.

Charles was shocked when she told him the story of Emma and Daniel.

'Amazing that Louisa knew this sort of thing might be on the cards,' he mused.

'Even Louisa would never have predicted this.'

235

'No . . . but the family-being-torn-apart bit.'

She said nothing.

'You must be very upset. You don't think he did it, do you?'

'No,' Annie said tiredly. 'I'm sure he didn't.'

'I must say . . . although I suppose you can never tell—Ted Bundy was charm personified by all accounts—but Daniel didn't seem the type to attack a vulnerable girl. He seemed too . . .'

'Thanks for likening our son to a serial killer!' Annie interrupted, but she was pleased Charles thought as she did about their son.

Daniel had liked his father too. The evening they met hadn't started well. Annie couldn't find the bar Charles had suggested—part of a new and expensive Spanish tapas restaurant off Charlotte Street, very near Richard's office—but the frontage was subtle and easy to miss.

At six thirty, the small, plush bar was almost empty. Solid brown-leather armchairs sat around in the low light, the decor warm wood, with modern art decorating the walls. Charles was already there, a bottle of champagne on ice and three glasses set out on the table in front of him. He'd got up quickly to greet her and shake Daniel's hand, and Annie had been immediately struck by their physical similarity—both tall, slim, long-legged, with the same wavy hair (although Daniel's was auburn, Charles's fair), cut below the ear.

She had filled the first awkward moments by wittering on about how hard it had been to find the bar, but soon the two men had relaxed, each obviously intrigued by the other's presence. They had talked about theatre and wine and the state of the nation, the conversation flowing easily enough through neutral territory and the first bottle of champagne. Annie had wondered if they would even mention the fact that they were father and son. But she felt it wasn't up to her to do so for them. In the end, it was Charles who had taken the plunge.

'So . . . it's hard to believe we're the same flesh and blood.'

Daniel had nodded. 'It must have been a shock for you, not knowing about me till now.'

Charles had given a short laugh. 'Understatement of the decade! But I'm glad we're in touch. I don't like the idea of a son out there I haven't met.'

'Nor me,' Daniel replied. 'I . . . it's been a relief to me . . . meeting you.'

Annie thought relief was an odd word to use. Maybe he meant it was a relief to find that his parents weren't as her mother had implied they might be: feckless or violent or criminals.

As they silently acknowledged each other as father, mother and son, Annie felt the sudden presence of a ghost family hovering. The three of them, together for the first time, the only bond their DNA, yet, by biological definition, still absolutely a family. She wondered if the others sensed it too.

When Daniel disappeared off to the men's room, Charles had turned to her, his expression bewildered.

'Not sure what to do with all this now. I mean, I like him, he seems rather special. But do I see him again? Do we try and bond in some way?'

'That's up to both of you.'

'What do you feel? Is it working, having him at home like a real son? Would you say you love him?'

She'd wanted to object to the word 'real', but she understood what he was asking.

'I suppose I keep trying to see him as the baby I remember loving, but it's elusive. So I'm just getting to know him as he is now . . . seeing where it goes. It isn't quite love, not yet.'

'But you're enjoying it? Him?'

She'd hesitated. 'I would if I was allowed to,' she'd muttered, seeing Daniel coming through the door towards them.

Now, in Charles's quiet flat, the windows were open to the warm night air, three butter-coloured pedestal candles on the coffee table casting the only light. She had been there a while now, sipping the chilled champagne, opening her heart to him, while he listened in silence. It was such a relief to talk to someone who did not judge.

'I spoke to my solicitor about Daniel, after we met last week,' Charles said. 'I wanted to know what the situation was about leaving him money.'

'He says he doesn't want money, that's not why he came looking for me . . . despite what my mother thinks.'

Charles gestured, his arms wide. 'Look, I hope I'm not about to peg it, but when I do, I should at least like to leave him something. Without there being any hassle about it,' he added.

'You should do that then.'

'Yes, I will. But William—that's my solicitor— said I should first make sure he's mine. You know, get a test?' He obviously saw her lowering brow, because he hurried on sheepishly, 'For what it's worth, I said I totally trusted that he was mine, but William says you can't be too careful. Of course, it's all academic if he's disappeared.'

'William couldn't be more right, Charles. It's so hard to get a good class of bastard these days,' she said, relishing her angry sarcasm.

He roared with laughter. 'Ooh, we are sharp tonight!'

'Sorry. It's just that nothing about this, except my own private relationship with Daniel, has been anything but trouble. No one sees him as a person, as Daniel. He's a predatory half-brother; seducer; home wrecker. Feckless, sponging and dangerous, if you listen to my mother—although she's rescinded that since she found out you're the father.'

'Did I ever meet your mother? She sounds terribly sensible.'

She shook her head, smiling. 'Not. But seriously, if they would just see him for who he is.'

'It's not an easy situation to deal with.'

Or that difficult, she thought stubbornly.

'But what if he doesn't ever get in touch with me again, Charles? Do I let him just walk away? I thought I was enhancing my family when Daniel came back, but it seems instead that I've done the opposite. And now I'm in danger of losing both sons.'

Charles must have heard the distress in her voice, because he got up quickly from the chair he'd been lounging in and came and sat beside her on the sofa. As she began to cry he took her in his arms and held her close. For a moment she resisted, not wanting to seem so weak in front of him. But he didn't let her go, and in the end she gave in, resting her body against his, her cheek pressed to the laundered softness of his pale blue shirt. As the sobs gradually lessened in his comforting embrace, she felt him drop a gentle kiss on her forehead. She lifted her face to his. For a moment they looked silently at each other. Charles raised an eyebrow.

'Not a good idea.' She pulled away.

Charles grinned, 'Oh, I don't know—seems rather splendid from where I'm sitting.'

'Stop it,' she said, smiling too. 'I suppose I'd better get back to my recalcitrant husband.'

'I suppose you better had.'

Richard was fast asleep when she got home. She was relieved. Something potentially dangerous had happened with Charles.

She knew she would never give in to an infidelity, but still . . . it was a moment of nostalgia which reminded her of her youth, their bodies stretched out naked together on a similarly warm summer night.

*　　　*　　　*

'Mrs Delancey?'

'Mercedes, hello.'

'You come over today, yes?' She sounded anxious.

'Today?' Annie wracked her brains. She was walking to the bakery, her mind still on the previous evening with Charles.

'The bed, it come soon. We waiting for you.'

She groaned silently. The bed. Of course. Her mother was getting a new bed and had asked her daughter to come and supervise the exchange.

240

Neither Eleanor nor Mercedes had the slightest faith in delivery men—not even if they *were* from Peter Jones. Eleanor was sure they were criminals who would try cheat her or steal all her valuables. Mercedes just didn't understand a word they said.

'I'm on my way. Tell Mother half an hour . . . no, *half* an hour, Mercedes,' she repeated loudly as she retraced her steps back home to fetch the car. 'I'll be there very soon,' she added, enunciating the words carefully in the face of the housekeeper's continuing fluster. Why can't she learn English? she huffed to herself. She's been with Mother for almost twenty-five years, she does nothing but watch English-speaking television when she's not working, and talks daily to my mother—whose only word of Spanish appears to be 'Mercedes'— but she still can't understand a bloody word I say.

'At last, darling. I thought you'd forgotten,' said Eleanor when Annie arrived, offering her cheek to be kissed.

Annie wasn't going to admit this was true. 'Are they here?'

'Not yet. They said between twelve and five.'

Annie looked at her watch. It was barely twelve-thirty. She gave a small sigh at the prospect of spending the whole day with her mother.

'How are you, Mother?' she asked, thinking of all the things she had to do at the bakery.

Eleanor chuckled. 'Looking forward to a good night's sleep.'

'Haven't you been sleeping?'

Her mother harrumphed. 'That mattress is like Brighton beach. Of course I'm not sleeping.' She waved her hand dismissively at her daughter. 'I'm well aware that I'm old, and that old people don't

241

sleep, but I don't see why I can't do something to improve the situation.'

'Quite right. Mercedes sounded a bit panicky when she rang.'

'Mercedes is Mediterranean, darling. Everything's a drama to her. The smallest domestic problem and it's *"Madre mia, madre mia, terribile, terribile"*, as if the world's about to end. It's very aggravating.'

They sat and talked for a while, Eleanor in her wing-back chair, Annie on the brown sofa. Mercedes brought them lunch: Ryvita with thin slices of ham and tomato, coffee in tiny blue porcelain cups and a Bendicks mint each—her mother's daily favourite.

'So, you still haven't introduced me to the Carnegie boy,' Eleanor said as she carefully folded and smoothed the foil from her chocolate into a thin silver ribbon.

'Charles?' Annie asked.

'I thought you said he was called Daniel.'

'Daniel, yes. Daniel isn't a Carnegie, Mother. His name is Gray.'

'Don't be obtuse, darling, you know what I mean. Gray?' Eleanor paused to consider this. 'Rather a nondescript name. I don't know any Grays.'

'No, well, never mind. He seems quite happy with it.'

'But his father *is* Charles Carnegie,' insisted Eleanor. 'You'd have thought he'd prefer to have the Carnegie name than be saddled with a name like Gray, wouldn't you?' She pronounced Daniel's surname as if she'd just sucked a lemon.

Annie gave up. 'He's going up to Edinburgh. He won't be back till September now.' She didn't say that she didn't know if she would ever see him again, let alone have the chance to introduce him to her mother.

'Well, in the autumn perhaps. Caro was stunned when I told her.' Eleanor chuckled with satisfaction. 'She says Charles is immensely rich, so if the boy plays his cards right he'll be set for life.' Her smile had a cynical tinge. 'Obviously no fool.'

Annie didn't bother to contradict her. There was little point challenging her mother's default position, that people were fundamentally no good unless they had a title or a lot of land. As she sat opposite her in the quiet drawing room, she couldn't help wondering what processes went on in her mother's head. What had she been like when she was young, before Annie's father died? Had she been happy then? Had she been kinder? All Annie remembered was afterwards, when her mother became more proud, more fixated with maintaining appearances. No one was going to look down on Eleanor Westbury and her daughter just because she was forced to earn a living. She told nobody about Ralph's appalling debts at the time, just pretended she wanted something to occupy her life now that she was a widow. And because of this stubborn pride, Annie had been intensely aware that her unwanted pregnancy had hit her mother particularly hard.

The bed arrived just after three. Annie shut her mother in the drawing room and dealt with the men herself. The Vi-Spring divan, queen-size, looked almost garishly modern against the mahogany furniture, set of antique bird prints and faded Regency stripes of her mother's bedroom.

'Try it ... go on,' Annie insisted with a smile,

243

after she and Mercedes had made up the bed with the new, box-fresh sheets and duvet cover.

Her mother, looking like an excited schoolgirl, sat on the edge of the mattress and heaved her legs up, settling luxuriously against the new, plump goose-down pillows. Her face broke into a broad grin.

'Heaven!' She pointed Annie to the other side of the bed. 'Lie down, darling. You have to try it. Caro was right. This mattress is blissful. I shall sleep like a log tonight.'

Annie was about to resist, but she loved her mother being happy. She stretched out next to her, her head on the cool, white smoothness of Egyptian cotton. She had to admit, the bed was very comfortable. As they lay side by side, Eleanor giggled.

'I bet you want one too, now!'

Annie found herself not only coveting a spanking new Vi-Spring bed, but also having a strong desire just to roll over on her side and go to sleep then and there.

'Mmm . . . wake me up tomorrow,' she murmured, closing her eyes for a moment.

Her mother chuckled again, and began pulling herself upright and off the bed, tweaking the turquoise-blue patchwork quilt Annie and Richard had given her for her seventieth birthday. 'Much as I appreciate your efforts on my behalf this afternoon, darling—and you have been marvellous—I'm not sharing my new bed with anyone!' She stood smiling down at her daughter, pushing her hairband back into place. 'You look a bit peaky. You're not coming down with something, are you?'

Annie opened her eyes and saw the genuine concern in her mother's eyes. It made her want to cry.

'No . . . no, I'm fine, Mother. Just a lot on at the moment.'

Eleanor nodded. 'You do too much.'

'Could say the same about you,' Annie replied, and forced herself away from the seductive pull of firm springs and fresh bed linen.

'I don't know what you're talking about,' Eleanor declared with a disingenuous smile.

17

Ed sat on alone in the bar. He'd sent the others home and the place was closed up to the outside world. He was in the tiny office in the basement, next to the kitchen. In the day it was like an inferno, hot from the ovens, pungent with the smells of frying food and disinfectant from the loos, reverberating with the sounds of clanging pans and barked orders of the bad-tempered Cypriot chef. But now it was just murky and depressing, perfectly suited to his mood.

Things had hit rock-bottom in the last few days. Emma refused to go back to her flat, refused to go to work, refused, in fact, to do anything but lie in his bed and cry. He was at his wits' end.

'What are you going to do?' she kept nagging him. To which he kept replying, 'What can I do?'

He felt helpless in the face of her distress. But short of stabbing Daniel—which even he could see wasn't much of a solution—what could be done?

'Please come round and talk to her, Mash,' he'd pleaded with his sister. She'd agreed to drop by after work, but it hadn't helped one bit.

'Come on, Emms, get up.' Marsha, in no-nonsense mode, had pulled his girlfriend out of bed and made her shower and get dressed in tracksuit bottoms and a T-shirt. She'd made her eat some toast and drink some tea, and Emms had looked better for a while, he'd thought. So he'd suggested they watch a movie to take their minds off the situation. Crap idea that turned out to be!

She'd immediately pulled a face. 'Why won't anyone take me seriously? You all expect me to get on with my life, just totally forget what that bastard Daniel did to me. But I can't . . . I really, really can't.' She'd begun to cry again and Mash had lost her rag.

'For Christ's sake, Emms. OK, if what you say happened, happened, then it must have been horrible. But at worst it was a drunken grope, surely? Daniel's not a monster . . .'

Emma'd got really hysterical then, and he'd started shouting at his own sister. She obviously didn't believe a word of what Emms said. This had shocked him—Marsha knew her better than anyone did, and she was always on his side—the best and most loyal sister anyone could have. Scrupulously fair too. Whatever their parents' faults, they'd all been brought up to be fair, Lucy to the point of mania sometimes. So he'd found himself asking: Do I believe Emma? He hadn't hesitated when she'd expressed a desire to be with him in the wake of the Lewis fiasco; he'd simply grabbed the opportunity. Marsha had reminded him of the risks—broken heart, jealousy, loss of face—but he'd been a willing lamb to the slaughter. I love her, he reminded himself as he sat alone in the cold glare of the neon strip-light. I've always loved her. But do I trust her?

He got up and gathered his jacket from the hook on the back of the door. Switching the light out, he made his way up the narrow stairs in the glow from the street. The bar key-ring was heavy with all its various keys and clanked loudly against the glass door as he undid the lock and fastened it securely behind him. The street was almost empty and he realised it was after two. He shivered. What shall I do if I can't believe her? The thought of her kissing Daniel made him almost throw up. And then there was his mother.

*   *   *

Annie was seeing a client in Chelsea about a fiftieth-birthday cake that morning. But she had time before that, and as she pulled on her pink Chanel jacket she knew what she wanted to do first.

It was mid-morning and she had a choice of tables in Ed's Islington bar; he wouldn't be busy for another hour or so. She was tired; she hadn't slept well. Richard had rung to say he was staying in town overnight. The merger was gathering pace, he had to work late, be in the office early. He told her he was staying with Andrew, an accountant friend who had a small flat above a pub, five minutes' walk from Richard's office. Andrew lived in Dorset and spent three nights a week in town, but Annie couldn't bring herself to ask if Andrew would be there. She was tormented for most of the

247

night by the thought that this was an excuse for her husband to spend the whole night with tasty Kate.

A waiter, blond and skinny and looking as if he should still be in fifth form, came over to take her order.

'Is Ed Delancey here?'

The boy looked round. 'Uh, yeah, he was a minute ago. Shall I find him?'

She nodded, and he wandered off through the door which led down to the kitchens, leaving her waiting nervously.

'Mum, hi.' Ed's greeting was cool. He sat down at her table.

He looks as tired as I feel, she thought.

'I haven't got long,' Ed added, constantly monitoring the activity in the cafe as he spoke, although there were only three other tables occupied.

'I know, but I wanted to see you, darling. To touch base.' In her nervousness, she had lost track of what she'd planned to say, her mind so taken up with her errant husband.

Ed sighed. 'It's all a mess.'

'I know, and I'm so sorry. I know I've handled it badly. How's Emma getting on?' She forced herself to ask the question, although Marsha had already told her the answer.

'Emma's not getting on, Mum. Not at all.'

She hesitated, agonising over how to respond. Should I rehash the whole thing, now? Here? Is there any point? She decided there wasn't.

'I miss you, darling. Very much. I hate all this coming between us. Can we try and get past it? Will you come round soon . . . have supper?'

She watched his face soften.

'Oh, Mum . . . that's not going to be easy. Emms . . .'

The boy-waiter came over and stood looking apologetic until Ed noticed him.

'Yes?'

'Uh, there's a problem with the till printout . . . it's not . . .'

'I'll be right there,' Ed said, and the boy disappeared back to the other side of the bar.

'I'd better go.' He was already on his feet. 'I'll call you. Do you want a coffee or something?'

She shook her head. 'Thanks, but no, I have to be at a meeting.' She wanted desperately to hug him to her, but she knew she couldn't do that in front of the others. So she just laid a hand on his arm. 'Love you,' she whispered as he turned away.

At least he didn't yell at me, she thought, her heart a bit lighter as she made her way to Highbury and Islington Underground. He knows I love him. Whatever's happened, he must know that.

*   *   *

The client in Chelsea wanted a cake for her husband's fiftieth, which was to be marked by a grand party in September, to be held in a marquee in the substantial garden behind their Chelsea Embankment house. She told Annie the cake had to be in the shape of the knot garden her husband had apparently planted nearly twenty years ago, and which was his pride and joy. But she was not happy with Annie re-creating it in icing sugar without first seeing the real thing.

'You see what I mean?' Veronica Mather stood

beside Annie as they contemplated the knot garden from the large sash window in the first-floor bedroom, which her host had flung wide. 'It's best seen from here first, so you get the real impact of the design. I'm sorry to drag you all this way, but you'll admit, it would have been hard to get a proper idea from a photograph.'

Annie gazed down at the square of garden, set at the end of the paved terrace. It was bordered by the traditionally immaculate box hedges, the green rows inter-woven in four lozenge-shapes joined by three concentric circles. Between the hedges were fine-gravel paths, and the centres of the lozenge shapes had been planted up with lavender, while the smaller sections contained other herbs. Annie recognised pink lamb's ear and the dark green spikes of spearmint leaves. It was pretty, certainly a faultless example of the genre, but to Annie, taming nature to such a neurotic degree seemed a bit pointless.

'Philip designed it himself. He prefers to call it a *parterre*,' Veronica was saying with a roll of her eyes. 'But I can't see there's much difference.' She turned to Annie. 'Shall we go down and you can see it at close quarters? The lavender and box smell divine together.'

Veronica insisted Annie stay for a glass of wine. She brought the bottle out onto the York-stone terrace, and seemed to have all the time in the world, detaining Annie for another hour with minuscule details of the impending party. And Annie found she was happy to comply. The cake would be good for business, because between them they could create something spectacular.

By the time she left the house on the

Embankment she was quite drunk. She began to walk unsteadily up towards the King's Road and, on impulse, called Charles.

'I'm in the area, two sheets to the wind after half a bottle of wine on an empty stomach. Do you fancy a cup of coffee somewhere? I can't go back to the office like this.'

'Come over,' Charles laughed. 'I'm waiting for the plumber to finish unblocking the sink, and I'm bored to bloody death.'

By the time Annie had found a taxi and arrived at Charles's flat, the plumber was packing his stuff into a worn canvas bag. She lay back on the sofa, puffed out by the climb up the stairs in her inebriated state.

'Daft client,' she complained. 'Had to show me her grisly knot garden, when a photo would have done just as well. Then wouldn't let me go.'

Charles disappeared, to arrive back a moment later with more wine and two glasses. 'I need to catch up,' he said, as Annie groaned.

But she drank the soft white burgundy appreciatively. 'Better than Veronica's,' she said. This is fun, playing hooky with Charles Carnegie, she thought. Blast Richard. Nothing so great in my life that I need to rush home for right now.

'Louisa still in France?'

'Yup. I'll probably join her next week.'

'Try to sound more enthusiastic!'

But Charles didn't laugh. He seemed to be deciding whether he should tell her something or not. 'To be honest, Annie, Louisa and I aren't . . . well, we aren't exactly seeing eye to eye at the moment.'

'Seeing eye to eye? About what? What do you

251

mean?' She was having trouble focusing on what he was saying.

Charles shrugged. 'It's been a bit rocky for a while. You know, the usual thing with Louisa.'

'Not sure I do.'

Charles gave her a frustrated glance.

'Too much wine. You mean you're having an affair?'

Charles shook his head vehemently. 'I'm most certainly not. No, I told you about her . . . her mad turns. She can be so tricky. And, well, I suppose I've rather had enough of it. We had another row about Daniel the other night and it was the last straw in a long line of last straws.'

She pulled a face. 'Oh, I see. Didn't take too kindly to you meeting up with your long-lost son, eh?'

'It wasn't that. I never told her. She was just so crazy about the whole thing. I'm not sure I can cope with her moods any more.'

Annie tried to marshal her wandering senses.

'You'll lose half your money if you divorce her,' was all she could think of to say.

'Oh, Annie, I don't give a stuff about the money.' He sighed. 'But obviously it would be a nightmare for all sorts of reasons—not least because she's so unstable. God knows what she'd do if I said I was leaving her.'

'You never know, she might be relieved.'

He looked at her as if the idea hadn't crossed his mind.

'Relieved? You think so?'

'I really have no idea. Sorry, that was a stupid thing to say.'

Neither spoke for a while, the problem of

252

Charles's marriage seeming suddenly too complex for both of them. He got up and put on a CD of Sonny Boy Williamson. The soft blues harmonica lulled Annie and stopped, for once, the tormenting thoughts about Richard spinning around her brain.

'Keep it to yourself . . . don't mention it to no one else,' she sang along. 'This song seems a tad too close to the bone.'

Charles obviously hadn't been listening to the lyrics. 'How do you mean?'

'Oh, nothing . . . just seems to be a song about cheating.'

'I told you, I'm not cheating.'

'Not you . . .'

He cocked his head, his expression curious.

'Not me either,' she muttered, embarrassed suddenly.

They listened in silence to the music.

'Talking of cheating, has that Emma come clean yet?'

She shook her head. 'Nope. Doesn't seem likely she will. And Daniel still hasn't called.'

'Not sure I'd call either, under the circs. Too complicated.'

Story of your life . . . and mine for that matter, she thought.

The alcohol didn't seem to be working any more. She was feeling headachy and depressed. For the first time in her life, she had no plan. In the past, when faced with trauma she'd buried it, covering the grave with ranks of distracting blooms. Now there seemed nothing, no panacea, that would do the job successfully.

Charles reached over from his chair and held his hand out towards her. She took it.

'I'd better get home.'

She got up, and Charles got up with her. 'Dance with me,' he said, pulling her close against him and beginning to sway to the plaintive, sexy rhythms of Sonny Boy's harmonica. The movement itself was comforting, and she went with it, making no attempt to extricate herself. It seemed safe in this separate reality, with this man who was both deeply familiar and a complete stranger, listening to music from a different time and culture—and easier to stay than to go.

For a while they danced, her head on his shoulder, their bodies hot and close on the muggy summer afternoon.

'Kiss me,' he said softly. 'Kiss me like you did all those years ago on the grass.'

'You don't even remember it,' she retorted, but she held his gaze for what seemed like a long moment.

'Oh, but I do . . . I do.'

She didn't have time to answer, because Charles bent swiftly and kissed her upturned face. The kiss was urgent, needy, and it took her completely by surprise, lifting her up in a sudden fierce whirlwind of desire. Her body responded almost without her permission, as if it remembered that first time too, when their lips, cold from the orange ice lollies, had come together. After a while, he drew her towards the bedroom. Breathless and weak, she followed him.

As she lay down he began to undress her slowly, covering each bit of skin that he laid bare with soft kisses. She helped him, caressing his body in return, unbuttoning his shirt and lifting it away from his tanned shoulders, until they were both naked on the cover of the bed. He pulled away and she saw him stare down at her.

'You're beautiful,' he whispered.

But something about the moment brought her up short. Her breathing sounded loud and ragged in the quiet bedroom. What the hell am I doing? She pushed him gently off her and sat up, clutching the bedcover to her nakedness.

'Charles! We can't. This is crazy!'

'Is it?' He looked surprised, as if she'd brought him round from a trance. 'Why?'

She stroked his cheek; his blue eyes were still bright with desire.

'Because it would be revenge sex, that's why.'

'Revenge? Revenge on whom?'

'On Richard, for a start, who I'm convinced is having an affair. On Louisa, perhaps, for being such a pain about Daniel.'

He sighed, looking disappointed, but gallantly got off the bed and put on his dressing gown.

'Not sure what it's got to do with anyone else.' He sat down beside her. 'My fault. Sorry, Annie, got a bit carried away there.'

'It wasn't just your fault,' she said shakily, getting up and attempting to dress herself, pulling at her buttons, straightening her skirt, trying to smooth her ruffled hair. Her lips felt bruised and on fire, her body as if it were coming down off a high. Then she sat down hard on the bed next to him, unable to do any more.

Charles looked as let down as she felt. 'You know,' he said, 'since meeting you again, and knowing about the boy, I've felt quite strange.' He frowned, his expression puzzled. 'I keep wondering how it would have been . . . if you'd told me back then. Would we have made a go of it, d'you think?'

Annie shook her head.

'It's fantasy, Charles . . . a fantasy that negates our other families, our real lives.'

'Oh, I know, I know . . . but I still find you very attractive.' He shot her a boyish grin.

'You had your chance,' she replied tartly. Just take thirty-five years to let me know you fancy me, why don't you, she thought. For a second she had a flashback of her eighteen-year-old self, waiting, waiting for him to ring. When she didn't hear from him the day after their night together, she told herself he was busy getting ready to go away. It was inconceivable to her that he wouldn't call. Then, when she realised he must have gone without phoning her, she told herself he would call from the French house. And when August dragged on and there was no phone call, she thought perhaps he would be waiting to see her when he got back at the end of the month. That August was the longest month of her life. September dragged by in an increasing miasma of despair. She wondered if her mother had forgotten to give her messages, but she knew that any contact from Charles Carnegie would be greeted with a fanfare by Eleanor. She would look for him when she was out, terrified she would bump into him on the Knightsbridge streets with his arm round another girl. That summer night had meant so much to her, and in her innocence she couldn't believe he hadn't cared too. It did not occur to her for a single second that she was already carrying his baby. Sitting on the bed next to him now, she felt again the agony of that teenage rejection.

'You won't let this silly mistake come between us,

will you?' Charles was still bent, dishevelled, on the bed. He looked up, brushing his hair back off his face in a gesture reminiscent of Daniel.

'Better stick to the Ritz in future,' she replied, as casually as she could manage, and he chuckled.

'The Ritz . . . perfect. You're so sensible, Annie. I love that about you.'

She almost ran down the worn, red-carpeted stairs from Charles's flat. She was lightheaded and slightly nauseous from too much wine. All she wanted was to get home and stand under a powerful stream of hot water, to wash away her foolishness. How could she have done that to Richard? However bad things are between us, he doesn't deserve that, she told herself. The thought of him knowing made her feel ill.

She hailed a taxi at the bottom of Queen's Gate, and immediately got out a mirror to check her face. She saw the taxi driver glance at her in his rear-view mirror. He knows what I've been up to. I look so wrecked and guilty. She reached in the bottom of her bag for her mobile. Three missed calls in the last hour, two from her mother's number and one from Richard. She didn't bother to listen to the message from him, he could wait. What does Mother want? She listened to the first voicemail. But it wasn't her mother's voice.

'Mrs Delancey . . . iss Mercedes . . . please come quick . . . iss your mother.'

The Spanish housekeeper sounded frantic. Annie felt her stomach turn over. She listened to the next one, also from Mercedes, which said exactly the same thing. This wasn't Mercedes being 'Mediterranean'—this sounded serious. Had her mother had a fall? She shouted through the glass to the taxi driver to take her to Cadogan Gardens as quickly as he could.

She checked to see when Mercedes had called; it was only fifteen minutes ago. She dialled Eleanor's number repeatedly as the taxi changed direction, but it was always engaged. The taxi driver, despite her desperate exhortations, seemed incapable of going more than three miles an hour. It was a ten-minute journey at most, but the lights were all against them and Pelham Street had a massive queue leading up to the junction at Brompton Cross. By the time she got to the flat she was almost fainting with anxiety.

The buzzer let her into the building without anyone answering the intercom. She flew upstairs. Dr Graham opened the door.

'Annie, come in.'

'Mother . . . what's happened?' she gasped, breathless.

The doctor didn't say anything at first, just drew her through to the drawing room. Mercedes was nowhere to be seen, but she thought she heard her talking hysterically in Spanish in the far reaches of the large flat.

'Where is she? What's happened?'

'Annie, sit down. I'm afraid I've got bad news. Your mother . . . I think she must have had a heart attack.'

'Where have they taken her? Which hospital is she in?'

'She, er, I'm afraid she didn't come round,' the doctor said slowly, looking anxiously at her face. She stared at him. She'd always thought Rob Graham looked uncannily like Colin Firth. He had the same soulful, hesitant look in his brown eyes.

He'd been her mother's doctor for a decade, and Annie was convinced Eleanor was a little in love with him.

'Didn't come round? I don't understand . . .' She jumped up. 'I must go to her.'

Dr Graham put a restraining hand on her arm. 'I'm sorry, Annie. Your mother died about an hour ago. I'm so sorry.'

'Died? Mother can't have died,' she said stubbornly, and pulled herself free from the doctor's hand. 'She had a new bed yesterday.'

'I'm so sorry,' Rob Graham repeated.

'Where is she?' She wasn't sure she was understanding any of what the doctor was telling her.

'She's in the bedroom.'

Annie almost ran down the passage. Her mother's room was at the end of the L-shaped flat. She passed Mercedes' door, and the housekeeper, red-eyed, poked her head out nervously, as if she'd been listening out for her.

'Ah, Mrs Annie . . . *su madre, iss terribile, terribile* . . . I very sorry . . . I call you, but you no answer.'

She patted the housekeeper's arm, but kept on going. The bedroom was very silent. Her mother lay propped against the puffy goose-down pillows on the brand-spanking-new, queen-size Vi-Spring divan. She was fully clothed, covered to her chin by the turquoise-blue patchwork quilt. Her eyes were closed, her hands by her sides. Annie stood silently looking down at her. Eleanor Westbury had gone, that much was clear. The face looked blank, empty; strangely, indefinably devoid of life. She reached out and laid her hand on her mother's cheek. It was still powdery, but cool, with the coldness of death. She heard Dr Graham behind her.

'What happened?' she asked, turning to the doctor. Her heart felt slow and heavy, as if it were having trouble pumping blood around her body. She wanted to sit down, but she couldn't move.

'From what I can gather, Mercedes went out to the supermarket, as she always does, while your mother was having her afternoon nap. When she came back, Eleanor wasn't up, which was unusual apparently. At first she thought she might have gone out, but your mother always told her what she was doing, so after a while she tiptoed to the bedroom to see if she was alright, and that was when she found her. She says she was already dead.'

'But why? There wasn't anything wrong with her heart, was there?'

Rob Graham shook his head. 'Not that I was aware. She hadn't been to see me for some time, so I don't know, but perhaps there was some underlying health problem that caused her heart to fail.'

Annie felt exasperated. 'I saw her only yesterday. This is a new bed, new sheets, new pillows. All new. We made it up and I lay next to her. Right there. She was fine, really happy. Surely I'd have known if she was so ill.' She was talking almost to herself.

'Heart problems don't always show up.' He paused, then said gently, 'Annie, I'm afraid there will have to be a post-mortem.'

'NO . . . no, you can't cut my mother up!'

Rob put his head on one side, his brown eyes full of pity. 'We don't have a choice. It's the law. If someone dies unexpectedly, then the cause of death has to be established. I have to refer it to the coroner.'

'But don't you need my consent for that?'

'No, unfortunately not. Annie, we need to know why Eleanor died. You don't think so now, but you *will* want to know eventually. These things are important.'

She nodded slowly, acknowledging that the doctor was right. Her mobile phone, which she realised she was still clutching in her left hand, began to buzz. She didn't even look to see who it was, just answered it automatically.

'Annie . . . thank God I've got you. Listen, I got a call . . .'

'I'm here,' Annie replied dully. 'I know. Mother's dead, Richard.'

'I'm on my way. I should be at the flat in about ten minutes,' her husband said. 'Is Dr Graham still there?'

'Yes. Hurry, please hurry,' she begged, then burst into tears.

18

Richard was stalwart. So kind and supportive. All the tensions between them had been put aside in her hour of need, but guilt sat like a lowering backdrop to the much greater distress about her mother. I don't deserve him. Now he lay against her back in bed, his arm warm and protective round her body. She was very still, almost not wanting to breathe, because breath meant life, which meant thought, and she couldn't bear to think. There had been so many times over the years when she had wished her mother was not her mother, times when she almost wished her dead, definitely imagining, on occasion, that she would be relieved when she was gone. She's dead, she thought. She's really dead, and I'll never see her again. She was very far from feeling relieved.

'I should have known there was something wrong,' she whispered. 'Maybe if I hadn't been so wound up in my own problems . . .'

'People have heart attacks out of the blue all the time, Annie. Someone at work, much younger than your mother, had one last year. Peter. Remember? I told you. He seemed fine until he wasn't.'

She sat up in bed. 'It just seems impossible that she could die that quickly. And she was in such a good mood about her bed.' She looked down at her husband. 'Can you believe she's dead?'

'Not really.'

'She had such spirit. She was so tough. It doesn't seem possible that she's gone.'

'She was eighty-two,' Richard pointed out.

'That's not old these days . . . if I'd got there more quickly.'

'She was already dead, Annie, when Mercedes found her.'

They talked on for a while, until Richard's responses became more monosyllabic and in the end stopped altogether, and Annie heard his breathing take on the slower rhythms of sleep. But she doubted she would sleep. Her heart seemed to have sped up and taken over her whole body with its hammering. Her brain was on a relentless loop: she was dying and I was naked in bed with Charles

262

Carnegie. That moment, the moment when I came to my senses . . . was that the moment she died? she asked herself. Was Mother warning me to stop, in a last act of unusual kindness . . . or disapproval? Had she needed Annie *in extremis*? Was she frightened, knowing she was about to die? The questions tormented her thoughts.

*   *   *

'What do you think we should do?' Marsha asked Ed as they walked away from the house. 'I feel so helpless, seeing Mum like this.'

'Me too. I don't know . . . I suppose with death you just have to go through it. She was pretty old.'

'Yeah. But maybe that doesn't count when it's your mother. And Mum seems to blame herself.'

'That's dumb. She wasn't there.'

'It's weird, thinking Grandma's dead.'

Ed didn't reply for a moment. 'I do feel upset, but she wasn't really the sort of person who allowed you to be close. I always felt she was judging me a bit,' Ed said.

'She wasn't warm and fuzzy, I grant you. But I never felt judged.'

'Yeah, but you were her favourite, Mash. You and Dad. You could do no wrong.'

It pained Marsha that Ed, once again, was feeling second best.

'Mum definitely felt judged.' Marsha turned to look at him. 'I don't think they had such a great relationship.'

'She seems pretty cut up about her dying though. She must have loved her.'

They walked in silence for a while. It was

beginning to rain, and Marsha stepped up the pace.

'You can love someone and still not like them very much,' Marsha commented.

'I know that,' Ed muttered, and Marsha wondered who he was referring to.

'So is Emms staying with you forever?'

'Not sure . . . she doesn't seem to want to go anywhere yet.'

He turned and saw the question in his sister's eyes, but he said no more.

'At least Grandma's death has meant you and Mum have made it up a bit.'

Ed nodded. 'Puts things into perspective.' Or at least shook him and Emma off the obsessive track they'd found themselves on since the night of the party. Thank God she's stopped crying, he thought. But nothing had been resolved about Daniel.

*   *   *

'I was right, it was a heart attack.' Dr Graham's voice on the phone was gentle. 'Her arteries were in a bad way, I'm surprised she didn't have any symptoms.'

'She never was very keen on vegetables—she always told Mercedes they gave her wind,' Annie told him sadly. She was sitting at her desk at home. She'd said to Jodie that she would not be in for a few days, there was so much to organise: the funeral, Mercedes' future, the flat, probate. 'If you'd known, could you have done anything?'

'At her age, probably not a lot. The last time I saw her was over a year ago, and her blood pressure was up a bit, but that's natural at eighty-plus.' He paused. 'She was lucky in a way, to go like that . . . peacefully.'

'It's just she seemed so well the day before.' She spoke almost to herself, repeating the same sentence for maybe the fiftieth time since her mother died. She still couldn't believe she was not still sitting there in her wing-back chair, wearing her padded navy hairband and silk polo-neck. 'Do you think it was quick, when she went?'

'I expect so,' said Rob cautiously.

'And she wasn't in pain?'

'Perhaps for a moment or two,' the doctor said, honestly. 'But it wouldn't have been for long.'

*   *   *

As she stood in the front pew of Chelsea Old Church, the coffin within arm's reach, Marsha felt shock rather than sadness. Shock that inside that panelled oak casket, a single wreath of white roses resting on its polished surface, was the dead body of her grandmother.

She'd never been to a funeral before. Her father's mother had died when she was only five—she hardly remembered her. And Gramps's funeral happened the week of her GCSEs. He lived in Lancaster and they hadn't let her go.

She clutched her mother's arm with one hand, the crumpled paper containing her eulogy in the other. The church was packed—Grandma was obviously a bit of a hit with her Chelsea set—the smart, black-clad congregation mostly over seventy-five. She felt sick with anxiety at having to talk in front of all these people. Lucy, leaning

265

across her mother, gave her an encouraging nudge. 'OK?' she mouthed.

Marsha's nod was hesitant. She glanced sideways at Ed, solemn and silent between Dad and Mercedes, who was kitted out in an impressive black mantilla, her face puffy from prolonged weeping. Poor Mercedes.

They began the first hymn, chosen by her grandmother in the detailed plan for her own funeral. Marsha still couldn't get her head around the idea of planning your own funeral and found herself stumbling through the half-familiar words. Church had been a sporadic thing when she was young. Dad keen, Mum not so keen.

'Bread of heaven, bread of heaven, feed me till I want no more; Feed me till I want no more.' The voices swelled behind her. These people certainly knew their hymns.

She checked on her mother, who was standing in total silence, and squeezed her hand tight. Marsha hadn't seen her cry yet, and that worried her. Maybe she did it in private—her mother wasn't given to displays of emotion—but it didn't seem quite normal to be dry-eyed in front of your mother's coffin.

The vicar, a portly man with the plummy drone she associated with religious discourse, was signalling to her. She felt her stomach flutter. She got up and went to the lectern, smoothing out the piece of paper in front of her. A sea of curious faces, pale against the uniform black funeral weeds, stared back at her.

'My grandmother,' she began, hearing the shake in her voice, 'was not someone to be messed with.' She heard the laughter with relief. 'But to me she was everything a grandmother should be . . .'

She felt as if she was talking forever, and skipped a couple of paragraphs of her typed sheet. When she came to the end, she looked over at her mother. She felt tears welling behind her eyes, but not so much for her grandmother, more for the desolate, lonely figure of her mum. She looks so bereft, she thought, as she made her way back to the pew. Her mother reached to kiss her gently on the cheek as she sat down.

'Are you OK?' Marsha whispered. But her mother didn't reply, just clutched Marsha's hand, holding tight to Lucy's on the other side.

'Death of death, and hell's destruction . . .' As the last hymn ended, Marsha began to feel calmer. The eulogy was over and she realised she was absolutely starving.

*　　　*　　　*

'Wonderful send-orf,' A bluff old gentleman, whose name she thought might be Gerald, told Annie as he bent slowly to retrieve his umbrella from the hall stand in her mother's flat. 'Eleanor must be in seventh heaven.'

She looked at him quizzically and the old man chuckled.

'Well, you never know with Eleanor . . . she usually got what she wanted. Perhaps she bullied the Almighty into fast-tracking her up to the seventh level. Sorry, sorry, no offence meant, but you know what I mean . . . she was always the star of the show.' He held out his hand. 'Thank you so much, Annie. I'll miss the old girl, you know.'

At last they were all gone.

'God, that was quite a marathon.' Marsha kicked off her black heels and wiggled her toes into the faded-rose drawing-room carpet.

'Well, we started out at nine this morning and it's now nearly five,' Richard pointed out with his usual precision. 'Your speech was brilliant,' he added to his daughter. 'Not an easy thing to get right.'

Annie was only half listening. It was just the family who had sat behind in the cortège on the interminable journey to Putney Vale, the traffic up Putney High Street almost stationary as usual. Mercedes had gone home to finish making the smoked-salmon sandwiches for the wake. The crematorium passed off without incident, a quick dispatch to the majestic strains of Bach's St Matthew Passion, rendered tinny and ridiculous by the crematorium sound system. She had felt as cold as death as her mother's body rolled off behind the dull blue curtains, but still no tears. My mother, the redoubtable Eleanor Westbury, reduced to a jar of ashes? It seemed impossible . . . ludicrous.

She looked around at her family now and it was as if there were a veil between her and them. They wouldn't understand how I'm feeling, she thought. It was a longing . . . not for her mother as such, but for *a* mother, any mother, who might hold her, keep her safe, give her the love Eleanor had never been able to show, and now never would. It was like a huge hole had opened up inside her chest.

'Tea?' Ed was suggesting. But Mercedes was ahead of him and appeared in the doorway with a tray holding Aunt Alice's massive silver teapot, pale green polka-dot Royal Albert china cups and

268

saucers, a silver milk jug, matching sugar bowl complete with tongs, and a saucer of thinly sliced lemon halves. Annie hadn't seen the set in thirty years—Eleanor used to bring it out for her 'girls', to show them how to preside over a tea table properly, despite the fact that almost no one 'took tea' by the sixties. Now the thought of her mother's anachronistic rituals made her sad.

'What will happen to Mercedes?' Lucy whispered when the Spanish housekeeper had gone back to the kitchen to clear up.

'Mother has left her a good chunk of money. She says she'll go back to Spain to be near her daughter.'

Ed poured the tea, smiling as he offered her a cup; her hand shook as she received it. They were all being so kind. Emma hadn't turned up to the funeral—she was ill, Ed said. She didn't believe that for a second, but she was grateful not to have to deal with the girl. Daniel's name had not been uttered by any of them since Eleanor's death. She'd texted him to tell him the news, but he hadn't responded. She sighed and pushed the painful thought to the back of her mind.

19

It was nearly two weeks since her mother had died, and still Annie hadn't been able to cry. The numb emptiness that settled in the day she stood beside Eleanor's coffin had not gone away. It frightened her, because she felt that if she gave way, even a little, she would be consumed by such sorrow that she might be fatally overwhelmed. To avoid any chance of this, she filled her days with constant, almost frantic activity that kept her busy from morning till night; it provided a certain sort of comfort.

She would manage to sleep, at most, for four or five hours, yet her body seemed to have a false energy which propelled her through the day. She was up at six and walking on the Heath, then swimming, the gym. She stayed long hours at the bakery, and when she got home she cooked, sometimes late into the night. Endless, elaborate, largely uneaten meals, including cakes, puddings, biscuits, which Richard surreptitiously consigned to the freezer. But cooking, as always in her life, was therapy of a kind.

Richard, as co-executor of Eleanor Westbury's estate along with her lawyer, Leo Silver, began to deal with probate while she responded to the letters of condolence, many eulogising her difficult mother. There were no surprises in the will. Eleanor had left the Cadogan Gardens flat and the bulk of her money to her daughter, with small bequests to the three grandchildren, and a sizeable legacy for Mercedes. She'd told Annie what she was doing over a decade ago, then never mentioned it again. In Eleanor's strict code of etiquette, it was very vulgar to dwell upon one's money.

*　　　*　　　*

'Jamie . . . are you busy?'

She heard him groan on the other end of the line. 'Uh, no, just lying here sound asleep, seeing

270

as it's six thirty in the bloody morning.'

'God, is it?' Annie looked at her watch. 'I'm so sorry . . . I didn't realise it was so early.'

'I can hear traffic. Are you out?'

'I'm walking to the gym. I'm not sleeping much these days.'

'Clearly.'

'Do you mind if I run something by you?' She heard her friend heave himself out of bed.

'Nope, I'm awake now. Go ahead.'

She paused as she crossed the road. 'You know the Carnegie thing? The day Mother died?'

'Yes . . . you and him stark naked and just about to get it on when your mother calls from the Astral Plain . . . Don't do it, Anneee, don't do it. *That* Carnegie thing?'

'I wish I'd never told you the last bit,' she muttered.

'And?'

'I think I should tell Richard. I don't think it's fair . . .'

She heard a loud spluttering.

'Do *not*! Do absolutely NOT tell Richard a single thing. You're trying to absolve your guilt by 'fessing up. I get it. But it's unforgivably selfish. The poor man might never get over it. Men, as a rule, don't.'

She thought about this for a moment. 'I thought it was the right thing to do. He's my husband. Shouldn't I be honest with him?'

Jamie harrumphed. 'No, you certainly should not. Honesty is a very overrated commodity—it should carry a government health warning. For "honesty" read "selfishness".'

'I don't mean to be selfish.'

She heard him sigh. 'I know, I know, of course you don't. But this really isn't the time to be making decisions like this.'

'Maybe not.'

'Oh, darling . . . you sound so miserable. Fuck the gym. Come over and bring some croissants. I'll put the coffee on.'

'No . . . thanks, Jamie. I'd better get going.'

*　　　*　　　*

'Annie.' Richard was looking at her with concern that night. 'Sit down will you? I can clear up later, it's definitely my turn.'

She turned to him. 'It's OK, I've started now.'

But Richard came up behind her and put his arms round her body, pinning her yellow rubber-gloved hands by her side. 'Please . . . stop.'

She stood tense in his embrace. She didn't know why, but the pressure of his body against hers was almost unbearable these days. She felt so raw and irritable and, frankly, mad. She wanted to shake him off, but she knew she couldn't do that. So she waited, waited until he let her go. Richard, unwittingly, still held her tight, both of them stranded stiffly next to the open dishwasher.

'I wish you'd talk to me. You seem so . . .'

'Mad?' she suggested softly.

'No . . . no, of course not. Just closed up and miserable. I know it's been hard, losing your mother so suddenly, but don't you think you should talk about it? You haven't cried since the day she died. And you're not sleeping. Please . . . tell me what's going on.'

She gently shook him off, and stubbornly

272

resumed rinsing the plates.

'I'm fine, really,' she replied. 'I just need a bit of time.'

'Me and the children are worried about you. We don't know how to help.'

She tried to summon up a smile for him. 'Sorry . . . sorry.'

'Don't be sorry. We're just concerned for you. Is it Daniel?' Richard asked. 'Has he still not been in touch?'

She shut the door of the dishwasher carefully, pulling off the rubber gloves and laying them over the edge of the sink.

'No, he hasn't, but it's not just Daniel. I don't know . . .' She couldn't articulate the mess that churned around her brain, didn't even want to try.

'Let's go up,' he was saying, holding out his hand to her. 'I'll run you a bath and we can get an early night.'

Later, as they lay in bed, Richard reached for her, letting his hand gently stroke her bare shoulder. She didn't move, but he must have taken this as a signal, because he leaned over and kissed her on the lips. Don't push him off. What's wrong with you? You know you love him. But she felt so tight inside, wound up like a clock, holding on . . . to what she didn't know.

'Please, Richard, don't . . . I can't.'

He drew back, his face neutral. But his hand still rested on hers. 'Let me hold you at least, Annie,' he said, pulling her over until she rested in the crook of his arm, her head on his bare chest. 'We all need cuddles.'

For a while they lay in silence and she found some comfort in his embrace, a slow, almost imperceptible letting go in what she knew to be a place of safety. He reached and turned off the light.

'I'm so sorry if I let you down over Daniel,' she heard Richard say softly. 'I've been a worse brat than my son, and with less excuse.'

She didn't know what to say.

'But I thought I'd lost you, lost the Annie I knew. It was pathetic, I admit that. But I couldn't cope. Not with Daniel, and certainly not with that Carnegie man.'

She could still hear the edge of jealousy, which he was obviously struggling to control.

'It's not as if I've behaved rationally either.' She thought of Charles and winced. Do *not* tell him; Jamie's ringing command echoed in her brain. She looked over at the shadow of his profile. 'I thought I was losing you altogether, not just the Richard I used to know.'

She heard Richard swallow. 'Yes, well . . . at one stage . . .'

The sleepy, almost tender mood in the room changed in an instant, as if sparked up by a bolt of lightning. That tone, that's what he sounded like on the bench by the sea that night, when he looked so distressed. She sat upright.

'At one stage? What do you mean?'

She turned the bedside light back on. Richard was still lying flat on his back, his hands clasped across his chest. He reached for his glasses and slowly pulled himself up against the wooden headboard. He wouldn't look at her.

'Richard?'

He sighed heavily, the long breath out sounding unnaturally loud. Her heart was hammering.

274

'Annie . . . you're not going to like this, but I . . . I really have to tell you something. I didn't want to, but we shouldn't have secrets, should we, not after all we've been through.' He paused but she found she couldn't speak to urge him on as she wanted. 'I . . . I had sex . . . with someone else.' The words seemed dragged by force from somewhere deep within him.

'Kate.'

He looked surprised. 'Kate?' Then horrified. 'Kate at the office? God, no! She's a child.'

She waited. So not Kate then. She felt sick.

'The lawyers hired an expert in Belgian tax law because of this merger . . . and this woman came over for a couple of days . . .'

'When you stayed out all night? Saying you were at Andrew's?'

He shook his head. 'No, this was weeks ago . . . before Cornwall. The night you saw Carnegie the second time. I tried to tell you, but that Morag woman interrupted us and then I just couldn't.' His expression was abject.

All this time, when I was beating myself up about Daniel, he was off shagging a Belgian tax expert?

'So this has been going on all summer?'

Again, he looked horrified. 'No . . . no, Annie, of course not. It was just once. I was drunk, we'd worked really late and I walked her back to her hotel . . . it meant nothing, absolutely nothing.'

'What's her name?' she asked, without knowing why. What the hell do I care what she's called?

'Marie. She was . . .'

'What? What was she, Richard? Good in bed?'

She saw him wince. 'Don't.'

'Well, was she . . . better than me?'

He reached for her hand but she slapped him off. The bastard, the bloody, bloody bastard. Her whole body, every single cell, was alight with rage.

'Why are you telling me this now, Richard? In fact, if it was only one night and meant nothing, why are you telling me at all?'

'I thought . . . it's been tormenting me. I feel so guilty. It was such a terrible thing to do. I thought I owed it to you to be honest. No more secrets.'

She heard Jamie's words again: You're just trying to absolve your guilt—and her own betrayal came back to her with sharp, uncomfortable clarity. I'm going to tell him about Charles. Why not? Why should she suffer, imagining her husband crawling all over that woman's body and let him off scot free? He's already jealous of Charles—it'll hurt and it serves him right!

'You just want to be forgiven.'

He nodded. 'Do you think you can . . . forgive me?'

'You shouldn't have told me. I didn't need to know.'

She glared at him, Charles's name on the tip of her tongue. But won't he feel better if I tell him? Won't it let him off the hook?

'I was drunk, I promise to God, Annie, it meant nothing. I hardly remember it.'

Yeah, right, she thought, her mind reeling as she tried to take in what he was telling her. She heard him groan softly.

'It was so difficult between us after Daniel turned up. You were—'

'Don't you dare start blaming Daniel for this. Or me. What you did was inexcusable.'

He didn't reply.

'So what if I was a pain to live with? We're married, aren't we? Married people do that to each other sometimes. It isn't a bloody charter for you to go out and shag the first available bit of skirt. Cheating on me ... just because I wasn't paying you enough attention? And you made *me* feel so guilty. I thought you were drinking and being mean because I'd brought Daniel into the house, when in fact you were just suffering from a shed-load of your own guilt.'

'I know ... I know that.'

She could tell he was thoroughly contrite. She felt almost sorry for him. Almost. But I stopped, she thought. He didn't. That's the difference.

'I think we've been lucky, you and me, with our marriage.' He spoke softly as if he was nervous of being too confrontational. 'It's never been challenged before. Even when the work stuff was difficult and the children were small, we've always pulled together. Maybe we got complacent.'

She knew he was probably right. It had never entered her head that either of them could be unfaithful. And yet, tempted by Charles and his playful seductiveness, she had been on the verge of succumbing.

She got up.

'Where are you going? Annie, please ... don't go.'

'I want to be on my own.'

'But if you sleep in Marsha's room, Lucy will know something's up.'

She hesitated.

'You're not going to tell Ed and the girls, are you?'

'Of course I'm not.' She was suddenly too tired

277

to do anything, and she sat back down on the bed. The thought of them knowing this about their father was too awful to contemplate. She wanted to cry, but she didn't want him to comfort her. She wanted to hit him, but she knew she couldn't. She wanted to indulge in the searing, uncomplicated pain of his betrayal, but she knew she didn't have the right.

'Annie?' She heard his voice as if from a long way away.

'Don't speak to me.' She lay down and turned her back to him, hearing his sorrowful sigh with stern indifference.

*   *   *

Jamie sat on Eleanor's barely used divan, watching Annie as she stood by her mother's chest of drawers holding a roll of black plastic bags.

'Christ, darling . . . he waits nearly thirty years and then picks a Belgian tax inspector!'

'Expert, not inspector. And it's not funny.'

'Well, it is a bit. I mean it's not as if you weren't just as keen to get your leg over Chelsea Charlie, if Mother hadn't intervened.'

She groaned. 'Don't start that again. No, I know. But still. It's bloody upsetting.'

'I'm sure it is, but not fatal.'

'No, not fatal, I suppose,' she conceded.

'Did you sort it out?'

She shook her head. 'Not really. Well, we're speaking, sort of. So as not to upset Lucy. Although I think she's given up on us being anything more than civil these days.'

She glanced nervously around the room. She'd

278

been putting this day off; it seemed sacrilege to go through her mother's things.

'Creepy, isn't it?' Jamie followed her gaze and gave a theatrical shudder.

'What if there's private stuff, like diaries, letters, in here.'

'You read 'em, darling! Well . . . perhaps not if it's your mother. But I reckon you're safe. Eleanor didn't strike me as a reflective person exactly.'

She smiled ruefully. 'No, I suppose not.'

Her mother's clothes were all immaculately kept, each item encased in clear plastic pockets, neatly stacked; Mercedes' work no doubt. There were the big knickers of the old; strange antique corsets; stockings rolled and bagged; piles of identical navy and cream silk polo-necks; elbow-length satin gloves from the fifties with buttons at the wrist; leather and gold-chain belts, all redolent of musty lavender, mothballs and another era. There was no sign of any papers. Richard had taken a whole pile away from the drop-leaf desk in the study, but nonetheless, Annie opened each drawer gingerly, terrified she might stumble across some dark and unpalatable secret.

'It's sad,' Jamie said, shaking the clothes free of their pockets so they could be taken in bin bags to the charity shop. 'All this reminds us of her, of course, but it's also strangely impersonal. This could belong to anyone really.'

The more the wardrobe and cupboards emptied, the more Annie began to agree. There's absolutely nothing that's even remotely personal to her here. No letters, cards, diaries (not even engagement diaries), photographs or albums—only yearbooks of the 'finished' girls from the school. No sign of

279

the pictures her grandchildren had drawn her when they were little, or the crooked clay models and constructions made of egg boxes and loo rolls they had given her with such pride. She found a V&A Museum address book beside her mother's chair in the drawing room, and on the rosewood table by the window were a few photographs in silver frames: her wedding to Ralph, Annie and Richard's wedding, a group shot of the children in late childhood, faces from the summer ball, one of Eleanor with the Queen at a charity night.

'Maybe she thought she was dying and chucked it all away,' Jamie suggested.

But Annie was bemused. Everyone keeps things of sentimental value. Everyone except her mother, it seemed.

'But she wasn't ill. Shall I ask Mercedes? My mother would never have lugged the bin bags down to the basement on her own.'

'Just seems so odd . . . to strip your life down to a few silk polo-necks. She must have been terrified of just this. You going through her things.'

Annie sat down on the bed. She felt so tired. And confused. Richard's confession had shocked her to the core, it made little difference that she was hardly in a position to judge him.

Jamie was looking at her intently. 'You've lost a lot of weight.'

'Have I?' she said absentmindedly. 'Maybe Mother just never cared about anything enough to keep it, Jamie. She just threw things away all the time.'

'Poor Annie . . . did you hope you might discover some proof that she, I don't know, loved you or something?'

She stared straight ahead. 'Like what though?'

'Not sure, but you hear of it, don't you? Letters, stashes of mementos kept carefully in a drawer that reveal that the dead person really cared.'

She smiled. 'You've been watching too many sci-fi soaps.'

'I'm sure she loved you, Annie, in her own sweet—or in Eleanor's case not-so-sweet—way. Surely you don't need proof.'

But she did. Not necessarily that her mother had loved her, but who her mother was. She realised she had absolutely no idea. All she knew was Eleanor's lifelong imperative to appear in the right place at the right time, with the right people, dressed in the right frock, saying the right thing with the right accent and the 'proper' social values. What did Mother really feel about me? Or about Daddy . . . about life in general? Her cronies at the funeral had been effusive about what a 'character' she'd been, how no event was complete without her. Could Eleanor Westbury's life really be reduced to her obsession with class and social status?

'It's all too late,' she said bleakly. 'We can speculate all we like, but we'll never know for sure now.'

Jamie looked at her sympathetically. 'You know you're very loved, don't you? And you know how to love other people,' her friend stated firmly. 'So somewhere along the line, you must have been shown how. That's usually down to the parents, isn't it?'

She hadn't thought about this before.

'I suppose you're right . . . I do know how to love, although not always very successfully.'

281

Mercedes was in her mother's study, packing into carrier bags the books Annie had said she didn't want. The housekeeper, with her resolute Catholic faith in the decisions of the Almighty, had remained surprisingly cheerful during the dismantling of what had come to be her home over the last twenty years. With the money Eleanor had left her she was now able to get a small flat in the village in Murcia, southern Spain, where her daughter and grandchildren lived, and perhaps that helped. Annie took a deep breath. Let's hope she understands what I'm asking.

'Mercedes, did my mother throw things away a lot recently?' She mimed putting something in the wastepaper basket.

'You need bag?' Mercedes asked, reaching over for a roll of black plastic bags that sat on the desk.

'No . . . no, I . . . my mother, she have clear-out? Papers and things?' Annie unconsciously raised her voice in pigeon English, in the mistaken notion that volume equalled clarity. She opened the top drawer of the desk and mimed picking something up, tearing it in pieces, then chucking it in the bin. She heard Jamie sniggering behind her.

The Spanish woman looked concerned. 'You lost something, Señora? *Ella nunca me deja abrir el escritorio, nunca.*'

'She says your mother never let her open the desk. Never.' Jamie said.

Annie turned to her friend in astonishment. 'Since when do you speak Spanish?'

Mercedes was looking anxiously between them.

'Since Luca . . . you remember him, about five years ago? My teacher at Berlitz said I had a real flair. And then just as I was getting the hang of it, the miserable little sod buggered off back to Seville.'

She vaguely recalled a smoulderingly handsome anaesthetist who had flitted through Jamie's life at some point, but it was hard to keep up. 'You might have mentioned it!'

'Too much fun seeing you do your dodgy Marcel Marceau act.'

But, even in her own language, Mercedes had no idea what they were talking about. She said Annie's mother often threw stuff away, she was an obsessively tidy person, but no more so recently. Annie didn't know whether she was pleased or disappointed. The thought of her mother knowing she didn't have much time left and deciding to cleanse her life was depressing enough, but perhaps more upsetting was the thought that she'd never found anything she received of a personal nature worth keeping.

'You'd have thought I'd have noticed that she didn't have any stuff around,' she said sadly, as they made their way downstairs to the car with the last bag of Eleanor's clothes.

'You would, if you'd been close,' he said. 'But you weren't.'

She was forced to agree. Not only had she not been close to her mother, she wasn't even sure if she'd liked her much. And did Mother really like me, she wondered.

* * *

283

She'd tried Daniel's phone again on the way home from her mother's flat, hoping against hope that this time he would pick up. She tried every two days or so, but she knew in her heart that it was hopeless. She climbed the stairs to find Richard soaking in his nightly bath.

'Did you see anything amongst Mother's papers that was at all personal?' she asked.

Richard reached for his glasses and put them on, rubbing the steam off the lenses and peering up at his wife.

'Uh . . . no, I don't think so. You saw what I took.'

She stood in the doorway, so bewildered that she was talking almost to herself. 'It's just so strange. Nothing, not even a letter from my father, or me, or anyone . . . nothing the children gave her.'

Richard pulled himself up in the water, looking in concern at her. 'What can I say? Eleanor was Eleanor, Annie. It just wasn't in her to be sentimental.'

'Is it sentimental to keep stuff about the people you love? Isn't it just normal, what people do who want to remember?'

'Maybe she didn't,' he said.

'I can't bear it.' Something suddenly snapped inside her. The mess she'd been wading through in her mind for weeks now parted like the Red Sea and she knew what she had to do. She turned and shot back into the bedroom.

'Annie?' she heard her husband call anxiously after her.

'I . . . I need to . . .'

She grabbed her overnight bag from the top of the cupboard and began to fill it with a pair of jeans, some T-shirts, a sweater, underwear and toiletries.

Richard appeared in the door to the bathroom, a towel wrapped round his body like a toga. 'Annie, what on earth are you doing?'

She turned to him, knowing her blue-grey eyes were sparking crazily. 'I think I'll go to Marjory's . . . just for a few days,' she said.

'At this time of night?' His voice was sharp with concern. 'Have you asked her?'

She shook her head miserably. 'I just feel a bit desperate, Richard.'

'It's me, isn't it? What I told you the other night.'

'No . . . well, yes, that didn't help, but it's not just that. It's everything.' She battled to control her voice. 'It's not about you, Richard. It's me . . . I'm so sorry,' she replied.

'Don't go, Annie, please. Not in this state.'

She sat down heavily on the bed, suddenly too tired to even move. 'I just need a break. Just for a few days.'

'OK, ring Marjory, set it up if you have to. If she's OK with it, I'll take you down in the morning.' His voice was firm and she found herself becoming calmer as he spoke.

Later, when Richard had turned the light out, she heard him say, 'I always thought you'd be relieved when Eleanor died. She's been the bane of your life, Annie. Isn't it a relief . . . to be free of all that bullying and criticism?'

'She was my mother,' she whispered sadly. 'How can I be relieved?'

20

Marjory received Annie, as always, with open arms. She didn't ask questions, although Annie was sure Richard would have said something to the old lady before he went back to London. The house was so restful, so quiet, so free from all the recent pressures. A sanctuary.

For most of the first day, Annie slept like the dead. The bedroom she called her own, unchanged since the days she'd slept there waiting for Tom to be born, was like a child's room: tiny faded rosebuds on the cotton curtains, a single bed with pink candlewick bedspread, a white chest of drawers, an upright wicker chair. But the very simplicity of the sparse furnishings seemed to soothe her. When she eventually came downstairs that evening, feeling almost drugged, Marjory had prepared a large pot of boeuf bourguignon. An open bottle of red wine and two glasses stood ready on the wooden table.

'I thought you needed feeding up,' Marjory said with a smile.

Annie sat down at the table and watched silently while the old lady picked over a large butterhead lettuce, dropping the vibrant green leaves into a battered blue metal colander. When she had enough, she held the colander under the running cold tap until the salad was rinsed clean.

'This is from the garden,' Marjory said, indicating the lettuce. 'But I planted so many that most have run to seed. I think I'm going a bit dotty—I forget there isn't still a houseful of people.' She spoke wistfully, and Annie realised she must have loved the time when there were two or three girls filling the old rectory at any one time, plus their friends and relatives to be accommodated. She remembered most meals with at least six or seven people round the large kitchen table.

Marjory waved at the wine. 'Help yourself.'

As Annie poured two glasses, the old lady set about the salad dressing, spooning Dijon mustard and white wine vinegar into the bottom of the deep wooden salad bowl—the same one Annie remembered from three decades ago—grinding salt and black pepper into the mix, then slowly beating in thick olive oil from a large green tin.

'We *could* eat outside,' Marjory said. 'You'd probably be warm enough, but I'm afraid my tiresome joints don't appreciate the evening chill any more.'

Annie said nothing much. She knew she didn't have to. She sipped the wine slowly, waiting, with the first real appetite she had experienced in a long time, for the meal to be ready. Marjory set a wide-rimmed willow-pattern bowl down in front of Annie, with a generous helping of the hot, rich stew. She gave her a side plate for the tossed lettuce, and pushed the breadboard with a stick of French bread towards her.

'Eat . . . eat,' Marjory urged, waiting until she saw Annie lift the first forkful of meat to her mouth before starting on her own bowl.

They ate in an easy silence. Annie wanted the delicious meal to go on forever. No pressure, no demands, no thought. Marjory's nurturing acceptance, the warmth of the kitchen, the steady tick-ticking of the station clock on the wall beside the dresser, the kick of the Beaujolais, and the body of Pablo, the silver tabby cat rubbing soft against her bare leg . . . it felt almost miraculous to her.

It was Annie who broke the silence. 'Did you never want children of your own?' She'd always wondered, but never dared ask before.

Marjory laughed. 'Never, not once,' she replied. 'I valued my freedom too much. I wanted to sleep all day and party all night. Paint when the mood took me. Have affairs, smoke too much, get tipsy.'

Annie looked astonished.

'Oh, I wasn't always an old woman, dear.'

'No . . . no, I know that. I just . . . you were so good with us all. So . . . so loving and supportive. I suppose I'd always thought we were the children you never had.'

'You were grown up, all you girls,' Marjory pointed out. 'I didn't have to change your nappies or feed you in the night and worry about you. Different thing entirely.'

'My mother—'

'Don't talk tonight, dear,' Marjory interrupted, seeing Annie yawn. There was cheese and apples to follow the stew, but Annie was unable to eat another thing. 'Go to bed and rest, you can tell me tomorrow.'

The following day she woke early, but this time without the crushing sense of dread that had dogged her since her mother died. She felt like a child as she jumped out of bed and drew back the thin rosebud curtains. The sun was just beginning to spread through the leaves of the apple trees in the orchard beneath her window, reflecting off the

288

heavy dew to make the grass shine like glass. She dressed quickly and tiptoed outside, pulling on a pair of Marjory's wellington boots and an old brown wool gardening jacket as she went. The summer air was heavenly: crisp, sharp and invigorating, and Annie took long, deep breaths, filling her lungs with as much as she could until her head was almost dizzy with it.

Nothing had changed for her, she knew that, but this was a magical place which seemed to protect her now, as it always had, from the real world. She thought back to the first time she had come here. Even then it had been a haven, safe from her mother's disapproval and panic about her unwanted pregnancy; Marjory never judged.

She walked down the drive and across the road to the field opposite, climbing to the highest point to look across the flat salt marshes to the sea. This was where she had come, almost every day throughout that dreary winter of 'sixty-six, to dream of what might become of her. But none of her dreams had included the baby growing so confidently inside her.

Marjory was up when she got back, grinding coffee beans in the kitchen.

'I thought we could go outside this morning,' she said. 'The sun hits the terrace about now, and it's even hot enough for *my* old bones.'

They took the cafetière, toast, butter and homemade blackcurrant jam out to the rusty wrought-iron table on the flagstones by the sitting-room window. It was indeed hot, and Annie basked, feeling the warmth seep in, healing her exhausted body.

'I'm so sorry about your mother. It must be hard.

If you want to talk about it . . .'

But Annie found it difficult to speak. The old lady had donned a droopy blue cotton sun hat and dark glasses, and she couldn't see much of her face. But she heard from the intonation that Marjory was waiting for her to explain why she was here.

'I didn't like her much,' she blurted out, unable to contain herself any longer. 'And I often fantasised about her dying and leaving me in peace. But now she's gone I'm tormented. I feel she's cheated me, dying so suddenly like that. I didn't have time to . . . well, to find out that she loved me. I didn't have time to forgive her.' She suddenly felt intensely angry with her mother.

Marjory was silent for a moment. 'I doubt she'd have said what you wanted her to say, even if she'd lived to be a hundred.'

'But where does that leave me?' Annie cried. 'I've tried all my life not to be like her. I've tried to make up for giving Daniel away by being the perfect mother to the other three. But it's all gone horribly wrong. Daniel won't speak to me, Ed's tormented, Richard had an affair with some Belgian piece of work, and to top it all, as Mother lay dying, I was seriously contemplating getting my leg over Charles Carnegie . . . as Jamie puts it.'

Marjory raised her eyebrows. 'Oh, dear.'

'I didn't . . . you know . . . but we nearly did,' she muttered, shamefaced. She watched Marjory's sympathetic but amused expression.

'Jamie thought it was funny too, but it's not.'

'What you're saying isn't, it's your turn of phrase that makes me smile,' she said. 'You make it sound like Armageddon.'

290

'That's what it feels like, Aunt Best. I've had this hole in my chest for days now, like a bottomless pit of anxiety. I have to keep busy all the time, or I feel I might slide into it, be consumed by it. It's so frightening.'

'Poor you. But from what you say, your mother was a bit of a narcissist. They're tricky in the general scheme of things, but as a parent ... ? Being a mother is all about unselfishness.' The old lady paused. 'She would never have changed, Annie.'

'But I was worse. Nothing in the world's more selfish than giving up your baby. I don't want to end up like my mother, with my children only wanting me to live so they have a chance to forgive me.'

'Stop being so melodramatic, dear. The thing with Daniel only blew up in the spring—you can't expect to tidy it away so soon. Why isn't he speaking to you, by the way?'

Annie hung her head and told Marjory about Emma's accusation. 'I've ruined it by not believing him. Or at least not showing clearly enough that I *did* believe him. Because I do, I honestly do.'

There was silence at the table but for the far-off sound of a car a way down the lane.

'It sounds to me as if your main problem with all this is guilt. Plain, old-fashioned guilt,' Marjory pronounced, looking her steadily in the eye.

Annie nodded sadly.

'Everyone makes mistakes, Annie. That's life. You can only do what you're capable of at the time. It's easy to see giving Daniel up as a mistake now, but at the time you never wavered. You were adamant you didn't want him. I'm not saying this

291

to be harsh, just pointing out the truth,' she added, but Annie winced at her words nonetheless.

'That makes me a pretty worthless mother.'

'It makes you what you were: a frightened, bullied teenager in an era of ridiculous social mores.' Marjory reached over and took Annie's hand in her own.

'So what do I do now?'

Marjory patted her encouragingly. 'Where do you want me to start? There's Eleanor. She's dead, not a lot you can do about that. Richard? Not much to do there either . . . what's done is done. No point in any tit-for-tat confession nonsense.' Marjory paused. 'What else?'

'Tip of the iceberg!'

'Poor Ed will have to sort his girlfriend out himself, I'm afraid. It's Daniel that concerns me.'

'And me.'

The familiar thought of him carrying away a second rejection, thinking he hadn't measured up to her expectations, was too much for her. Finally, after weeks of unconsciously manning the barricades, she lost control and the pent-up tears flowed freely.

Marjory let her cry herself to a standstill.

'You said I might never know Daniel properly, but I do, I really *do*. I want desperately to be part of his life. And I want him to know that I believe him about Emma . . . totally.' She began to sob afresh. 'But he won't answer his phone and I don't know how to get through to him.'

'You know where he is,' Marjory said. 'Why don't you go to him? Tell him what you've just told me.'

She looked at her friend blankly. 'Go to him? Up in Edinburgh, you mean?'

Marjory nodded. 'You say he's not answering his phone, and you don't know where he's staying in London. But his play will be advertised. Surely you can find him there.'

She made it sound so simple. And as Annie began to think about it, she realised it *was* simple. Finding him, at least.

Annie slept that afternoon, a hot, damp, exhausted sleep riven with dreams of Baby Tom. She couldn't find him; he was there in her arms one minute, then Daniel himself was holding him. She didn't want him to hold him for some reason, but although she kept begging him to give the baby back, Daniel just walked away. She woke herself with her cry. Two people, the baby and the man—never reconciled in her mind. And she'd failed to adequately protect either of them as a good mother should.

* * *

They waited at the front door for the taxi that would take Annie to the station. She had stayed another day with Marjory, her tired brain floating between the past and the present as she mused on her mother's life, and the problems in her own. It was with reluctance that she embraced her friend when the taxi drew into the gate.

'Thank you . . . for everything, Aunt Best.'

The old lady seemed physically frail in her arms, but also tough and certain in the love she conveyed to Annie as she hugged her in return. Love that was as close to a mother's love as Annie had ever experienced, and a benchmark for her relationship with her son. 'No point in forgiving your mother,

293

dear,' Marjory was saying quietly as she released her friend, 'unless you can forgive yourself.'

She returned to London with a sense of calm and determination. The central core of anxiety was fading. She still had no energy, but she no longer felt on the edge of madness. As soon as she got home, she checked online for the details of Daniel's play: tomorrow was the last night.

'What do you hope to do up there?' Richard asked, when he found her in the bedroom, packing afresh, barely an hour after she'd got back.

'I need to find him, Richard. I need to tell him I believe him,' she said.

'But what if you go all that way and he won't see you?'

'He won't be able to avoid me. His play is on, he has to be there.'

'OK . . . well, it's up to you.' She noticed her husband didn't put up any objection, on the back foot since his confession and not about to challenge her. 'For what it's worth, I hope you get a chance to talk to him.'

'Thanks.' He sounded sincere, and she knew that he was finally making an effort to support her over Daniel.

'When you get back, Annie, can we try and start again? Put all this behind us?' He looked and sounded wretched.

She gazed at him for a moment and, despite the hurt, her heart went out to him. She loved him, there had never been any doubt about that. 'I hope we can.'

He smiled tentatively at her, perhaps afraid she might reject him, and held out his hand. She took it in her own and for a moment they stood quietly together, the fight gone out of both of them.

'Good luck in Scotland,' he said.

*   *   *

Edinburgh was cold, the wind from the east slicing down the wide avenues of grey neo-classical buildings and making it feel more like November than August. She had packed in the muggy warmth of London, and her thin knitted jacket was no match for the Scottish weather. She arrived in the city after two, and checked into a hotel north of Princes Street, which, at such late notice and at the height of the festival, had cost her an eye-watering sum. She didn't care. Daniel's play wasn't on till nine, so she had the afternoon to kill. She tried his mobile again, and again got voicemail. She didn't leave a message; she was frightened he might manage to evade her if he knew she was in town.

She wandered the streets, bought a dark green wool shawl to wrap over her jacket, had tea and a teacake in a small, crowded tearoom along the Royal Mile, got a ticket to the play. Everywhere was packed and loud with enthusiastic festival-goers, hanging out, drinking, making their way between venues, the atmosphere vibrant with laughter and expectation. She felt awkward and out of place. In other circumstances I'd have enjoyed this, she thought, but now I just want to get through this evening, see Daniel. The jollities set her teeth on edge. Every few minutes she looked at her watch, but time passed excruciatingly slowly, not least because there was no guarantee that she would find her son that night.

The theatre, when she eventually got there, was

small and claustrophobic. The chairs were of grey moulded plastic, crammed onto a raised platform, the walls covered in dusty black drapes. Annie reckoned the space could seat around a hundred. She'd walked in the rain across to the Old Town, up the hill, carrying the umbrella the hotel had lent her, wishing she could see her son immediately. She was intensely curious about what his work would be like. As she waited for the play to begin, she searched the half-full theatre for him, sure he would be somewhere in the audience. But if he was there, she didn't see him.

Called *The Sneeze*, the play was a farcical black comedy, based on a series of random events beginning with a sneeze. It was sharp and edgy and very funny. As soon as the prolonged and enthusiastic applause had died down, Annie hurried to the entrance, where a young girl dressed in black was sitting yawning behind the desk.

'I'm looking for Daniel Gray.'

The girl didn't respond for a moment, just stared blankly at Annie with large, tired eyes.

'Daniel . . . yeah . . . he just left.'

She must have looked stricken, because the girl added, 'But he'll be at the Assembly Rooms, I reckon. He and Gillen go there most nights.'

The pavement was crowded, but the rain had stopped. Annie nearly missed her son. She'd almost forgotten how beautiful he was, even in the half-light, dressed in jeans and a crumpled blue shirt. He was leaning against the wall of the venue, huddled in an intense conversation with a tall, very thin man with a shaved head and thick dark eyebrows that threatened to overwhelm his strong face. Both were smoking. I never knew he smoked, she thought, hesitating for a moment before going up to Daniel and tentatively touching his arm. He swung round.

'Annie!'

She saw the surprise on his face, then a wariness descend.

'I didn't know you were up,' he went on. 'You should have said.'

'Hi, I'm Annie Delancey.' She reached out to shake his friend's hand.

'Sorry ... this is Gillen Dare, my director.' Daniel's voice was jumpy, and his friend must have noticed because Gillen was looking at her curiously, his bright eyes boring into her, taking her all in.

'The play was fantastic,' Annie said, summoning up her social skills when all she wanted to do was talk in private to her son. But despite her anxiety, she had found herself quickly immersed in the witty, ridiculous farce. 'Really funny. The audience seemed to love it,' she added.

The two men beamed. 'Yeah ... better pace than the other two performances, and the house was much more responsive tonight,' Gillen said. 'Last night they were half asleep, but this lot got it. Hope the reviews—if it gets reviewed—reflect their enthusiasm.' He looked at his friend, but Daniel said nothing, just stared off down the broad street.

At another time, Annie would have liked to talk more to Gillen about the play, but Daniel must have been feeling as she was, because his silence was heavy and constraining. After a few moments, Gillen dropped his cigarette on the pavement and ground it with the toe of his black boot.

297

'I'll leave you to it,' he said. 'I have to go and talk to Calum about clearing out our stuff tomorrow . . . see you later?' He bowed slightly to Annie. Daniel nodded briefly, and waved his hand at his friend as Gillen disappeared back into the building.

'Why did you come?' Daniel said, as soon as they were alone. She sensed a controlled anger in his words, and flinched.

'Can we go somewhere?' she asked.

Daniel looked away. 'Umm . . .'

'We could try my hotel. It'd be quiet.'

He nodded. 'OK.'

The journey back was almost silent as they joined the noisy stream of people making their way down the Mound towards the lights and jostle of Princes Street. Behind them the castle was lit up and glowing gold as it perched like a fairy kingdom over the gardens below, the gothic spike of Scott's Monument piercing the night sky to the right, the eerie strains of a bagpipe lament carried on the wind from somewhere in the Old Town. For a moment Annie was absorbed in the beauty of the panorama in front of her, wanting to share her pleasure with her tall son striding along beside her. But Daniel's face looked shuttered and oblivious to his environment.

There were few people in the dimly lit hotel bar by the time they got there and Annie and Daniel had a choice of armchairs. Daniel ordered a beer, she a glass of wine.

'You asked me why I came up here,' Annie began, when the drinks were settled on the low glass table between them. 'You didn't answer my messages, that's why.' She tried, unsuccessfully, not to sound hurt. She wanted to add, 'even when I told you my mother had died,' but she refrained. She hadn't come all this way to blame him.

Daniel looked straight at her. 'Look, we met each other, we had a go at making it work. And if it had been just us, it might have been OK ... perhaps. But it wasn't. I don't blame your family, you all did the best you could, but I don't see any point in pursuing it, with Emma's accusation always standing between us.'

She felt he had rehearsed this speech many times. And it was clear that he was trying to control his own hurt and anger, and failing just as she had.

'I'm so glad I met you, Annie. It was incredibly important to me, and I'll always be grateful to you for that.'

'Are you saying you don't want any contact with me any more?' Her voice was sharp, she couldn't help it.

Daniel sighed. 'I don't see the point.'

'So you're just going to give up at the first hurdle?' She didn't mean to sound so upset, but why should she hide her distress? Why should he think that she wasn't affected by his rejection?'

'I didn't say that,' Daniel replied, taking a long gulp of beer.

'You did. You said you didn't see the point in continuing our relationship.'

'Annie, your son's girlfriend—who is also your daughter's best friend and flatmate, and someone the family've known for decades—accused me of sexual harassment. Whatever you actually believe, you have to take someone's side, and that, for all practical purposes, will have to be Emma's.'

'Not if she's lying. I don't believe her. Never have, never will.'

Daniel raised his eyebrows at her. 'So if I told you now that it was true, that I did come on to her in a drunken frenzy, what would you say?'

She didn't hesitate. 'I'd say you were lying.'

Daniel looked taken aback, then his face slumped. 'God, Annie.'

'Look, I can't *make* you believe me, Daniel. Of course you're right that we have a problem with Emma. I haven't seen her since it happened, and don't particularly want to. And yes, she's Ed's girlfriend.' She paused. 'But that's a separate issue. It doesn't alter the fact that I know you didn't do anything to her.'

For what seemed like a long moment, Daniel stared at the floor. When he raised his head, she saw a new determination in his eyes.

'Annie . . . there's something I want to tell you.'

She waited while he fiddled nervously with the label on his beer bottle, hoping he wasn't going to suddenly confess. He looked so serious.

'I should have told you sooner, and I would have done, but then this thing happened, and, well, that changed everything. Anyway . . . the thing is, I'm gay.'

She stared at him in astonishment. 'Gay? My God . . . why didn't you say something when Emma accused you? You could have sorted the whole thing out in a second.'

He shrugged. 'I did try, in the park. Then Ed rang. I don't know . . . perhaps I wanted you to believe that I could never have done that to Emma, gay or straight . . .' He gave her a rueful smile.

She said nothing, tired of repeating her assurances on that score.

'And would it have made any difference?' he went on. 'As I hadn't said anything before that, the others—certainly Ed—might have thought I was just making it up, trying to wriggle out of the situation. And anyway, just because a person is gay doesn't mean that they still couldn't have a moment of madness with the opposite sex. It would never happen with me, but it does happen.'

'Have you always known you're gay?'

'As long as I remember any sexual feelings at all . . .'

He was looking at her anxiously, seeing how she was taking it.

'Did you think I'd disapprove? Is that why you didn't tell me?'

He shrugged. 'Dad's a total homophobe. He didn't say much before Mum died, because she was always fine with it. But afterwards, well, it got quite nasty. He'd go on about "bad blood" . . . shit like that. That's why we barely see each other now. And finding you, I suppose I didn't want to rock the boat, risk you thinking less of me in any way.'

'Oh, Daniel. It makes no difference to me at all. I'm glad I know.' And I'm glad I persuaded him that I believe him about Emma before he told me, she thought.

The barman came over and asked if they wanted anything else. 'No, we're fine.' Her wine was disgusting—tinny and warm—but she didn't want to waste valuable time complaining.

'When I went in search of you,' Daniel was saying, his voice lowered as another couple sat down at a table near theirs, 'I didn't expect you to love me . . . that can't be manufactured overnight. But I so wanted you to think I was special in some way. Not because I'm any different from anyone else, I don't mean that, but because . . . I don't know, I just wanted to be special to you. And for a while there, I felt I was.' He stared across at her, his expression suddenly vulnerable. He cleared his throat. 'And then this bloody party . . . Emma . . . and it was like a house of cards.' He looked away.

'You *are* very special to me, Daniel,' Annie said quietly. 'Why do you think I'm here?'

Daniel didn't reply. The silence dragged on, and she felt they were both just tired of it all. He must have thought about this almost as obsessively as she had. She wanted to speak, but there seemed so much to say, too much; she had no idea where to start. In the end it all came down to something very simple: she was his mother.

'Daniel . . . when you were born, maybe it was true that I didn't want you, or want the drama that would have been our life if I'd kept you. But that didn't alter how much I found myself loving you.' She paused, remembering. 'I loved every inch of you . . . I knew you so well back then.' She looked across at her son, and in that moment, as she saw the tears fill his light eyes, she finally married the two people, the baby and the man. Tom was finally Daniel, not just in fact, but in her heart. 'I gave you away. But that doesn't mean I didn't love you as much as it is possible to love another human being in the time I had with you. I loved you just as deeply as I love my other children.'

There was a long silence. Neither looked at the other. Annie took a sip of her wine, just for something to do, and instantly regretted it.

302

'I'm kind of jealous of them, Marsha and the others, I'll admit that,' he muttered. 'It all seems so cosy, so perfect for them. They have you and Richard, they belong. You all belong.' He stopped and shook his head. 'But there's no point going down this road.'

'I wish I could change that.'

Daniel shot his mother a rueful grin. 'Christ, I'm maudlin. Feeling sorry for myself. It's pathetic. Please, don't indulge me, I'm just tired.'

She smiled. 'I'm glad we've had the chance to talk, to air how we both feel.'

'Hmm . . . so long as it's not an excuse for you to wallow in guilt for another thirty years.'

'Can't promise that . . .'

'I understand why Ed thought I'd done it,' Daniel went on, almost to himself. 'If I'd have been him, I'd have thought exactly the same. The girls were wonderful . . . are wonderful. I like you all so much. But you must see what an awkward position we're left in. Without Emma retracting her accusation—which she might not even remember the whole truth about, she was so drunk—there will always be a question in their minds.'

She nodded, 'I know what you're saying, of course I do. But what about you and me?' She looked hard at her son. 'I want you in my life, Daniel. I want to know you. It's as simple as that.'

'Thanks, Annie,' Daniel replied tiredly. 'And thanks for coming. That means everything to me.' He looked at his watch in a determined way. 'Listen, I've got to get back. There's a party . . . last night knees-up.' He wiped his hands across his face. 'Strange to think it's over. So much work and

303

only three performances.'

'You must be so proud of it.'

He nodded, his frown lifting. 'I am. Gillen did such a great job. He's a major talent.'

'As are you. Will you come back to London now?'

He hesitated. 'Not sure. There's something else I haven't told you, Annie. Gillen and I, we're together . . . have been since the spring. It sort of built as we worked on the play together. But he's Scottish, he lives up here, so we haven't seen much of each other. He was coming back and forth when I had the flat, but now we're thinking we might stay in Edinburgh, find a place together. And it could be easier to get the next project off the ground up here.'

Annie tried not to show her disappointment. 'It's a long way.'

'I'll be down a lot. Stoke Newington beckons!'

'I'd say come to ours when you're down, but perhaps we should leave that plan on ice for the moment.' They both laughed.

'Yeah . . . not falling into that trap again in a hurry.'

'I'm sorry it . . .'

He held up his hand. 'Stop! No more apologies, no more recriminations. Let's just take it slowly. See each other when we can, not make any plans.'

Which is what I should have done from the start, she thought.

'As long as we do see each other. I'm not going to beg, but please don't disappear on me again.'

He smiled apologetically. 'OK, that wasn't very grown-up. Gillen told me so in no uncertain terms, but I had my stupid pride.'

'We said no more apologies.' She got up. Daniel put down the empty beer bottle he'd been cradling like a comfort blanket during their talk, and stood up too.

'OK, but just one more. I'm so sorry about your mother. I should have called you. Are you alright? . . . Stupid question.'

'I haven't been, but it's getting better, I suppose. Never easy, as you know, when you lose your mother—whatever the relationship. But she was in her eighties . . .' She kept saying that to people, to show that she was OK about it, but in fact she couldn't see what difference it made, her mother being old.

He nodded and leaned forward to kiss her on the cheek. 'Thank you for coming all this way, Annie,' he repeated. 'I'd been falling apart over the Emma thing, not knowing what to do about you.'

'Even if you stay in Edinburgh, you'll keep in touch with me? Promise?' she asked.

'Scout's honour,' he replied, holding up three fingers as if taking an oath. And she had to believe him.

'And your father—Charles—just to say that if you choose to see him again, it'll have to be without me being involved.'

Daniel looked puzzled and was just about to say something, but she hurried on. 'Nothing sinister . . . I just think it's best if you both have your own relationship now.' She knew that she couldn't use Daniel as an excuse to see Charles again.

'OK . . .' He was looking at her closely but she bent her head, digging in her bag for her mobile and scrolling through the contacts.

'I'll text it to you . . . Charles's number.'

'Thanks.'

They said goodbye, and as she walked up to her room she hoped Daniel would keep in touch with Charles, even if he would never meet her mother now. Eleanor had chosen not to see the baby, and now she would have no chance to know the man.

*   *   *

The train home the next morning was dreary, the journey soporific. She dozed on and off, only to wake to more rain-soaked fields and grey northern towns. She was longing to ring Daniel, but she didn't want to hassle him. I just have to trust I've done enough. But she knew she would have few chances to see him if he stayed in Scotland. And suddenly her life seemed very empty. Her mother, she now realised, had been a massive presence. As she rattled down the east coast, there were things she knew she would have relayed to Eleanor: things about Daniel, Edinburgh, the play. Would she have mentioned he was gay? Yes, definitely. After the way her mother had denied Uncle Terence's homosexuality, however, she could imagine the chilly response she'd have received.

Her phone rang and she grabbed it eagerly, hoping it was Daniel. It was Charles. They'd only spoken once, briefly, since her mother's death. He'd wanted to get together, she had refused.

'I'm on a train,' she warned him. 'We might lose connection.'

'How are you?' he asked.

'I'm alright. You?'

'Oh, you know. Louisa's back tomorrow. Dreading it. How did it go with your mother's funeral?'

'Not sure I remember much about it. But OK, I guess.'

She told him about Daniel. He didn't seem particularly surprised or even interested that Daniel was gay.

'Credit to you, Annie, you're a stayer, going all that way just to say you care. Hope Daniel appreciates it.'

'That's not why I did it. My motives were entirely selfish!'

'Maybe, but selfish in a good way. Annie, before I lose you to a tunnel, I want to say something. I can't get what happened between us out of my head. I know we were both stressed out by stuff that day, and the wine probably didn't help, but you can't deny there was something there. I don't know . . . it just felt right to me.'

Her heart sank. 'No, Charles, no. It felt *good* in the moment, I won't deny that. But not right. It wasn't right.'

'Well, OK. Not right in the moral sense perhaps, but I haven't felt that desire for anyone for so long.'

'That's such a man thing to say!' She exclaimed. 'Of course you haven't. You've been married for twenty-five years. You can't live on the edge of that sort of desire for someone you see every day in washing-up gloves and the like, it wouldn't be human.'

She heard him sigh. 'OK, fair enough. But I wanted you to know that for me it was real.'

'Get a grip, Charles.'

He laughed. 'Maybe it's the masochist in me. Maybe the fact that you're always so rude to me is a turn-on! I shall get a whip.'

'I said "grip", not "whip",' she replied, beginning to giggle. At that point, mercifully, the train went into a tunnel and the connection was lost before Charles could reply. As she gazed out at the blackened brick walls and saw only her own reflection staring back, she understood how dangerously seductive his ability to make her laugh was. Taking nothing seriously, including himself, he was the antithesis of her husband's probity. And when things had been so complicated at home, she'd found she enjoyed it more than she should. Is that what drove Richard into the arms of the Belgian? A bit of giggling over a few glasses of good wine? She was still angry with him. She knew she had to come to terms with what he had done, considering Charles, but however much she tried not to picture it, she was still devastated by the thought of her own husband having sex with another woman. How would they be able to trust each other in the future?

21

'Mike, hi.' Marsha walked through the door held open by her brother's flatmate. 'Sorry, I know it's early . . .'

Mike looked wasted, but that was nothing new. She wasn't sure if he'd just got up or never been to bed, because his stained sweatpants, black vest and patchy stubble were pretty much the only way she'd ever seen him.

He grunted, checking his mobile, which he

clutched in one hand. 'Ten thirty . . . not so early. Um, the others aren't up yet. Do you want tea or something? I've just put the kettle on.'

She shook her head.

'I can wake them if you like?'

'Thanks.' She sat down on the sofa. She could hardly contain her fury.

Ed emerged first. 'Sis? What are you doing here? What's up?' He sat down in the only armchair and stared bleary-eyed at her.

'I need to talk to you . . . both.'

Ed glanced towards the bedroom. 'She'll be up in a minute. She's awake.'

'Good.'

'You look totally hacked off. Something happened? Tell me . . .'

'I'll wait till Emma's here.'

Ed pulled a face, glancing warily at her. 'OK. I'll just get some coffee going. Want some?'

She shook her head, watching him pad through to the kitchen in his T-shirt and tracksuit bottoms. What will this do to him? She didn't want her brother hurt, but she wasn't going to let Emma get away with it for a minute longer. If they split up as a consequence, wasn't that better in the long run for Ed? She was sick and tired of making excuses for her friend. Ever since she could remember, she had let Emma off the hook every bloody time. Because it was generally accepted that Emms was Emms and couldn't really help behaving badly. But was that really true?

Emma finally appeared from the bedroom wearing one of Ed's sweatshirts and a pair of faded pink pyjama bottoms. Even in her dishevelled state, with her hair tousled and her dark eyes rimmed with smudged mascara, she still looked unreasonably beautiful. This was the first time Marsha had spoken to her since their row. When she saw her, Emma didn't flinch, just raised an eyebrow slightly before sitting in the chair her boyfriend had just vacated and rubbing one eye with the back of her hand.

'Hi.'

'Hi.'

Ed popped his head round the kitchen door. 'Coffee, Emms?'

She nodded. 'Please.'

Marsha waited, not looking at Emma, until her brother was back in the room, carrying two mugs. Emma scrunched around, drawing her legs up under her and hiding her hands in her sleeves in a childlike gesture very familiar to Marsha. She *is* still a child, she couldn't help thinking, and was annoyed that the thought slightly diminished her anger.

'OK . . .' She drew in her breath, let it out slowly. 'I talked to Mum last night. She's just back from Edinburgh, seeing Daniel's play.' She paused.

'Brilliant, I'm sure,' Ed muttered, a slightly sneering edge to his tone.

'Don't know, Mum didn't say. But that's not the interesting part of her trip. The interesting part, the truly fascinating part, is that Daniel told her he's gay.'

There was a stunned silence. Emma dropped her head, wouldn't look at either of them.

'Gay?' Ed looked bewildered. 'Did she believe him?'

Marsha nodded. 'Well, yes, she did, especially seeing as he introduced her to his partner—the

310

man he's just about to set up house with.'

Ed looked at his girlfriend. 'Emms?'

When she finally met his gaze, she looked, if anything, defiant, not contrite, as Marsha had expected.

'So what?' she shot at Ed. 'Just because he's gay doesn't mean he didn't attack me.'

'Oh, for Christ's sake, Emma!' Marsha exploded. 'Stop it, will you? Just drop the act.'

Emma glared at her. 'Great friend you turned out to be. Daniel's clever, he's just conned your poor mum . . . all of you, with his smooth talk and his Oxbridge blah.'

'Emma—' Ed's voice was very low and Marsha's heart went out to him '—please. It seems pretty unlikely that a gay guy in a relationship would come onto a girl . . .'

Emma began to cry. 'Go on,' she sobbed, 'take Daniel's side.' She blinked her tear-filled lashes at him. 'What can I do? If you think I'm capable of lying like that, you should dump me, never speak to me again, babe, because it would be a terrible thing to do.'

Marsha looked at Ed and saw the uncertainty in his eyes, and the love. Good job, Emma!

'Don't say that,' he whispered.

'Well, it's horrible, you all suspecting me when *I'm* the victim in all this.'

'Now you know how Daniel felt,' Marsha snapped.

Emma's look was pained. 'I don't understand why you're being so vile, Mash. We're best friends . . . at least we were. You should be on my side.' She took a theatrical breath. 'Ed says you're jealous. You had the hots for Daniel when you met

311

him at that party, and he chose me. You can't bear that, can you?'

Bitch! She shot a glance at her brother, who looked immediately sheepish. Obviously they'd been finding every reason under the sun in the time since the party to blame anyone but Emma for the debacle.

'None of what you've just said changes the fact that Daniel is in a committed relationship with a man,' she said, tight-lipped. 'Can't you see what you're doing? You're being so bloody selfish. Mum's been really upset, and it's still causing problems between her and Ed.'

'I'm sorry about your mum,' Emma's voice began to rise in a crescendo of self-pity. 'But it isn't my fault. They weren't speaking before all this happened. And what was I supposed to do? Let him attack me and say nothing, just because it would cause problems in the family? Why should he get away with it?' She slid deeper into the chair, her arms crossed defensively round her body, her head bowed.

Marsha let out a long sigh. She found it almost impossible to imagine being friends with Emma, sharing a flat, while this huge lie hung between them.

'So you're sticking to your story?'

'Mash, it doesn't necessarily mean he didn't do it ...' Marsha could see the agony of doubt in her brother's eyes as he slouched awkwardly against the wall behind his girlfriend, cradling a cup of coffee in both hands. 'He could be bi ...'

'Yeah ... yeah, of course he could be bi,' She hated the sarcasm in her own voice. 'But he's not, Ed. He's not fucking bisexual, is he? He's GAY!'

She turned back to Emma. 'See what you're doing? You're making a total fool of this guy—' she indicated her brother '—who's stood by you through thick and thin, believing every lying word that comes out of your mouth. Do you think that's right?'

No one spoke. Emma was sobbing quietly. One more go, Marsha thought, taking a deep breath. Just one more attempt to make her see sense.

'Emma, look at me.'

Emma didn't respond, her head buried firmly in the arm of the chair.

'Emma!'

Finally she raised her face, pale and wet with tears. 'Leave me alone, will you?

'I'll leave you alone when you tell me the truth. This is *me* you're talking to, Emma. Don't forget, I know you through and through. And I know for an absolute fact that you're lying right now.'

Emma didn't reply, just gave her a hostile stare.

'Please.' Marsha's tone softened. 'Please don't drag this out any longer, Emms. It's not fair on any of us.'

'I think you've said enough,' Ed told her, moving purposefully to sit on the arm of Emma's chair. He wouldn't meet her eye as he stroked his girlfriend's dark hair, and Marsha didn't know what to think. Was he prepared to take her word against all reasoning? Was he that besotted?

She got up, finally admitting defeat. 'I'm out of here.' As she gathered her jacket in silence, Emma suddenly spoke. Her voice was small and she didn't look at either of them, fiddling with the edge of her sleeve as she spoke.

'OK . . . listen. Maybe it wasn't quite how I

313

said . . .'

Marsha held her breath.

'I don't know . . . I was drunk and I fell asleep, and . . . well, I woke up and Daniel was there and he was trying to get me up off the sofa, and, well . . .' Emma fell silent, still mashing the cuff of her sleeve between her fingers.

'And well what?' Ed sounded cautious, as if he were trying to make sense of what he was hearing. Marsha felt a terrible pity for him.

She watched as Emma gazed up at him. Her face no longer held any trace of the previous defiance. 'And, I don't know . . . I suppose in my drunken state I *thought* he was coming on to me, and I was half-asleep and I sort of . . .'

'Kissed him.' Ed wasn't asking, and Emma nodded miserably.

Marsha felt sorry for both of them. She didn't want to be there any longer. She didn't want to witness her brother's humiliation.

'And he didn't . . . you know . . . he didn't do anything except push me away and hold me off.' She paused, dropping her head again. 'And I was angry, I suppose.'

Marsha saw the small shrug. The indulgence of beauty, she thought, must be so corrupting to the beautiful.

'And then I freaked that Daniel'd tell you all what I'd done . . . and you were ill . . .' Emma was saying.

'And I believed you . . .' Ed said slowly.

'I'm sorry, babe, I'm so sorry . . .' Emma muttered. 'I wished I'd never said anything almost as soon as I'd said it. But then you jumped on Daniel, and it got so horrible and I felt trapped. I just didn't know how to tell you.'

Ed turned away and went and threw himself on the sofa.

Emma looked up at Marsha now. 'I'm so sorry, Mash, I didn't think . . . your mum and the whole Daniel thing; it's been so difficult knowing I'm to blame.'

Marsha didn't know what to say. She thought back to Emma's distress—clearly real enough, but with a different cause—on the morning after the party. Then the subsequent tearful accusations. She felt almost in awe of her friend's performance. It was a terrible thing to do to anyone, but there was no point in telling Emma this now. She knew.

'Listen, I think I'll get going,' she muttered. But neither Ed nor Emma responded to her as she made her way out of the flat with relief, leaving the ominous silence behind her.

*　　　*　　　*

Annie lay in bed that night, her eyes burning with tiredness, but determined to stay awake till Richard got home. He had told her he'd be late—it was the final day of the deal and there was to be a get-together to celebrate. But Annie couldn't relax. Would she be there? He'd said it had just been one night, but wasn't he bound to say that? Her friend Helen, who lived in Cumbria, had an unfaithful husband. When she learnt about the other woman, he'd sworn blind that it was over, and she believed him. In fact he never gave her up for a second.

Her brain told her that carrying on behind her back would never be Richard's modus vivendi, but her heart refused to be certain as she unwillingly reran an image of his hands all over that woman's breasts. She'd been so wound up in Daniel's disappearance and her mother's death that she'd had no time to feel the full extent of her jealousy. But it's cruelly insidious, jealousy, and it must have sensed she now had space in her life to really suffer.

When he did come in, she lay still, eyes tight shut.

'Annie ... are you awake?' He spoke in a dramatic whisper that even people three streets away would have been able to hear.

She gave up all pretence. 'It's after one.' She hated the injured-wife pitch of her voice.

'Sorry ... sorry, darling, I did warn you it might be a late one.' He flopped into bed. 'It's done! The deal's done.'

'Great ... so who were you with?'

'Oh, Kate, Larry, Mike ... all the gang from the other team.'

'Marie?'

There was silence. 'Of course not Marie.' His voice was hurt and suddenly sober. She felt his arm come round her, smelt the blast of brandied breath. 'You don't trust me, do you?'

She didn't answer. She realised that, in fact, she probably trusted him more than she trusted herself.

'Annie, please. I don't blame you, of course. But I told you, it was just one night ... a dreadful mistake I'll regret for the rest of my life. I'd never, ever do it again.' He pulled at her shoulder, trying to turn her to face him. 'Look at me, Annie, please look at me.'

She turned reluctantly, feeling on the verge of tears.

'But, Richard ... what if, in the future, something else happens, something difficult that neither of us can cope with, will we both do the same thing again?'

There was a leaden pause.

'Both?'

Oh, God. She felt a dull thud in her stomach and for a split second she was on the verge of confessing. But how could she ever explain what had happened between her and Charles? She didn't understand it herself. It was so caught up with Daniel, with their past, with some fantasy about what they might have had together. Did she want to burden her husband's brain with similar images to the ones currently tormenting her own?

'I mean me being mad and obsessed with Daniel.'

His body relaxed and he laughed softly. 'God, for a moment there, I thought you were going to tell me you'd had it off with Charles Carnegie.' She heard him groan. 'Boy, was I jealous of him. Jealous of Daniel too, but that wasn't as bad as thinking of you falling in love with Charles again.'

She winced. 'God forbid.' And her words were heartfelt.

*   *   *

The Indian restaurant on the Holloway Road was almost empty when Annie and Richard walked in. Soft jazz played in the dim, red-walled room, rich with the aroma of fragrant Indian spices and sizzling meat.

'Mmm . . .' Richard sniffed appreciatively as he took his seat. 'I'm famished.'

They ordered a bottle of red wine as they waited for Ed. It had been he who'd requested the meal.

'He won't bring Emma, will he?'

Marsha had told her what happened at the flat two days before, but Ed hadn't talked to her himself, only texted to say he wanted to meet. And Emma had made no attempt to be in touch.

'I somehow doubt it.'

Annie saw Ed's familiar figure as he pushed open the restaurant door. He looked pale and strained as he sat down, his smile perfunctory. But she was so happy to see him.

Richard poured his son some wine and piled manfully into the silence. 'How's work?'

'Fine. You know . . . yeah, not so bad at the moment. The end of the summer's quiet because everyone's still away. September'll be mayhem.'

For a while they talked about roadworks in Islington, the refurbishment of Richard's office, and a new TV series about celebrities in the jungle which Ed said was brilliant. Annie waited patiently for her son to tell them what he'd really come to say.

It was only after they'd ordered the food and the waiter had laid a plate of poppadoms and a selection of chutneys on the table that Ed drew a white envelope from the inside pocket of his jacket.

'For you, Mum.' He handed it to her. 'From Emma.'

She opened the card. It had a pretty, neutral pen-and-wash illustration of three poppies on the front. Inside, Emma had written:

318

Dear Annie, Richard and Lucy,

I am writing to apologise to you all. I have explained to the others what went on between me and Daniel at the party, so I'm sure you don't need to hear it again. There is no excuse for the lie I told, or for expecting you to believe me.

I know that everyone has been hugely upset by what I did, and that your relationship with Daniel and with Ed has been badly affected. I can only apologise again.

Please, if you want to talk to me, yell at me, whatever, I am happy to meet up. Your family has been amazing to me over the years—supporting me through so many difficult times—and you don't deserve this sort of behaviour from me. I know that I have forfeited your respect now, and I'm not asking you to forgive me.

Love, Emma

Annie closed the card and passed it to Richard. Ed was looking at her expectantly.

'It's a heartfelt apology,' Annie said.

Ed sighed. 'She's her own worst enemy.'

Annie looked at him closely. 'What does this mean for you two?'

'Oh, it's over, Mum. I . . . well, I suppose part of me never believed in it as a long-term thing . . . a girl like Emma sticking with me.'

Annie was about to object, but he held up his hand. 'And oddly, I think I could have got past her coming on to Daniel when she was drunk and half-asleep.' He gave a short laugh. 'Not easily—I'm not pretending the thought didn't make me feel sick at the time. But it was the lie that really scared

319

me. And that she could keep it up so convincingly and for so long, even when she could see the consequences.'

Richard laid the card down on the table. 'She's not a bad person.'

'She's not, but she's potentially a very dangerous one ... as we've all found out to our cost,' said Annie.

'What will Marsha do?' Richard asked. 'Can they still be friends and flatmates?'

For a moment they all sat in silence, considering the implications.

'I hope they can get back on track, now that Emms has finally confessed,' Ed said.

'I suppose it's not as if Marsha doesn't know her, and, to a certain extent, know what she's capable of,' Annie commented. 'And you? Can you be friends?'

Ed gave her a wry smile. 'I'm doing my best to get past what she did. I mean, I've known her all my life, practically. So maybe ... in time.' He paused. 'But I'm not in love with her any more.'

Annie tried not to let the relief show on her face.

'I think she should write to Daniel too,' Richard said.

'She has, but she needs his address, if you could give it to me.'

When Richard got up to go to the loo, Ed turned to Annie. 'Do you think you'll ever be able to forgive her, Mum?'

Annie didn't answer for a moment. 'I probably already have, but an incident like this changes the way you think about someone. I know she's got what they call "issues", and I've always had sympathy for her because of her background. But it'll be hard to trust her after this.'

She reached across the table and put her hand on top of his for a moment. 'It's great to see you, darling. I'm so sorry about all this. I handled everything so badly.'

Ed stared at her, then dropped his eyes, but she could see the emotion in them.

'I'm sorry too, Mum. I've been vile to you. I just got so jealous of him, I didn't know what to do with myself.'

'It's understandable.'

He shrugged. 'Is it? I'm not proud of myself.'

As Annie and Richard walked off to look for a taxi, after dinner, she took her husband's arm.

'I'm so relieved she wrote,' she said.

'Me too. It was a proper apology.'

'And at least Ed's over her,' Annie added. 'I was worried he'd soldier on, making the best of it and being thoroughly miserable.'

Richard laughed. 'God, it's not easy being a parent, is it? Watching them make mistakes you can't do anything about.'

'No . . . you just want them all to be perfectly happy, every minute of every day, forever and ever,' Annie heard the wistfulness in her voice, but she felt at least the family had achieved a resolution of sorts. There was still a note of fragility in the reunion between her and Richard, between her and Ed, between her and her elder son. But it was, nonetheless, a reunion.

*　　　*　　　*

Ed lay alone in bed that night, and felt like shit. Part of him was relieved it was done, relieved that

Emma had finally stepped up to the plate and apologised to his mother. Part of him was still shocked by her manipulation of him and everyone else. Most of him just missed her like hell. He'd seen the relief on his mother's face when he told her he wasn't in love with Emma any more, but that wasn't quite the truth. The thought that she was gone, that he'd never make love to her again, never watch her beautiful face as she slept, never feel that swell of pride in just being with her . . .

He got up and went through to the sitting room to retrieve his mobile from the table. He punched in Marsha's number.

'It's me.' He kept his voice low.

'I know,' Marsha replied. She sounded half asleep.

'Listen . . . just seen Mum and Dad. Gave them Emms's apology card.'

'How did Mum take it?'

'She was good. Yeah . . . sort of calmer than I thought she'd be.' He paused. 'That's not really why I rang, Mash. I . . . I wanted to say how sorry I am . . . for doubting you.'

He heard a tired sigh.

'It's OK. I know why you did. But thanks anyway.'

'I should have trusted you.'

'It doesn't matter now, Ed. You did what you thought was right at the time. None of us were sure of anything.'

'I miss her.'

'I think she misses you too.'

He felt a sharp pain in his gut as the fact that she was gone hit him again. 'Is she there now?'

'No, she's staying at her mum's for a bit. We thought we both needed a break.'

'I suppose we all make mistakes,' he said. 'The whole family's been overheated by this Daniel thing. Perhaps she was just acting out for the rest of us.'

'Don't go all psychobabble on me, Eddie,' he heard his sister laugh. 'But maybe you're right. It's not such a daft idea.'

*　　　*　　　*

Annie rang Daniel the next morning. He took her call at once.

'How was your trip south?'

'Good . . . it was good,' she told him.

'We've had a fantastic review in *Time Out* for the play. It's only short, but the guy clearly loved it. Gillen's over the moon.' He gave a chuckle. 'I'm over the moon.'

'You both deserve it. Send me the link and I'll have a read.' She was almost reluctant to bring up the subject of Emma, it seemed like old news. But he would want to be told.

'Scary,' he said when she'd finished. 'But she's young, Annie. I hope you'll forgive her.'

'Not that young.' She was aware of the edge in her voice and took a deep breath. 'But yes . . . yes, of course I'll forgive her. I already have, I suppose. I'm just not sure I want to spend too much time with her. She makes me nervous.'

He gave a short laugh. 'Makes *you* nervous!'

'Anyway, I wanted to let you know.'

'Sure . . . it's a massive relief that none of you will have any doubts about me on that score any

323

more. Please give my best to the others . . .'

As she put the phone down, she felt a tide of relief flood through her body.

Epilogue

'Hurry up, Annie!' Richard called up the stairs. 'We're going to be late.' She took a final look at herself in the long mirror: the fitted, knee-length black dress, heavy amber necklace, black satin pumps, and decided she didn't look too bad. She patted her hair, sprayed a short burst of perfume at her neck and wrists and grabbed her evening bag from the bed. It was December and her birthday, but Richard had begged her to come with him to an important client dinner. 'We can do the birthday at the weekend,' he'd told her.

Annie didn't mind. She had always dreaded the social pressure from the big, lavish birthday parties of her childhood. The only thing she remembered loving was the raspberry jellies in waxed paper cases.

'What are they like . . . these clients?' she asked Richard, as the taxi made its way south across London.

'Oh, you know. Ken Turnbull's an old-school entrepreneur. He lives to build up companies and sell them on. Rich as Croesus, of course. David, his partner, is younger and a bit on the shady side—shirt's too shiny, tan looks fake.'

'Should be a barrel of laughs,' she commented.

'Ken drinks too much,' Richard added, 'and never stops talking about himself. You just have to hang on his every word.'

'At least we're going to the Rib Room,' she said. 'Good choice.'

'Not mine.'

She left her coat with the girl at the reception desk, and was ushered by the maître d' ahead of Richard to their table. She had thought, when Richard had said the Rib Room, that it would remind her too much of her mother. She hadn't been here since her mother's birthday. But she found herself silently greeting the restaurant like a long-lost friend; it was good to be back.

Then she saw them.

'Mum!' Marsha leapt up from the long table and hugged her mother, laughing with pleasure. 'Happy Birthday!'

Lucy, recently back from Africa and tanned and thin from her months at the orphanage, followed suit. Then Ed, wrapping his mother in a long, insistent embrace. And it was then that she noticed Marjory Best, resplendent in emerald green, Jamie grinning broadly in his sharp Tommy Hilfiger suit, and sitting between her two friends, Daniel.

She closed her eyes momentarily, to push back the tears. In the months since the summer, she had seen Daniel whenever he was down from Edinburgh. He'd been round to the house too— sometimes with Gillen—and the rest of the family were gradually beginning to relax with him. She knew that her three would never be as close to him as they were to each other. And she'd also accepted that *she* felt differently about Daniel to the way she felt about the others. No less strongly, but in a different way. She knew that when she'd first met Daniel again she'd unconsciously tried to make up for the lost years, and it seemed to the rest of the family that she loved him *more* than she loved them. But none of that mattered now; she was lucky, it had worked out for them all.

It had been much easier with the family since Emma and Ed had broken up. Marsha was still in touch with Emma, but their meetings were awkward, Marsha said. Emma had stayed at her mother's house and Marsha now had a new flatmate. Annie knew it would take time to rebuild their friendship.

'I ... I can't believe this!' She turned to her husband, who was grinning from ear to ear, his cheeks pink with excitement. 'Ken Turnbull? David with the shiny shirt and the dodgy tan?'

Richard shrugged happily. 'I did know a Ken Turnbull once. He was a drunk too.'

She moved to kiss the others, then was told firmly by Marsha to sit down. In front of her place was a pile of presents and cards. She felt completely overwhelmed. Nothing had prepared her for the experiences she had gone through in the last year, but she realised in that moment that she was happier than she had ever been. She had survived, and so had her family, warts and all ... her family that now, however tentatively, included Daniel as a welcome guest.

'Here's to my mother,' she said, raising her glass of champagne and realising, finally, that with all she had, she no longer cared to be angry with Eleanor Westbury.

After the second course there was a pause. Annie was a little drunk by now, but it was as much from an overload of pleasure as from the champagne. Richard whispered to Marsha, Lucy winked, Ed waved to the maître d'. And suddenly the lights of the restaurant dimmed a little, and Annie saw Jodie and Carol, dressed in their best, walking slowly towards the table, carrying between them a large cake glowing fiercely with scores of candles. The cake was in the shape of a huge rose. Pink and melting, the sugar petals glistened temptingly in the candle-flames.

Faintly, as if from another room, Annie was aware of voices singing an enthusiastic 'Happy Birthday'. But she was far away, her eyes resting in turn on the people round the table, all there specifically in her honour: her three dear children; the woman who had shown her what mothering was really about; her best friend; her loving husband; the two capable women she worked with . . . and Daniel, the beautiful son she had thought she would never see again.

She realised as she watched them that they had all, in their separate ways, taught her something vital. It was that she, Annie Delancey, despite her mother's lifelong efforts, wasn't perfect. She could never be; it was pointless to try. But they loved her anyway, as she loved them. She pressed the knife through the soft crunch of the pink sugar petals, her eyes closed tight as a child, and wished she would always remember that.

Acknowledgements

Tangled Lives would not be the book it is without the generous help and support of the following people: Jane Wood, Robyn Karney, Katie Gordon and the whole team at Quercus, Laura Morris, Don Boyd, Clare Boyd, Kate Boyd, Jane Bow, Barbara Roddam, Shelley Borkum, Judie Sandeman-Allen, Paul Hallam, Jonathan David, Carmen Wheatley and Suzie Ladbrooke. Thank you all very much.